THE YEAR'S **BEST**
MYSTERY AND
SUSPENSE
STORIES
1995

Other Books by Edward D. Hoch

THE YEAR'S **BEST**
MYSTERY AND SUSPENSE STORIES
1995

EDITED BY **EDWARD D. HOCH**

Walker and Company
New York

FOR **JUNE AND LEN MOFFATT**

First published in the United States of America in 1995 by Walker Publishing
Company, Inc.

Published simultaneously in Canada by Thomas Allen & Son Canada,
Limited, Markham, Ontario

Library of Congress Catalogue Card Number: 83-646567 series
ISBN 0-8027-3266-6

CONTENTS

CONTENTS

INTRODUCTION

The year 1994 was a particularly rewarding one for readers of the mystery short story, with a number of fine original anthologies joining the leading mystery magazines in offering various forms of literate ingenuity. Among general magazines, *Playboy* continued to use occasional crime fiction, and I was delighted to see three crime stories—by Muriel Spark, Elmore Leonard, and Joyce Carol Oates—in the pages of *The New Yorker*. There were even several new mystery magazines, distributed through subscription and mystery bookshops, though it was too soon to tell how lasting or successful these might be.

During the year I served as a judge for the Golden Mysteries short story contest held in conjunction with the fiftieth anniversary of the Mystery Writers of America. I also chaired the MWA Edgar committee judging the year's best published short stories. If many of the stories I read, on both committees, seem to have shifted from detective fiction to crime fiction, it is perhaps a sign of our changing tastes. Some writers, including John Dickson Carr's biographer, Douglas G. Greene, have argued that the term "crime fiction" is so broad as to be almost useless. Nearly all the classic writers have dealt with crime in their novels and stories. Perhaps we need a new term to suggest the ingenuity and surprise that have replaced detection in the plots of many modern mystery writers.

Speaking of new terms, the British anthologists Michael Cox and Jack Adrian have suggested the word "mystorical" for a mystery story set in a past era. You'll find two examples in the following pages, by Doug Allyn and P. M. Carlson. You'll also find tales about— But I don't want to give anything away. The fun is finding out for yourself just how clever some of these authors can be.

Again this year there were so many stories I liked that I had to omit a story of my own. My special thanks to Doug Greene and Marv Lachman, who helped with the bibliography and necrology in the Yearbook section, and to my wife, Patricia, who read every mystery magazine and anthology and offered her usual valuable suggestions.

—*Edward D. Hoch*

THE YEAR'S **BEST**
MYSTERY AND
SUSPENSE
STORIES
1995

DOUG ALLYN

THE DANCING BEAR

The vagaries of the alphabet have placed Doug Allyn, 1985 winner of MWA's Robert L. Fish award for most promising first story, at the beginning of this volume, and Batya Swift Yasgur, this year's Fish winner, at the end. Allyn has more than fulfilled the promise of that first story, with numerous Edgar nominations and five previous appearances in this series. This year, with an intriguing historical mystery quite different from his usual tales, he finally won the top prize. The Mystery Writers of America named "The Dancing Bear" as its Edgar winner for best short mystery of the year.

The inn was a sorry place with walls of wattle and daub and a lice-ridden thatch roof in dire need of repair. The light within was equally poor, no proper candles, only tallow bowls and even a few Roman lamps that were probably cast aside when the last legions abandoned these Scottish borderlands to the Picts six hundred years ago. Still, logs were blazing in the hearth, the innkeeper had recently slaughtered a hog, and there were guests to entertain. I was content to strum my lute and sing for sausages and a place near the fire. The few coins to be earned in such a hovel weren't worth the risk. With five kings contending in Scotland, and the Lionheart abroad, banditry ruled the roads.

The guests were a mixed lot, a peddler of tinware, an elderly man and his wife on a pilgrimage to Canterbury, a crew of thatchers drifting south in search of work, two farm boys taking an ox to market.

The only person of any substance was a young soldier, a returned crusader from the boiled look of him. He wore a well-crafted chain-mail shirt beneath his linen surcoat, and his broadsword was German steel, carried in a bearskin sheath across his back in the old Scottish style. He was tall, with unkempt, sandy hair and a scraggly blond beard. His skin was scorched scarlet as a slab of beef, and his eyes were no more than slits. Perhaps they'd been narrowed by the desert sun. Or perhaps they'd seen too much.

He kept to himself, away from the camaraderie of the fire, though he did applaud with the others when I made up a roundelay that described each of the guests in a verse. But his countenance darkened again when I sang "The Cattle Raid at Cooley," an Irish war ballad popular in this border country. The innkeeper was an affable fellow, but I noticed he kept a weather eye on the moody young soldier. As did I.

But he was no trouble. As I gently plucked the opening notes to "The Song of Roland," the crusader lowered his head to the table and dozed off. The ballad is a hymn to the fallen stalwarts of mighty Charlemagne who died for honor. It's a song I sing well, but barely a quarter through it, I noticed the eyes of my listeners straying. Annoyed, I followed their glances.

In the shadows in the corner, the young soldier was on his feet. And he was dancing, shuffling round and round in the smoky darkness. At first I thought he was responding to my music, but his eyes were clenched tight and his steps were graceless. If he was hearing music, it was not mine. My voice died away, but still he danced, lost within himself. And we watched, in silence, bewitched. And for just a moment I felt a feather touch of a memory. There was something familiar about his movements, something I'd seen before. But I could not call it to mind. After a time I quietly took up my song again, though to little effect. I doubt anyone heard a word.

The young crusader stumbled back into his seat and his slumber before I finished singing, but the sense of fellowship around the fire was gone. Uneasy, avoiding each other's eyes, we each of us found places, wrapped our cloaks about us, and so to sleep. But not for long.

Living on the road has sharpened my senses, if not my wits.

Sometime in the night I heard a muffled footstep and snapped instantly awake, my glance flicking about the room like a bat.

Movement. In the corner. As my eyes adjusted to the dark, I could see the young soldier. Dancing. His eyes were partly open, but there was no light in them, no awareness. And his face was a twisted mask of anguish. And yet he danced, shuffling in a mindless circle like a . . .

Bear.

And I remembered where I'd seen this dance before. In the marketplace of Shrewsbury when I was a boy. It was a feast day and there was a fair, with jugglers and minstrels and a puppet show. And near the village gate was a man with a chained bear, a great brown hulk of a brute with a mangy coat. The man would prod it with a stick and sing a doggerel verse, and the bear would rear upright and shuffle in a circle, pawing the air. And the man would swat it and caper about as though the two were dancing.

I was enchanted, awed by the power this ragamuffin minstrel had over his monstrous beast. When he worked the crowd, I paid him my only copper to see the bear dance again. And I gradually lost my fear of the animal and moved closer. Only then did I realize why the minstrel had no fear of it. The bear's claws had been ripped out, and his eyes seared with coals. He was blind.

I cried all the way home and poured out my heart to my father. Who cuffed me for whining. Perhaps rightly. But later that night I hid a blade beneath my jerkin and skulked back to the marketplace, determined to rescue the bear somehow. But the fair was finished and they were gone. I never saw him again. Until tonight. For the young soldier's dance reminded me strongly of the ghost bear of my boyhood. He too shuffled in his circle, blind to his surroundings. The difference was that if the soldier opened his eyes, he could see.

When I opened mine again, he was gone. As were the thatchers and the farm boys and even their ox. Only the old pilgrims and I had slept past the dawn, and they were packing to leave as I stirred myself. Perhaps I could have stayed another night, earned another meal, but the inn felt haunted to me now. I slung my lute o'er my shoulder, bade the innkeeper good day, and set out.

The day was fine, a brassy October morn, heather crunching beneath my shoes and curlews crying. I'd summered to the north in Strathclyde, singing in inns and village fairs, but winter was on the wing, and I wished to be far south of these border hills when it came. In England. Perhaps even at home in Shrewsbury.

Or perhaps not. A mile or so from the inn, I came to a fork in the trail. The young soldier was resting there, seated comfortably on a knoll above the path, his blade across his knees.

"Good morning, minstrel," he nodded. "I've been waiting for you."

"Good morning to you," I said. In the light of day he seemed older. Not his face, which despite his beard was boyish and unseamed, but his eyes. . . . "Waiting?" I said. "Why?"

"To offer you employment," he said. "I journey west to the Clyde, to a town called Sowerby. A small place, but lively. I should like to hire you to perform there, and a troubador of your skill will surely find other work as well."

"Thank you, no," I said. "I'm traveling south."

"To those of us who drift on the wind, one road is much like another, is it not? Come with me. I have need of your talent, and I can pay. In advance if you like." He rose, blotting out the sun with his shoulders. And for a moment he was again the blinded bear of my boyhood. And my dreams. And he was asking for my help.

"Keep your money," I said with a shrug, offering him my hand. "I'm Tallifer of Shrewsbury, minstrel and poet. And the price of my company is a riddle. Why does a man dance like a bear in the dark when no music plays?"

"I am Arthur Gunn," he said, accepting my hand. "Of Clyde, and the Holy Land. I, ah, danced last night?"

"That you did. A curious thing to see," I said as we set off on the path to the west. "Tell me the story of it."

"You should have taken the coins," he smiled. "There's nought wondrous about it. I followed the cross and King Richard to Acre, and I was captured by Saracens in a raid in ninety-one south of Caesarea, myself and a dozen more."

"People say they are cruel captors."

"Not unlike ourselves," he said dryly. "They led us east, into the wastes. By chance, one of the captured was a bastard son of Hugh of Burgundy, and so a band of French horse dogged us like hounds.

"And after a few days, the Saracens began to kill us. Not from malice, but to save water. Each night when we camped the guards would look us over and slaughter those who looked too weak to go on before giving water to the rest. I was young and very afraid, so when they approached me, I would rise and shuffle about to show I was hale. And worthy of a sip of water. Of living another day. As the chase stretched on, we all went half mad from thirst and exhaustion. And if a man fell on the trail and was killed, I would dance over him. To prove I was stronger, you see. That I was still alive. So my friends died, and I . . . danced."

He fell silent, his face dark with memories.

"It must have been terrible," I said. "What happened?"

"On the twelfth day, young Burgundy died, and I knew the pursuit would end when they found him. I had wasted a bit so my shackles were not so tight, nor did the guards check as closely as before, for they were exhausted, too. That night I chewed my arm and dripped blood onto my ankle till it was oily enough to slip my chain. I must've fled into the desert, though I honestly don't remember. The French said I was dancing when they found me. Alone, on the sand."

"Perhaps it will pass now that you are returned?"

"It has abated somewhat," he agreed. "It only happens when I drink too much, or get overtired. With luck the winds of Scotland will blow my ghosts away altogether."

"I hope so," I said earnestly. "A happier question. What song do you wish me to sing? To your family? Or a lass, perhaps?"

"I've no family, and as for a lass, I'm not sure," he said, brightening. "Before I left, my best friend and I fought over a woman, a tanner's daughter we'd both lain with. Nearly killed each other, but by God she was worth the fight. Hair dark as a raven's wing, eyes like opals, and a heat about her . . ."

"You still care for her, then?"

"Who knows?" He shrugged. "It's been long years. I lost to Duncan fair and square and went off crusading. I expect they are married now with a brood. Whatever their situation, I want you to make up a song to suit it as you did last night. And whether it's a wedding gift or a peace offering, say the trouble between us is forgotten, and I would be his friend again."

"And if he chooses not to forget the trouble?"

"Then perhaps you'll have to sing a dirge for one of us," he said mildly.

"That's all very well for you," I grumbled. "But dirges are difficult to sing. And if you kill each other, who will pay me?"

Sowerby was larger than I expected, a walled market town sprawled haphazard along a riverbank, with a branch of the Clyde running through it. The village gate was guarded but open, and we passed through without being challenged. Within, all was abustle. There were two smithies with hammers ringing and sparks dancing aloft, a tannery, an alehouse, and a pottery shop with goods displayed on planks in front. A water-driven gristmill was built into the town's outer wall, rumbling like distant thunder as its great wheel turned.

The village houses were mostly thatch or wattle and daub, with a few built of stone. In the south corner, the castle keep loomed above all, a crude but substantial blockhouse built of stone atop a natural hill in the Norman style. Its corners were outset so archers could sweep its walls.

Two herds of horses were tethered just outside the inner ward gate, with guardsmen and merchants looking them over.

"Horse traders," Arthur offered, "from Menteith and Lennox if I recall their livery right. We've come at a good time, minstrel. There will be celebrating—"

"Arthur! Arthur Gunn?" A guards captain stepped away from a group of traders and strode toward us. He was a striking man, half a head taller than Gunn, bearded and dark as a Saracen. He wore a brimmed steel helmet and the livery of Sowerby over a mailed coat. His fist grasped the hilt of his broadsword as he came, from habit, I hoped.

He halted in front of Arthur, looking him over, his face un-

6

readable. And then before Arthur could react, the captain seized him by the waist and lifted him aloft.

"God's eyes, Arthur," he grinned, "I thought you'd be dead with your head on a pike by now."

"I may be yet," Arthur said. "Or have you forgotten what happened the last time we spoke?"

The smile remained on the captain's face, but it no longer lit his eyes. "No," he said, lowering Arthur to the ground. "I've not forgotten. A word, Arthur, alone."

They wandered off a few paces, heads together, the captain whispering earnestly. I busied myself examining a row of pots, trying to appear uninterested, but I whirled about with my hand on my dirk when I heard Arthur shout.

But he was laughing. Both of them were, arm in arm, tears streaming, laughing like boys at the greatest joke in the world. I think Arthur would've fallen if the captain hadn't held him up. It appeared my song of peace wouldn't be needed. Just as well. Yet I'd have felt better about it if the burly guard captain's laughter had been less fierce.

"Tallifer, this is the old friend I told you about, Duncan Pentecost. A captain now, Duncan?"

"Aye. Promotion comes easy when the best men are off to the Holy Land. You've come at a good time, minstrel. Laird Osbern and his lady have come down from Pentland to look at stock. There's a feast tonight, and our steward's beside himself trying to organize an entertainment. His name's Geoffrey. Tell him I sent you and that you come highly recommended."

"You're most kind," I said.

"Not at all. Arthur says you're a fine singer, and his word has always been good with me. And now I'd best get back to the mounts before Simon of Lennox skins my lord's marshal out of his house and first-born daughter. I'll see you both tonight at the feast. And, Arthur, welcome home."

He strode back to the horse traders.

"A fair-sized man," I observed.

"So he is," Arthur agreed. "If we'd had trouble, it might have ended as it did before. Still, I was glad for your company, Tal-

7

lifer. And I wish to pay you for the song, even though you didn't have to sing it."

"No need," I said. "With your friend's help I'll find profit enough to make my trip worthwhile. And as you said, to those who drift with the wind, one road's the same as another. I'd better be off in search of Geoffrey the steward."

"And I'll find our lodging," Arthur said. "Duncan offered us beds in a barracks room in the castle. You'll stay with me?"

"Are you sure you want me to? Isn't there someone else here you must see?"

"Someone else?"

"The woman, you clot. The one you and Duncan fought over. Is she his wife now?"

"No," he said, trying not to grin and failing. "He's unmarried. And the woman . . . is dead, minstrel. Forget her. I'll see you later."

He strode off, chuckling quietly to himself. Crazed by grief over his lost love, no doubt. Hair dark as a raven's wing . . . I shook my head and set off to find Laird Osbern's steward.

The evening feast was a small one, a courtesy to the traders who'd gathered rather than a display of wealth by the Laird of Pentland and Sowerby, Solmund Osbern. There was food aplenty, but plain. Cold plates of venison and hare and partridge, wooden bowls of thick bean porridge flavored with leeks and garlic. The laird and his family sat at the linen-draped high table, a small army of them, four grown sons, their wives, the local reeve, and a priest. Two low tables of rude planks extended from the corners of the high table to form a rough horseshoe shape, which was appropriate since horses were the topic of the day.

In England, strict protocols of station would have been rigidly observed, but these Scots were more like an extended family, with jests and gibes flying back and forth between high and low tables. Indeed, I'd seen Laird Osbern himself that afternoon haggling like a fishmonger with a red-bearded trader from Lennox over a yearling colt. The laird was on in years, nearly sixty, folk said. He was gaunt of face and watery-eyed, but still formidable for all that. He'd gotten the best of the bargaining without adding the weight of his title to the scales.

His sons were a dour crew, wary and hard-eyed as bandits. They were dressed in coarse wools, little better than commoners'. They conversed courteously enough with their guests but kept wary eyes on them. They were fiercely deferential to their sire, though less so to his lady, I thought.

Lady Osbern was clearly not the laird's first wife, for she was a strikingly handsome woman younger than his sons. Richly clad in fur-trimmed emerald velvet, she had the canny eyes and grace of a cat. She stayed demurely at Osbern's elbow, saying little and that only to her husband, but I doubt there was a man in the room who wasn't aware of her. Or a woman either.

As I'd been hired last, I sang last, for such are the protocols of minstrelsy. I wasn't displeased at the order of things, since Scots afeeding can be a damned surly audience. Later, with full bellies and oiled with ale, they're a ready and roisterous crowd. I won them over early with a maudlin love ballad I'd learned in Strathclyde, then followed with "The Cattle Raid at Cooley." Even Laird Osbern joined in at the last chorus, with a full, if unsteady, baritone, and the guests roared their approval at the finish.

To a wandering singer like myself, such times are the true compensation for my craft, fair payment for the chancy life of the road, the loneliness, the lack of home and family. I was glowing like a country bridegroom, singing at my best, the circle of rowdy Scots cheering me on. And so chose my best tune next, "The Song of Roland." A mistake.

Half through it I began to hear murmurs and muffled laughter. I glanced behind me as I strolled the room. It was Arthur. He'd been sitting at low table with Duncan Pentecost, but now he was up, his face flushed with wine, eyes closed, dancing his mindless shuffle, round and round, my bear on a chain. It would've been funny if it were not for the agony so plain in his face. I skipped to the last verse of the song, thinking that if I ended it quickly, he might end his dance. But I was too late.

A trader from Menteith, a wiry rat of a man, staggered from his seat and began capering about Arthur, making sport of him.

With a roar, Duncan Pentecost vaulted a table, seized the wretch by the throat, and hurled him back amongst his friends.

In a flash men were up, blades drawn, squaring off, ready for slaughter.

"*Hold!*" Laird Osbern roared. "I'll hang the first man who draws blood in my hall. Sheath your blades, sirs, or by God's eyes, ye'll answer to me and my sons."

"Your captain struck me for no good reason," the rat-faced trader complained.

"You were mocking a better man than you'll ever be," Duncan said. "And if you and your lot want satisfaction, come ahead on, one at a time or all together—"

"Shut your mouth, Duncan," Osbern snapped. "These men are guests. I've given you no leave to fight anyone. Now, what's wrong with this lad? Is he mad?"

"No, my lord," I said hastily, seizing Arthur's arm. He had stopped circling and was looking about, confused. "He's newly home from the Holy Land. He has no head for wine."

"Then see him to bed and let him sleep it off. As for you, Duncan, hie yourself up to keep tower and relieve the watchman there. The night air will cool your temper."

For a moment I thought Pentecost was going to refuse and charge into the traders. But he didn't. He visibly swallowed his anger, then nodded. "Yes, my lord. As you say." He wheeled and stalked out.

"And that, sirs, is the end to it. We can't fall to brawling in front of our good ladies like a pack of damned Vikings. We're friends here. So," he said, raising his tankard, "will you join me, gentlemen? Here's tae us. Wha's like us?"

In the hallway I heard the roar of approval as Osbern's guests answered his toast. The din seemed to startle Arthur into awareness.

"What's happened?" he mumbled, blinking.

"Nothing," I said, leading him into the barracks room and easing him down on a pallet. "Everything's all right."

"The laird was shouting at Duncan," he said, frowning, trying to remember. "Was there trouble because of me?"

"Nothing that can't be mended. Go to sleep, Arthur, we'll put things right in the morning."

But apparently he couldn't wait. Later that night, I woke to the scuff of a footstep, and saw Arthur go out.

In the morning his bed was empty. I stirred myself and set off for the kitchen, in search of news and perhaps a crust of bread. But before I reached it, I heard shouts of alarm, and a guardsman pounded down the corridor past me. I followed him at a walk. Trouble finds me quick enough without hurrying toward it.

A crowd was clustered near the mill tower in the outer bailey wall. I threaded through them close enough to see. It was Arthur, my bear. He lay crumpled against the stone wall, his limbs twisted at impossible angles, his body broken like a crushed insect in the muddy street. His cloak was torn and bloodstained, and his poor face was shattered, bits of bone and teeth gleaming bloody in the morning sun.

There was a stir behind me as Duncan Pentecost thrust his way through the crowd. He was hatless and bleary-eyed, doubtless roused from sleep after his long night watch. He knelt beside Arthur's body and gently closed his friend's eyes with his fingertips. Then he tugged Arthur's bloody cloak up to cover his head and turned to face the crowd. And those near him took a step back at the killing rage in his eyes. The others parted as Laird Osbern strode up with two of his sons and several of the Lennox and Menteith traders. "What's happened here?" Osbern asked.

"My friend's been beaten to death," Duncan said coldly. "And I tell you now, my lord, the cowards who did this will not see their pigsty homes again."

"You accuse us of this killing, captain?" the red-bearded Lennoxman said, outraged.

"Perhaps not you personally, Simon of Lennox. But my friend was a soldier. It would take several men to break him like this. And he had no enemies here but your lot."

"We had no trouble with him, Pentecost. Only with you."

"But I was out of your reach last night. Perhaps some of you chanced on Arthur and took out your anger on him."

"Gentlemen," I interjected quietly. "Before this goes further, I think you should look at the body more closely. Arthur was not killed here."

"What do you mean?" Duncan said, whirling to face me as I knelt near the corpse. "Of course he was. And what would a singer know of such matters anyway?"

"I was a soldier before I was a singer," I said, rising. "I've seen death many times in many guises. And I tell you Arthur was not killed where he lies now."

"I don't care if he was killed in Araby," Simon of Lennox said. "I'll not have my men accused of murder by—"

"Curb your tongues and tempers a moment," the laird snapped. "You, minstrel, why do you say he was not killed here?"

"He's been brutally savaged, my lord, and his limbs are broken. If it had happened here, there would be blood spattered on the wall and the ground. But only his cloak is blood-soaked."

"He's right," Laird Osbern's eldest son put in. "There is no blood about, or at least not enough for the damage done."

"True enough," the laird said, eyeing me shrewdly. "You arrived with the dead man, didn't you, minstrel? He was your friend?"

"Yes, my lord, he was."

"And you know no one else here, no friends or kinsmen?"

"No, lord."

"Then perhaps I see a way past this," Osbern nodded. "The traders planned to leave at midday. If I delay them, it might be said I'm making an excuse to seize their property. Since you are a stranger here, with neither friends *nor* allies," he added pointedly, "perhaps you can be relied on to give a fair accounting. My son Ruari will stay with you to lend you authority. Go where you like, question whom you like. If you discover who has done this to your friend, they shall pay dearly for it. But, minstrel, take care not to accuse anyone falsely. For that would be as great an offense as this. Do you understand?"

"Yes, my lord," I said, swallowing. "I will do what I can."

"And do it quickly," Osbern said. "I'll not risk war with Lennox over one death, however unfortunate. At midday, we'll have done with this whether you discover anything or no. And now, shall we see to our breakfast, gentlemen? I'd hate to hang a man on an empty stomach."

He strode off, trailed by the others. Duncan held back a moment, but at Osbern's pointed glance, he followed.

Young Osbern and I looked each other over warily. He was a bull of a youth, beetle-browed and round-shouldered, with a shaggy mane of dark hair. He wore the plain leather jerkin and pants of a yeoman. Save for his boots, which were finely made, he looked quite ordinary. He'd spoken up boldly about the blood, though, and his eyes were clever as a ferret's.

"So, minstrel," he said, "whom shall we talk to first?"

"The dead man," I said, kneeling beside Arthur's body. I pulled his cloak away from his face and swallowed. It was terrible to see. His skull was crushed, the bone showing clearly through the gash.

"His face has been smashed like a melon," Ruari said, wincing.

"And yet there's very little bleeding from it," I said. "I think he was probably dead already when this occurred."

"His cloak is quite soaked," Ruari said, reaching past me to tug the cloak from beneath the body. Beneath it his coat of mail gleamed dully, except in the small of his back, where it was darkly stained. "Odd. His armor appears intact."

"So it does," I said, tugging the mailed shirt up above the bloodstain, to reveal a puncture wound in the small of his back. "There. That is how he was killed."

Ruari knelt, gingerly touching the hole with his fingertips, in part, I think, to show he wasn't afraid. "I've seen this sort of wound before," he said slowly, "or one similar to it. A spike dagger, needle-bladed to slide through chain mail. That's why his armor is unmarred."

"Who would have such a blade?"

"I don't know," Ruari said. "It's an uncommon weapon. I doubt any of the traders own one."

"What about your father's men?"

"Nor them either," he said. "The blade's too thin to be of use

in a fight. A man at arms might carry one into battle to finish a
fallen enemy, but it's good for little else."

"Aye," I said. "And Arthur wore no helmet. Since he was
struck from behind, he could have been killed as easily with a
broadsword, or even with a cudgel. Why use a dagger at all?"

"Or break his bones after? Someone must have hated him
greatly."

"Perhaps not. Perhaps he wasn't beaten. His bones could have
been broken in a fall."

"From the mill tower, you mean? Not likely. A man might
break a limb, but not much more."

"But suppose he fell from the castle keep, and struck hard on
the slope above us? He might tumble outward to land where he
lies now."

"The keep? But what would he be doing there?"

"I don't know. What's directly above us?"

"The armory. But it would've been locked last night."

"Then perhaps I'm wrong. But if he did fall from above, there
should be a mark of some kind on the rocks. He would have
struck with great force."

"Aye, so he would," Ruari nodded thoughtfully, looking up
at the rocky face that slanted steeply down from the stone
towers above. "And it would have to be somewhere near the
foot of the wall . . ."

He was climbing before he finished his thought, scrambling
up the cliff face like a Barbary ape. A few rods below the ashlar
facing of the wall he paused, glanced down to get his bearings,
then began inching to his left among the rocks.

And then he stopped. He turned cautiously and looked down
at me. And raised his hand. And even in the deep shadows of
the keep above, I could see his palm was stained with blood.

It was still an hour until noon when Ruari and I strode together
into the great hall. The tables were as generously laden with cold
game and trenchers as they had been the previous evening, but
the mood was taut as a strung bow and no one was eating much.
The traders from Lennox and Menteith were seated together,
shoulder to shoulder, as though they were ringed by wolves.

And perhaps rightly, for there were a half dozen men-at-arms arrayed behind Laird Osbern, Duncan Pentecost was guarding the door, and armed yeomen were posted at intervals around the room. Save for Lady Osbern, who sat at her husband's left, no women were present at all.

"Father, gentlemen," Ruari began, but the laird waved him to silence.

"Have you discovered the truth of what happened to the crusader?" he asked.

"I'm not sure. Perhaps."

"Then let the minstrel tell it. If trouble comes from what is said here, on his head be it. Come, stand by me."

Ruari glanced at me, shrugged, and did as he was bid. Leaving me alone in the center of the room. "Now, minstrel, what did you find?"

"We found, my lord, that Arthur Gunn was murdered, struck from behind with a thin blade. A spike dagger."

"A spike dagger?" Osbern echoed, frowning.

"Yes, my lord. And further, he was not killed in the street where he was found. He was killed in the keep, either in the armory or near it, and his body thrown from the wall there."

"The keep? But there was no one up there, save my family and—"

"And Duncan Pentecost," I finished, "who was on duty there." I sensed a movement from behind me, where Duncan stood at the door.

"But Duncan was the lad's friend," Osbern scoffed. "He stood up for him at the feast, ready to fight half the room on his behalf."

"That is true, my lord. Duncan was his friend. In fact, he was the only close friend he had here. And thus the only one he would likely have gone to visit in the night. Where Duncan stood watch. In the keep tower."

"But the stairway guard—"

"Admitted to me that he had a bit too much ale last night," Ruari put it. "He likely was asleep when the crusader went past."

"But even so, Duncan and the crusader were friends."

"And sometimes even friends can fall out," I said quietly. "Over a woman."

"Enough!" Lady Osbern's voice cracked like a whip. "Duncan, will you just stand there and let this English vagabond dirty your name with his lies? He's all but called you murderer—"

"Gentlemen, I am not armed," I said, backing away. "Nor have I accused anyone."

"Duncan! Hold your place, sir!" Laird Osbern snapped. "Madam, forgive me for being such a lout. You're quite right, our hall is no fit place for such talk. And as you gentlemen of Lennox and Menteith have been found blameless, you are no doubt eager to be on your way, are you not?"

"Yes, my lord," Simon of Lennox said hastily, arising. "We have imposed on your hospitality too long already. By your leave we shall be off straightaway."

"Of course. Godspeed to you, Simon, and to all of you. My dear," Osbern said, smiling benignly at his lady, "all this talk has upset you. Perhaps you should retire and rest a bit. Alwyn! See your stepmother to her rooms. As to this other matter, Ruari, minstrel, Duncan, come with me."

He turned and stalked from the hall. I followed, and Ruari pointedly fell into step between Pentecost and myself. Osbern led us a considerable distance from the great hall to a tower guardroom with arrow slits for windows and an oaken door.

"Ruari, wait out here and see we're not interrupted. By anyone." He closed the door and turned slowly to face us.

"And now, sirs, we are quite alone. And I will have the truth, from both of you. Minstrel, what did you find up there?"

"Bloodstains on the stones, my lord, near the armory. And on the wall. Arthur was killed there, and his body thrown down."

"I see. And you, Duncan, what have you to say?"

"It was . . . as the minstrel says, my lord," Pentecost said, swallowing. "Arthur and I fell out years ago, before he went crusading. And last night . . . we argued again."

"And you stabbed him from behind? Dishonorably? With a spike dagger? Is that what you are telling me?"

"Yes, my lord."

"I see. And you carry such a blade ordinarily, do you?"

"No, lord, I was . . . he found me in the armory, and we argued, and as he turned to leave, I, ah, I seized the dagger from a workbench. And struck him."

"You seized the dagger. You didn't draw your own blade and order your friend to defend himself? And yet a few hours earlier you were ready to fight *for* him. But never mind. This Arthur Gunn came upon you in the armory, you argued, and you killed him. From behind," Laird Osbern said, moving closer to Pentecost until their faces were only inches apart. "And was there, by chance, a witness to any of this, Duncan?"

"Witness, my lord?"

"I'm asking if you were alone when he found you."

"Yes, my lord," Pentecost said, avoiding the old man's eyes. "Quite alone. I'd gone there to get out of the wind."

"Enough," Osbern said, turning away. "You've killed a man who was my guest, Duncan. I could have you gutted in the courtyard for that alone. But that would only cause my—family further upset. So I offer you a sporting chance, Pentecost. Go from this place, now. Take a mount, but no weapons. In two hours' time, armed men will follow. With orders to kill you on sight. Unless, of course, you have something further to offer in your defense. A mitigating circumstance, perhaps?"

"No, my lord. I have nothing more to say. Now or ever."

"Then be off. Forgive me if I don't wish you luck."

Duncan turned without a word and stalked out. Osbern eyed me for a moment in silence, then shrugged. "So, minstrel, are you satisfied that justice has been done for your friend's death?"

"Yes, my lord. And he wasn't a friend, really, only a companion of the road."

"I see. He behaved strangely last night, but he seemed harmless enough. People tell me you've been at court, minstrel. In London?"

"Yes, lord."

"Then you must have seen many beautiful women. And what do you think of my lady?"

I hesitated a heartbeat. I've been wounded in battle and once I was trapped in a burning stable, but I've never felt nearer death than at that moment. It was in the old man's eyes. I wondered if I would leave the room alive.

"Your wife is truly lovely, my lord. Her hair gleams like a raven's wing, her eyes glow like opals."

"Spoken like a poet," Osbern said dryly, "but that wasn't my point. Any fool can see she's beautiful. It's her . . . deportment that troubles me. Speaking out of turn as she did today, for example. She's not nobly born, you see. She was only a tanner's daughter. But as my sons are grown and the succession is assured . . . I indulged myself and married for love. And even now, God help me, I do not regret it. Still, a man of my station must maintain certain standards, must he not?"

"As you say, my lord."

"I have an aunt," he said, musing to himself more than to me. "A horse-faced old crone, married to the church. She is abbess of a grim little convent in the highlands north of Pentland. Perhaps I'll send my lady there for a rest. And to learn proper behavior. A few months with my aunt would teach a mule manners. As to the matter of your friend's death, there's still one minor point that troubles me. This woman Duncan and his friend fought over. What do you know of her?"

"Only that she is dead," I said carefully. "Arthur told me she died long ago."

"Did she indeed? What a pity. She must have been very comely to cause all this trouble from beyond the grave."

"We do not know for certain that the argument *was* over the woman, my lord. We have only Duncan's word for that. Perhaps they fought over something else. Men sometimes kill each other over a penny or a look. Or nothing at all."

"So they do," he nodded, satisfied. "You've a glib tongue, minstrel. And you're quick with a song as well. And will you sing of what happened here?"

"No, my lord," I said positively. "A friend murdering a friend over a trifle is no fit subject for a song. It's best forgotten."

"Truly," he said, gazing out the arrow slit. "Best forgotten. Will you be tarrying long in this country, do you think?"

"No, lord. My home is far to the south, and winter is coming on. I'd best be on my way."

"Very wise," he said, without looking at me. "Godspeed to you, minstrel."

I strolled out of Sowerby that afternoon at a leisurely pace, whistling as I went. Until I was out of sight of the watchtower. Then I plunged into the wood and struck hard to the east, running full out as long as I could, then slowing to a steady, mile-eating trot. I found a stream just at dusk, but instead of using the ford, I waded downstream until well after moonrise, finally leaving it many miles below where I'd entered.

Was I being overcautious? Perhaps. But I'd seen Ruari and a band of men-at-arms set out after Duncan in far less time than the two hours the old laird had promised. And I had little doubt that when they'd finished with him, they'd be hunting me.

The old laird knew damned well Duncan hadn't killed his friend over nothing. Arthur had gone to the keep looking for Duncan in the middle of the night. And found him in the armory. But not alone. He was almost certainly with Lady Osbern. Perhaps she'd even struck the blow that killed him. And now Arthur was dead, and Duncan soon would be. And I was the last one who might spread the tale. A proud old man with a young, passionate wife fears the sound of laughter more than death itself. He will do anything, even murder, to stop it.

I maintained my killing pace all through the night and the next day. Late that evening, I forded the Tweed into England. Perhaps Osbern's men would not pursue me so far south, but the Tweed is only a river and the border only a line on a map. And Laird Osbern was a tall man with a long reach. I pushed on through the night.

The morning broke clear, a golden October dawn that melted away the shadows and my fears. As the sun climbed slowly through the morn, my spirits rose with it. I was exhausted but too numb to feel much pain. And so I walked on.

And just before midday, a breeze came wafting out of the east, swirling leaves and dirt into a dust devil that seemed to dance ahead of me on the road, leading me on. On a whim, I tried to join in with it, whirling round and round, capering about like a mating partridge. Or a dancing bear.

I shuffled in a circle until my legs finally gave way and I sank to my knees in the road. Still the dust devil danced on ahead. Beckoning me to follow. But not to the south and home.

To the west. Toward Ireland. A land of poets, they say.

I knew of no towns that lay in that direction. But there was a path of sorts. And to those who drift with the wind, one road is much like another.

ROBERT BARNARD

THE GENTLEMAN IN THE LAKE

Despite its title, Robert Barnard's tale of murder in the Lake District of England bears little resemblance to Raymond Chandler's lady in a similar body of water. It's a pleasure to welcome Barnard back for his third appearance in this series, with one of the year's Edgar nominees. It appeared in both Ellery Queen's Mystery Magazine *and in the British anthology* Midwinter Mysteries 4, *at just about the time Barnard was winning CWA's Golden Handcuffs Award for his outstanding contribution to crime fiction.*

There had been violent storms that night, but the body did not come to the surface until they had died down and a watery summer sun sent ripples of lemon and silver across the still-disturbed surface of Derwent Water. It was first seen by a little girl, clutching a plastic beaker of orange juice, who had strayed down from the small car park, over the pebbles, to the edge of the lake.

"What's that, Mummy?"

"What's what, dear?"

Her mother was wandering round, drinking in the calm, the silence, the magisterial beauty, the more potent for the absence of other tourists. She was a businesswoman, and holidays by the Lakes made her question uncomfortably what she was doing with her life. She strolled down to where the water lapped onto the stones.

"*There*, Mummy. *That.*"

She looked toward the lake. A sort of bundle bobbed on the

surface a hundred yards or so away. She screwed up her eyes. A sort of *tweedy* bundle. Greeny-brown, like an old-fashioned gentleman's suit. As she watched she realized that she could make out, stretching out from the bundle, two lines . . . *Legs.* She put her hand firmly on her daughter's shoulder.

"Oh, it's just an old bundle of clothes, darling. Look, there's Patch wanting to play. He has to stretch his legs too, you know."

Patch barked obligingly, and the little girl trotted off to throw his ball for him. Without hurrying the woman made her way back to the car, picked up the car phone, and dialed 999.

It was late on in the previous summer that Marcia Catchpole had sat beside Sir James Harrington at a dinner party in St. John's Wood. "Something immensely distinguished in Law," her hostess Serena Fisk had told her vaguely. "Not a judge, but a rather famous defending counsel, or prosecuting counsel, or *something* of that sort."

He had been rather quiet as they all sat down: urbane, courteous in a dated sort of way, but quiet. It was as if he was far away, reviewing the finer points of a case long ago.

"So nice to have *soup,*" said Marcia, famous for "drawing people out," especially men. "Soup seems almost to have gone out these days."

"Really?" said Sir James, as if they were discussing the habits of Eskimos or Trobriand Islanders. "Yes, I suppose you don't often . . . *get it.*"

"No, it's all melons and ham, and pâté, and seafood cock-tails."

"Is it? *Is* it?"

His concentration wavering, he returned to his soup, which he was consuming a good deal more expertly than Marcia, who, truth to tell, was more used to melons and suchlike.

"You don't eat out a great deal?"

"No. Not now. Once, when I was practicing. . . . But not now. And not since my wife died."

"Of course you're right: People don't like singles, do they?"

"Singles?"

"People on their own. For dinner parties. They have to find another one—like me tonight."

"Yes . . . Yes," he said, as if only half understanding what she said.

"And it's no fun eating in a restaurant on your own, is it?"

"No . . . None at all. . . . I have a woman come in," he added, as if trying to make a contribution of his own.

"To cook and clean for you?"

"Yes . . . Perfectly capable woman. . . . It's not the same, though."

"No. Nothing is, is it, when you find yourself on your own?"

"No, it's not. . . ." He thought, as if thought was difficult. "You can't *do* so many things you used to do."

"Ah, you find that too, do you? What do you miss most?"

There was a moment's silence, as if he had forgotten what they were talking about. Then he said: "Travel. I'd like to go to the Lakes again."

"Oh, the Lakes! One of my favorite places. Don't you drive?"

"No. I've never had any need before."

"Do you have children?"

"Oh yes. Two sons. One in medicine, one in politics. Busy chaps with families of their own. Can't expect them to take me places . . . Don't see much of them. . . ." His moment of animation seemed to fade, and he picked away at his entrée. "What *is* this fish, Molly?"

When, the next day, she phoned to thank her hostess, Marcia commented that Sir James was "such a sweetie."

"You and he seemed to get on like a house on fire, anyway."

"Oh, we did."

"Other people said he was awfully vague."

"Oh, it's the legal mind. Wrapped in grand generalities. His wife been dead long?"

"About two years. I believe he misses her frightfully. Molly used to arrange all the practicalities for him."

"I can believe that. I was supposed to ring him about a book I have that he wanted, but he forgot to give me his number."

"Oh, it's two-seven-one-eight-seven-six. A rather grand place in Chelsea."

But Marcia had already guessed the number after going through the telephone directory. She had also guessed at the name of Sir James's late wife.

"We can't do much till we have the pathologist's report," said Superintendent Southern, fingering the still-damp material of a tweed suit. "Except perhaps about *this*."

Sergeant Potter looked down at it.

"I don't know a lot about such things," he said, "but I'd have said that suit was dear."

"So would I. A gentleman's suit, made to measure and beautifully sewn. I've had one of the secretaries in who knows about these things. A gentleman's suit for country wear. Made for a man who doesn't know the meaning of the word 'casual.' With a name tag sewn in by the tailor and crudely removed . . . with a razor blade probably."

"You don't *get* razor blades much these days."

"Perhaps he's also someone who doesn't know the meaning of the word 'throwaway.' A picture seems to be emerging."

"And the removal of the name tag almost inevitably means—"

"Murder. Yes, I'd say so."

Marcia decided against ringing Sir James up. She felt sure he would not remember who she was. Instead, she would call round with the book, which had indeed come up in conversation—because she had made sure it did. Marcia was very good at fostering acquaintanceships with men, and had had two moderately lucrative divorces to prove it.

She timed her visit for late afternoon, when she calculated that the lady who cooked and "did" for him would have gone home. When he opened the door he blinked, and his hand strayed toward his lips.

"I'm afraid I—"

"Marcia Catchpole. We met at Serena Fisk's. I brought the book on Wordsworth we were talking about."

She proffered Stephen Gill on Wordsworth, in paperback. She had thought as she bought it that Sir James was probably not used to paperbacks, but she decided that, as an investment, Sir James was not yet worth the price of a hardback.

"Oh, I don't . . . er . . . Won't you come in?"

"Lovely!"

She was taken into a rather grim sitting room, lined with legal books and Victorian first editions. Sir James began to make uncertain remarks about how he thought he could manage tea.

"Why don't you let me make it? You'll not be used to fending for yourself, let alone for visitors. It was different in your generation, wasn't it? Is that the kitchen?"

And she immediately showed an uncanny instinct for finding things and doing the necessary. Sir James watched her, bemused, for a minute or two, then shuffled back to the sitting room. When she came in with a tray, with tea things on it and a plate of biscuits, he looked as if he had forgotten who she was, and how she came to be there.

"There, that's nice, isn't it? Do you like it strong? Not too strong, right. I think you'll enjoy the Wordsworth book. Wordsworth really *is* the Lakes, don't you agree?"

She had formed the notion, when talking to him at Serena Fisk's dinner party, that his reading was remaining with him longer than his grip on real life. This was confirmed by the conversation on this visit. As long as the talk stayed with Wordsworth and his Lakeland circle it approached a normal chat: He would forget the names of poems, but he would sometimes quote several lines of the better-known ones verbatim. Marcia had been educated at a moderately good state school, and she managed to keep her end up.

Marcia got up to go just at the right time, when Sir James had got used to her being there and before he began wanting her to go. At the door she said: "I'm expecting to have to go to the Lakes on business in a couple of weeks. I'd be happy if you'd come along."

"Oh, I couldn't possibly—"

"No obligations either way: We pay for ourselves, separate rooms *of course,* quite independent of each other. I've got business in Cockermouth, and I thought of staying by Buttermere or Crummock Water."

A glint came into his eyes.

"It would be wonderful to see them again. But I really couldn't—"

"Of course you could. It would be my pleasure. It's always better in congenial company, isn't it? I'll be in touch about the arrangements."

Marcia was in no doubt she would have to make all the arrangements, down to doing his packing and contacting his cleaning woman. But she was confident she would bring it off.

"Killed by a blow to the head," said Superintendent Southern when he had skimmed through the pathologist's report. "Some kind of accident, for example, a boating accident, can't entirely be ruled out, but there was some time between his being killed and his going into the water."

"In which case, what happened to the boat? And why didn't whoever was with him simply go back to base and report it, rather than heaving him in?"

"Exactly. . . . From what remains, the pathologist suggests a smooth liver—a townee, not a countryman, even of the upper-crust kind."

"I think you suspected that from the suit, didn't you, sir?"

"I did. Where do you go for a first-rate suit for country holidays if you're a townee?"

"Same as for business suits? Savile Row, sir?"

"If you're a well-heeled Londoner that's exactly where you go. We'll start there."

Marcia went round to Sir James's two days before she had decided to set off north. Sir James remembered little or nothing about the proposed trip, still less whether he had agreed to go. Marcia got them a cup of tea, put maps on his lap, then began his packing for him. Before she went she cooked him his light supper (wondering how he had ever managed to cook it for himself) and got out of him the name of his daily. Later on she rang her and told her she was taking Sir James to the Lakes, and he'd be away for at most a week. The woman sounded skeptical but uncertain whether it was her place to say anything. Marcia, in any case, didn't give her the opportunity.

She also rang Serena Fisk to tell her. She had an ulterior motive for doing so. In the course of the conversation, she casually asked: "How did he get to your dinner party?"

"Oh, I drove him. Homecooks were doing the food, so there was no problem. Those sons of his wouldn't lift a finger to help him. Then Bill drove him home later. Said he couldn't get a coherent word out of him."

"I expect he was tired. If you talk to him about literature you can see there's still a mind there."

"Literature was never my strong point, Marcia."

"Anyway, I'm taking him to the Lakes for a week on Friday."

"*Really?* Well, you are getting on well with him. Rather you than me."

"Oh, all he needs is a bit of stimulus," said Marcia. She felt confident now that she had little to fear from old friends or sons.

This first visit to the Lakes went off extremely well from Marcia's point of view. When she collected him, the idea that he was going somewhere seemed actually to have got through to him. She finished the packing with last-minute things, got him and his cases into the car, and in no time they were on the M1. During a pub lunch he called her "Molly" again, and when they at last reached the Lakes she saw that glint in his eyes, heard little grunts of pleasure.

She had booked them into Crummock Lodge, an unpretentious but spacious hotel that seemed to her just the sort of place Sir James would have been used to on his holidays in the Lakes. They had separate rooms, as she had promised. "He's an old friend who's been very ill," she told the manager. They ate well, went on drives and gentle walks. If anyone stopped and talked, Sir James managed a sort of distant benignity that carried them through. As before, he was best if he talked about literature. Once, after Marcia had had a conversation with a farmer over a drystone wall he said:

"Wordsworth always believed in the wisdom of simple country people."

It sounded like something a schoolmaster had once drummed

into him. Marcia would have liked to say, "But when his brother married a servant he said it was an outrage." But she herself had risen by marriage, or marriages, and the point seemed to strike too close to home.

On the afternoon when she had her private business in Cockermouth she walked Sir James hard in the morning and left him tucked up in bed after lunch. Then she visited a friend who had retired to a small cottage on the outskirts of the town. He had been a private detective, and had been useful to her in her first divorce. The dicey method he had used to get dirt on her husband had convinced her that in his case private detection was very close to crime itself, and she had maintained the connection. She told him the outline of what she had in mind, and told him she might need him in the future.

When, after a week, they returned to London, Marcia was completely satisfied. She now had a secure place in Sir James's life. He no longer looked bewildered when she came round, even looked pleased, and often called her "Molly." She went to the Chelsea house often in the evenings, cooked his meal for him, and together they watched television like an old couple.

It would soon be time to make arrangements at a Registry Office.

In the process of walking from establishment to establishment in Savile Row, Southern came to feel he had had as much as he could stand of stiffness, professional discretion, and awed hush. They were only high-class tailors, he thought to himself, not the Church of bloody England. Still, when they heard that one of their clients could have ended up as an anonymous corpse in Derwent Water, they were willing to cooperate. The three establishments that offered that particular tweed handed him silently a list of those customers who had had suits made from it in the last ten years.

"Would you know if any of these are dead?" he asked one shop manager.

"Of course, sir. We make a note in our records when their obituary appears in the *Times*."

The man took the paper back and put a little crucifix sign

THE GENTLEMAN IN THE LAKE

against two of the four names. The two remaining were a well-known television newsreader and Sir James Harrington.

"Is Sir James still alive?"

"Oh, certainly. There's been no obituary for him. But he's very old: We have had no order from him for some time."

It was Sir James that Southern decided to start with. Scotland Yard knew all about him, and provided a picture, a review of the major trials in which he had featured, and his address. When Southern failed to get an answer from phone calls to the house, he went round to try the personal touch. There was a For Sale notice on it that looked to have been there for some time.

The arrangements for the Registry Office wedding went without a hitch. A month after their trip, Marcia went to book it in a suburb where neither Sir James nor she was known. Then she began foreshadowing it to Sir James, to accustom him to the idea.

"Best make it legal," she said in her slightly vulgar way.

"Legal?" he inquired from a great distance.

"You and me. But we'll just go on as we are."

She thought about witnesses, foresaw various dangers, and decided to pay for her detective friend to come down. He was the one person who knew of her intentions, and he could study Sir James's manner.

"Got a lady friend you could bring with you?" she asked when she rang him.

" 'Course I have. Though nobody as desirable as you, Marcia love."

"Keep your desires to yourself, Ben Brackett. This is business."

Sir James went through the ceremony with that generalized dignity that had characterized him in all his dealings with Marcia. He behaved to Ben Brackett and his lady friend as if they were somewhat dodgy witnesses who happened to be on his side in this particular trial. He spoke his words clearly, and almost seemed to mean them. Marcia told herself that in marrying her he was doing what he actually wanted to do. She didn't risk any celebration after the ceremony. She paid off Ben Brackett, drove

Sir James home to change and pack again, then set off for the Lake District.

This time she had rented a cottage, as being more private. It was just outside Grange—a two-bedroom stone cottage, very comfortable and rather expensive. She had taken it for six weeks in the name of Sir James and Lady Harrington. Once there and settled in, Sir James seemed, in his way, vaguely happy: He would potter off on his own down to the lakeside, or up the narrow abutting fields. He would raise his hat to villagers and tourists, and swap remarks about the weather.

He also signed, in a wavering hand, anything put in front of him.

Marcia wrote first to his sons, similar but not identical letters, telling them of his marriage and of his happiness with his dear wife. The letters also touched on business matters: "I wonder if you would object if I put the house on the market? After living up here I cannot imagine living in London again. Of course the money would come to you after my wife's death." At the foot of Marcia's typed script Sir James wrote at her direction: "Your loving Dad."

The letters brought two furious responses, as Marcia had known they would. Both were addressed to her, and both threatened legal action. Both said they knew their father was mentally incapable of deciding to marry again, and accused her of taking advantage of his senility.

"My dear boys," typed Marcia gleefully. "I am surprised that you apparently consider me senile, and wonder how you could have allowed me to live alone without proper care if you believed that to be the case."

Back and forth the letters flew. Gradually Marcia discerned a subtle difference between the two sets of letters. Those from the MP were slightly less shrill, slightly more accommodating. He fears a scandal, she thought. Nothing worse than a messy court case for an MP's reputation. It was to Sir Evelyn Harrington, MP for Finchingford, that she made her proposal.

Southern found the estate agents quite obliging. Their dealings, they said, had been with Sir James himself. He had signed all the letters from Cumbria. They showed Southern the file, and he noted the shaky signature. Once they had spoken to Lady Harrington, they said: A low offer had been received, which demanded a quick decision. They had not recommended acceptance, since, though the property market was more dead than alive, a good house in Chelsea was bound to make a very handsome sum once it picked up. Lady Harrington had said that Sir James had a slight cold, but that he agreed with them that the offer was derisory and should be refused.

Southern's brow creased: Wasn't Lady Harrington dead?

There was clearly enough of interest about Sir James Harrington to stay with him for a bit. Southern consulted the file at Scotland Yard and set up a meeting with the man's son at the House of Commons.

Sir Evelyn was a man in his late forties, tall and well set up. He had been knighted, Southern had discovered, in the last mass knighting of Tory backbenchers who had always voted at their party's call. The impression Sir Evelyn made was not of a stupid man, but of an unoriginal one.

"My father? Oh yes, he's alive. Living up in the Lake District somewhere."

"You're sure of this?"

"Sure as one can be when there's no contact." Southern left a silence, so the man was forced to elaborate. "Never was much. He's a remote bugger . . . a remote sort of chap, my father. Stiff, always working, never had the sort of common touch you need with children. Too keen on being the world's greatest prosecuting counsel. . . . He sent us away to school when we were seven."

Suddenly there was anger, pain, and real humanity in the voice.

"You resented that?"

"*Yes.* My brother had gone the year before and told me what that prep school was like. I pleaded with him. But he sent me just the same."

"Did your mother want you to go?"

"My mother did as she was told. Or else."

"That's not the present Lady Harrington?"

"Oh no. The present Lady Harrington is, I like to think, what my father deserves. . . . We'd been warned he was failing by his daily. Dinner burnt in the oven, forgetting to change his clothes, that kind of thing. We didn't take too much notice. The difficulties of getting a stiff-necked old . . . man into residential care seemed insuperable. Then the next we heard he's married again and gone to live in the Lake District."

"Didn't you protest?"

"Of course we did. It was obvious she was after his money. And the letters he wrote, or she wrote for him, were all wrong. He would *never* have signed himself 'Dad,' let alone 'Your loving Dad.' But the kind of action that would have been necessary to annul the marriage can look ugly—for *both* sides of the case. So when she proposed an independent examination by a local doctor and psychiatrist, I persuaded my brother to agree."

"And what did they say?"

"Said he was vague, a little forgetful, but perfectly capable of understanding what he'd done when he married her, and apparently very happy. That was the end of the matter for us. The end of *him.*"

Marcia had decided from the beginning that in the early months of her life as Lady Harrington she and Sir James would have to move round a lot. As long as he was merely an elderly gentleman pottering around the Lakes and exchanging meteorological banalities with the locals there was little to fear. But as they became used to him there was a danger that they would try to engage him in conversation of more substance. If that happened, his mental state might very quickly become apparent.

As negotiations with the two sons developed, Marcia began to see her way clear. Their six weeks at Grange were nearing an end, so she arranged to rent a cottage between Crummock Water and Cockermouth. When the sons agreed to an independent assessment of their father's mental condition and nominated a doctor and a psychiatrist from Keswick to undertake it, Marcia phoned them and arranged their visit for one of their first days in the new cottage. Then she booked Sir James and herself into Crummock Lodge for the relevant days. "I'll be busy getting the cottage ready," she told the manager. She felt distinctly pleased with herself. No danger of the independent team talking to locals.

"I don't see why we have to move," complained Sir James when she told him. "I like it here."

"Oh, we need to see a few places before we decide where we really want to settle," said Marcia soothingly. "I've booked us into Crummock Lodge so I'll be able to get the new cottage looking nice before we move in."

"This is nice. I want to stay here."

There was no problem with money. On a drive to Cockermouth Marcia had arranged to have Sir James's bank account transferred there. He had signed the form without a qualm, together with one making the account a joint one. Everything in the London house was put into store, and the estate agents forwarded Sir James's mail, including his dividend checks and his pension, regularly. There was no hurry about selling the house, but when it did finally go Marcia foresaw herself in clover. With Sir James, of course, and he was a bit of a bore. But very much worth putting up with.

As Marcia began discreetly packing for the move Sir James's agitation grew, his complaints became more insistent.

"I don't want to move. Why should we move, Molly? We're happy here. If we can't have this cottage we can buy a place. There are houses for sale."

To take his mind off it, Marcia borrowed their neighbor's rowing boat and took him for a little trip on the lake. It didn't take his mind off it. "This is lovely," he kept saying. "Derwent Water has always been my favorite. Why should we move on? I'm not moving, Molly."

He was beginning to get on her nerves. She had to tell herself that a few frazzled nerves were a small price to pay.

The night before they were due to move, the packing had to be done openly. Marcia brought all the suitcases into the living room and began methodically distributing to each one the belongings they had brought with them. Sir James had been dozing when she began, as he often did in the evening. She was halfway through her task when she realized he was awake and struggling to his feet.

"You haven't been listening to what I've been saying, have you, Molly? Well, have you, woman? I'm not moving!"

Marcia got to her feet.

"I know it's upsetting, dear—"

"It's not upsetting because we're staying here."

"Perhaps it will only be for a time. I've got it all organized, and you'll be quite comfy—"

"Don't treat me like a child, Molly!" Suddenly she realized with a shock that he had raised his arm. "Don't treat me like a child!" His hand came down with a feeble slap across her cheek. "Listen to what I say, woman!" Slap again. "I am not moving!" This time he punched her, and it hurt. "You'll do what I say, or it'll be the worse for you!" And he punched her again.

Marcia exploded with rage.

"You *bloody* old bully!" she screamed. "You brute! That's how you treated your wife, is it? Well, it's not how you're treating me!"

She brought up her stronger hands and gave him an almighty shove away from her even as he raised his fist for another punch. He lurched back, tried to regain his balance, then fell against the fireplace, hitting his head hard against the corner of the mantelpiece. Then he crumpled to the floor and lay still.

For a moment Marcia did nothing. Then she sat down and sobbed. She wasn't a sobbing woman, but she felt she had had a sudden revelation of what this man's—this old monster's—relations had been with his dead wife. She had never for a moment suspected it. She no longer felt pity for him, if she ever had. She felt contempt.

She dragged herself wearily to her feet. She'd put him to bed, and by morning he'd have forgotten. She bent down over him. Then, panic-stricken, she put her hand to his mouth, felt his chest, felt for his heart. It didn't take long to tell that he was dead. She sat down on the sofa and contemplated the wreck of her plans.

Southern and Potter found the woman in the general-store-cum-newsagent's at Grange chatty and informative.

"Oh, Sir James. Yes, they were here for several weeks. Nice enough couple, though I think he'd married beneath him."

"Was he in full possession of his faculties, do you think?"

The woman hesitated.

"Well, you'd have thought so. Always said, 'Nice day,' or 'Hope the rain keeps off,' if he came in for a tin of tobacco or a bottle of wine. But no more than that. Then one day I said, 'Shame about the Waleses, isn't it?'—you know, at the time of the split-up. He seemed bewildered, so I said, 'The Prince and Princess of Wales separating.' Even then it was obvious he didn't understand. It was embarrassing. I turned away and served somebody else. But there's others had the same experience."

After some minutes Marcia found it intolerable to be in the same room as the body. Trying to look the other way, she dragged it through to the dining room. Even as she did so she realized that she had made a decision: She was not going to the police, and her plans were not at an end.

Because, after all, she had her "Sir James" all lined up. In the operation planned for the next few days, the existence of the real one was anyway something of an embarrassment. Now that stumbling block had been removed. She rang Ben Blackett and told him there had been a slight change of plan, but it needn't affect his part in it. She rang Crummock Lodge and told them that Sir James had changed his mind and wanted to settle straight into the new cottage. While there was still some dim light, she went into the garden and out into the lonely land behind, collecting as many large stones as she could find. Then she slipped down and put them into the rowing boat she had borrowed from her neighbor the day before.

She had no illusions about the size—or more specifically the weight—of the problem she had in disposing of the body. She gave herself a stiff brandy, but no more than one. She found a razor blade and, shaking, removed the name from Sir James's suit. Then she finished her packing, so that everything was ready for departure. The farming people of the area were early to bed as a rule, but there were too many tourists staying there, she calculated, for it to be really safe before the early hours. At pre-

cisely one o'clock she began the long haul down to the shore. Sir
James had been nearly six foot, so though his form was wasted,
he was both heavy and difficult to lift. Marcia found, though,
that carrying was easier than dragging, and quieter, too. In three
arduous stages she got him to the boat, then into it. The worst
was over. She rowed out to the dark center of the lake—the
crescent moon was blessedly obscured by clouds—filled his
pockets with stones, then carefully, gradually, eased the body
out of the boat and into the water. She watched it sink, then
made for the shore. Two large brandies later, she piled the cases
into the car, locked up the cottage, and drove off in the direction
of Cockermouth.

After the horror and difficulty of the night before, everything
went beautifully. Marcia had barely settled into the new cottage
when Ben Brackett arrived. He already had some of Sir James's
characteristics down pat: his distant, condescending affability,
for example. Marcia coached him in others, and they tried to
marry them to qualities the real Sir James had no longer had:
lucidity and purpose.

When the team of two arrived, the fake Sir James was working in the garden. "Got to get it in some sort of order," he explained in his upper-class voice. "Haven't the strength I once
had, though." When they were all inside, and over a splendid
afternoon tea, he paid eloquent tribute to his new wife.

"She's made a new man of me," he explained. "I was letting
myself go after Molly died. Marcia pulled me up in my tracks
and brought me round. Oh, I know the boys are angry. I don't
blame them. In fact, I blame myself. I was never a good father
to them—too busy to be one. Got my priorities wrong. But it
won't hurt them to wait a few years for the money."

The team was clearly impressed. They steered the talk round
to politics, the international situation, changes in the law. "Sir
James" kept his end up, all in that rather grand voice and distant
manner. When the two men left, Marcia knew that her problems
were over. She and Ben Brackett waited for the sound of the car
leaving to go back to Keswick, then she poured very large whis-
kies for them. Over their third she told him what had happened
to the real Sir James.

"You did superbly," said Ben Brackett when she had finished.
"It was bloody difficult."

"I bet it was. But it was worth it. Look how it went today. A
piece of cake. We had them in the palms of our hands. We won,
Marcia! Let's have another drink on that. We won!"

Even as she poured, Marcia registered disquiet at that "we."

Sitting in his poky office in Kendal, Southern and Potter sur-
veyed the reports and other pieces of evidence they had set out
on the desk.

"It's becoming quite clear," said Southern thoughtfully. "In
Grange we have an old man who hardly seems to know who the
Prince and Princess of Wales are. In the cottage near Cockermouth we have an old man who can talk confidently about politics and the law. In Grange we have a feeble man, and a corpse
which is that of a soft liver. In the other cottage we have a man
who gardens—perhaps to justify the fact that his hands are *not*
those of a soft-living lawyer. At some time between taking her
husband on the lake—was that a rehearsal, I wonder?—and the
departure in the night, she killed him. She must already have
had someone lined up to take his place for the visit of the medical team."

"And they're there still," said Potter, pointing to the letter
from the estate agents in London. "That's where all communications still go."

"And that's where we're going to go," said Southern, getting
up.

They had got good information on the cottage from the Cockermouth police. They left their car in the car park of a roadside
pub, and took the lane through fields and down toward the
northern shore of Crummock Water. They soon saw the cottage,
overlooking the lake, lonely . . .

But the cottage was not as quiet as its surroundings. As they
walked toward the place they heard shouting. A minute or two
later they heard two thick voices arguing. When they could dis-
tinguish words, it was in a voice far from upper-crust:

"Will you get that drink, you cow? . . . How can I when I can
hardly stand? . . . Get me that drink or it'll be the worse for you

tomorrow. . . . You'd better remember who stands between you and a long jail sentence, Marcia. You'd do well to think about that *all the time*. . . . Now get me that scotch or you'll feel my fist!"

When Southern banged on the door there was silence. The woman who opened the door was haggard-looking, with bleary eyes and a bruise on the side of her face. In the room behind her, slumped back in a chair, they saw a man whose expensive clothes were in disarray, whose face was red and puffy, and who most resembled a music hall comic's version of a gentleman.

"Lady Harrington? I'm Superintendent Southern and this is Sergeant Potter. I wonder if we could come in? We have to talk to you."

He raised his ID toward her clouded eyes. She looked down at it slowly. When she looked up again, Southern could have sworn that the expression on her face was one of relief.

BRENDA MELTON BURNHAM

THE TENNIS COURT

*A resident of Arizona, Brenda Melton Burnham is a writer
new to this series. Here she contributes a fine tale of a long-
ago summer when the war made everything different. It was
another of this year's Edgar nominees.*

I settle into the familiar contours of the wicker chair as the first
sliver of sun appears over the eastern mountains. The screen
door squeals its usual complaint, and Leah steps onto the porch,
her entire concentration focused on the tray in her hands.

She arrives at the table and sets her burden down without
spilling it, always a triumph to be savored; then pours my coffee
and hands me the mug before dropping into the chair beside
me. She reminds me of myself at twelve, all legs and eagerness;
physically racing to catch up with her mind while emotionally
still clinging to childhood.

"Gonna be another hot day," Leah says, using her grown-up
voice as she picks up her glass of milk.

"A scorcher," I agree.

We sip our refreshments in our best tea party manner. I can
usually last longer than my granddaughter at this game of Let's
Pretend; I've had years of adulthood in which to practice.

Sixty yards in front of us, across the slope of grass turning
brown in the August heat, the men of the family bend their ener-
gies—and their backs—to the cause of tearing out the old tennis
court. The noise of the heavy jackhammers echoes against the
foothills.

"I was your age when my grandfather built this court," I say, even though I know I've said it many times before.

Nineteen forty-two saw countries at war and families in turmoil. Our family was no different. My father and Uncle Theo joined the army in the spring. When they left for training, my mother and my aunt packed up their children and returned here, to their father's farm.

I fell asleep to the sound of my mother and her three sisters as they laughed and talked among themselves. I woke in the morning to the same sounds—as though they had continued, unceasing, throughout the night. Bras and panties hung from the clothesline in the mud room. Lipsticks and powder lay atop the dresser scarves, next to the old inlaid brushes and tortoiseshell combs. Chinese checkers and dominoes decorated the side table in the living room, always ready and waiting for a quick game.

In the early mornings, before the sun reached the valley, my grandfather went fishing on the river at the back of the farm. Often one or more of his daughters accompanied him as they had done when they were young.

In the evenings, after dinner, we sat on the porch to catch the air and listen to Gabriel Heater on the radio. I helped turn the crank on the ice cream maker. We watched my seven-year-old sister and Aunt Marge's five-year-old twins chase fireflies.

Always, *always* my grandfather had dominated this house, these lives. Even when he wasn't present, his shadow was. But 1942, in the Krueger household, was to be the year of the women.

"C'mon, Sonia," they would call to me. "If you want to go with us, you'd better hurry."

And of course I wanted to go with them. Every morning I examined my flat child's chest for signs of a bosom. I tried to brush my hair in a pageboy the way Aunt Trudy, the youngest of the sisters, did. Aunt Inga taught me to play cribbage and the strategy for winning at dominoes. Aunt Marge showed me how to use her nail polish. My mother let me stay up after the younger kids had been put to bed.

"I'm coming," I would call with one last glance in the mirror.

"Have you got the rackets, Inga?"

"Don't forget the balls this time, Liz."

Every afternoon we headed for the park in town where I watched my sister and the twins while the four women played tennis. I had never realized how beautiful they were with their blond hair and white teeth and strong, healthy bodies.

Soldiers and civilian personnel from the nearby military base realized it as well. There was always a contingent of them waiting to challenge the Krueger women. My mother, Marge, and Inga had no favorites and soundly defeated most comers, but Trudy was soft on a thin, dark, intense young man named Ira Glass.

It was a day like all other days as we headed home. Early June, perhaps, when the sun still promised a summer that would last forever. The car seats burned the backs of my legs, and my throat tasted of dust. The other women were teasing Trudy.

"You should've had that last point, Trudy. Don't give away the game just because you give away your heart."

"Tennis matches start with love. They don't always end that way."

"Oh, Ira, my wonderful one."

Trudy protested loudly and they all laughed.

When we got home, Grandfather waited on the porch. "Where have you been?" he shouted in German.

"Speak English, Poppa," Marge said.

"Playing tennis," Inga said. "At the park."

"Tramps! Strumpets! Parading yourselves in front of those men!"

"Oh, Poppa, don't be ridiculous," my mother said.

I huddled back with the little kids, trying to be ignored.

"Was it hot that summer, Gram?" Leah asks.

"Hotter even than now," I reply.

The heavy pounding of the jackhammers ceases just as the sun pops over the ridge. My daughter comes out of the house with a pitcher of lemonade to refresh the laboring men before they begin the effort of removing the moss-stained chunks of concrete.

* * *

Trudy had worked as a druggist's assistant in town and Inga as a secretary. Within a week of each other they were fired from their jobs. I was shooed from the room both times and was forced to listen at the door.

". . . a sympathizer," Trudy sobbed.

"Silly man," my mother said.

"If only Poppa wouldn't insist on aggravating them."

"They're afraid," Marge scoffed. "That's all. It's the war."

"Besides," Inga said, "it gives us more time to be together."

And always the young men waited at the courts. More and more now Trudy and Ira were a pair. He gave her a pin, a gold tennis racket with a tiny ball of glittering stones. She gave him a silver ring she'd worn as a child; he wore it on a chain around his neck.

Some nights Trudy slipped out the side door after everyone had gone to bed, and I knew she went to meet Ira. I discovered this by accident one night when I got up to go to the bathroom. When I came out, my mother was waiting in the hall.

"What's wrong?" I whispered.

"Nothing. Go back to bed."

"But I saw Trudy . . ."

My mother focused a hard look on me. "Yes? What did you see?"

"Nothing."

My mother put her arm around my shoulder and kissed the top of my head. "It isn't easy growing up, *liebchen*," she murmured into my hair.

"Were you happy that summer?" my granddaughter asks.

"Oh yes," I reply. "Yes, I was happy."

Throughout the whole time, my grandmother cooked. A short, round woman, she left the sanctuary of her kitchen only to feed her precious birds, calling to them in her native tongue. "Come, my pretty ones, come see what I have for you. Come, come."

July days melted one into the other. The temperature continued to soar. My grandfather seemed to shrivel with the heat while the women plumped out and grew taller and stronger. On the court their faces shone with perspiration. The tennis dresses whipped around their thighs. They were Valkyries . . . Amazons. I thought they were indomitable.

One day, as we walked to the car, a woman ran up and spat in Inga's face. "Nazi bitch!" she screamed, her face twisting with the ugly words.

Inga calmly wiped her cheek with the towel she had been carrying while my mother and Marge marched along beside her, their expressions closed and inscrutable. Trudy and I and the little kids stumbled alongside, silent with shock.

Another time, as we were driving past, a gang of boys threw rocks at us.

"You mustn't let it upset you, Sonia," Marge said to me. "They don't know who to take their anger out on."

"But we're Americans. Aren't we?"

"Of course we are."

"Even though some people forget it," Inga added.

"Were you surprised when your grandpa decided to build the tennis court?" Leah asks.

"You might say that," I acknowledge.

Out on the lawn the men finish their lemonade and bend to their labors once again. They tie handkerchiefs about their heads to keep the sweat out of their eyes. Their bodies glisten with moisture.

When we came down to breakfast that morning in early August, Grandfather was outside, astride his tractor. Behind him the huge disks chopped up the once-green lawn.

"What's he doing?"

"What in the world . . ."

"He's tearing up the whole yard."

"You want to play tennis, *ja?*" he called out to them. "Fine. I build you a tennis court."

The women looked at each other and said things with their eyes.

The next day the Gruener brothers arrived and agreed to pour a concrete slab when Grandfather had the ground ready.

"Does this mean we won't be going to town anymore?" I asked. The women glared at me.

"No need," Grandfather said.

Our outings took on a desperate air those last days.

"We can always invite people over to play," Inga suggested.

"Can't you see it?" Marge said. "Poppa standing at the gate, checking everyone as they come through?" She laughed.

"He'll never let Ira come," Trudy said. She nibbled at the corners of her stubby red fingertips.

Her sisters didn't answer.

"Oh god, what'll I do?" she cried out.

"Everyone must've been pretty excited," Leah remarks.

"It was a pretty exciting time."

Already the heat is building. In front of us, their muscles bulge as the younger men load the concrete pieces on the flatbed truck.

Every day Grandfather worked, harrowing, leveling, then building the forms for the concrete slabs. Every day the women's voices grew shriller.

"You really needn't tear up the yard like this for us," my mother, being the eldest, said at dinner. "Why don't you put in a flower bed for Momma?"

"Momma has enough flower beds."

"We don't mind going into town."

"Even when someone spits on you?"

The women darted glances at one another. "We do have friends there," Marge said.

"Invite them here."

"Poppa," my mother said, "we *like* going to the park."

"I will not have my family spit on." Grandfather's fist crashed onto the table. Dishes rattled. One of the twins began to cry. Grandmother decided to make coffee cake so it would be ready for breakfast the next morning. "I will not have my daughters behaving like sluts. Do you hear me? You will play here or you will play nowhere."

Trudy jumped up and ran from the room.

In town the next day Trudy and Ira took the car while the others played tennis. Afterward, as we were driving home, she said, "It's decided. We'll go tonight and be married over in Slocum County." Her eyes glittered, and she bit her lip nervously.

"Trudy, are you sure?"

"Of course I'm sure. I love him. He loves me."

"Then bring him home. Poppa will give in when he knows you're serious."

"No. He won't. And you know it. He still has one foot on German soil."

"But you can't sneak off . . ."

"If you don't want to help me, you don't have to. I'll do it by myself."

"We'll help you," Inga said.

"I'll bet you couldn't wait until the court was finished, right?" Leah prompts.

"It seemed to happen very fast." I close my eyes and let the heat seep into my bones.

"How do I look?" Trudy twirled, fluffing her hair, showing off her soft white dress. The little gold racket pin gleamed at her breast.

"You look beautiful," I said. The others nodded.

They all hugged each other, then my mother and Trudy slipped out the bedroom door and down the dark stairs. I rushed to the window and watched my youngest aunt disappear across the lawn.

And saw the other figure step out of the barn behind her.

"Someone else is out there," I whispered.

The others rushed over. "You're seeing things, *liebchen*," Inga said.

"No, no, I'm not!"

The door opened and my mother came in, her face pale. "Poppa was waiting by the barn. He's following her. He must've known about them all along."

"How could he know?"

45

"How did he know about the spitting? It's a small town. I tell you he knows."

"What'll we do?"

"What can we do?"

"Why didn't you go after her?"

"It was too late." My mother shrugged her shoulders and shook her head. "It was too late the minute Trudy stepped out the door."

We sat in the silent bedroom and waited, our ears straining to hear a strange noise among the night sounds, afraid to speak for fear of missing it.

There was no missing it when it came. Trudy raced back across the wet grass, slamming the screen door behind her, pounding up the stairs and into the room. Her hair hung in tangles. A huge red mark ran across her cheek. Dark stains covered her dress. The bodice was ripped and the tiny pin gone.

"Oh, Liz," she cried, "I'll never see him again," and fell into my mother's arms.

"Trudy, did you and Ira—" Inga paused. "You aren't pre—"

Marge turned to me, bumping Inga with her elbow. "Go to bed, Sonia."

"But I want . . ."

"Go to bed," my mother said.

"I still don't understand why you never played tennis, Gram," my granddaughter says.

One of the men—is it Max? or Charley? I can't tell—stops digging and kneels to work at the dirt with his hands.

I never heard Grandfather come back. I woke late the next morning. No air moved through the silent house. Dressing was an effort. My clothes felt heavy on my body as I walked down the stairs. Mother and Marge and Inga were down by the dock. My sister and the twins dug ditches in the mud, something they weren't normally allowed to do. The women talked of the heat and answered the little kids' questions about bugs and dirt and trees. From the front yard we could hear the sounds of the Gruener brothers pouring the concrete slab for the tennis court.

* * *

"I've always hated this court," I whisper. To Leah? To myself? To the past? "Always."

The kneeling man—it is Max; I can see the bright cloth tied about his head—calls to the other men. They gather around him. I hear their exclamations but can't make out the words.

My mother discovered Trudy's body when she went upstairs to check on her. The coroner's report said "suicide while of an unsound mind." It was assumed she had gotten the sleeping pills when she was working at the drugstore.

Two MP's from the army base came to the house a week later. Ira Glass had gone AWOL, and they were trying to locate him.

"But I don't understand," Leah persists, her eyes full of the innocence of youth. "If you hated it so much, why did you wait until now to tear it out?"

All the men scrape at the earth with their hands.

"Pour me another cup of coffee, will you, dear?" I say.

The morning the heat wave broke, my mother and Inga went fishing with my grandfather. When the boat returned to the dock two hours later, only the women were aboard. They came ashore silently, their backs erect, their wet clothes dripping on the soft green grass.

"Poppa had a strike and had started to reel it in," they said, "when he dropped his pole and clutched at his chest."

"He must've had a heart attack," they said.

"He was overboard before we could catch him," they said.

"It was downstream where the current was strongest. That was where he always liked to fish, you remember," they said.

"We went in to help him, but he never came up," they said.

The police decided against dragging the river. His body surfaced four days later several miles away. He was buried in the family plot next to Trudy.

* * *

They're all gone now . . . Trudy . . . Mother . . . Marge. Inga, who never married, died a week ago. After the funeral I asked my son Karl and my son-in-law Max, Leah's father, both stalwart, upright men, to tear out the tennis court.

Now the men walk up to the porch in a group. They let Karl lead.

"We found—" he begins, then stops to take a deep breath. "There were bones under the concrete, Mother." He holds out something. "And this." A set of dog tags. And a tiny silver ring.

I take the small objects in my hands. They are still cool from the dark, damp soil. I am aware of so many things. The heat from the sun, the river singing in the distance. The contours of the old wicker chair. Of debts owed and the debts paid.

My granddaughter, unusual for her, sits silent beside me.

"Mother," Karl says softly, fearful of startling me. "We'd better call the police, don't you think?" He looks at me. Waits. A good son.

"Yes," I answer. "You're right. We must."

P. M. CARLSON

THE EIGHTH WONDER OF THE WORLD; OR, GOLDEN OPINIONS

Since publishing her first novel ten years ago, P. M. (Patricia McEvoy) Carlson has become a prolific mystery writer and has assumed an active role in writers' organizations. She is a past president of Sisters in Crime and has held various posts in Mystery Writers of America. Most of her novels concern academic sleuth and statistician Maggie Ryan, but here she tries something different—a historical mystery in which actress Bridget Mooney uncovers dirty dealings in the building of the Brooklyn Bridge.

I scrambled from the stage door, coughing and gasping, heedless of the damage to my beautiful bustled frock. Most miserable hour that e'er time saw! I reckon I'd never been in such a fix. Smoke billowed about me, and sparks rained down. I smelt a dreadful odor and realized that a lock of my unkempt red hair had caught fire. As I knelt to douse it in a puddle of meltwater, I could hear shrieks, thin and terrible against the background roar of the colossal furnace behind me.

The Brooklyn Theatre had caught fire just moments ago, and flames were already lapping at the dark heavens.

The screams behind me tore at my heart, but I stiffened the sinews, summoned up the blood, and crawled gasping along the filthy alley. I heard new cries—the shouts of men on the street ahead, firemen and curiosity seekers who were pouring from

49

nearby saloons and hotels. Legs booted for the December weather pounded by; lanterns bobbed. When I reached the street I tried to stand but my scorched lungs were unable to sustain me and the world swam as I fell against a post.

Clarity returned moments later, and I could again hear the screams and shouts and thudding boots on the cold street. Now I was moving swiftly, being carried along by a pair of strong arms belonging to a sturdy fellow of some twenty years. He wore a cheap rough laborer's coat but his smile was a treasure of kindliness.

"Feeling better, missy?" he asked solicitously.

"Oh, sir, my gratitude is boundless!" I gasped as elegantly as I could. His face registered sudden respect. Perhaps I should remind you that I had recently been tutored in elocutionary skills by the esteemed English actress Mrs. Fanny Kemble, the greatest of her generation.

"Excuse me, madam," he said in confusion, and for a moment I feared that he would bow and drop me. "You won't take it the wrong way, I hope, but for a moment I thought you were a mere actress."

Pleased that he now thought me a lady, I said, "I remain grateful."

My hearty rescuer had borne me a block away from the inferno, and now paused. "Are you better, madam? I can leave you here with your permission, and go back for another poor soul."

Well, I ask you, would any young lady, weakened by smoke and fear, want to be abandoned on the cold street in front of a dry-goods store? The prospect was so dreadful that I was weighing several desperate and perhaps improper means of clinging to my rough-clad hero when I heard a woman's voice call, "Harry! Harry Supple, is that you?"

"Yes, ma'am," said my young man, turning to a carriage that pulled up beside us.

"Harry, it's a dreadful fire! Is it Dieters Hotel?"

The newcomer's voice was educated, and the carriage lanterns gleamed against a shiny painted gig. Well, I reckoned that the well-bred voice and glossy paint signified places far more comfortable than this cold street. I decided to swoon again as Harry Supple answered, "It's the Brooklyn Theatre, ma'am. I was just going back to help the firemen, for I fear there are people dying. But here's this poor lady I rescued with her frock and hair all scorched, and in a faint again, poor thing. A fine lady, too."

"Put her in the carriage, Harry," commanded the lady. "She is well-dressed. I'll take her home. Your strong arms are needed here."

Quickly, Harry placed me in the carriage and vanished into the night. The lady tapped the horse with her whip, for she herself was driving, and we moved rapidly away from the dreadful conflagration. I remained limp, with my eyes closed, but I was aware that the lady drove only a few blocks before halting again, calling for servants to help her carry me in.

I was laid on a bed with smooth sheets, and my face and arms were cleansed with moistened cotton cloths amidst soft exclamations about my scorched hair and frock. Then the lady and her maids began to discuss removing the frock, to attend to my needs more easily. Since a pocket that I had sewn into my bustle contained a few items that I preferred not to reveal to the public, I emitted a little moan and fluttered my eyelashes.

"She's coming round," said the educated lady.

It was my cue to open my eyes and say feebly, "Oh . . . what lovely place is this? Am I in heaven, and these the Lord's own angels?" Unfortunately the effect I intended was rather ruined by a spasm of coughing that overtook me.

"Poor dear!" said the educated woman briskly. "You have survived your ordeal, and I believe that when you have taken more good, fresh air, you will be able to return to your home."

In the lamplight, I saw that she was a strong woman in her thirties with a pug nose, lively features, and a beautiful smile. I said, "Thank you for your kindness, madam," paused to make sure I had no more coughing to do, and added, "Oh—I remember, the fire! The dreadful fire!"

"Yes. What happened?" The lady's face was as filled with curiosity as the maid's.

"Oh, madam, it was so quick!" I replied. "One of the border curtains high above the stage blew against the flame of a border light, and caught instantly. In a few moments the entire theater was ablaze!"

"How dreadful!"

"Yes—yes, it was. You are so kind to me, madam, in this hour of misfortune. Permit me to introduce myself. I am Miss Mooney, of a landed Irish family, friends to the Kemble and Sartoris families of England."

Oh, I know, I know, we weren't really landed, unless you count the muddy gutters of St. Louis where Papa spent much of his time. But we were Irish, weren't we? And I certainly knew Kembles and Sartorises. I also knew President Grant—in fact, his daughter Nellie had provided me with the lovely frock I was wearing—but his administration had crumbled in such a flurry of frauds and bribery that I did not wish to mention him until I knew more about this household.

The kind lady said, "I am Mrs. Roebling, and it is a pleasure to make your acquaintance, dear Miss Mooney, though I regret the tragic circumstances of our meeting. Were you attending the spectacle tonight?"

In fact, I had been in the spectacle tonight. But looking around the solid respectability of this room, I hesitated to admit it. Laboring folks like Harry Supple were fascinated by those of us in the limelight, and the higher classes, the noble families of England and the wealthy and politically powerful on both sides of the Atlantic, toasted us. The great actress Mrs. Kemble had married into Southern landed gentry, and her sister Mrs. Sartoris, an opera singer, had wed an English noble. But between Supple and Sartoris lay a large middle class of respectable burghers, the men who ran the shops and built the bridges of the nation, and many of them looked askance at those in my profession until they became rich enough to view us as their playthings.

Bridges! That was it, bridges! On my way to the ferry, I had seen this fine lady often, talking to the workers who were building the great span over the East River. "Mrs. Roebling," I said, "are you by any chance related to the illustrious man who is constructing the splendid bridge to Brooklyn?"

Mrs. Roebling beamed. "Yes. My husband is the Chief Engineer."

I clasped my hands. "What a noble work it is, Mrs. Roebling! When I crossed the East River on the ferry, it was stirring indeed to see those two great towers rising like anthems to the sky!" It was true—the two giant structures rose from the river and upward, ever upward, taller than anything for miles around, except for Trinity Church in Wall Street.

Mrs. Roebling leaned back in the bedside chair and smiled sadly. "They were not built without cost, dear Miss Mooney."

"Oh, yes, I have heard of the dreadful caisson disease that has afflicted the Chief Engineer."

"It is dreadful indeed. These last four years my poor husband has suffered so much that he cannot bear to speak to people, nor stir from his room. I write his instructions for him, and carry them to the workmen. And yet, despite the pain and exhaustion, his mind remains clear."

"That is good news, for I had heard that it affects the mind as well."

Mrs. Roebling scowled. "That is not true, Miss Mooney! Who has been telling you such rubbish?"

"A gentleman admirer of mine. But of course you know best, Mrs. Roebling, and I will endeavor to correct his misapprehension when next I see him."

Mrs. Roebling leaned toward me and asked urgently, "Who is your admirer, Miss Mooney? Who is spreading these rumors? Is it Abram Hewitt, the ironmonger?"

She was so intent, looking at me like a hound at a rabbit hole, that I forgot my own difficulties and sat up on the bed. "Mrs. Roebling, please do not distress yourself! I have no desire to sow dissension between the Chief Engineer and the others devoted to the bridge."

"Dissension aplenty has already been sown!" Mrs. Roebling snorted. She looked me over carefully, then sighed. "Ah, well, it cannot be Abram Hewitt. That prim fellow is incapable of behaving in a manner that would lead a lady to describe him as her admirer. Miss Mooney, you would find it difficult to believe the trials we suffer, trying to accomplish what we were chosen to do! The great bridge stands unfinished while the politicians quarrel. This affair with the cable wire—"

Well, that made me prick up my ears, because my admirer was in fact in the wire business. I asked, "What affair with the cable wire?"

"That hypocritical fellow Hewitt is a trustee of the bridge company, as you may know. And he says that those connected with the bridge must not bid on the cable, thus disqualifying my husband's brothers! Yet people believe in his saintliness!"

"You mean Mr. Hewitt has prevented the Roebling wire company from furnishing the wire for the cables?"

"Exactly! Mr. Hewitt said he personally would not bid for the contract. But he's an ironmonger, his company doesn't manufacture wire! Of course he won't bid personally! His cronies will bid instead!" She looked at me earnestly. "It is not merely the unfairness to my brothers-in-law that distresses me. It is the fear that Mr. Hewitt's friends will provide a slipshod product for my—for *our* great bridge!"

Well, naturally Mrs. Roebling would think that Roebling wire would build a better bridge. Still, for such a proper lady, she seemed very knowledgeable. I tried to console her. "That is dreadful, Mrs. Roebling. But surely the opportunity to contribute to this marvel of our age will inspire the company to provide only the best wire! Besides, if Mr. Hewitt values his reputation, he will see to it that his friend's product is excellent."

She said darkly, "Mr. Hewitt is one of Tilden's chief supporters."

"Tilden? They say he has just been elected President of the United States! That is—"

"It is still contested," Mrs. Roebling reminded me. "In any case, just now Mr. Hewitt has great power among seekers of patronage. For all his saintly posing, I prefer the corrupt followers of President Useless S. Grant!"

Well, I was relieved that I had not admitted to my acquaintance with the Grant family. I idly smoothed the skirt of the lovely dress Nellie Grant had given me, then gasped in shock. I reckon I've never seen a skirt so ratty-looking. The white muslin flounces were caked with mud and soot, and burn marks streaked the splendid mandarin yellow foulard.

Mrs. Roebling saw my dismay and exclaimed, "Oh, my dear

Miss Mooney, here I've been chattering on about my problems while you are the one with troubles!"

"My poor frock! Besmeared as black as Vulcan!"

She picked up a fold of the skirt and inspected it in the lamplight. "The muslin is easily washed," she declared briskly, and turned to the servant. "As for the foulard—Bessie, didn't you boil up the mixture for scorch marks last week? Onion juice, vinegar, white soap, and fuller's earth? And bring the scissors, so we can repair Miss Mooney's coiffure."

I stood to peek into a glass, and for a moment did not realize that the bedraggled Medusa-like creature reflected there was my usually sprightly self. "Oh, my goodness, what will Lloyd think!" I gasped unthinkingly.

When I'd first noticed the border curtain catching fire, I had roused the other actors. Then I'd lit out for the dressing room to exchange my flimsy theatrical costume for my beloved Nellie Grant dress, with its bustle pocket filled with my souvenirs and with a few bracelets I found lying about, left behind by other actresses who were fleeing the blazing theater. There had not been time to arrange my hair, and the long auburn tresses looked sorry indeed, burnt and damp and snaky with dirty snow. No wonder Harry Supple had not assumed I was a lady.

Slowly I became aware that Mrs. Roebling was regarding me with great suspicion.

"Mrs. Roebling, what is it?" I inquired anxiously, concerned about her sudden change of demeanor.

She asked in a tight voice, "Did you say Lloyd? Is that the name of your admirer, the man who is maligning my husband's ability?"

"Mrs. Roebling, I know that your husband is able! The proof stands proudly in the East River, poised to link these two great cities!"

"It is Lloyd, then," said Mrs. Roebling. "Mr. J. Lloyd Haigh."

I said feebly, "I am sorry, Mrs. Roebling. He appeared to be honorable in all other matters."

And indeed he did appear honorable, my Lloyd. He was a handsome gentleman of some fifty years, with twinkling honest eyes. He was a fine vocalist, a jolly man who was always ready with a compliment that could make a young lady shiver with pleasure. He was also eager to be of assistance in business matters, and had purchased a few old deeds and papers that Aunt Mollie had bequeathed me, giving me over a thousand dollars for them with the explanation that a gentleman of good reputation could use them to obtain loans from a bank, but that a young lady wouldn't wish to trouble herself to learn about interest and repayment and similar tedious matters. Don't you think that was kind of him? Yes indeed. His generosity had enabled me to take a room in an excellent hotel instead of the dirty inn where the other actors stayed. He spoke often of marriage but I put him off.

"Honorable!" Mrs. Roebling exclaimed. She was combing my unsightly hair and gave the comb an angry and painful jerk to emphasize her point. "Those of us who know something of the wire business are aware of certain underhanded practices by Mr. J. Lloyd Haigh's company! But I fear that is of no interest to the bridge trustees."

I waited until the comb was safely through the next red tress before saying, "What you say is shocking, Mrs. Roebling. It is difficult to believe such things of a fine gentleman."

"Oh, yes, he's most persuasive. You aren't the first lady to believe him, and gentlemen are just as gullible. During the bidding, each firm submitted samples of their wire for testing by Colonel Paine with his new device. Mr. Haigh's samples did well. But I suspect Haigh did not manufacture them at his own mill. Instead, he purchased them from a reputable firm, and submitted them as his own."

"Dear me!"

"Of course Mr. Abram Hewitt is trying to assure his success also. Mr. Hewitt cleared out the Tweed Ring from the bridge project, only to arrange for his own friends to profit from it. It makes the Chief Engineer so angry! I believe he would have been up and about years ago except for the nervous exhaustion the politicians inspire in him."

"Poor fellow," I said, reflecting that Mrs. Roebling herself must be able to deal with politicians rather skillfully, or a sick man would not still be in charge of the great bridge. "If a member of the public may offer a suggestion, would it be possible for all the wire to be tested before it is used on the bridge?"

"Yes! Indeed, that may be the answer, testing all the wire!" She thought a moment, smiled, and I breathed a sigh of relief for her kinder mood, for she had finished with the comb and was picking up the scissors. "If Haigh's firm is chosen, we could enforce his honesty, couldn't we?" She snipped carefully. "Still, Miss Mooney, if Mr. Haigh mentions matrimony, be certain to inquire about Miss Jennie Hughes before you accept."

"Accept! Goodness, no, I have no intention of marrying anyone! My aunt Mollie had a little money from her father, and after she married Uncle Mike she wanted to buy a"—I had to feign a fit of coughing, because I almost said "a saloon"—"to buy a pleasant riverside property, but they said a married lady couldn't sign for it, her husband had to sign for it."

"That is true." Mr. Roebling clipped my singed locks into a fringe across my forehead. "A wife cannot enter into a contract, although a single woman can."

"So Uncle Mike signed for the property, and then he mortgaged it, and spent the money. And soon the bank foreclosed and sold Aunt Mollie's property." I didn't tell her that Uncle Mike had lost the money gambling with the sporting men who work in the saloon, but Aunt Mollie had to take up copying for a trade. From then on she made more private arrangements with bankers, and frequently warned me that for a poor girl marriage was a snare, no different from being a bound servant or a tart, excepting of course in the eyes of the Lord, and the Lord didn't often pay the bills, did He?

Hastily, I added to Mrs. Roebling, "Of course, with a fine husband like the Chief Engineer, marriage is an excellent arrangement."

"Of course," said Mrs. Roebling. "And yet I have heard other stories much like your aunt Mollie's. Someday we must ask them to change the laws. The difficulty is that we wives have so many duties, we cannot easily spare the time. Meanwhile, you are wise to stay clear of Mr. Haigh. There, Miss Mooney, that is the best we can do with your hair."

"Oh, thank you! It looks quite fashionable," I said, and indeed it appeared much less pitiful and mangy. "You are the kindest lady in the world! And Mr. Harry Supple is one of the kindest men."

"Yes, Harry's a good lad, one of our most trusted riggers. He used to be a sailor, and is good on the wire ropes."

"Do thank him for me, as I was too enfeebled to do so. Now, I have imposed too long on your good graces. My cough is much improved, and my hair is respectable again."

"But your frock, Miss Mooney!"

"I would gladly accept a jar of your mixture to clean scorch marks."

She and Bessie gave me several jars, and an old traveling cape to ward off the winter winds, as my cloak had been abandoned to the blaze. Mrs. Roebling drove me to my fine hotel, saying she would return to the scene of the fire to see if she could help other poor souls.

The next day I rose early, donned the Roebling cape and a feather-trimmed bonnet that dipped low enough in front to hide most of my damaged hair, and hurried to the site of the great fire. The scene was ghastly, the stench worse. Well over a hundred people had perished, and the firemen were still carrying bodies from the smoldering wreckage. I saw our stage manager, who was delighted that I had survived, but sad to inform me that two of our company had perished, Mr. Murdoch and Mr. Burroughs.

"Oh, no!" The world grew blurry, and I turned and staggered away from the dismal scene. Murdoch and Burroughs were fine boisterous young actors, and we'd had many a jolly hour backstage trading yarns about growing up in St. Louis or Zanesville.

"Bridge, my sweet! Is it you?" cried a gentlemanly baritone.

I turned, and Mr. J. Lloyd Haigh, devilishly handsome in his fine, dark cape and checked trousers, ran across to me from the door of the Market National Bank and well nigh hugged my head off. "Oh, Bridget, I was sick with worry!" cried my sweet-scented dandy.

I bowed my head against his elegant woolen cape. "Yes, I would not spend another such a night, though 'twere to buy a world of happy days! But please, Lloyd, I can't bear it here any longer!"

Lloyd pulled out a snowy handkerchief and tried to dry my tears. "Now, now, Bridget, you are safe with me! Let us walk by the river. Tell me, did your aunt Mollie's business papers burn?"

"No, Lloyd, they are safe."

"Good. Bridget, you are the dearest creature in the world!"

Even through my tears, I could feel the heat of his ardent gaze, and I allowed him to steal a kiss in honor of the great emotion we both felt at my narrow escape. Then he led me away from the scene of the calamity. When we reached the streets near the East River we paused to watch the bridge workers. The great towers, solid and yet airy with their handsome Gothic arches, stood proudly against the gray December sky. Thin ladders stretched the entire height of each tower. Near us stood the stone anchorage building, gray and massive, its top platform spiky with derricks. A few wire ropes had been slung from it to the very top of the two great towers, and thence to the New York side far away. Their scarves blowing in the wind, the laborers were laying slats between these first wire ropes, building themselves a narrow footbridge across the sky. I wondered if handsome Harry Supple was one of the nimble figures I saw scurrying high among the slender wire ropes.

I said, "Lloyd, is it true that your firm might provide the wire for this astonishing bridge?"

"Yes indeed!" He beamed at me. Lloyd had fine teeth and a most engaging smile. "The trustees of the Bridge Company have an excellent opinion of me. That is the most important thing in the world, Bridget, a good opinion. I am fortunate."

Well, I think that riches are more important than good opinion, because generally if a body has money, the good opinion follows along after. As one of Shakespeare's shiftier characters says, "I have bought golden opinions from all sorts of people." But sometimes it's more comfortable not to argue. I said, "It is important indeed. But isn't it true that the Chief Engineer has an interest in a rival firm?"

"Why, what a pert creature you are, my little Bridget, to be so interested in complicated business matters!"

59

I smiled the way I smiled when I played Juliet, and hoped that my poor hair did not look too bristly in the daylight. "Sir, when a gentleman proposes marriage, of course a young lady is interested in his prospects!"

"Ah, my sweet, of course! Well, my prospects are excellent. Naturally, the Chief Engineer favors his brothers' firm in Trenton. My mill, however, is located here in Brooklyn. Therefore I have the strong support of the editor of the Brooklyn *Eagle*, who is also a trustee of the bridge company. I have also another powerful friend among the trustees. Good opinion, Bridget, that is the secret! For when those who hold this good opinion of me gain nationwide power, my prospects will be boundless!"

"You are a supporter of Mr. Tilden, then?"

"A most loyal supporter! And soon my loyalty will be rewarded!" He was glowing with enthusiasm, and I could see that he had reason. If Lloyd helped Tilden's cause, Abram Hewitt and the other Tilden enthusiasts among the trustees would favor giving him the contract, and it would matter little who made the better wire. The Roeblings, I decided, might well lose this skirmish.

"Your loyalty to Tilden is financial also?" I hazarded.

"Naturally. What a lot of questions you ask, you sweet vixen!"

"Then your reward will be financial also!" I clapped my gloved hands and favored him with my sauciest smile.

It was too much for dear Lloyd, who pulled me into the shadowed privacy of the doorway of a saloon that had not yet opened and attempted to steal another kiss. "Yes, my reward will certainly be financial. And more, I hope, when you are my dear wife, and the queen of Brooklyn!"

Sweet-scented though he was, Lloyd was becoming far too ardent for the early morning of a day when I had much to mourn and much to do, seeing as I was out of work again. So, recollecting what Mrs. Roebling had told me, I giggled fetchingly and said, "Mr. Haigh, sir, I have not yet accepted your kind proposal! First I must confer with Miss Jennie Hughes!"

Well, that gave him a turn! His breath sort of hitched, and then he laughed heartily. "That was merely an attempt at blackmail, Bridget, I swear! Scurrilous people told her to say we had wed! I never married Miss Hughes, I never told her I would! She knew I was married already! You mustn't believe silly rumors!"

Hang it, this was worse than I'd expected. I needed to know more. I laughed heartily, too. "That is a great relief, Lloyd! I know it's true that many people do scurrilous deeds for the sake of money. Still, a charge of bigamy is serious!"

"It's false!" he exclaimed, clasping both my hands in his and gazing at me most sincerely. "I'm not a bigamist. I divorced my first wife in Connecticut! Bridget, my sweet, these falsehoods pain me all the more, for now I have met you, my truest love! Your bright eyes, your russet hair, the hint of freckles on the loveliest nose in the nation!"

I smiled demurely while I calculated. If he'd divorced his first wife, there must have been a second one, and not Jennie Hughes, for he said he hadn't married her. That made Jennie the third, at least, who claimed to have married him. I silently thanked Aunt Mollie, and Mrs. Roebling, for saving me from becoming a bigamist's fourth wife, surely a fate worse than death, and twice as ignoble.

I wriggled from Lloyd's embrace back to the street and started for the ferry landing. "Come, Lloyd, let us not be precipitous! A young lady must keep her reputation pure. You yourself have taught me the importance of good opinion. I will consider your kind offer."

"Bridget, I will do anything!" he cried sincerely. "I will go down on bended knee!"

Well, I must admit I like to see a handsome gentleman on bended knee, but gentlemen have other virtues, too. I squeezed Lloyd's hand gratefully, and by the time the ferry reached New York he had promised me a new velvet traveling dress in exchange for another of Aunt Mollie's old papers. An emerald-green dress, I decided, because green looked splendid with my hair, what there was of it.

Several days later, after much diligent searching, I had only two offers of work, one from a troupe that proposed to tour to Chicago with two Boucicault melodramas, and another from a Water Street dance hall. Since the duties in Water Street included more than dancing, I chose the touring troupe, and bade my Lloyd a tearful farewell, promising that I'd give him my answer soon.

Oh, I know, I know. Lloyd was a goodly apple rotten at the core, and a proper young lady would have snubbed such a dishonorable fellow; but it's so difficult to find honorable men in these times. And even if you find one he may up and get caisson disease, and lounge about moaning in an upstairs room while you build his bridges for him. My skills did not run to engineering, so it seemed prudent to pursue my chosen profession while selecting my gentlemen admirers for their generous hearts. And hang it, Lloyd did offer pretty compliments, and elegant green velvet traveling dresses, and useful business assistance whenever I found one of Aunt Mollie's commercial papers! Besides, when Tilden became president, and Abram Hewitt was running Washington, who could guess what splendors lay ahead for my Lloyd, and for his good friends?

But Tilden did not become president. Clever as he was, Abram Hewitt's skills at bribery were no match for those of the party of Lincoln and Grant, and Rutherford B. Hayes overcame popular defeat to triumph in the electoral college by a majority of one. It was many months before I returned to New York and encountered Mr. J. Lloyd Haigh again, and I expected him to bear signs of his disappointment as I sent in a note to his John Street office. But when he emerged he was his old ebullient self, handsome and wreathed in smiles.

"Bridget Mooney!" he cried. "I am delighted! Delighted!"

"I too, Lloyd!"

"You are the most beautiful creature in the world, Bridget!" He looked at me all hot-eyed. "May I beg the pleasure of escorting you to dinner?"

I carefully deployed my parasol in order to keep his enthusiastic attentions at bay and said, "I had hoped to take a constitutional to see the great bridge. They are calling it the eighth wonder of the world!"

"Of course, my sweet!" He offered his arm and we strolled along to observe the work at the New York anchorage. Atop the great stone boxlike structure, workmen with their sleeves rolled up in the June warmth were working with a thick, tautly stretched wire cable that came all the way from Brooklyn, crossing the tops of the towers to this anchorage, looping around an iron horseshoe-shaped holder, and then returning to Brooklyn as it had come. Lloyd explained that it was but one part of the enormous cable that would support the bridge. Working behind the great steel anchor bars, the laborers—one of them was my kindly hero, Harry Supple—attached the cable's horseshoe-shaped holder to a sturdy wire rope that ran over some pulleys back to a great machine. They started the machine. Amidst the ensuing noise and smoke, I saw the machine slowly easing the cable into position so they could attach it to the anchor bars.

Lloyd was observing with interest, too. He shouted, "Dangerous operation! If something gave way it would catapult that iron horseshoe across the river, and the cable too! The pull at the hoisting machine is seventy tons!"

I looked at the taut cable stretching all the way to Brooklyn. Seventy tons of tension. "You must be proud to be associated with such an achievement," I shouted.

"Indeed I am!"

"There's such a lot of wire in each cable! It must be very profitable to have such a contract."

"Yes, but—" A cloud flitted across his handsome face.

"But not as profitable as it should be?"

"Hush, little Bridget! It's no concern of yours!"

"The Chief Engineer has set unfair standards?" I hazarded. "Perhaps he is testing the wire?"

"Don't trouble yourself about it, Bridget!"

"I am troubled only for your sake! I worry so, Lloyd!"

I gave him my most anxious look, which put him in a more confiding spirit. "Fear not, I can manage the Chief Engineer, although he is implacable, Bridget! He has Colonel Paine check every wire, right at my mill. And he substitutes Roebling wire whenever he's allowed. Not in the cables, of course, but do you see the wire rope that attaches the cable to the hoisting machine?"

"The one that runs over the pulleys?"

"Yes. That's Roebling wire." He gestured at a woman's figure on the anchorage, and I recognized Mrs. Roebling in earnest conversation with the assistant engineers. "And he has his wife deliver letters to the bridge trustees, trying to undermine the good opinion I enjoy among them!"

The good opinion, and perhaps the profits, too. I said, "Your friends among the trustees will stand by you, surely."

"They will! I have my ways!" He beamed at me. "Fear not, Bridget, my profits are secure!"

"I'm certain they are, Lloyd!" I was tired of hollering and turned my attention to the anchorage. With many groans, the great machine had eased its seventy-ton load into place between two anchor bars. Quickly, the workmen drove in a thick steel pin to fasten it securely to the anchor bars. I must admit, I was impressed at the minds that had conceived this bridge, and the methods of building it, wire by wire and stone by stone. I was impressed also by the workmen. Harry Supple's sturdy forearms glistened in the sun. He had driven in the steel pin that locked the straining cable to the anchor bars. It all made me proud to be a part of this glorious age.

It didn't seem so glorious a few days later. I was in Water Street, reassuring myself that the dance hall would still hire me if the theater companies did not, when a great cannon sound boomed and crashed through the air. It was a noise to harrow up the soul. People began to shriek. Several ladies nearby, including some reputed harlots, fell to their knees to pray for forgiveness for their sins. With prickling spine, I hastened toward the great noise. There were shouts that there had been an accident at the bridge, and a crowd was forming at the anchorage. Someone was wounded. I ran to fetch a doctor I knew, then asked various gentlemen in the crowd what had occurred. Some said a cable had snapped; some said a bridge tower had fallen; some agreed with the young ladies in Water Street, and believed it was the Second Coming. There were many reports of falling stones, and of a fifty-foot-high splash of water in the East River that had drenched the passengers on the Fulton Ferry.

It was not until the next day that the newspapers pieced together what had happened. While workmen were trying to fasten a new cable to the anchor bars, it had broken away from the machine, shot as though from a catapult toward the Brooklyn shore. It had sheared off a chimney, leaped clean over the great tower, and smashed rowboats before splashing into the middle of the river. Two men working on the anchorage had been wounded, and two killed.

One of the dead was my own dear hero, Harry Supple.

The cause of the accident was the failure, not of the cable wire itself, but of the wire rope that attached it to the hoisting machine. Someone had made sure the reporter knew that the wire that failed had been manufactured by the Roebling company.

The engineers investigated, and issued a report stating their belief that it had accidentally been cut by the sharp iron rim of its own pulley wheel.

Yes, you're right, of course. I knew better, too. I vowed by my aunt Mollie's shade to avenge dear Harry's death. But what could a young lady do? Mr. J. Lloyd Haigh had powerful friends, and no one would choose to believe the observations of a temporarily penniless actress if the esteemed Mr. Haigh denied them. I soon discarded any notion of joining Miss Jennie Hughes and a few of his other wives in publicly attacking his virtue. Many would prefer to believe his protestations of blackmail, and my own spotless reputation might be damaged. Besides, the bridge company trustees doubtless knew the story already, and had granted him the contract despite his nefarious behavior. After all, he had damaged mere ladies, not the gentlemen whose good opinions counted.

My brother, before he was killed by the Rebels, had taught me marksmanship, and the army-issue Colt revolver I carried in my bustle was well-oiled and reliable. Still, I reckoned there were more fitting ways to deal with a low-down skunk who had so thoughtlessly struck down the flower of heroism with a seventy-ton slingshot. Lloyd's proudest achievement was the golden opinion others held of him. That would be my target.

I hocked my emerald-green traveling dress—after all, June is too warm for velvet, don't you think?—and accosted a lad, a street urchin of about my height, with the offer to purchase better garments for him if he would allow me to have his. Once he overcame his natural tendency to flee from a lady whose sanity had deserted her, he agreed.

The next day I dressed in the urchin's smelly clothes, tied up my hair to tuck into his soiled cap, and strutted into Mr. J. Lloyd Haigh's mill in South Brooklyn. I spied a foreman who was clearly as Irish as I was. "Me name is Mike O'Rourke, sir," I told him in Papa's best dialect, "just over from the old country, and in need of a job."

"No jobs here, lad," he said kindly. "Try up at the bridge."

"Whisht and haven't I been up there already? Please, sir!"

"This is no work for a boy."

"Sure and I can learn, sir! That gentleman over there—" I indicated the Chief Engineer's assistant, Colonel Paine, who was testing every coil of wire before it was loaded on a flatbed wagon. "He looks at the wire and writes on a paper. That's simple."

My countryman howled with laughter. "Not so simple, lad! We test the wire in many ways. If it's good wire, then we give it a certificate and it may be loaded on. If it's bad wire, it's discarded onto that pile in the yard. Now, would you know good wire from bad? Off with you, now!"

I looked curiously at the flatbed wagon. "What happens to the good wire, sir? Does it go in the bridge?"

"That's right, they drive it straight to the bridge."

"And what happens to the bad wire?"

He glanced at the pile in the yard. "You're a curious puppy, Mike O'Rourke! I suppose they sell it for other purposes."

"What if they send bad wire to the bridge?"

"Well, it won't have a certificate, will it? We caught them one night exchanging bad wire for the good wire they'd stored here overnight. Now the certified wire goes straight to the bridge, no waiting overnight, so they can't switch it, can they?"

Since I myself, a mere female, could think of several ways to switch it, I decided to investigate further. The certificate was clearly the crucial item; Colonel Paine handed it to the teamster. I bade farewell to the Irish foreman, stuck my hands in my pockets, and sauntered off in the direction of the bridge. Not long after, the flat wagon loaded with wire passed me. I followed and soon saw it turn into the yard of another building where rejected wire was stored. Hiding behind the fence, I watched Mr. J. Lloyd Haigh's men unload the good wire onto a second wagon, replace it with rejected wire, and send the flatbed wagon loaded with the bad wire on toward the bridge, together with the certificate belonging to the good wire that had been left behind.

What would they do with the wagonload of good wire, now that it had no certificate? I slithered an arm through the fence and hooked an apple from the lunch pail of one of Lloyd's men. I had scarce finished it when a teamster climbed into the wagon seat and drove the load of good wire toward the gate. I had to run to keep up with the horses, and was near enough to see them turn into the yard of the building where Colonel Paine tested the wire. Sure enough, soon the same good wire was tested again. I was watching the inspector sign another certificate for it when something jerked me back by the collar.

"You're still about?" cried the Irish foreman, not so kindly as before. "Off with you now, little rascal!" He fetched me a whack with his hand so I skedaddled.

Next day, attired in my serviceable black frock, I intercepted Mrs. Robeling as she started for the bridge. "Forgive me, Mrs. Roebling, but I have important information for you."

She did not pause. "Good day, Miss Mooney. I saw you recently with Mr. J. Lloyd Haigh, against my advice. I fear I have no time for any friend of his." She stalked on stonily.

I hastened along after her. "Hear me out, Mrs. Roebling! I know that your assessment of Mr. Haigh is correct! Please count me a friend of the late heroic Harry Supple, not of a man we both know to be a crook!"

She hesitated, still suspicious, but gracious again. "Miss Mooney, I cannot converse at present, because I have urgent engineering specifications for the laborers on the bridge." She gestured to the packet of papers she carried.

"My message is for them also, and for the Chief Engineer, and for the many members of the public who will tread the bridge in future years. The wire Mr. Haigh is delivering to the bridge has not in fact been approved by Colonel Paine."

She looked shocked. "Oh, you are mistaken, Miss Mooney!

Colonel Paine certifies each load of wire, and it is not accepted at the bridge without a certificate!"

"But does Colonel Paine accompany each load from the mill to the bridge? Does he know that it is driven into a building where Mr. Haigh's men exchange the certified wire for wire he has rejected? Does he see the rejected wire continue to the bridge with his certificate, while the good wire is returned to the mill, there to be tested and certified again? Why, some of that wire has probably been tested a dozen times, and has produced a dozen certificates for Mr. Haigh to use on rejected wire!"

"And all the bad wire worked into the bridge cables!" Mrs. Roebling clapped her hand to her mouth in dismay.

"Do you mean it is too late? That the bridge could collapse, and kill hundreds?" In the back of my mind I heard again the horrid thin shrieks from the burning theater.

"Well," said Mrs. Roebling, "there is a margin of safety, of course, and if we can add good wire to the cables—some two hundred wires each, or even a hundred and fifty—" An enthusiasm glowed in her eyes as she began to calculate, as though solving the engineering problem was her true joy.

I reminded her, "First, you must get the good wire."

"True, Miss Mooney." She looked dejected again. "We have tried so often to convince the trustees that we should change contractors, to no avail! Mr. Abram Hewitt holds Haigh's mortgage, you know, and as he himself lost so much in the Tilden campaign, he has no wish for Haigh to default on his payments."

So that was the source of the "good opinion" Lloyd enjoyed. I said, "Another difficulty is that we are ladies, Mrs. Roebling, and the trustees will not value our observations as highly as those of men."

"That is true, Miss Mooney. We must get a gentleman—I know. The Chief Engineer will send Colonel Paine himself, with some trusted colleagues, to witness the replacement of the certified wire by the bad wire."

"A good plan! Here, I've written the address on this card. Colonel Paine can hide behind the fence there and observe what is done. He and his colleagues can testify to the trustees, and then you and the Chief Engineer can advise them as to the best engineering solution."

"Yes. Surely even Mr. Hewitt will not agree to a swindle that endangers the public! Will you testify against Mr. Haigh as well?"

"Oh, madam, I am eternally grateful to you for so kindly rescuing me, and would assist you if I could, but I obtained this information in a manner that might compromise my reputation. I truly believe that the testimony of a gentleman like Colonel Paine is more likely to bring the desired result."

Mrs. Roebling's pleasant pug-nosed face hid a shrewd knowledge of the world. "I see, Miss Mooney. I would not wish your reputation harmed by Mr. Haigh's falsehoods, for your sake, and because such an event would damage our case. I am grateful for the information, and will not bring your name into the matter."

In fact, I was concerned with more than my reputation. A great advantage of having Mr. Haigh as an eager suitor, rather than a jaded husband, was his generosity. I feared that if he lost the bridge-wire contract he would be as poor as I, and so I hastened to ask my shifty admirer to underwrite two new costumes I would need in order to join a touring production of *Two Roses*.

We struck a bargain for the costumes, Lloyd and I. He agreed to pay the dressmaker's bill in exchange for another of Aunt Mollie's old papers and a dozen kisses, and I departed for Buffalo and Syracuse, fully expecting that he would be disgraced before I returned. But no such thing occurred. When I arrived in New York at the end of August, he still held the wire contract for the great bridge.

I arranged to encounter Mrs. Roebling as she left the bridge yard, and asked if our plan had failed.

"Goodness, no!" she exclaimed. "Dear Miss Mooney, you are concerned because as yet there has been no public notice of this affair. You must be patient—the bridge trustees will make it public at an appropriate time. Meanwhile, the soundness of the bridge is assured. The trustees were at last convinced of Mr. Haigh's duplicity, and have agreed that he must replace all the bad wire not yet worked into the cables, and must add one hundred fifty wires per cable to assure its strength, all at his own expense. Further, our inspectors now accompany the loads of certified wire from Mr. Haigh's mill all the way to the bridge yard. Fear not, Miss Mooney, the great bridge is sound!"

"I am glad to hear it, Mrs. Roebling. Are the trustees convinced at last that Mr. Haigh is a scoundrel?"

"Oh, yes!" She laughed merrily. "Do you know, the man had the cheek to tell the trustees that he wasn't anxious about the money it would cost him, he cared only that they should hold a good opinion of him. One of them replied that it was now the unanimous opinion of the trustees that he was a"—her dark eyes sparkled as she looked about to make certain that no one could overhear her before she whispered—"a damned rascal!"

"How shocking!" I exclaimed. "And at a meeting of gentlemen, too! But aren't you disappointed that Mr. Haigh has not been publicly shamed?"

"When dealing with the politicians among the bridge trustees, compromise is often necessary, especially when the news would shame them, too," said Mrs. Roebling philosophically. "Someday they will make Mr. Haigh's fraud public. Meanwhile, it is my job to build the eighth wonder of the world!"

I held Mrs. Roebling in the highest esteem, and soon gained further evidence that her assessment of the situation was accurate. When I next saw Lloyd, his splendid voice and hot eyes were as delightful as ever, but he had begun to pinch pennies and I soon found it more agreeable to cultivate other acquaintances. Besides, don't you think a young lady should avoid too close an association with a man who is about to be publicly shamed?

But as the months wore on, I realized that the bridge trustees were not going to put Lloyd's disgrace in the newspapers. No doubt Mrs. Roebling was correct, and they feared that reporters might not follow their lead in assigning all the blame to Haigh, so their own foolish complicity in allowing his fraud would be exposed. They might call him a rascal in a private meeting, but publicly he still basked in the golden opinion of his colleagues.

So, for dear dead Harry's sake, I took the riskier road.

I donned a black wig and a veiled hat and went to the bank.

Two banks, in fact, both favored by my clever Lloyd, the Market National Bank and the Grocers' Bank. I claimed that I was a lady from Baltimore who had been swindled by Mr. Haigh, that in exchange for a consideration he had given me a bank draft signed by C. Sidney Norris and Company and it had proved to be a forgery.

I left both banks in a state of excited confusion, particularly the Grocers' Bank, where the manager had blanched when I mentioned C. Sidney Norris and whispered to his assistant, "Didn't we loan Haigh money on a draft from Norris?"

Quickly, I slipped away and changed from my proper wig and veil to a vulgar red dress, rouged my cheeks and painted my lips, and was lounging against the building across the street from Lloyd's office when the police came for him. I hoped to be an invisible part of the passing crowd, but Lloyd's ardent eyes were sharp and he shrieked when he saw me. "There! There she is! Officer, arrest her! She gave me the forged paper!"

The officer glanced my way and was not impressed. "Not likely, sir. She's a common harlot."

Lloyd jumped up and down pathetically while both officers restrained him. "She did it! She did it!"

I hoisted my skirt an inch and gave them a glimpse of my ankle along with a lewd wink. "And Oi'll do it again if ye want, sir," I said in a low-down accent, "jist as long as ye pay!"

The officer laughed. "Be off with you, duckie!"

I scampered away.

Oh, come now! Surely you aren't surprised to learn that Aunt Mollie's lovely commercial papers were questionable! In the copying trade my aunt had done many jobs of work for bankers, and became quite skillful at various signatures. From time to time she would bring home an extra copy and slip it into a box that she bequeathed to me, and that I'd kept for purely sentimental reasons, although from time to time brute necessity forced me to sell a bank draft or two to a kindly business adviser such as dear Lloyd. Gentlemen like Lloyd are often eager to assist a young lady who is confused by commercial papers, and will purchase them from her so that she will be spared the unpleasantness of banking transactions. Lloyd had paid me a total of two thousand eight hundred fifty-two dollars for Aunt Mollie's commercial papers. Wasn't that kind of him? And then, because no bank would question a gentleman of such golden reputation, he had borrowed a hundred twenty-five thousand dollars on them from the two banks.

The gentlemen at the banks were not amused to see their assets turn to dust. Mr. J. Lloyd Haigh's arrest upon a charge of forgery was prominently featured in the newspapers, along with his matrimonial escapades and, at last, his bridge-wire frauds. Trustee Abram Hewitt, of course, was not mentioned.

Lloyd protested vigorously, but as the expenses of making good on the bridge contract had nearly bankrupted him, none of those gentlemen whose golden opinions he had bought in earlier days appeared to defend him.

I know, I know, a proper young lady would never do such a low-down thing to a gentleman admirer. But I've well nigh given up on being proper. Besides, don't you think people should be stopped from marrying so many young ladies and ruining their reputations, and from catapulting handsome heroes to cruel death, and from weakening the cables of the great bridge, which could collapse and kill as many folks as perished in that dreadful Brooklyn Theatre inferno? I know those crimes are not as serious as swindling the gentlemen who run banks, but I'm just a foolish Missouri girl with no sense, who hopes never to hear those agonized shrieks again.

Mr. J. Lloyd Haigh was sent to Sing Sing to repent and break rocks. Mrs. Roebling built her bridge and cared for her invalid. My life for the next two years was singularly uneventful, and it was not until the spring of 1883, after a run of good luck in St. Louis, that I returned to New York with my friend Hattie and my ten-month-old niece Juliet James. Wearing one of my new Worth dresses from Paris, I called on Mrs. Roebling. We chatted, and I asked her what she would do now that her bridge was finished.

"No more bridges!" she said vehemently. "I have a son to raise, and after that I may study the law." In fact, some years later, I heard that Mrs. Roebling had earned a diploma from New York University's law program for women. Her essay won a prize. It concerned the unfairness of the law to married women like my aunt Mollie, who could not own property, while single women could. She thought the gentlemen of the legislature ought to change the law. But they didn't, not for the longest time.

Before we parted, she again expressed her gratitude for my assistance in the matter of the wire fraud, and gave me tickets to the official opening ceremonies for her great bridge.

A wondrous sight it was, and is to this day, Mrs. Roebling's bridge: noble towers pierced by Gothic arches and linked by soaring cables, as graceful and melodious as a song. I reckon I've never seen a finer sight!

Hattie, little Juliet, and I joined a vast crowd to watch President Chester Arthur, Governor Grover Cleveland, the mayor of New York, the mayor of Brooklyn, and Mr. Abram Hewitt of the spotless reputation, who all gave addresses to honor the opening of the eighth wonder of the world. Mr. Hewitt specifically declared that Mrs. Roebling represented "all that is admirable in human nature, and all that is wonderful in the constructive world of art." But the most enthusiastic applause came when he stated that all the money raised had been "honestly expended."

The mayor of Brooklyn praised the beauty and stateliness of the bridge. "Not one shall see it," he declared in ringing tones, "and not feel prouder to be a man!"

Yes indeed.

BRENDAN DUBOIS

THE NECESSARY BROTHER

*With his fourth appearance in this series Brendan DuBois
brings us another of his vivid and memorable New Hampshire
tales, this one about a son and brother on a visit home for the
holidays. But this brother, and this visit, are a bit different.
The story was another of this year's Edgar nominees.*

I still have the problem of last evening's phone call on my mind
as I wait for Sarah to finish her shower this Thursday holiday
morning in November. From my vantage point on the bed I see
that the city's weather is overcast, and I wonder if snow flurries
will start as I begin the long drive that waits for me later in the
morning. The bedroom is large and is in the corner of the building, with a balcony that overlooks Central Park. I pause between
the satin sheets and wait, my hands folded behind my head, as
the shower stops and Sarah ambles out. She smiles at me and I
smile back, feeling effortless in doing that, for we have no secrets
from each other, no worries or frets about what the future may
bring. That was settled months ago, in our agreement when we
first met, and our arrangement works for both of us.

She comes over, toweling her long blond hair with a thick
white towel, smile still on her face, a black silk dressing gown
barely covering her model's body. As she clambers on the bed
and straddles me, she drops the towel and leans forward, envel-
oping me in her damp hair, nuzzling my neck.

"I don't see why you have to leave, Carl," she says, in her
breathless voice that can still make my head turn. "And I can't

believe you're driving. That must be at least four hours away. Why don't you fly?"

"It's more like five," I say, idly caressing her slim hips. "And I'm driving because flying is torture this time of year, and I want to travel alone."

She gently bites me on the neck and then sits back, her pale blue eyes laughing at me. With her long red fingernails she idly traces the scars along my side and chest, and then touches the faint ones on my arms where I had the tattoos removed years ago. When we first met and first made love, Sarah was fascinated by the marks on my body, and it's a fascination that has grown over the months. At night, during our love play, she will sometimes stop and touch a scar and demand a story, and sometimes I surprise her by telling her the truth.

"And why are you going?" she asks. "We could have a lot of fun here today, you and me. Order up a wonderful meal. Watch the parades and old movies. Maybe even catch one of the football games."

I reach up and stroke her chin. "I'm going because I have to. And because it's family."

She makes a face and gets out of bed, drawing the gown closer to her. "Hah. Family. Must be some family to make you drive all that way. But I don't understand you, not at all. You hardly ever talk about them, Carl. Not ever. What's the rush? What's the reason?"

I shrug. "Because they're family. No other reason."

Sarah tosses the towel at my head and says in a joking tone, "You're impossible, and I'm not sure why I put up with you."

"Me too," I say, and I get up and go into the steamy bathroom as she begins to dive into the walk-in closet that belongs to her.

I stay in the shower for what seems hours, luxuriating in the hot and steamy water, remembering the times growing up in Boston Falls when showers were rationed to five minutes apiece because of the creaky hot water that could only stand so much use every cold day. Father had to take his shower before going to the mills, and Brad was next because he was the oldest. I was fortunate, being in the middle, for our youngest brother, Owen, sometimes ended up with lukewarm water, if that. And Mother, well, we never knew when she bathed. It was a family secret.

I get out and towel myself down, enjoying the feel of the warm heat on my lean body as I enter the bedroom. Another difference. Getting out of the shower used to mean walking across cold linoleum, grit on your feet as you got dressed for school. Now it means walking into a warm and carpeted bedroom, my clothes laid out neatly on my bed. I dress quickly, knowing I will have to move fast to avoid the traffic for the day's parade. I go out to the kitchen overlooking the large and dark sunken living room, and Sarah is gone, having left breakfast for me on the marble-top counter. The day's *Times* is there, folded, and I stand and eat the scrambled eggs, toast, and bacon while drinking a large glass of orange juice and a cup of coffee.

When I unfold the *Times* a note falls out. It's in Sarah's handwriting. *Do have a nice trip,* it says. *I've called down to Raphael. See you when you get back. Yours, S.*

Yours. Sarah has never signed a note or a letter to me that says love. Always it's "yours." That's because Sarah tells the truth.

I wash the dishes and go into the large walk-in closet near the door that leads out to the hallway. I select a couple of heavy winter jackets, and from a combination-lock box similar to a fuse box, take out a Bianchi shoulder holster, a 9mm Beretta, and two spare magazines. I slide on the holster and pull a wool cardigan on and leave and take the elevator down, whistling as I do so.

Out on the sidewalk by the lobby Raphael nods to me as I step out into the brisk air, his doorkeeper's uniform clean and sharp. My black Mercedes is already pulled up, engine purring, faint tendrils of exhaust eddying up into the thick, cold air. Raphael smiles and touches his cap with a brief salute. There is an old knife scar on his brown cheek, and though still a teenager, he has seen some things that could give me the trembling wakeups at two A.M. In addition to his compensation from the building, I pay Raphael an extra hundred a week to keep his eyes open for me. The doorkeepers in this city open and close lots of doors, and they also open and close a lot of secrets, and that's a wonderful resource for my business.

Raphael walks with me and opens the door. "A cold morning, Mr. Curtis. Are you ready for your drive?"

I slip a folded ten-dollar bill into his white-gloved hand, and it disappears effortlessly. "Absolutely. Trunk packed?"

"That it is," he says as I toss the two winter coats onto the passenger's seat and buckle up in the warm interior. I always wear seat belts, a rule that, among others, I follow religiously. As he closes the door, Raphael smiles again and says, "*Vaya con Dios,*" and since the door is shut, I don't reply. But I do smile in return and he goes back to his post.

I'm about fifteen minutes into my drive when I notice the Thermos bottle on the front seat, partially covered by the two coats I dumped there. At a long stoplight I unscrew the cap and smell the fresh coffee, then take a quick drink and decide Raphael probably deserves a larger Christmas bonus this year.

As I drive I listen to my collection of classical music CDs. I can't tell you the difference between an opus and a symphony, a quartet or a movement, or who came first, Bach or Beethoven. But I do know what I like, and classical music is something that just seems to settle into my soul, like hot honey traveling into a honeycomb. I have no stomach for, nor interest in, what passes as modern music. When I drive I start at one end of my CD collection and in a month or so I get to the other end, and then start again.

The scenery as I go through the busy streets and across the numbered highways on my way to Connecticut is an urban sprawl of dead factories, junkyards, tenements, vacated lots, and battered cars with bald tires. Not a single pedestrian I see looks up. They all stare at the ground, as if embarrassed at what is around them, as if made shy by what has become of their country. I'm not embarrassed. I'm somewhat amused. It's the hard lives in that mess that give me my life's work.

I drive on, humming along to something on the CD that features a lot of French horns.

Through Connecticut I drive in a half-daze, listening to the music, thinking over the phone call of the previous night and the unique problem that it poses for me. I knew within seconds of hanging up the telephone what my response would be, but it still troubles me. Some things are hard to confront, especially when they're personal. But I have no choice. I know what I must do and that gives me some comfort, but not enough. Not nearly enough.

While driving along the flat asphalt and concrete of the Connecticut highways, I keep my speed at an even sixty miles per hour, conscious of the eager state police who patrol these roads. Radar detectors are still illegal in this state and the police here seem to relish their role as adjuncts to the state's tax collection department. They have the best unmarked cars in the region, and I am in no mood to tempt them as I drive, drive along.

Only once do I snap out of my reverie, and that's when two Harley-Davidson motorcycles rumble by, one on each side, the two men squat and burly in their low seats, long hair flapping in the breeze, goggles hiding their eyes, their denim vests and leather jackets looking too thin for this weather, their expressions saying they don't particularly care. The sight brings back some sharp memories: the wind in my face, the throb of the engine against my thighs, the almost Zenlike sense of traveling at high speed, just inches away from the asphalt and only seconds away from serious injury or death, and the certainty and comfort of what those motored bikes meant. Independence. Willing companions. Some sharp and tight actions. I almost sigh at the pleasurable memory. I have not ridden a motorcycle for years, and I doubt that I ever will again.

I'm busy with other things.

Somewhere in Massachusetts the morning and mid-morning coffee I have drunk has managed to percolate through my kidneys and is demanding to be released, and after some long minutes I see a sign that marks a rest area. As I pull into the short exit lane I see a smaller sign that in one line sums up the idiocy of highway engineering: NO SANITARY FACILITIES. A rest area without a rest room. Why not.

There's a tractor-trailer parked at the far end of the lot, and the driver is out, slouched by the tires, examining something.

Nearly a dozen cars have stopped and it seems odd to me that so many drivers have pulled over in this empty rest area. All this traffic, all these weary drivers, at this hour of this holiday morning?

I walk past the empty picnic tables, my leather boots crunching on the two or three inches of snow, when a man comes out from behind a tree. He's smoking a cigarette and he's shivering, and his knee-length leather coat is open, showing jeans and a white T-shirt. His blond hair is cut quite short, and he's to the point: "Looking for a date?"

The number of parked and empty cars now makes sense and I feel slightly foolish. I nod at the man and say, "Nope. Just looking for an empty tree," and keep on going. Some way to spend a holiday.

I find my empty tree and as I relieve myself against the pine trunk, I hear footsteps approach. I zip up and turn around and two younger men are there. One has a moustache and the other a beard, and both are wearing baseball caps with the bills pointed to the rear. Jeans, short black leather jackets, and sneakers mark their dress code. I smile and say, "No thanks, guys. I'm all set," as I walk away from the tree.

The one with the scraggly moustache laughs. "You don't understand, faggot. We're not all set."

Now they both have knives out, and the one with the beard says, "Turn over your wallet, 'fore we cut you where it counts."

I hold up my empty hands and say, "Jeez, no trouble, guys." I reach back and in a breath or two, my Beretta is in my hand, pointing at the two men. Their pasty-white faces deflate, like day-old balloons losing air, and I give them my best smile. They back up a few steps but I shake my head, and they stop, mouths still open in shock.

"Gee," I say. "Now I've changed my mind. I guess I'm not all set. Both knives, toss them behind you."

The knives are thrown behind them, making clattering noises as they strike tree branches and trunks before hitting the ground. The two young men turn again, arms held up, and the bearded one's hands are shaking.

"Very good," I say. I move the Beretta back and forth, scanning, so that one of the two is always covered. "Next I want those pants off and your wallets on the ground, and your jackets. No arguing."

The one with the moustache says, "You can't—"

I cock the hammer back on the Beretta. The noise sounds like a tree branch cracking from too much snow and ice.

"You don't listen well," I say. "No arguing."

The two slump to the ground and in a matter of moments the clothing is in a pile, and then they stand up again. Their arms go back up. One of the two—the one with the moustache—was not wearing any underwear and he is shriveled with cold and fear. Their legs are pasty white and quivering and I feel no pity whatsoever. I say, "Turn around, kneel down, and cross your ankles. Now."

They do as they're told, and I can see their bodies flinch as their bare skin strikes the snow and ice. I swoop down and pick up the clothing and say, "Move in the next fifteen minutes and you'll disappear, just like that."

I toss the clothing on the hood of my car and pull out a set of car keys and two wallets. From the wallets I take out a bundle of bills in various denominations, and I don't bother counting it. I just shove it into my pants' pocket, throw everything into the car, and drive off.

After a mile I toss out the pants and jackets, and another mile after that, I toss out the car keys and wallets.

Too lenient, perhaps, but it is a holiday.

Ninety minutes later I pull over on a turn-off spot on Route 3, overlooking Boston Falls, the town that gave me the first years of my life. By now a light snow is falling and I check my watch. Ten minutes till one. Perfect timing. Mother always has her Thanksgiving dinner at three P.M., and I'll be on time, with a couple of free hours for chitchat and time for some other things. I lean against the warm hood of the Mercedes and look at the mills and buildings of the town below me. Self-portrait of the prodigal son returning, I think, and what would make the picture perfect would be a cigarette in my hand, thin gray smoke curling above my head, as I think great thoughts.

But I haven't smoked in years, and the thoughts I think aren't great, they're just troubled.

I wipe some snow off the fender of the car. The snow is small and dry, and whispers away with no problem.

A few minutes later I pull up to 74 Wall Street, the place where I grew up, a street with homes lining it on either side. The house is a small Cape Cod that used to be a bright red and now suffers a covering of tan vinyl siding. In my mind's eye, this house is always red. It's surrounded by a chain-link fence that Father put up during the few years of retirement he enjoyed before dying ("All my life, all I wanted was a fence to keep those goddamn dogs in the neighborhood from pissing on my shrubs, and now I'm going to get it."). I hope he managed to enjoy it before coughing up his lungs at Manchester Memorial. Father never smoked a cigarette in his life, but the air in those mills never passed through a filter on its journey to his lungs. Parked in front of the house is the battered tan Subaru that belongs to my younger brother Owen and the blue Ford pickup truck that is owned by older brother Brad.

On Owen's Subaru there is a sticker on the rear windshield for the Society for the Protection of New Hampshire Forests, and on Brad's Ford is a sticker for the Manchester Police Benevolent Society. One's life philosophy, spelled out in paper and gummed labels. The rear windshield of my Mercedes is empty. They don't make stickers for what I do or believe in.

Getting out of the car, I barely make it through the front door of the house before I'm assaulted by sounds, smells, and a handful of small children in the living room. The smells are of turkey and fresh bread, and most of the sounds come from the children yelling, "Uncle Carl! Uncle Carl!" as they jump around me. There are three of them—all girls—and they belong to Brad and his wife, Deena: Carey, age twelve; Corinne, age nine; and the youngest, Christine, age six. All have blond hair in various lengths and they grasp at me, saying the usual kid things of how much they miss me, what was I doing, would I be up here long, and of course, their favorite question:

"Uncle Carl, did you bring any presents?"

Brad is standing by the television set in the living room, a grimace pretending to be a smile marking his face. Deena looks up to him, troubled, and then manages a smile for me and that's all I need. I toss my car keys to Carey, the oldest.

"In the trunk," I say, "and there's also one for your cousin."

The kids stream outside and then my brother Owen comes in from the kitchen holding his baby son, Todd, and he's followed by his wife, Jan, and Mother. Owen tries to say something, but Mother barrels by and gives me the required hug, kiss, and why-don't-you-call-me-more look. Mother's looking fine, wearing an apron that one of us probably gave her as a birthday gift a decade or two ago, and her eyes are bright and alive behind her glasses. Most of her hair is gray and is pulled back in a bun, and she's wearing a floral print dress.

"My, you are looking sharp as always, Carl," she says admiringly, turning to see if Owen and Brad agree, and Owen smiles and Brad pretends to be watching something on television. Jan looks at me and winks, and I do nothing in return.

Mother goes back into the kitchen and I follow her and get a glass of water. When she isn't looking I reach up to a shelf and pull down a sugar bowl that contains her "mad money." I shove in the wad that I liberated earlier this day, and I return the bowl to the shelf, just in time to help stir the gravy.

As she works about the stove with me Owen comes in, still holding his son, Todd, and Jan is with him. Owen sits down, looking up at me, holding the baby and its bottle, and it gurgles with what seems to be contentment. Owen's eyes are shiny behind his round, wire-rimmed glasses, and he says, "How are things in New York?"

"Cold," I say. "Loud. Dirty. The usual stuff."

Owen laughs and Jan joins in, but there's a different sound in her laugh. Owen is wearing a shapeless gray sweater and tan chinos, while Jan has on designer jeans and a buttoned light pink sweater that's about one button too many undone. Her brown hair is styled and shaped, and I can tell from her eyes that the drink in her hand isn't the first of the day.

"Maybe so," she says, "but at least it isn't boring, like some places people are forced to live."

Mother pretends to be busy about the stove and Owen is still smiling, though his eyes have faltered, as if he has remembered some old debt unpaid. I give Jan a sharp look and she just smiles and drinks, and I say to Owen, "How's the reporting?"

He shrugs, gently moving Todd back and forth. "The usual. Small-town stuff that doesn't get much coverage. But I've been thinking about starting a novel, nights when I get home from meetings. Something about small towns and small-town corruption."

Jan clicks her teeth against her glass. "Maybe your brother can help you. With some nasty ideas."

I finish off my water and walk past her. "Oh, I doubt that very much," I say, and I go into the living room, hearing the sound of Jan's laughter as I go.

The three girls have come back and the floor is a mess of shredded paper and broken boxes, as they ooh and aah over their gifts. There's a mix of clothing and dolls, the practical and the playful, because I know to the penny how much my older brother Brad makes each year and his budget is prohibitively tight.

His wife Deena is on the floor, playing with the girls, and she gives me a happy nod as I come in and sit down on the couch. She is a large woman and has on black stretch pants and a large blue sweater. I find that the more I get to know Deena, the more I like her. She comes from a farm family and makes no bones about having dropped out of high school at age sixteen. Though she's devoted utterly and totally to my brother, she also has a sharp rural way of looking at things, and though I'm sure Brad has told her many awful stories about me, she has also begun to trust her own feelings. I think she likes me, though I know she would never admit that to Brad.

Brad is sitting in an easy chair across the way, intent on looking at one of the Thanksgiving Day parades. He's wearing sensible black shoes, gray slacks, and an orange sweater, and pinned to one side is a turkey button, probably given to him by one of his daughters. Brad has a thin moustache and his black hair is slicked back, for he started losing it at age sixteen. He looks all right, though there's a roll of fat beginning to swell about his belly.

"How's it going, Brad?" I ask, sending out the first peace feeler.

"Oh, not bad," he says, eyes not leaving the screen.

"Detective work all right? Got any interesting cases you're working on?"

"Unh-hunh," and he moves a glass of what looks like milk from one hand to the other.

"Who do you think will win the afternoon game?" I try again.

He shrugs. "Whoever has the best team, I imagine."

Well. Deena looks up again, troubled, and I just give her a quiet nod, saying with my look that everything's all right, and then I get up from the couch and go outside and get my winter coats and overnight bag and bring them back inside. I drop them off upstairs in the tiny room that used to be my bedroom so many years and memories ago, and then I look into a mirror over a battered bureau and say, "Time to get to work," and that makes me laugh. For the first time in a long time I'm working gratis.

I go downstairs to the basement, switching on the overhead fluorescents, which *click-click-hum* into life. Father's old workbench is in one corner, and dumped near the workbench is a pile of firewood for the living room fireplace. The rest of the basement is taken up with boxes, old bicycles, and a washer and dryer. The basement floor is concrete and relatively clean. I go upstairs fast, taking two steps at a time. Brad is in the living room, with his three girls, trying to show some enthusiasm for the gifts I brought. I call out to him and he looks up.

"Yeah?" he says.

"C'mere," I say, excitement tingeing my voice. "You won't believe what I found."

He pauses for a moment, as if debating with himself whether he should ever trust his younger brother, and I think his cop curiosity wins out, for he says " 'Scuse me" to his daughters and ambles over.

"What's going on?" he says in that flat voice I think cops learn at their service academy.

"Downstairs," I say. "I was poking around and behind Father's workbench there's an old shoe box. Brad, it looks like your baseball card collection, the one Mother thought she tossed away."

For the first time I get a reaction out of Brad and a grin pops into life. "Are you sure?"

"Sure looks like it to me. C'mon down and take a look."

Brad brushes by me and thunders downstairs on the plain wooden steps, and I follow close behind, saying, "You've got to stretch across the table and really take a close look, Brad, but I think it's them."

He says, "My God, it's been almost twenty years since I've seen them. Think of how much money they could be worth . . ."

In front of the workbench Brad leans over, casting his head back and forth, his orange sweater rising up, treating me to a glimpse of his bare back and the top of his hairy buttocks, and he says, "Carl, I don't see—"

And with that I pick up a piece of firewood and pound it into the back of his skull.

Brad makes a coughing sound and falls on top of the workbench, and I kick away his legs and he swears at me and in a minute or two of tangled struggle, he ends up on his back. I straddle his chest, my knees digging into his upper arms, a forearm pressed tight against his throat, and he gurgles as I slap his face with my free hand.

"Do I have your attention, older brother?"

He curses some more and struggles, and I press in again with my forearm and replay the slapping. I'm thankful that no one from upstairs has heard us. I say, "Older brother, I'm younger, faster, and stronger, and we need to talk; if you'll stop thrashing around, we'll get somewhere."

Another series of curses, but then he starts gurgling louder and nods, and I ease up on the forearm and say, "Just how stupid do you have to be before you stop breathing, Brad?"

"What the hell are you doing, you maniac?" he demands, his voice a loud whisper. "I'm gonna have you arrested for assault, you no-good—"

I lean back with the forearm and he gurgles some more and I say, "Listen once, and listen well, older brother. I got a phone call last night from an old friend saying my police-detective brother is now in the pocket of one Bill Sutler. You mind telling me how the hell that happened?"

His eyes bug out and I pull back my forearm and he says, "I don't know what the hell you're talking about, you low-life biker."

Two more slaps to the face. "First, I'm no biker and you know it. Second, I'm talking about Bill Sutler, who handles the numbers and other illegal adventures for this part of this lovely state. I'm talking about an old friend I can trust with my life telling me that you now belong to this charming gentleman. Now. Let's stop dancing and start talking, shall we?"

Brad's eyes are piggish and his face is red, his slick black hair now a tangle, and I'm preparing for another struggle or another series of denials, and then it's like a dam that has been ruptured, a wall that has been breached, for I feel his body loosen underneath me, and he turns his face. "Shit," he whispers.

"Gambling?" I ask.

He just nods. "How much?" I ask again.

"Ten K," he says. "It's the vig that's killing me, Carl, week after week, and now, well, now he wants more than just money."

"Of course," I say, leaning back some. "Information. Tip-offs. Leads on some investigations involving him and his crew."

Brad looks up and starts talking and I slap him again, harder, and I lean back into him and say in my most vicious tone, "Where in hell have you been storing your brains these past months, older brother? Do you have even the vaguest idea of what you've gotten yourself into? Do you think a creature like Bill Sutler is going to let you go after a couple of months? Of course not, and if he ever gets arrested by the state or the feds, he's going to toss you up for a deal so fast you'll think the world is spinning backward."

He tries to talk but I keep plowing on. "Then let's take it from there, after you get turned over. Upstairs is a woman who loves you so much she'd probably go after this Sutler guy with her bare hands if she could, and you have three daughters who think you're the best daddy in the Western Hemisphere. Not to mention a woman who thinks you're the good son, the successful one, and a younger brother who wishes he could be half the man you pretend you are. Think of how they'll all do, how they'll live, when they see you taken away to the state prison in orange overalls."

By now Brad is silently weeping, the tears rolling down his quivering cheeks, and I feel neither disgust nor pity. It's what I expected, what I planned for, and I say, "Then think about what prison will be like, you, a cop, side by side with some rough characters who would leap at a chance to introduce you to some hard loving. Do I have your attention now, older brother? Do I?"

He's weeping so much that he can only nod, and then I get off his chest and stand up and he rolls over, in a fetal position, whispering faint obscenities, over and over again, and I don't mind since they're not aimed at me.

"Where does this guy Sutler live?" I ask.

"Purmort," he says.

"Get up," I say. "I'm going to pay him a visit, and you're going to help."

Brad sits up, snuffling, and leans back against the wooden workbench. "You're going to see him? Now? An hour before Thanksgiving dinner? You're crazy, even for a biker."

I shrug, knowing that I will be washing my hands momentarily. They look clean, but right now they feel quite soiled. "He'll talk to me, and you're going to back me up, because I'm saving your sorry ass this afternoon."

Brad looks suspicious. "What does that mean?"

"You'll find out, soon enough."

Before Brad can say anything, the door upstairs opens up and Deena calls down, "Hey, you guys are missing the parade."

I look at Brad and he's rubbing at his throat. I reply to Deena, "So we are, so we are."

Fifteen minutes later I pull into Founder's Park, near the Bellamy River, in an isolated section of town. Of course it's deserted on this special day and I point out an empty park bench, near two snow-covered picnic tables. "Go sit there and contemplate your sorry life."

"What?"

"I said, get out there and contemplate your sorry life. I'm going to talk to this Sutler character alone."

"But—"

"I'm getting you out of trouble today, older brother, and all I ask from you is one thing. That you become my alibi. Anything comes up later today or next week that has to do with me, you're going to swear as a gentleman and a police officer that the two of us were just driving around at this time of the day, looking at the town and having some fond recollections before turkey dinner. Understand?"

Brad looks stubborn for a moment and says, "It's cold out there."

I reach behind me and pull out the Thermos bottle that Raphael had packed for me, so many hours and places ago. "Here. I freshened it up at the house a while ago, before we left. Go out there and sit and I'll be back."

That same stubborn look. "Why are you doing this for me?"

I lean over him and open the door. "Not for you. For the family. Get out, will you? I don't want to be late."

At last he steps out and walks over to the park bench, the Thermos bottle in his humiliated hands, and he sits down and stares out at the frozen river. He doesn't look my way as I pull out and head to Purmort.

I've parked the Mercedes on a dirt road that leads into an abandoned gravel pit, and I have a long wool winter coat on over my cardigan sweater. The air is still and some of the old trees still have coverings of snow looking like plastic casts along the branches. There's a faint maze of animal tracks in the snow, and I recognize the prints of a rabbit and a squirrel. I'm leaning against the front hood of the Mercedes as a black Ford Bronco ambles up the dirt path. It parks in front of my car and I feel a quick tinge of unease: I don't like having my escape routes blocked, and then the unease grows as two men get out of the Bronco. I had only been expecting one.

The man on the right moves a bit faster than his companion and I figure that he's Bill Sutler. My guess is correct, and it is he who begins to chatter at me.

"Let me start off by saying I don't like you already for two reasons," he says in a gravelly tone that's either come from throat surgery or too many cigarettes at an early age. He's just a few inches shorter than me, and though his black hair is balding, he has a long strip at the back tied in a ponytail. Fairly fancy for this part of the state. His face is slightly pockmarked with old acne scars, and he has on a bright blue ski jacket with the obligatory tattered ski passes hanging from the zipper. Jeans and dull orange construction boots finish off his ensemble.

"Why's that?" I say, arms and legs crossed, still leaning against the warm hood of my Mercedes, my boots in the snow cover.

"Because you pulled me out of my house on Thanksgiving, and because of your license plates," he says, pointing to the front of my Mercedes, talking fast, his entire face seemingly squinting at me. "You're from New York, and I hate guys from New York who think they can breeze in here and throw their weight around. You're in my woods now, guy, and I don't care what games you've played back on your crappy island. We do things different up here."

His companion has stepped away from the passenger's side of the Bronco and is keeping watch on me. He seems a bit younger but he's considerably more bulky, with a tangle of curly hair and a thick beard. He's wearing an army fatigue coat and the same jeans/boot combination that Sutler is sporting. I note that the right pocket of his coat is sagging some, from the weight of something inside.

I nod over to the second man. "That your muscle, along to keep things quiet?"

Sutler turns his head for a moment. "That there's Kelly, and he's here because I want him here. I tell him to leave, he'll leave. I tell him to break every finger on your hands, he'd do that, too.

So let's leave him out of things right now. Talk. You got me here, what do you want?"

I rub at my chin. "I want something that you have. I want Brad Curtis's *cojones,* and I understand you have them in your pocket."

Sutler smirks. "That I do. What's your offer?"

This just might be easy. "In twenty-four hours, I settle his gambling debt," I say. "I also put in a word to a couple of connected guys, and some extra business gets tossed your way. You get your money, you get some business, and I get what I want. You also never have any contact or dealings with him again, any time in the future."

"You're a relation, right?"

I nod. "His brother."

"Younger or older?"

"Younger."

Sutler smirks again, and I decide I don't like the look. "Isn't that sweet. Well, look at this, younger brother. The answer is no."

I cock my head. "Is that a real no, or do you want a counteroffer? If it's a counteroffer, mention something. I'm sure I can be reasonable."

He laughs and rocks back on his heels a bit and says, "Little one, this isn't a negotiation. The answer is no."

"Why?"

That stops him for a moment, and there's a furtive gesture from his left hand, and Kelly steps a bit closer. "Because I already told you," he says. "I don't like you New York guys, and I don't trust you. Sure, you'd probably pay off the money, but everything else you say is probably crap. You think I'm stupid? Well, I think you're stupid, and here's why. I got something good in that nitwit detective, and you and your New York friends aren't going to take it away. I got him and my work here on my own, and I don't need your help. Understand?"

"Are you sure?"

Another laugh. "You think I'm giving up a detective on the largest police force in this state for you? The stuff he can feed me is pure gold, little one, and it's gonna set me for life. There's nothing you have that can match that. Nothing."

He gestures again. "And I'm tired of you, and I'm tired of this crap. I'm going back home."

"Me too," I say, and I slide my hand into the cardigan, pull out my Beretta, and blow away Kelly's left knee.

Kelly is on the ground, howling, and the echo of the shot is still bouncing about the hills as I slam the Beretta into the side of Sutler's head. He falls, and I stride over to Kelly. Amid his thrashings on the now-bloody snow, I grab a .357 revolver from his coat and toss it into the woods. In a matter of heartbeats I'm back to Sutler, who's on the ground, fumbling to get into his ski jacket. I kick him solidly in the crotch. He yelps and then I'm on him, the barrel of the Beretta jamming into his lips until he gags and has a couple of inches of the oily metal in his mouth. His eyes are very wide and there's a splotch of blood on his left cheek. I take a series of deep breaths, knowing that I want my voice cool and calm.

"About sixty seconds ago I was interested in negotiating with you, but now I've lost interest. Do you understand? If you do, nod your head, but nod it real slow. It's cold and my fingers are beginning to get numb."

His eyes are tearing and he nods, just like I said. "Very good," I say, trying to place a soothing tone in my voice. "I came here in a good mood, in a mood to make a deal that could help us both, and all you've done since we've met is insult me. Do you think I got up early this morning and drove half the day so a creature like you can toss insults my way? Do you?"

Though I didn't explain to him the procedure for shaking his head, Sutler shows some initiative and gently shakes it. Kelly, some yards away, is still groaning and occasionally crying. I ignore him because I want to, and I think Sutler is ignoring him because he has to.

"Now," I continue. "If you had some random brain cells in that sponge between your ears, I think you would have figured out that because this matter involves my brother, I might have a

personal interest in what was going on. But you were too stupid
to realize that, correct?"

Another nod of the head, and saliva and blood are beginning
to drip down the barrel of the Beretta. "So instead of accepting
a very generous offer, you said no and insulted me. So you left
me no choice. I had to show you how serious I was, and I had
to make an impression."

I gesture over to the sobbing hulk of his companion. "Take a
look at Kelly if you can. I don't know the man, I have nothing
against him, and if the two of us had met under different circumstances, we might have become friends."

Well, I doubt that, but I keep my doubts to myself. I am making a point. "But I had to make an example," I continue, "and
in doing so, I've just crippled Kelly for life. Do you understand
that? His knee is shattered and he'll never walk well again for
the next thirty or forty years of his life because of your ill manners and stubbornness. Now. You having rejected my offer,
here's my counteroffer. Are you now interested?"

Another nod, a bit more forceful. "Good. Here it is. You forget the gambling debt. You forget you ever knew my brother,
and you take poor Kelly here to a hospital and tell them that he
was shot in a hunting accident or something. I don't care. And
if you ever bother my brother or his family, any time in the
future, I'll come back."

I poke the Beretta in another centimeter or two, and Sutler
groans. "Then I'll find out who counts most in your life—your
mother, your wife, your child, for all I know—and I'll do the
same thing to them that I did to Kelly. Oh, I could make it permanent, but a year or two after the funeral, you usually get on
with life. Not with this treatment. The person suffers in your
presence, for decades to come, because of you. Now. Is the deal
complete?"

Sutler closes his teary eyes and nods, and I get up, wiping the
Beretta's barrel on his ski jacket. Sutler is grimacing and the
crotch of his pants is wet and steaming in the cold. Kelly is
curled up on his side, weeping, his left leg a bloody mess, and I
take a step back and gently prod Sutler with my foot.

"Move your Bronco, will you?" I ask politely.

* * *

My brother's face is a mix of anger and hope as he climbs back into my Mercedes, rubbing his hands from the cold. His face and ears are quite red.

"Well?" he asks.

"Piece of cake," I say, and I drive back to the house.

Dinner is long and wonderful, and I have a sharp appetite and eat well, sitting at the far end of the table. My nieces good-naturedly fight over the supposed honor of sitting next to me, which makes Mother and Deena laugh, and even Brad attempts a smile or two. I stuff myself and we regale each other with stories of holidays and Christmases and Thanksgivings past, and Owen bounces Todd on his knee as Jan smiles to herself and sips from one glass of wine and then another.

I feel good belonging here with them. Though I know that none of them quite knows who I am or what I do, it's still a comfortable feeling. It's like nothing else I experience, ever, and I cherish it.

Later, I take a nap in my old bedroom, and feeling greasy from the day's exertions and the long meal, I take a quick shower, remembering a lot of days and weeks and years gone past as I climb into the tiny stall. It seems fairly humorous that I am in this house taking a weak and lukewarm shower after having remembered this creaky bathroom earlier this morning, back at my Manhattan home. That explains why I am smiling when I go back into my old bedroom, threadbare light green towel wrapped around my waist, and I find Jan there, waiting for me, my brother Owen's wife.

Her eyes are aglitter and her words are low and soft, but there's a hesitation there, as if she realizes she has been drinking for most of the day and she has to be careful in choosing each noun and verb. She's standing by an old bureau, jean-encased hip leaning up against the wood, and she has something in her hands.

"Look at this, will you," she says. "Found it up here while I was waiting for you."

I step closer and I can smell the alcohol on her breath, and I also smell something a bit earthier. I try not to sigh, seeing the eager expression on her face. I take her offering and turn it over. It's an old color photograph, and it shows a heavyset man with a beard and long hair in a ponytail sitting astride a black Harley-Davidson motorcycle. He's wearing the obligatory jeans and leather vest. His arms are tattooed. The photo is easily a decade old, and in those years the chemicals on the print have faded and mutated, so that there's an eerie yellow glow about everything, as if the photo were taken at a time when volcanic ash was drifting through the air.

I look closely at the photo and then hand it back to my sister-in-law. About the only thing I recognize about the person is the eyes, for it's the only thing about me that I've not changed since that picture was taken.

"That's really you, isn't it?" she asks, that eager tone in her voice still there. With her in my old room, everything seems crowded. There's a tiny closet, the bureau, a night table, and lumpy bed with thin blankets and sheets. A window about the size of a pie plate looks out to the pale-green vinyl siding of the house next door.

"Yes, that's me," I say. "Back when I was younger and dumber."

She licks her lips. "Asking questions about you of Owen is a waste of time, and your mother and Brad aren't much help either. You were a biker, right?"

I nod. "That's right."

"What was it like, Carl?" she asks, moving a few inches closer to me. I know I should feel embarrassed, standing in my old bedroom with my sister-in-law, just wearing a towel, but I'm not sure what I feel. I just know it's not embarrassment. So instead of debating the point, I answer her question.

"It was like moving to a different country and staying at home, all at the same time," I say. "There was an expression, something about being free and being a citizen. Being free meant the bike and your friends and whatever money you had for gas and food, and the time to travel anywhere you wanted, any time, with no one to stop you, feeling the wind in your hair and face.

Being a citizen meant death, staying at home, paying taxes, and working a forty-hour week. That's what it was like."

She gives me a sharp-toothed smile. "You almost make it sound like a Boy Scout troop. Way your older brother talks, I figure you've been in trouble."

I shrug. "Comes with the territory. It's something you get used to. Being free means you run into a lot of different people, and sometimes their tempers are short and their memories are long. Sometimes you do some work for some money that wouldn't look good on a job application form."

"So that explains the scars?" she asks.

"Yeah, I guess it does."

"So why did you change? What happened? From the picture, I can tell you've had your tattoos taken off."

I look around and see that my clothes are still on the bed where I left them. "I got tired of having my life depend on other people. Thing is, you run with a group, the group can sometimes pull you down. What the group accomplishes can come back at night and break your windows, or gnaw on your leg. And I didn't want to become a citizen. So I chose a bit of each world and made my own, and along the way I changed my look."

"And what do you do now? Everyone says consulting work, but they always have an uncomfortable look on their face when they mention that, like they have gas or something. So what's your job?"

I pause and say, "Systems engineer."

Her eyes blink in amusement. "A what?"

"Systems engineer. Sometimes a system needs an outside pressure or force to make a necessary change or adjustment. That's what I do. I'm an independent contractor."

"Sounds very exciting," she says, arching an eyebrow this time. "You should talk some to your younger brother. Maybe pass some of that excitement along. Or maybe you're the brother who got it all in this family."

I now feel an aching sorrow for Owen, and I try not to think of what their pillow talk must be like at night. "Guess you have to work with what you've got."

"Unh-hunh," she says. "Look, you must be getting cold. Are you going to get dressed, or what?"

I decide she wants a show, or wants something specific to happen, so I say, "Or what, I suppose." I turn to the bed and drop the towel and get dressed, and I hear a hush of breath coming from her. After the underwear, pants, and boots, I turn, buttoning my shirt, and she's even closer and I reach to her and she comes forward, lips wet, and then I strike out and put a hand around her throat. And I squeeze.

"Jan," I say, stepping forward and looking into her eyes, "you and I are about to come to an agreement, do you understand?"

"What are you doing, you—" and I squeeze again, and she makes a tiny yelping sound, and her nostrils begin to flare as she tries to breathe harder. She starts to flail with her hands and I grab one hand and press her against the bureau. It shakes and she tries to kick, but I'm pushing at her at an uncomfortable angle, and she can't move.

"This won't take long, but I ask that you don't yell. You try to yell and I'll squeeze hard enough to make you black out. Do you understand? Try blinking your eyes."

She blinks, tears forming in her eyes. My mind plays with a few words and then I say, "Owen and my family mean everything to me. Everything. And right now, by accident of marriage and the fact of my brother's love, you're part of this family. But not totally. My mother and Owen and even Brad come before you. You're not equal in my eyes, do you understand?"

She moves her head a bit, and I'm conscious that I might have to take another shower when I'm finished. "So that's where I'm coming from when I tell you this: I don't care if you love my brother or hate my brother, but I do demand this. That you show him respect. He deserves that. Stay with him or leave him tonight, I don't care. But don't toss yourself to those random men that manage to cross your path, especially ones related to him. If you can't stand being with him, leave, but do it with dignity. Show him respect or I'll hurt you, Jan."

"You're hurting me now," she whispers.

"No, I'm not," I explain. "I'm not hurting you. I'm getting your attention. In an hour you'll be just fine, but in a hundred years you're always going to remember this conversation in this dingy bedroom. Am I right?"

She nods and I say, "So we've reached an understanding. Agreed?"

Another nod and I let her go and back away, and Jan rubs at her throat and coughs. Then she whispers a dark series of curses and leaves, slamming the door behind her, and what scares me is that she isn't crying, not one tear, not one sign of regret or fear. I finish getting dressed, trying not to think of Owen.

Despite a lumpy bed and the too-silent surroundings of Boston Falls, I sleep fairly well that night, with none of those disturbing dreams of loud words and sharp actions that sometimes bring me awake. I get up with the sun and slowly walk through the living room to the kitchen. Sprawled across the carpeted floor in sleeping bags are my three nieces—Carey, Corinne, and Christine—and their shy innocence and the peacefulness of their slight breathing touches something inside of me that I wasn't sure even existed anymore.

Mother is in the kitchen and I give her a brief hug and grab a cup of coffee. I try not to grimace as I sip the brew; Mother, God bless her, has never made a decent cup of coffee in her life. I've been dressed since getting up and Mother is wearing a faded blue bathrobe, and as she stirs a half-dozen eggs in a mixing bowl she looks over at me through her thick glasses and says, "I'm not that dumb, you know."

I gamely try another sip of coffee. "I've always known that, ever since you found my collection of girlie magazines when I was in high school."

"Bah," she says, stirring the whisk harder. "I knew you had those for a while, and I knew boys always get curious at that age. I didn't mind much until your younger brother Owen was snooping around. Then I couldn't allow it. He was too young."

She throws in a bit of grated cheese and goes back to the bowl and says, "Are you all right, Carl?"

"Just fine."

"I wonder," she says. "Yesterday you were roaming around here like a panther at the zoo, and then you and Brad go off for a mysterious trip. You said it was just a friendly trip, but the two of you haven't been friends for years. You do something bad out there?"

I think about Kelly with the shattered leg and Bill Sutler with his equally ruined day, and I say, "Yeah, I suppose so."

Her voice is sharp. "Was it for Brad?"

Even Mother probably can see the surprise on my face, so I say, "Yes, it was for Brad."

"You hurt someone?"

I nod. "But he deserved it, Mom."

Then she puts down her utensils and wipes her hands on her apron and says, "That's what you do for a living, isn't it, Carl? You hurt people."

Right then I wish the coffee tasted better, for I could take a sip and gain a few seconds for a response, but Mother is looking right through me and I say, "You're absolutely right."

She sighs. "But yesterday was for Brad. And the money you send me, and the gifts for your nieces, and everything else, all comes from your job. Hurting people."

"That's right."

Mother goes back to the eggs, starts whisking again with the wire beater, and says, "I've known that for a very long time, ever since you claimed you quit being a biker. I just knew you went on to something different, something probably even worse, though you certainly dressed better and looked clean."

She looks over again. "Thank you for the truth, Carl. And I'll never ask you again, you can believe that. Just tell me that what you do is right, and that you're happy."

So I tell her what she wants to hear, and she gives me another hug, and then there's some noise as the kids get up.

And then after breakfast it's time to go, and though Jan hangs back and says nothing, the kids are all over me, as is Mother, and even Deena—Brad's wife—gives me a peck on the cheek. Owen shakes my hand and I tell him to call me, anytime, making sure that Jan has heard me. And then there's the surprise, as Brad shakes my hand for the first time in a very long year or five.

"Thanks," he says. "And, um, well, come by sometime. The girls do miss you."

With that one sentence playing in my mind, I drive for over an hour, not bothering with the music on my CD player, for I'm hearing louder music in my head.

Later that night I'm in my large sunken tub, a small metal pitcher of vodka martinis on the marble floor. Sarah is in the tub with me, suds up to her lovely and full chest, and her hair is drawn up around her head, making her look like a Gibson girl from the turn of the century. I talk for some minutes and she laughs a few times and then reaches out with a wet and soapy foot and caresses my side. Like myself, she's holding a glass full of ice cubes and clear liquid.

"Only a guy like you, Carl, could travel hours to your family's home on a holiday weekend and bring your work with you," she says.

I sink a bit in the tub, feeling the hot water relax my back muscles. It had snowed some on the way back, and I'm still a bit tense from the drive.

"It wasn't work," I say. "It was a favor, a family thing."

"Mmmm," she says, sipping from her glass. "So that makes it all right?"

I shrug. "It just makes it, I guess."

"A worthwhile trip, then?"

"Very," I say, drinking from my own glass, enjoying the slightly oily bite of the drink. She sighs again and says, "You never really answered me, you know."

I close my eyes and say, "I didn't know I owed you an answer."

She nudges me with her foot. "Brute. From Thursday morning. When I asked you why you went there. And all you could say was family. Is that it, Carl? Truly?"

I know the true answer, which is that the little group of people in that tiny town are the only thing I have that is not bought or paid for in blood, and that keeping that little tie alive and well is important, very important to me. For if that tie were broken, then whatever passes for a human being in me would shrivel up and rot away, and I could not allow that. That is the truth, but I don't feel like debating philosophy tonight.

So I say, "Haven't you heard the expression?"

"What's that?"

I raise my drink to her in a toast. "Even the bad can do good."

Sarah makes a face and tosses the drink's contents at me, and then water starts slopping over onto the floor, and the lovely evening gets even lovelier, and there's no more talk of family and obligations, which is just fine.

ED GORMAN

SEASONS OF THE HEART

Author, editor, and publisher Ed Gorman has lived much of his life among the farmlands of Iowa, and he makes fine use of a farm setting in this novelette, marking his fourth appearance in these annual volumes. "Seasons of the Heart" was published in Ellery Queen's Mystery Magazine *and in the anthology* Partners in Crime.

In the mornings now, the fog didn't burn off till much before eight, and the dew stayed silver past nine, and the deeper shadows stayed all morning long in the fine red barn I'd helped build last year. The summer was fleeing.

But that wasn't how I knew autumn was coming.

No, for that all I had to do was look at the freckled face of my granddaughter Lisa, who would be entering eighth grade this year at the consolidated school ten miles west.

For as much as she read, and when she wasn't doing chores she was always reading something, even when she sat in front of the TV, she hated school. I don't think she'd had her first serious crush yet, and the girlfriends available to her struck her as a little frivolous. They were town girls and they didn't have Lisa's responsibilities.

This particular morning went pretty much as usual.

We had a couple cups of coffee, Lisa and I, and then we hiked down to the barn. It was still dark. You could hear the horses in the hills waking with the dawn, and closer by the chickens. Turnover day was coming, a frantic day in the life of a farmer.

You take the birds to market and then have twenty-four hours to clean out the chicken house before the new shipment of baby chicks arrives. First time I ever did it, I was worn out for three days. That's when my daughter Emmy read me the Booker T. Washington quote I'd come to savor: "No race can prosper till it learns that there is as much dignity in tilling a field as writing a poem." Those particular words work just as well as Ben-Gay on sore muscles. For me, anyway.

The barn smelled summer sweet of fresh milk. Lisa liked to lead the animals into the stalls; she had her own reassuring way of talking to them in a language understood only by cows and folk under fourteen years of age. She also liked to hook them up.

The actual milking, I usually did. Lisa always helped me pour the fresh milk into dumping stations. We tried to get a lot of milk per day. We had big payments to make on this barn. The Douglas fir we'd used to build it hadn't come cheap. Nor had the electricity, the milking machines, or the insulation. You've got to take damned good care of dairy cattle.

I worked straight through till Lisa finished cleaning up the east end of the barn. This was one of those days when she wanted to do some of the milking herself. I was happy to let her do it.

Everything was fine till I stepped outside the barn to have a few puffs on my pipe.

Funny thing was, I'd given up both cigarettes and pipe years before. But after Dr. Wharton, back in Chicago when I was still with the flying service, told me about the cancer, I found an old briar pipe of mine and took it up again. I brought it to the farm with me when I came to live with Emmy. I never smoked it in an enclosed area. I didn't want Lisa to pick up any secondhand smoke.

The chestnut mare was on the far hill. She was a beauty and seemed to know it, always prancing about to music no one else seemed to hear, or bucking against the sundown sky when she looked all mythic and ethereal in the darkening day.

And that's just what I was doing, getting my pipe fired up and looking at the roan, when the rifle shot ripped away a large chunk of wood from the door frame no more than three inches to my right.

I wasn't sure what it was. In movies, the would-be target always pitches himself left or right, but I just stood there for several long seconds before the echo of the bullet whining past me made me realize what had happened.

Only then did I move, running into the barn to warn Lisa, but she already knew that something had happened.

Lisa is a tall, slender girl with the dignified appeal of her mother. You wouldn't call either of them beauties, but in their fine blond hair and their melancholy brown eyes and their quick and sometimes sad grins, you see the stuff of true heartbreakers, a tradition they inherited from my wife, who broke my heart by leaving me for an advertising man when Emmy was nine years old.

"God, that was a gunshot, wasn't it?"

"I'm afraid it was."

"You think it was accidental, Granddad?"

"I don't know. Not yet, anyway. But for now, let's stay in the barn."

"I wonder if Mom heard it."

I smiled. "Not the way she sleeps."

She put her arms around me and gave me a hug. "I was really scared. For you, I mean. I was afraid somebody might have— Well, you know."

I hugged her back. "I'm fine, honey. But I'll tell you what. I want you to go stand in that corner over there while I go up in the loft and see if I can spot anybody."

"It's so weird. Nobody knows you out here."

"Nobody that I know of, anyway."

She broke our hug and looked up at me with those magnificent and often mischievous eyes. "Granddad?"

She always used a certain tone when she was about to ask me something that she wasn't sure about.

"Here it is. You've got that tone."

Her bony shoulders shrugged beneath her T-shirt, which depicted a rock-and-roll band I've never heard of. They were called The Flesh Eaters and she played their tapes a lot.

"I was just wondering if you'd be mad if I wrote it up."

"Wrote what up?"

"You know. Somebody shooting at you."

"Oh."

"Mrs. Price'll make us do one of those dorky how-I-spent-my-summer-vacation deals. It'd be cool if I could write about how a killer was stalking my granddad."

"Yeah," I said, "that sure sounds cool all right."

She grinned the grin and I saw both her mother and her grandmother in it. "I mean, I might 'enhance' it a little bit. But not a lot."

"Fine by me, pumpkin," I said, leading her over to the corner of the barn where several bales of hay would absorb a gunshot. "I'll be right back."

I figured that the shooter was most likely gone, long gone probably, but I wanted to make sure before I let Lisa stroll back into the barnyard.

I went up the ladder to the hayloft, sneezing all the way. My sinuses act up whenever I get even close to the loft. I used to think it was the hay but then I read a *Farm Bulletin* item saying it could be the rat droppings. For someone who grew up in the Hyde Park area of Chicago, rat droppings are not something you often consider as a sinus irritant. Farm life was different. I loved it.

I eased the loft door open a few inches. Then stopped.

I waited a full two minutes. No rifle fire.

I pushed the door open several more inches and looked outside. Miles of dark green corn and soybeans and alfalfa. On the hill just about where the mare was, I saw a tree where the gunman might have fired from. Gnarly old oak with branches stout enough for a hanging.

"Granddad?" Lisa called up from below.

"Yeah, hon?"

"Are you all right?"

"I'm fine. How about you?"

"God, I shouldn't have asked you if I could write about this for my class."

"Oh, why not?"

"Because this could be real serious. I mean, maybe it wasn't accidental."

"Now you sound like your grandmother."

"Huh?"

"She'd always do something and then get guilty and start apologizing." I didn't add that despite her apologies, her grandmother generally went right back to doing whatever she'd apologized for in the first place.

"I'm sorry if I hurt your feelings, Granddad."

Lisa never used to treat me like this. So dutifully. Nor did her mother. To them, I was just the biggest kid in the family and was so treated. But the cancer changed all that. Now they'd do something spontaneous and then right away they'd start worrying about it. There's a grim decorum that goes along with the disease. You become this big sad frail guy who, they seem to think, just can't deal with any of life's daily wear and tear.

That's one of the nice things about my support group. We get to laugh a lot about the delicate way our loved ones treat us sometimes. It's not mean laughter. Hell, we understand that they wouldn't treat us this way if they didn't love us, and love us a lot. But sometimes their dutifulness can be kind of funny in an endearing way.

"You 'enhance' it any way you want to, pumpkin," I said, and started to look around at fields sprawling out in front of me.

I started sneezing pretty bad again, too.

I spent ten minutes in the loft, finally deciding it was safe for us to venture out as soon as we finished with the milking for the day.

On the way out of the barn, I said, "Don't tell your mom. You know, about the gunshot."

"How come?"

"You must be crazy, kid. You know how she worries about me."

Lisa smiled. "How about making a bargain?"

"Oh-oh. Here it comes."

"I won't tell Mom and you let me drive the tractor."

Lots of farm kids die in tractor accidents every year. I didn't want Lisa to be one of them. "I'll think about it, how's that?"

"Then I guess I'll just have to think about it, too." But she laughed.

I pulled her closer, my arm around her shoulder. "You think I'm wrong? About not telling your mom?"

She thought for a while. "Nah, I guess not. I mean, Mom really does worry about you a lot already."

We were halfway to the house, a ranch-style house of blond brick with an evergreen windbreak and a white dish antenna east of the trees.

Just as we reached the walk leading to the house, I heard a heavy car come rumbling up the driveway, raising dust and setting both collies to barking. The car was a new baby-blue Pontiac with official police insignia decaled on the side.

I stopped, turned around, grinned at Lisa. "Remember now, you've got Friday."

"Yeah, I wish I had Saturday, the way you do."

We'd been betting the last two weeks when Chief of Police Nick Bingham was going to ask Emmy to marry him. They'd been going out for three years, and two weeks ago Nick had said, "I've never said this to you before, Emmy, but you know when I turned forty last year? Well, ever since, I've had this loneliness right in here. A burning." And of course my wise-ass daughter had said, "Maybe it's gas." She told this to Lisa and me at breakfast next morning, relishing the punch line.

Because Nick had never said anything like this at all in his three years of courting her, Emmy figured he was just about to pop the question.

So Lisa and I started this little pool. Last week I'd bet he'd ask her on Friday night and she'd bet he'd ask her on Saturday. But he hadn't asked her either night. Now the weekend was approaching again.

Nick got out of the car in sections. In high school he'd played basketball on a team that had gone three times to state finals and had finished second twice. Nick had played center. He was just over six five. He went three years to college but dropped out to finish harvest when his father died of a heart attack. He never got the degree. But he did become a good lawman.

"Morning," he said.

"Pink glazed?" Lisa said when she saw the white sack dangling from his left hand.

"Two of 'em are, kiddo."

"Can I have one?"

"No," he said, pulling her to him and giving her a kind of affectionate Dutch rub. "You can have both of 'em."

He wasn't what you'd call handsome, but there was a quiet manliness to the broken nose and the intelligent blue eyes that local ladies, including my own daughter, seemed to find attractive, especially when he was in his khaki uniform. They didn't seem to mind that he was balding fast.

Emmy greeted us at the door in a blue sweatshirt and jeans and the kind of white Keds she'd worn ever since she was a tot. No high-priced running shoes for her. With her earnest little face and tortoiseshell glasses, she always reminded me of those quiet, pretty girls I never got to know in my high school class. Her blond hair was cinched in a ponytail that bobbed as she walked.

"Coffee's on," she said, taking the hug Nick offered as he came through the door.

We did this three, four times a week, Nick finishing up his morning meeting with his eight officers then stopping by Donut Dan's and coming out here for breakfast.

Strictly speaking, I was supposed to be eating food a little more nutritional than donuts, but this morning I decided to indulge.

The conversation ran its usual course. Lisa and Nick joked with each other, Emmy reminded me about all the vitamins and pills I was supposed to take every morning, and I told him about how hard a time I was having finding a few good extra hands for harvest.

Lisa sounded subdued this morning, which caused Emmy to say, "You feeling all right, hon? You seem sort of quiet."

Lisa faked a grin. "Just all that hard work Granddad made me do. Wore me out."

Lisa was still thinking about the rifle shot. So was I. Several times my eyes strayed to Nick's holster and gun.

Just as we were all starting on our second cup of coffee, Lisa included, a car horn sounded at the far end of our driveway. The mail was here.

Wanting a little time to myself, I said I'd get the mail. Sometimes Lisa walked down to the mailbox with me, but this morning she was still working on the second pink glazed donut. The rifle shot had apparently affected her appetite.

After the surgery and the recuperation, I decided to spend whatever time I had left—months maybe or years, the doctors just weren't very sure—living out my Chicago-boy fantasy of being a farmer. Hell, hadn't my daughter become a farmer? I inhaled a relatively pure fresh air and less than two miles away was a fast-running river where, with the right spoon and plug and spinner, you could catch trout all day long.

I tried to think of that now, as I walked down the rutted road to the mailbox. I was lucky. Few people ever have their fantasies come true. I lived with those I loved, I got to see things grow, and I had for my restive pleasure the sights of beautiful land. And there was a good chance that I was going to kick the cancer I'd been fighting the past two years.

So why did anybody want to go and spoil it for me by shooting at me?

As I neared the mailbox, I admitted to myself that the shot hadn't been accidental. Nor had it been meant to kill me. The shooter was good enough to put a bullet close to my head without doing me any damage. For whatever reason, he'd simply wanted to scare me.

The mailbox held all the usual goodies, circulars from True Value, Younkers Department Store, Hy-Vee supermarkets, Drugtown, and the Ford dealer where I'd bought my prize blue pickup.

The number-ten white envelope, the one addressed to me, was the last thing I took from the mailbox.

I knew immediately that the envelope had something to do with the rifle shot this morning. Some kind of telepathic insight allowed me to understand this fact.

There was neither note nor letter inside, simply a photograph, a photo far more expressive than words could ever have been.

I looked away from it at first, then slowly came back to it, the edge of it pincered between my thumb and forefinger.

I looked at it for a very long time. I felt hot, sweaty, though it was still early morning. I felt scared and ashamed and sick as I stared at it. So many years ago it had been; something done by a man with my name, but not the same man who bore that name today.

I tucked picture into envelope and went back to the house.

When I was back at the table, a cup of coffee in my hand, I noticed that Emmy was staring at me. "You all right, Dad?"

"I'm fine. Maybe just getting a touch of the flu or something."

While that would normally be a good excuse for looking gray and shaken, to the daughter of a cancer patient those are terrifying words. As if the patient himself doesn't worry about every little ache and pain. But to tell someone who loves you that you suddenly feel sick . . .

I reached across the table and said to Nick, "You mind if I hold hands with your girl?"

Nick smiled. "Not as long as you don't make a habit of it."

I took her hand for perhaps the millionth time in my life, holding in memory all the things this hand had been, child, girl, wife, mother.

"I'm fine, honey. Really."

All she wanted me to see was the love in those blue eyes. But I also saw the fear. I wanted to sit her on my lap as I once had, and rock her on my knees, and tell her that everything was going to be just fine.

"Okay?" I said.

"Okay," she half-whispered.

Nick went back to telling Lisa why her school should have an especially good basketball team this year.

On the wall to the right of the kitchen table, Emmy had hung several framed advertisements from turn-of-the-century magazines, sweet little girls in bonnets and braids, and freckled boys with dogs even cuter than they were, all the faces and poses leading you to believe that theirs was a far more innocent era than ours. But the older I got, the more I realized that the human predicament had always been the same. It had just dressed up in different clothes.

There was one photograph up there. A grimy man in military fatigues standing with a cigarette dangling from his lips and an M-16 leaning against him. Trying to look tough when all he was was scared. The man was me.

"Well," Nick said about ten minutes later.

Emmy and Lisa giggled.

No matter how many times they kidded Nick about saying "Well" each time he was about to announce his imminent departure, he kept right on saying it.

Emmy walked him out to the car.

I filled the sink with hot, soapy water. Lisa piled the breakfast dishes in.

"Granddad?"

"Yes, hon?"

"You sure you don't want to tell Mom about the gunshot?"

"No, hon, I don't. I know it's tempting but she's got enough to worry about." Emmy had had a long and miserable first marriage to a man who had treated adultery like the national pastime. Now, on the small amount of money she got from the farm and from me paying room and board, Emmy had to raise a daughter. She didn't need any more anxiety.

"I'm going into town," I said as I started to wash the dishes and hand them one by one to Lisa, who was drying.

"How come?"

"Oh, a little business."

"What kind of business?"

"I just want to check out the downtown area."

"For what?"

I laughed. "I'll fill out a written report when I get back."

"I'll go with you."

"Oh no. This is something I have to do alone."

"Detectives usually have partners."

"I think that's just on TV."

"Huh-uh. In *Weekly Reader* last year there was this article on Chicago police and it said that they usually worked in teams. Team means two. You and me, Granddad."

I guessed I really wasn't going to do much more than nose around. Probably wouldn't hurt for her to ride along.

By the time Emmy got back to the kitchen, looking every bit as happy as I wanted her to be, Lisa and I had finished the dishes and were ready for town.

"When will you be back?"

"Oh, hour or two."

Emmy was suspicious. "Is there something you're not telling me?"

"Nothing, sweetheart," I said, leaning over and kissing her on the cheek. "Honest."

We went out and got in the truck, passing the old cedar chest Lisa had converted into a giant tool box and placed in the back of the pickup. She had fastened it with strong twine so it wouldn't shift around. It looked kind of funny sitting there like that but Lisa had worked hard at it so I wasn't about to take it out.

Twenty years ago there was hope that the interstate being discussed would run just east of our little town. Unfortunately, it ran north, and twenty miles away. Today the downtown is four two-block streets consisting of dusty red-brick buildings all built before 1930. The post office and the two supermarkets and the five taverns are the busiest places.

I started at the post office, asking for Ev Meader, the man who runs it.

"Gettin' ready for school, Lisa?" Ev said when we came into his office.

She made a face. Ev laughed. "So what can I do for ya today?"

"Wondering if you heard of anybody new moving in around here?" I said. "You know, filling out a new address card."

He scratched his bald head. "Not in the past couple weeks. Least I don't think so. But let me check." He left the office.

I looked down at Lisa. "You going to ask me?"

"Ask you what, Granddad?"

"Ask me how come I'm asking Ev about new people moving into town."

She grinned. "Figured I'd wait till we got back in the truck."

"No new address cards," Ev said when he came back. "I'll keep an eye out for you if you want."

"I'd appreciate it."

In the truck, Lisa said, "Is it all right if I ask you now?"

"I'm wondering if that shot this morning didn't coincide with somebody moving here. Somebody who came here just so they could deal with me."

"You mean, like somebody's after you or something like that?"

"Uh-huh."

"But who'd be after you?"

"I don't know."

The man at the first hotel had a potbelly and merry red suspenders. "Asian, you say?"

"Right."

"Nope. No Asians that I signed in, anyway."

"How about at night?"

"I can check the book."

"I'd appreciate it."

"Two weeks back be all right?"

"That'd be fine."

But two weeks back revealed no Asians. "Sorry," he said, hooking his thumbs in his suspenders.

"How come Asians?" Lisa said after we were back in the truck.

"Just because of something that happened to me once."

We rode in silence for a time.

"Granddad?"

"Yeah."

"You going to tell me? About what happened to you once?"

"Not right now, hon."

"How come?"

"Too hard for me to talk about." And it was. Every time I thought about it for longer than a minute, I could feel my eyes tear up.

The woman at the second motel wore a black T-shirt with a yellow hawk on it. Beneath it said, "I'll do anything for the

Hawkeyes." Anything was underlined. The Hawkeyes were the U of Iowa.

"Couple black guys, some kind of salesmen I guess, but no Asians," she said.

"How about at night?"

She laughed. "Bob works at night. He doesn't much like people who aren't white. We had an Asian guy, I'd hear about it, believe me."

The man at the third motel, a hearty man with a farmer's tan and a cheap pair of false teeth, said, "No Asian."

"Maybe he came at night?"

"The boy, he works the night shift. Those robberies we had a few months back—that convenience store where that girl got shot?—ever since, he keeps a sharp eye out. Usually tells me all about the guests. He didn't mention any Asian."

"Thanks."

"Sure."

"I'll be happy to ask around," he said.

"Cochran, right?"

"Henry Cochran. Right."

"Thanks for your help, Henry."

"You bet."

"You going to tell me yet?" Lisa said when we were in the pickup and headed back to the farm.

"Not yet."

"Am I bugging you, Granddad?"

I smiled at her. "Maybe a little."

"Then I won't ask you anymore."

She leaned over and gave me a kiss on the cheek, after which she settled back on her side of the seat.

"You know what I forgot to do today?" she said after a while.

"What?"

"Tell you I love you."

"Well, I guess you'd better hurry up and do it, then."

"I love you, Granddad."

The funny thing was, I'd never been able to cry much till the cancer, which was a few years ago when I turned fifty-two. Not even when my two best soldier friends got killed in Nam did I

113

cry. Not even when my wife left me did I cry. But these days all sorts of things made me cry. And not just about sad things, either. Seeing a horse run free could make me cry; and certain old songs; and my granddaughter's face when she was telling me she loved me.

"I love you, too, Lisa," I said, and gave her hand a squeeze.

That afternoon Lisa and I spent three hours raking corn in a wagon next to the silo, stopping only when the milk truck came. As usual Ken, the driver, took a sample out of the cooling vat where the milk had been stored. He wanted to get a reading on the butterfat content of the milk. When the truck was just rolling brown dust on the distant road, Lisa and I went back to raking the corn. At five we knocked off. Lisa rode her bike down the road to the creek where she was trying to catch a milk snake for her science class this fall.

I was scrubbing up for dinner when Emmy called me to the phone. "There's a woman on the line for you, Dad. She's got some kind of accent."

"I'll take it in the TV room," I said.

"This is Mr. Wilson?"

"Yes."

"Mr. Wilson, my name is Nguyn Mai. I am from Vietnam here visiting."

"I see."

"I would like to meet you tonight. I am staying in Iowa city but I would meet you at the Fireplace restaurant. You know where is?"

"Yes, the Fireplace is downtown here."

"Yes. Would seven o'clock be reasonable for you?"

"I have to say eight. There's a meeting I need to go to first."

"I would appreciate it, Mr. Wilson."

She sounded intelligent and probably middle-aged. I got no sense of her mood.

"Eight o'clock," I said.

After dinner, I took a shower and climbed into a newly washed pair of chinos and a white button-down shirt and a blue windbreaker.

In town, I parked in the Elks lot. Across the cinder alley was the meeting room we used for our support group.

The hour went quickly. There was a new woman there tonight, shy and fresh with fear after her recent operation for breast cancer. At one point, telling us how she was sometimes scared to sleep, she started crying. She was sitting next to me so I put my arm around her and held her till she felt all right again. That was another thing I'd never been too good at till the cancer, showing tenderness.

There were seven of us tonight. We described our respective weeks since the last meeting, exchanged a few low-fat recipes, and listened to one of the men discuss some of the problems he was having with his chemotherapy treatments. We finished off with prayer and then everybody else headed for the coffeepot and the low-fat kolaches one of the women had baked especially for this meeting.

At eight I walked through the door of the Fireplace and got my first look at Nguyn Mai. She was small and fiftyish and pretty in the way of her people. She wore an American dress, dark and simple, a white sweater draped over her shoulders. Her eyes were friendly and sad.

After I ordered my coffee, she said, "I'm sorry I must trouble you, Mr. Wilson."

"Robert is what most people call me."

"Robert then." She paused, looked down, looked up again. "My brother Nguyn Dang plans to kill you."

I told her about the rifle shot this morning, and the envelope later.

"He was never the same," she said, "after it happened. I am his oldest sister. There was one sister younger, Hong. This is the one who died. She was six years old. Dang, who was twelve at the time, took care of the funeral all by himself, would not even let my parents see her until after he had put her in her casket. Dang always believed in the old religious ways. He buried Hong in our backyard, according to ancient custom. The old ways teach that the head of a virgin girl is very valuable and can be used as a very powerful talisman to bring luck to the family members. Dang was certainly lucky. When he was fourteen, he

115

left our home and went to Saigon. Within ten years, he was a millionaire. He deals in imports. He spent his fortune tracking you down. It was not easy."

"Were you there that day?"

"Yes."

"Did you see what happened?"

She nodded.

"I didn't kill her intentionally. If you saw what happened, you know that's the truth."

"The truth is in the mind's eye, Robert. In my eye, I know you were frightened by a Cong soldier at the other end of our backyard. You turned and fired and accidentally shot Hong. But this is not what my brother saw."

"He saw me kill her in cold blood."

"Yes."

"But why would I shoot a little girl?"

"It was done, you know, by both sides. Maybe not by you but by others."

"And so now he's here."

"To kill you."

During my second cup of coffee, she said, "I am afraid for him. I do not wish to see you killed, but even more I do not wish to see my brother killed. I know that is selfish but those are my feelings."

"I have the same feelings." I paused and said, "Do you know where he is?"

"No."

"I looked for him today, after the envelope came."

"And you didn't find him?"

I shook my head. "For what it's worth, Mai, I never forgot what happened that day."

"No?"

"When I got back to the States, I started having nightmares about it. And very bad migraine headaches. I even went to a psychologist for a year or so. Everybody said I shouldn't feel guilty, that those accidents happen in war. Got so bad, it started to take its toll on my marriage. I wasn't much of a husband—or a father, for that matter—and eventually my wife left me. I'd look around at the other guys I'd served with. They'd done ugly things too, but if it bothered them, they didn't let on. I was even going to go back to Nam and look up your family and tell them I was sorry but my daughter wouldn't let me. At that point, she was ready to put me in a mental hospital. She said that if I seriously tried to go, she'd put me away for sure. I knew she meant it."

"Did you talk to the police today, about his taking a shot at you?"

"You've got to understand something here, Mai. I don't want your brother arrested. I want to find him and talk to him and help him if I can. There hasn't been a day in my life since when I haven't wanted to pick up the phone and talk to your family and tell them how sorry I am."

"If only we could find Dang."

"I'll start looking again tomorrow."

"I feel hopeful for the first time in many years."

I stayed up past midnight because I knew I wouldn't sleep well. There was a Charles Bronson movie on TV, in the course of which he killed four or five people. Before that day in Nam, when I'd been so scared that I'd mistaken a little girl for a VC, I had been all enamored of violence. But no longer. After the war, I gave away all my guns and nearly all my pretensions to machismo. I knew too well where machismo sometimes led.

Ten hours later, coming in from morning chores, I heard the phone ringing. Emmy said it was for me.

It was the motel man with the merry red suspenders. "I heard something you might be interested in."

"Oh?"

"You know where the old Sheldon farm is?"

"I don't think so."

"Well, there's a lime quarry due west of the power station. You know where that would be?"

"I can find it."

"There's a house trailer somewhere back in there. Hippie couple lived there for years but they moved to New Mexico last year. Guy in town who owns a tavern—Shelby, maybe you know him—he bought their trailer from them and rents it out

sort of like an apartment. Or thought he would, anyway. Hasn't
had much luck. Till last week. That's when this Asian guy rented
it from him."

The day was ridiculously beautiful, the sweet smoky breath of
autumn on the air, the horses in the hills shining the color of
saddle leather.

The lime quarry had been closed for years. Some of the equipment had been left behind. Everything was rusted now. The
whining wind gave the place the sound of desolation.

I pointed the pickup into the hills where oak and hickory and
basswood bloomed, and elm and ash and ironwood leaves
caught the bright bouncing beams of the sun.

The trailer was in a grassy valley, buffalo grass knee-deep and
waving in the wind, a silver S of creek winding behind the rusted
old Airstream.

I pulled off the road in the dusty hills and walked the rest of
the way down.

There was a lightning-dead elm thirty yards from the trailer.
When I reached it, I got behind it so I could get a better look at
the Airstream.

No noise came from the open window, no smoke from the
tin chimney.

I went up to the trailer. Every few feet I expected to hear a
bullet cracking from a rifle.

The window screens were badly torn, the three steps tilted
rightward, and the two propane tanks to the right of the door
leaned forward as if they might fall at any moment.

I reached the steps, tried the door. Locked. Dang was gone.
Picking the lock encased in the doorknob was no great trouble.

The interior was a mess. Apparently Dang existed on Godfather's pizza. I counted nine different cartons, all grease-stained,
on the kitchen counter. The thrumming little refrigerator
smelled vaguely unclean. It contained three sixteen-ounce bottles of Pepsi.

In the back, next to the bed on the wobbly nightstand, I found
the framed photos of the little girl. She had been quite pretty,
solemn and mischievous at the same time.

The photo Dang had sent me was very different. The girl lay on a table, her bloody clothes wrapped around her. Her chest was a dark massive hole.

I thought I heard a car coming.

Soon enough I was behind the elm again. But the road was empty. All I'd heard was my own nerves.

During chores two hours later, Lisa said, "You find him?"

"Find who?"

"Find who? Come on, Granddad."

"Yeah, I found him. Or found his trailer, anyway."

"How come you didn't take me with you? I'm supposed to be your partner."

I leaned on my pitchfork. "Hon, from here on out I'll have to handle this alone."

"Oh, darn it, Granddad. I want to help."

There was a sweet afternoon breeze through the barn door, carrying the scents of clover and sunshine.

"All that's going to happen is I'm going to talk to him."

"Gosh, Granddad, he tried to kill you."

"I don't think so."

"But he shot at you."

"He tried to scare me."

"You sure?"

"Pretty sure."

After washing up for the day, I went into the TV room and called Mai and told her that I'd found where her brother was staying.

"You should not go out there," she said. "In my land we say that there are seasons of the heart. The season of my brother's heart is very hot and angry now."

"I just want to talk to him and tell him that I'm sorry. Maybe that will calm him down."

"I will talk to him. You can direct me to this trailer?"

"If you meet me at the restaurant again, I'll lead you out there."

"Then you will go back home?"

"If that's what you want."

119

She was there right at eight. The full moon, an autumn moon that painted all the pines silver, guided us to the power station and the quarry and finally to the hill above the trailer.

I got out of the car and walked back to hers. "You follow that road straight down."

"Did you see the windows? The lights?"

He was home. Or somebody was.

"I appreciate this, Robert. Perhaps I can reason with my brother."

"I hope so."

She paused, looked around. "It is so beautiful and peaceful here. You are fortunate to live here."

There were owls and jays in the forest trees, and the fast creek silver in the moonlight, and the distant song of a windmill in the breeze. She was right. I was lucky to live here.

She drove on.

I watched her till she reached the trailer, got out, went to the door, and knocked.

Even from here, I could see that the man/silhouette held a handgun when he opened the door for her. Mai and I had both assumed we could reason with her brother. Maybe not.

"You up for a game of hearts?" Lisa said a while later.

"Sure," I said.

"Good. Because I'm going to beat you tonight."

"You sure of that?"

"Uh-huh."

As usual I won. I thought of letting her win but then realized that she wouldn't want that. She was too smart and too honorable for that kind of charity.

When she was in her cotton nightie, her mouth cold and spicy from brushing her teeth, she came down and gave me my goodnight kiss.

When Lisa was creaking her way up the stairs, Emmy looked into the TV room and said, "Wondered if I could ask you a question?"

"Sure."

"Are you, uh, all right?"

"Aw, honey. My last tests were fine and I feel great. You've really got to stop worrying."

"I don't mean physically. I mean, you seem preoccupied."

"Everything's fine."

"God, Dad, I love you so much. And I can't help worrying about you."

The full-grown woman in the doorway became my quick little daughter again, rushing to me and sitting on my lap and burying her tear-hot face in my neck so I couldn't see her cry.

We sat that way for a long time and then I started bouncing her on my knee.

She laughed. "I weigh a little more than I used to."

"Not much."

"My bottom's starting to spread a little."

"Nick seems to like it fine."

With her arms still around me, she kissed me on the cheek and then gave me another hug. A few minutes later, she left to finish up in the kitchen.

The call came ten minutes after I fell into a fitful sleep. I'd been expecting Mai. I got Nick.

"Robert, I wondered if you could come down to the station."

"Now? After midnight?"

"I'm afraid so."

"What's up?"

"A Vietnamese woman came into the emergency room over at the hospital tonight. Her arm had been broken. The doc got suspicious and gave me a call. I went over and talked to her. She wouldn't tell me anything at all. Then all of a sudden, she asked if she could see a man named Robert Wilson. You know her, Robert?"

"Yes."

"Who is she?"

"Her name is Nguyn Mai. She's visiting people in the area."

"Which people?"

I hesitated. "Nick, I can't tell you anything more than Mai has."

For the first time in our relationship, Nick sounded cold. "I need you to come down here, Robert. Right away."

Our small town is fortunate enough to have a full-time hospital that doubles as an emergency room.

Mai sat at the end of the long hallway, her arm in a white sling. I sat next to her in a yellow, form-curved plastic chair.

"What happened?"

"I was foolish," she said. "We argued and I tried to take one of his guns from him. We struggled and I fell into the wall and I heard my arm snap."

"I don't think Nick believes you."

"He says he knows you."

"He goes out with my daughter."

"Is he a prejudiced man, this Nick?"

"I don't think so. He's just a cop who senses that he's not getting the whole story. Plus you made him very curious when you asked him to call me."

"I knew no one else."

"I understand, Mai. I'm just trying to explain Nick's attitude."

Nick showed up a few minutes later.

"How's the arm? Ready for tennis yet?"

Mai obviously appreciated the way Nick was trying to lighten things up. "Not yet," she said, and smiled like a small, shy girl.

"Mind if I borrow your friend a few minutes, Mai?"

She smiled again and shook her head. But there was apprehension in her dark eyes. Would I tell Nick that her brother had taken a shot at me?

In the staff coffee room, I put a lot of sugar and Cremora into my paper cup of coffee. I badly needed to kill the taste.

"You know her in Nam, Robert?"

"No."

"She just showed up?"

"Pretty much."

"Any special reason?"

"Not that I know of."

"Robert, I don't appreciate lies. Especially from my future father-in-law."

"She phoned me last night and we talked. Turns out we knew some of the same people in Nam. That's about all there is to it."

"Right."

"Nick, I can handle this. It doesn't have to involve the law."

"She got her arm broken."

"It was an accident."

"That's what she says."

"She's telling the truth, Nick."

"The same way you're telling the truth, Robert?"

In the hall, Nick said, "She seems like a nice woman."

"She is a nice woman."

When we reached Mai, Nick said, "Robert here tells me you're a nice woman. I'm sorry if my questions upset you."

Mai gave a little half bow of appreciation and good-bye.

In the truck, I turned the heat on. It was two A.M. of a late August night and it was shivering late-October cold.

"Where's your car?"

"The other side of the building," Mai said.

"You'd better not drive back to Iowa City tonight."

"There is a motel?"

After I got her checked in, I pulled the pickup right to her door, number seventeen.

Inside, I got the lights on and turned the thermostat up to eighty so it would warm up fast. The room was small and dark. You could hear the ghosts of it crying down the years, a chorus of smiling salesmen and weary vacationers and frantic adulterers.

"I wish I had had better luck with my brother tonight," Mai said. "For everybody's sake."

"Maybe he'll think about it tonight and be more reasonable in the morning."

In the glove compartment I found the old .38 Emmy bought when she moved to the farm. Bucolic as rural Iowa was, it was not without its moments of violence, particularly when drug deals were involved. She kept it in the kitchen cabinet, on the top shelf. I had taken it with me when I left tonight.

In the valley, the trailer was a silhouette outlined in moon silver. I approached in a crouch, the .38 in my right hand. A white-tailed fawn pranced away to my left, and a raccoon or possum rattled reeds in a long waving patch of bluestem grass.

When I reached the elm, I stopped and listened. No sound whatsoever from the Airstream. The propane tanks stood like sentries.

The doorknob was no more difficult to unlock tonight than it had been earlier.

Tonight the trailer smelled of sleep and wine and rust and cigarette smoke. I stood perfectly still, listening to the refrigerator vibrate. From the rear of the trailer came the sounds of Dang snoring.

When I stood directly above him, I raised the .38 and pushed it to within two inches of his forehead.

I spoke his name in the stillness.

His eyes opened but at first they seemed to see nothing. He seemed to be in a half-waking state.

But then he grunted and something like a sob exploded in his throat and I said, "If I wanted to, I could kill you right now, but I don't want to. I want you to listen to me."

In the chill prairie night, the coffee Dang put on smelled very good. We sat at a small table, each drinking from a different 7-Eleven mug.

He was probably ten years younger than me, slender, with graying hair and a long, intelligent face. He wore good American clothes and good American glasses. Whenever he looked at me directly, his eyes narrowed with anger. He was likely flashing back to the frail, bloody dead girl in the photo he'd sent me.

"My sister told you why I came here?"

"Yes."

"You came to talk me out of it, that is why you're here?"

"Something like that. The first thing is, I want to tell you how sorry I am that it happened."

"Words."

"Pardon?"

"Words. In my land there is a saying, 'Words only delay the inevitable.' If you do not kill me, Mr. Wilson, I will kill you. No matter how many words you speak."

"It was an accident."

"I am a believer in Hoa Hao, Mr. Wilson. We do not believe in accidents. All behavior is willful."

"I willfully murdered a six-year-old girl?"

"In war, there are many atrocities."

Anger came and went in his eyes. When it was gone, he looked old and sad. Rage seemed to give him a kind of fevered youth.

"You were there, Dang. You saw it happen. I wasn't firing at her. I was firing at a VC. She got in the way."

He stared at me a long time. "Words, Mr. Wilson, words."

I wanted to tell him about my years following the killing, how it shaped and in many respects destroyed my life. I even thought of telling him about my cancer and how the disease had taught me so many important lessons. But I would only sound as if I were begging for his pity.

I stood up. "Why don't you leave tomorrow? Your sister is worried about you."

"I'll leave after I've killed you."

"What I did, Dang, I know you can't forgive me for. Maybe I'd be the same way you are. But if you kill me, the police will arrest you. And that will kill Mai. You'll have killed her just as I killed your other sister."

For a time, he kept his head down and said nothing. When he raised his eyes to me, I saw that they were wet with tears. "Before I sleep each night, I play in my head her voice, like a tape. Even at six she had a beautiful voice. I play it over and over again."

He surprised me by putting his head down on the table and weeping.

In bed that night, I thought of how long we'd carried our respective burdens, Dang his hatred of me, and me my remorse over Hong's death. I fell asleep thinking of what Dang had said about Hong's voice. I wished I could have heard her sing.

When I got down to the barn in the morning, Lisa was already bottle-feeding the three new calves. I set about the milking operations.

Half an hour later, the calves, the rabbits, and the barn cats taken care of, Lisa joined me.

"Mom was worried about you."

"Figured she would be," I said. "You didn't tell her anything, did you?"

"No, but Nick did."

"Nick?"

"Uh-huh. He told her about the Vietnamese woman."

"Oh."

"So Mom asked me if I knew anything about it."

"What'd you say?"

"Said I didn't know anything at all. But I felt kinda weird, Granddad, lying to Mom, I mean."

"I'm sorry, sweetheart."

At lunch, bologna sandwiches and creamed corn and an apple, Emmy said, "Dad, could I talk to you?"

"Sure."

"Lisa, why don't you go on ahead with your chores. Granddad'll be down real soon."

Lisa looked at me. I nodded.

When the screen door slapped shut, Emmy said, "Nick thinks you're in some kind of trouble, Dad."

"You know how much I like Nick, honey. I also happen to respect him." I held her hand. "But I'm not in any kind of trouble."

"Who's the Vietnamese woman?"

"Nguyn Mai."

"That doesn't tell me much."

"I don't mean for it to tell you much."

"You getting mad?"

"No. Sad, if anything. Sad that I can't have a life of my own without answering a lot of questions."

"Dad, if Nick wasn't concerned, I wouldn't be concerned. But Nick has good instincts about things like this."

"He does indeed."

"So why not tell us the truth?"

I got up from the table, picked up my dishes, and carried them over to the sink. "Let me think about it a little while, all right?"

She watched me for a long time, looking both wan and a little bit peeved, and finally said, "Think about it a little while, then."

She got up and left the room.

There were two carts that needed filling with silage. Lisa and I opened the trapdoor in the silo and started digging the silage out. Then we took the first of the carts over and started feeding the cows.

When that was done, I told Lisa to take the rest of the afternoon off. She kept talking about all the school supplies she needed. She'd never find time to get them if she was always working.

During the last rain, we'd noticed a few drops plopping down from the area of the living room. The roof was a good ten years old. I put the ladder against the back of the house and went up and looked around. There were some real bad spots.

I called the lumber store and got some prices on roofing materials. I told them what I wanted. They'd have them ready tomorrow morning.

There was still some work, so after a cup of coffee I headed for the barn. I hadn't quite reached it before the phone rang.

"For you, Dad," Emmy called.

"Robert?"

"I thought maybe you'd be gone by now, Mai. I went out and visited your brother last night. I don't know if he told you about it. I also don't know if it did any good. But at least I got to tell him I was sorry."

"I need to meet you at the hill above his trailer. Right away, please. Something terrible has happened."

"What're you talking about, Mai?"

"Please. The hill. As soon as possible."

"Can you drive?"

"Yes. I drove a little this morning."

"What's happened, Mai?"

"Your granddaughter. Dang has taken her."

As I was grabbing my jacket, and remembering that I'd left the .38 in the glove compartment, Emmy came into the room.

"I need to go out for a little while."

She touched my arm. "Dad, I don't know what just happened, but why don't you get Nick to help you?"

I'd thought about that, too. "Maybe I will."

I drove straight and hard to the hill. All the way there I thought of Dang. One granddaughter for one little sister. Even up. I should have thought of that and protected Lisa.

Mai stood by the dusty rental car.

"How do you know she's down there?"

"An hour ago, I snuck down there and peeked in the window. She is sitting in a chair in the kitchen."

"But she's still alive? You're sure?"

"Yes."

"Did you see if she's bleeding or anything?"

"I don't think he has hurt her. Not yet, anyway."

"I'm going in to get her."

She nodded to the .38 stuffed into my belt. "I am afraid for all of us, now. For Dang and for your granddaughter and for you. And for me."

She fell against me, crying. I was as tender as I could be but all I could think of was Lisa.

"I tried to talk him into giving her up. He says that he is only doing the honorable thing." More tears. "Talking won't help, Robert."

I went east, in a wide arc, coming down behind the trailer in a stand of windbreak firs. The back side of the Airstream had only one window. I didn't see anybody watching me.

I belly crawled from the trees to the front of the trailer. By now, I could hear him shouting in Vietnamese at Lisa. All his anger and all his pain were in those words. The exact meaning made no difference. It was the sounds he made that mattered.

I went to the door and knocked. His words stopped immediately. For a time there was just the soughing silence of the prairie.

"Dang, you let Lisa go and I'll come in and take her place."

"Don't come in, Granddad. He wants to kill you."

"Dang, did you hear me? You let Lisa go and I'll come in. I have a gun now but I'll drop it if you agree."

His first bullet ripped through the glass and screening of the front door.

I pitched left, rolling on the ground to escape the second and third shots.

Lisa yelled at Dang to stop firing, her words echoing inside the trailer.

Prairie silence again; a hawk gliding down the sunbeams.

I scanned the trailer, looking for some way to get closer without getting shot. There wasn't enough room to hide next to the three stairs; nor behind the two silver propane tanks; nor even around the corner. The bedroom window was too high to peek in comfortably.

"He's picking up his rifle, Granddad!" Lisa called.

Two more shots, these more explosive and taking larger chunks of the front door, burst into the afternoon air. I rolled away from them as best I could.

"Granddad, watch out!"

And then a cry came, one so shrill and aggrieved I wasn't sure what it was at first, and then the front door was thrown open and there was Dang, rifle fire coming in bursts as he came out on the front steps, shooting directly at me.

This time I rolled to the right. He was still sobbing out words in Vietnamese and these had the power to mesmerize me. They spoke exactly of how deep his grief ran.

Another burst of rifle fire, Dang standing on the steps of the trailer and having an easy time finding me with his rifle.

There was a long and curious delay before my brain realized that my chest had been wounded. It was as if all time stopped for a long moment, the universe holding its breath; and then came blood and raging, blinding pain. Then I felt a bone in my arm crack as a bullet smashed into it.

Lisa screamed again. "Granddad!"

As I lay there, another bullet taking my left leg, I realized I had only moments to do what I needed to. Dang was coming down from the steps, moving in to kill me. I raised the .38 and fired.

The explosion was instant and could probably be heard for miles. I'd been forced to shoot at him at an angle. The bullet had missed and torn into one of the propane tanks. The entire trailer had vanished inside tumbling gritty black smoke and fire at least three different shades of red and yellow. The air reeked of propane and the burning trailer.

I called out for Lisa but I knew I could never get to my feet to help her. I was losing consciousness too fast.

And then Dang was standing over me, rifle pointing directly down at my head.

I knew I didn't have long. "Save her, Dang. She's innocent, just the way your sister was. Save her, please. I'm begging you."

The darkness was swift and cold and black, and the sounds of Lisa screaming and fire roaring faded, faded.

The room was small and white and held but one bed and it was mine.

Lisa and Emmy and Nick stood on the left side of the bed while Mai stood on the right.

"I guess I'll have to do some of your chores for a while, Granddad."

"I guess you will, hon."

"That means driving the tractor."

I looked at Emmy, who said, "We'll hire a couple of hands, sweetheart. No tractor for you until Granddad gets back."

Nick looked at his watch. "How about if I take these two beautiful ladies downstairs for some lunch? This is one of the few hospitals that actually serves good food."

But it wasn't just lunch he was suggesting. He wanted to give Mai a chance to speak with me alone.

Lisa and Emmy kissed me, then went downstairs with Nick.

I was already developing stiffness from being in bed so long. After being operated on, I'd slept through the night and into this morning.

Mai leaned over and took my hand. "I'm glad you're all right, Mr. Wilson."

"I'm sorry, Mai. How things turned out."

"In the end, he was honorable man."

"He certainly was, Mai. He certainly was."

After I'd passed out, Dang had rushed back into the trailer and rescued Lisa, who had been remarkably unscathed.

Then Dang had run back inside, knowing he would die in the smoke and the flames.

"Tomorrow would have been our little sister's birthday," Mai said. "I do not think he wanted to face that."

She cried for a long time cradled in my good left arm, my right being in a sling like hers.

"He was not a bad man."

"No, he wasn't, Mai. He was a good man."

"I am sorry for your grief."

"And I'm sorry for yours."

She smiled tearily. "Seasons of the heart, Mr. Wilson. Perhaps the season will change now."

"Perhaps it will," I said, and watched her as she leaned over to kiss me on the forehead.

As she was leaving, I pointed to my arm sling and then to hers. "Twins," I said.

"Yes," she said. "Perhaps we are, Robert."

AUTHOR'S NOTE: For the farm details, I drew on memory and a fine book called *The American Family Farm*, Ancona/Anderson, Harcourt Brace Jovanovich, 1989. And thanks to Dr. Robert Drexler for his help with Vietnamese names.

WENDY HORNSBY

HIGH HEELS IN THE HEADLINER

Three years ago Wendy Hornsby, a professor of history at the University of California, Long Beach, won the MWA Edgar award for her brilliant and startling short story "Nine Sons." Here's another story that's just as startling in an entirely different way. It appeared in Malice Domestic 3, *and in a limited edition chapbook as* High Heels Through the Headliner. *With five well-reviewed novels to her credit and more novels and stories on the way, Wendy Hornsby could be the next big name in American mystery writing.*

"Exquisite prose, charming story. A nice read." Thea tossed the stack of reviews her editor had sent into the file drawer and slammed it shut. The reviews were always the same, exquisite, charming, nice. What she wanted to hear was, "Tough, gritty, compelling, real. Hardest of the hard-boiled."

Thea had honestly tried to break away from writing best-selling fluff. What she wanted more than anything was to be taken seriously as a writer among writers. To do that, she knew she had to achieve tough, gritty, and real. The problem was, her whole damn life was exquisite, charming, nice.

Thea wrote from her own real-life experience, such as it was. One day, when she was about halfway through the first draft of *Lord Rimrock, L.A.P.D.*, a homeless man with one of those grubby cardboard signs—WILL WORK FOR FOOD—jumped out at her from his spot on the median strip up on Pacific Coast Highway. Nearly scared her to death. She used that raw emotion, the fear like a cold dagger in her gut, to write a wonderful scene for Officer Lord Rimrock. But her editor scrapped it because it was out of tone with the rest of the book. Overdrawn, the editor said.

Fucking overdrawn, Thea muttered and walked up to the corner shop for a bottle of wine to take the edge off her ennui.

In her mind, while she waited in line to pay, she rethought her detective. She chucked Lord Rimrock and replaced him with a Harvard man who preferred the action of big-city police work to law school. He was tall and muscular with a streak of gray at the temple. She was working on a name for him when she noticed that the man behind her in line had a detective's shield hanging on his belt.

She gawked. Here in the flesh was a real detective, her first sighting. He was also a major disappointment. His cheap suit needed pressing, he had a little paunch, and he was sweating. Lord Rimrock never sweated. Harvard men don't sweat.

"Excuse me," she said when he caught her staring.

"Don't worry about it." His world-weary scowl changed to a smarmy smile and she realized that he had mistaken her curiosity for a come-on. She went for it.

"What division do you work from?" That much she knew to ask.

"Homicide. Major crimes." *He smiled out of the side of his mouth, not giving up much, not telling her to go away, either. She raised her beautiful eyes to meet his.* No. Beautiful was the wrong tone. Too charming.

"Must be interesting work," Thea said.

"Not very." *She knew he was flattered and played him like a* . . . She'd work out the simile later.

"What you do is interesting to me," she said. "I write mystery novels."

"Oh yeah?" He was intrigued.

"I suppose you're always bothered by writers looking for help with procedural details."

"I never met a writer," he said. "Unless you count asshole reporters."

She laughed, scratching the Harvard man from her thoughts,

dumping the gray streak at the temple. This detective has almost no hair at all.

Thea paid for her bottle of Chardonnay. The detective put his six-pack on the counter, brushing her hand in passing. Before she could decide on an exit line, he said, "Have you ever been on a ride-along? You know, go out with the police and observe."

"I never have," she said. "It would be helpful. How does one arrange a ride-along?"

"I don't know anymore." *The gravel in his voice told her he'd seen too much of life.* "Used to do it all the time. Damned liability shit now, though. Department has really pulled back. Too bad. I think what most taxpayers need is a dose of reality. If they saw what we deal with all day, they'd get off our backs."

Thea did actually raise her beautiful eyes to him. "I think the average person is fascinated by what you do. That's why they read mysteries. That's why I write them. I would love to sit down with you sometime, talk about your experiences."

"Oh yeah?" He responded by pulling in his paunch. "I just finished up at a crime scene in the neighborhood. I'm on my way home. Maybe you'd like to go for a drink."

"Indeed, I would." Thea gripped the neck of the wine bottle, hesitating before she spoke. "Tell you what. If you take me by the crime scene and show me around, we can go to my place after, have some wine and discuss the details."

Bostitch was his name. He paid for his beer and took her out to his city car, awkward in his eagerness to get on with things.

The crime scene was a good one, an old lady stabbed in her bedroom. Bostitch walked Thea right into the apartment past the forensics people who were still sifting for evidence. He explained how the blood-spatter patterns on the walls were like a map of the stabbing, showed her a long arterial spray. *On the carpet where the body was found, she could trace the contours of the woman's head and outstretched arms. Like a snow angel made in blood.*

The victim's family arrived. They had come to look through the house to determine what, if anything, was missing, but all they could do was stand around, numbed by grief. Numbed? Was that it?

Thea walked up to the daughter and said, "How do you feel?"

"Oh, it's awful," the woman sobbed. "Mom was the sweetest woman on earth. Who would do this to her?"

Thea patted the daughter's back, her question still unanswered. How did she feel? Scorched, hollow, riven, shredded, iced in the gut? What?

"Seen enough?" Bostitch asked, taking Thea's arm.

She hadn't seen enough, but she smiled compliantly up into his face. She didn't want him to think she was a ghoul. Or a wimp. To her surprise, she was not bothered by the gore or the smell or any of it. She was the totally objective observer, seeing everything through the eyes of her fictional detective character.

Bostitch showed her the homicide kit he kept in the trunk of his car, mostly forms, rubber gloves, plastic bags. She was more impressed by the name than the contents, but she took a copy of everything for future reference to make him happy.

By the time Bostitch drove her back to her house, Thea's detective had evolved. He was the son of alcoholics, grew up in Wilmington in the shadow of the oil refineries. He would have an ethnic name similar to Bostitch. The sort of man who wouldn't know where Harvard was.

In her exquisite living room, they drank the thirty-dollar Chardonnay. Bostitch told stories, Thea listened. All the time she was smiling or laughing or pretending shock, she was making mental notes. *He sat with his arm draped on the back of the couch, the front of his jacket open, an invitation to come closer. He slugged down the fine old wine like soda pop. When it was gone, he reached for the warm six-pack he had brought in with him and flipped one open.*

By that point, Bostitch was telling war stories about the old days when he was in uniform. The good old days. He had worked morning watch, the shift from midnight to seven. He liked being on patrol in the middle of the night because everything that went down at oh-dark-thirty had an edge. After work he and his partners would hit the early-opening bars. They would get blasted and take women down to a cul-de-sac under the freeway and screw off the booze before they went home. Not beer, he told her. Hard stuff.

"Your girlfriend would meet you?" Thea asked.

"Girlfriend? Shit no. I'd never take a girlfriend down there. There are certain women who just wet themselves for a cop in uniform. We'd go, they'd show."

"I can't imagine," Thea said, wide-eyed, her worldly mien slipping. She couldn't imagine it. She had never had casual sex with anyone. Well, just once actually, with an English professor her freshman year. It had been pretty dull stuff and not worth counting.

"What sort of girls were they?" she asked him.

"All kinds. There was one—she was big, I mean big—we'd go pick her up on the way. She'd say, 'I won't do more than ten of you, and I won't take it in the rear.' She was a secretary or something."

"You made that up," Thea said.

"Swear to God," he said.

"I won't believe you unless you show me," Thea said. She knew where in the book she would use this gem, her raggedy old detective joining the young cowboys in uniform for one last blowout with young women. No. He'd have a young female partner and take her there to shock her. A rite of passage for a rookie female detective.

The problem was, Thea still couldn't visualize it, and she had to get it just right. "Take me to this place."

She knew that Bostitch completely misunderstood that she was only interested for research purposes. Explaining this might not have gotten him up off the couch so fast. They stopped for another bottle on the way—a pint of scotch.

It was just dusk when Bostitch pulled up onto the hard-packed dirt of a vacant lot at the end of the cul-de-sac and parked. A small encampment of homeless people scurried away under the freeway when they recognized the city-issue car.

The cul-de-sac was at the end of a street to nowhere, a despoiled landscape of discarded furniture, cars, and humanity. Even weeds couldn't thrive. She thought humanity wouldn't get past the editor—overdrawn—but that was the idea. She would find the right word later.

Bostitch skewed around in his seat to face her.

"We used to have bonfires here," he said. "Until the city got froggy about it. Screwed up traffic on the freeway. All the smoke."

"Spoiled your fun?" she said.

"It would take more than that." He smiled out the window. "One night, my partner talked me into coming out here before the shift was over. It wasn't even daylight yet. Some babe promised to meet him. I sat inside here and wrote reports while they did it on the hood. God, I'll never forget it. I'm working away in my seat with this naked white ass pumping against the windshield in front of my face—bump, bump, bump. Funny as hell. Bet that messed up freeway traffic."

Thea laughed, not at his story, but at her own prose version of it.

"You ever get naked on the hood of the car?" she asked. She'd had enough booze to ask it easily. For research.

"I like it inside better," he said.

"In the car?" she asked. She moved closer, *leaning near enough to smell the beer on his breath. During his twenty-five years with the police, he must have had half the women in the city. She wanted to know what they had taught him. What he might teach her.*

She lapped her tongue lightly along the inner curve of his lips. Thea said, with a throaty chuckle, "I won't do more than ten of you. And I won't take it in the rear."

When he took her in his arms he wasn't as rough as she had hoped he would be. She set the pace by the eager, almost violent way she tore loose his tie, ripped open his shirt. His five-o'clock shadow sanded a layer of skin off her chin.

They ended up in the backseat, their clothes as wrinkled and shredded as the crime scene report under them. At the moment of her ecstasy the heel of Thea's shoe thrust up through the velour headliner. She looked at the long tear. *The sound of the rip was like cymbals crashing at the peak of a symphony, except the only music was the rhythmic grunting and groaning from the tangle of bodies in the backseat. She jammed her foot through the hole, bracing it against the hard metal roof of the car to get some leverage to meet his thrusting, giving him a more solid base to bang against.*

Bostitch seemed to stop breathing altogether. His face grew a dangerous red and drew up into an agonized sort of grimace that stretched every sinew in his neck. Thea was beginning to worry that she might have killed him when he finally exhaled.

"Oh Jesus," he moaned. "Oh sweet, sweet Jesus."

She untangled her foot from the torn headliner and wrapped her bare legs around him, trapping him inside her until the pulsing ceased. Maybe not, she thought. Pulsing, throbbing were definitely overused.

After the afterglow, what would she feel? Not shame or anything akin to it. She smiled with pride in her prowess. She had whipped his ass and left him gasping. Thea buried her face against his chest and bit his small, hard nipple.

"You're amazing," he said, still breathing hard.

She said nothing. That moment was definitely not the time to explain that it was her female detective, Ricky, or maybe Marty Tenwolde, who was amazing. Thea herself was far too inhibited to have initiated the wild sex that had left their automobile nest in serious need of repair.

When they had pulled their clothes back together, he said, "Now what?"

"Skid Row," she said. "I've always been afraid to go down there, but I need to see it for the book I'm working on."

"Good reason to be afraid." *The cop spoke with a different voice than the lover, a deep, weary growl that* something or other. "You don't really want to go down there."

"I do, though. With you. You're armed. You're the law. We'll be safe."

She batted her big, beautiful eyes again. Flattery and some purring were enough to sway him. He drove her downtown to Skid Row.

Thea had never seen anything as squalid and depraved. Toothless, stoned hookers running down the middle of the street. Men dry heaving in the gutter. *The smell alone made him wish she hadn't come along. He was embarrassed that she saw the old wino defecate openly on the sidewalk. But she only smiled that wry smile that always made the front of his slacks feel tight.*

There was a six- or seven-person brawl in progress on one corner. Thea loved it when Bostitch merely honked his horn to make them scatter like so many cockroaches.

"Seen enough?" he asked.

"Yes. Thank you."

Bostitch held her hand all the way back to her house.

"Will you come in?" she asked him.

"I'll come in. But don't expect much more out of my sorry old carcass. I haven't been that fired up since . . ."

"I thought for a minute you had died," she said. "I didn't know where to send the body."

"Felt like I was on my way to heaven." He slid a business card with a gold detective's shield from behind his visor and handed it to her. "You ever need anything, page me through the office."

So, he had a wife. A lot of men do. Thea hadn't considered a wife in the equation. She liked it—nice characterization. Bostitch called home from the phone on Thea's desk and told the wife he'd be out late on a case. Maybe all night.

"No wonder you fool around," Thea said when he turned his attention back to her. "It's too easy. Does your wife believe you?"

He shrugged. "She doesn't much bother anymore believing or not believing."

"Good line," Thea said. More than anything, she wanted to turn on her computer and get some of what she had learned on disk before she forgot anything. She had a whole new vocabulary: boot the door meant to kick it down, elwopp was life without possibility of parole, fifty-one-fifty was a mental incompetent. So many things to catalog.

"Where's your favorite place to make love?" she asked him.

"In a bed."

That's where they did it next. At least, that's where they began. Bostitch was stunned, pleased, by the performance Thea coaxed from him. He gave Thea a whole chapter.

All the next week she was his shadow. She stood beside him during the autopsy of the stabbing victim, professional and detached because female detective Marty Tenwolde would be. The top of the old lady's skull made a pop like a champagne cork when the coroner sawed it off, but she wasn't even startled. She was as tough and gritty as any man on the force. She was tender, too. After a long day of detecting, she took the old guy home and screwed him until he begged for mercy. Detective Tenwolde felt . . .

That feeling stuff was the hard part. Tenwolde would feel attached to her old married partner. Be intrigued by him. She couldn't help mothering him a bit, but she could by no stretch describe her feelings as maternal. Love was going too far.

Thea watched Bostitch testify in court one day. A murder case, but not a particularly interesting one. It was a garden-variety family shoot-out, drunk husband takes off after estranged wife and her boyfriend. Thea added to her new vocabulary, learning that dead bang meant a case with an almost guaranteed conviction.

Bostitch looked sharper than usual and Thea was impressed by his professionalism. Of course, he winked at her when he thought the jury wasn't looking, checked for her reaction whenever he scored a point against the defense attorney. She always smiled back at him, but she was really more interested in the defendant, a pathetic little man who professed profound grief when he took the stand in his defense. He cried. *Without his wife, he was only a shell occupying space in this universe. His wife had defined his existence, made him complete. Killing her had only been a crude way to kill himself.* If he had any style, he would beg for the death sentence and let the state finish the job for him. Thea wondered what it felt like to lose a loved one in such a violent fashion.

Detective Tenwolde cradled her partner's bleeding head in her lap, knowing he was dying. She pressed her face close to his ear and whispered, "My only regret is I'll never be able to fuck you again, big guy. I love your ragged old ass." Needed something, but it was a good farewell line. Tough, gritty, yet tender.

Out in the corridor after court, the deputy district attorney complimented Bostitch's testimony. Thea, holding his hand, felt proud. No, she thought, she felt lustful. *If he had asked her to, for his reward in getting the kid convicted, she would gladly have blown Bostitch right there on the escalator.* Maybe she did love him. Something to think about.

After court, Thea talked Bostitch into taking her to a Hungarian restaurant he had told her about. He had had a run-in with a lunatic there a year or so earlier. Shot the man dead. Thea wanted to see where.

"There's nothing to see," he said as he pulled into the hillside parking lot. "But the food's okay. Mostly goulash. You know, like stew. We might as well eat."

They walked inside with their arms around each other. The owner knew Bostitch and showed them to a quiet booth in a far-back corner. It was very dark.

"I haven't seen Laszlo's brother for four or five months," the owner said, setting big plates of steaming goulash in front of them. He had a slight accent. "He was plenty mad at you, Bostitch, I tell you. Everybody knows Laszlo was a crazy man, always carrying those guns around. What could you do but shoot him? He shot first. I think maybe his brother is a little nuts, too."

"Show me where he died," Thea said, her lips against Bostitch's juglike ear. He turned his face to her and kissed her.

"Let's eat and get out of here," he said. "We shouldn't have come."

There was a sudden commotion at the door and a big, fiery-eyed man burst in. The first thing Thea noticed was the shotgun he held at his side. The owner rushed up to him, distracted his attention away from Thea's side of the restaurant.

"Shh, Thea." Bostitch, keeping his eyes on the man with the shotgun, pulled his automatic from his belt holster. "That's Laszlo's brother. Someone must have called him, told him I was here. We're going to slip out the back way while they have him distracted."

"But he has a gun. He'll shoot someone."

"No he won't. He's looking for me. Once I'm out of here, they'll calm him down. Let me get out the door, then you follow me. Whatever you do, don't get close to me, and for chrissake stay quiet. Don't attract his attention." Bostitch slipped out of the booth.

She felt *alive. Adrenaline wakened every primitive instinct for survival. Every instinct to protect her man. If the asshole with the gun made so much as a move toward Bostitch, Tenwolde would grind him into dog meat. Bostitch was only one step from safety when Tenwolde saw the gunman turn and spot him.*

Dog meat was good, Thea thought. The rest she was still unclear about. That's when she stood up and screamed, "Don't shoot him. I love him."

Bostitch would have made it out the door, but Thea's outburst caused him to look back. That instant's pause was just long enough for the befuddled gunman to find Bostitch in his sights and fire a double-aught load into his abdomen. Bostitch managed to fire off a round of his own. The gunman was dead before he fell.

Thea ran to Bostitch and caught him as he slid to the floor, leaving a wide red smear on the wall.

His head was heavy in her arms.

"Why?" he sighed. His eyes went dull.

Tenwolde watched the light fade from her partner's eyes, felt his last breath escape from his shattered chest. She couldn't let him see her cry; he'd tease her forever. That's when she lost it. Bostitch had used up his forever.

"It's not fair, big guy," she said, smoothing his sparse hair. She felt a hole open in her chest as big as the gaping wound through his. Without him, she was incomplete. "You promised me one more academy-award fuck. You're not going back on your promise, are you?"

He was gone. Still, she held on to him, her cheek against his, his blood on her lips. "I never told you, Bostitch. I love your raggedy old ass."

CLARK HOWARD

SPLIT DECISIONS

The first of Clark Howard's nine previous appearances in this series was in the 1981 volume of Best Detective Stories of the Year, *with his Edgar-winning tale "Horn Man." Here he returns to the New Orleans scene with a tough tale of a small-time prizefighter and his world.*

Roy Britt was sitting in the doorway drinking milk from a carton when old Rainey arrived to open the poolroom.

"No work on the docks this morning?" Rainey asked. He was an old black man with cotton tufts for hair and a face like shiny saddle leather.

"Ice storm up in the Midwest," Roy said, standing. "Lot of the big rigs are waiting for the interstates to be cleared, I guess. They didn't put on no day help at all this morning."

"Come on in, then," Rainey said, unlocking the front door. "You can sweep the floor and brush down the tables."

"Okay. Thanks, Rainey."

Rainey did not acknowledge the thanks as he led Roy into the stale, musty air of the poolroom and began turning on lights. Roy finished his milk and tossed the carton into a trash can. He was a middleweight, slightly over the one-sixty limit, with scar tissue along the flesh just under each eyebrow. With a twenty-and-fourteen record, he had other scars too, some that showed, some that didn't. He hadn't had a fight in eight months, which was why he showed up at the docks every morning to try for day work unloading trucks.

"Start with the floor, let's get these stinking cigarette butts out of here," Rainey told him, unlocking an old brass National cash register and checking his drawer of starter cash. As Roy got a broom out of the utility closet, Rainey asked, "You in the mood for Wingy or Bix this morning?"

"Wingy sounds good," Roy replied.

Finishing with the register, Rainey turned to an old, beat-up hi-fi record player behind the counter and put on a 78 rpm of "St. James Infirmary" as written by W. C. Handy and rendered by Wingy Manone, a cornet player from right here in New Orleans who had lost an arm as a kid when he was run over by a streetcar named Burgundy. He had gone on to become a world-class Dixieland musician anyway.

As the achy blues of the number wafted in the dingy poolroom, Roy Britt closed his fighter's hands around the broom handle and began to sweep.

It was almost ten when the phone rang and Rainey turned from a racing form he was studying to answer it. "Pool hall."

Roy was at a back table, slowly dragging a soft-bristled brush across the green felt of the playing field. It pleased him to see how he could work the nap into a smooth, even texture completely devoid of fuzz or roughness that might throw a good shot off a thirty-second of an inch. As he worked, he heard the soft *click-click* of pool balls from another table where a hustler named Bumper was practicing with a custom stick. Backing that sound was another Dixieland record Rainey had put on. Everything considered, Roy liked the poolroom. There was something warm and cozy about it, like the locker rooms in some athletic clubs where he'd boxed as a kid. Seedy, shabby, but homey, too.

"Okay, I'll tell him," Roy heard Rainey say into the phone. The old black man hung up and shuffled back to where Roy was and said quietly, "Jack Kono wants to see you." He squinted suspiciously. "You ain't in no trouble, are you?"

"Not that I know of," Roy replied.

"Why Jack Kono sending for you, den?"

"Maybe he's got a fight for me," Roy said. "He's been putting together some matches for Legion Hall."

"If he wanted you for a fight, how come he didn't say so?" Rainey wanted to know.

Roy shrugged. "Who knows? Kono's got Cajun in him. They don't think like you and me." He picked some lint off the brush he was using. "Where does he want to see me?"

"Blue Creole at noon. He eatin' lunch there."

Nodding, Roy resumed brushing down the table. Old Rainey shuffled away, muttering, "Sho' hope you ain't in no trouble with Jack Kono."

When he finished the tables, Roy left the poolroom and walked down Canal Street to Sam's 24-Hour Grill. Sam, a rail-thin man with jailhouse tattoos on both forearms, was behind the counter filling saltshakers. "Hey, Roy," he said, bobbing his chin. "Benny's in the kitchen."

"Hey, Sam. Thanks."

Back in the kitchen, slicing tomatoes, was a young woman who would have had a drop-dead figure if she'd been twelve pounds lighter, but with the extra weight was kind of roundy. She had freckles that started at her hairline and, when she was dressed, disappeared between her breasts. When she was undressed, they didn't disappear at all. Her hair was a reddish color that Crayola hadn't named yet.

"Hi, baby," she said as Roy walked in.

"Verbenia, you don't owe no money to Jack Kono, do you?" Roy asked without preliminary.

"Lord, no." She rolled her eyes toward the ceiling. "You know I don't borrow at street rates. Why?"

"He wants to see me."

"Jack Kono?"

"Yeah. I thought maybe you run short of money or something without telling me."

"Well, think again."

"You haven't been betting the dogs or nothing, have you?"

"Roy." She stopped slicing and put one fist on her hip, the thin-bladed knife still in it. "Read my lips. I said I haven't borrowed from none of Jack Kono's loan sharks. Period." She resumed slicing. "Did you go see about that job? In the ad I cut out?"

Roy looked down at the tomatoes. "I was going to, but then

I got the message that Kono wanted to see me, an' I thought if you didn't owe him nothing, then maybe he had a fight for me or something—"

Benny stopped slicing again, her eyes becoming weary and knowing at the same time. "Roy, I thought we agreed you'd give up fighting and find a regular steady job so maybe you and me and Sugar can get out of the Quarter, move out to that new tract by the airport—"

"I know," he said. "But I got to see what Kono wants first, don't I? What do you want me to do, ignore the man, Verbenia?"

"Roy," she asked impatiently, "why can't you call me 'Benny' like ever'body else does? Why do you insist on calling me 'Verbenia'?"

Roy shrugged. "I like 'Verbenia.' I think it's pretty."

Benny shook her head in exasperation. "Well, I wish you could have knowed my daddy. Y'all would have got on real fine. Only two people in the world ever liked the name 'Verbenia.'" She pointed the slicing knife at the door. "Go on, get out of here; I got to finish getting ready for the lunch crowd."

"Okay. I'm gonna run home and put on my good shirt."

"Look around the neighborhood for Sugar while you're there," Benny said. "I got a feeling she's ditching school again."

"Okay. See you later." Roy kissed her on the cheek and sneaked in a quick feel of one thickset breast.

"Oh, stop it—"

"Bye," he said, going out the back door, "Verbenia."

They had a kitchenette apartment in a horseshoe-shaped building that had once been a high-class brothel in the days when customers arrived by carriage. There was still a long pole in front where the horses had been tethered. The courtyard was cobblestone set by slaves, and in its time had been a vine-covered and magnolia-filled place of gas-lit shadows, full of strange, alluring aromas that conjured up visions of the flesh, and fleeting glimpses of mysterious women behind numbered doors. That courtyard now, as Roy Britt walked briskly across it, was a dead, trash-littered place, uninviting and dreary by day, unlighted and dangerous by night.

When he let himself in, Roy found Sugar sprawled in front of the television, spreading mayonnaise on bread while she watched with riveted eleven-year-old eyes some dreadful horror special effects on the screen before her.

"Hey, Roy," she said with only a glance.

"Hey, Sugar. What you watching?"

"*Vampire Vixens of Venus.* What you doing home?"

"Changing shirts." He was already at the creaky chifforobe the three of them shared, unbuttoning his denim work shirt and replacing it with a wine-colored Western sport shirt with fake pearl buttons that Benny had given him for Christmas.

Now Sugar tore her eyes away from the television. This was not part of the regular drill around here. "What are you putting on your good shirt in daytime for? You only wear that shirt at night when you and Mama go out drinking."

"I'm going to see a man about some work," Roy said. He bobbed his chin at the television. "What's she doing to that poor guy?"

"Sucking his blood out through his thumb. It's called erotic horror. What kind of work?"

"A fight maybe."

"Really?" Her young face showed excitement. It was a face totally different from her mother's, with a café au lait complexion, light blue albino eyes, and tightly wired pitch-black hair that curled in a cluster on her head like a skullcap. "Who are you gonna fight?"

"Don't know. Not even sure that's what it's about."

Sugar sat up, cross-legged, still spreading mayonnaise. "I'd like to see you rematched with Sonny Boy Newton. I still think you whipped him that night. The judges giving him a split decision really sucked."

Roy shrugged. "Could've gone either way, I guess. I thought I whipped him, too. I really hate split decisions, you know? People think, hey, it's the best way to lose, because it was so close, one judge for you, two judges for the other guy. But it's really the worst way to lose, 'cause you know you came so near to winning. Makes you mad at yourself for not trying harder. I really hate split decisions." Roy was looking at himself in a yellow-stained mirror on the chifforobe door. He was twenty-and-fourteen, and six of his fourteen losses had been split decisions. For a while, a few years back, they had even introduced him as "Roy 'Hard Luck Kid' Britt."

"You'll kick his ass next time, Roy," said Sugar.

"You watch your language," he chastised. " 'Member, you're a young lady." Roy knelt next to her and took a bite of the mayonnaised bread. "Stay off the streets until after school's out," he cautioned. From his pocket he pulled several crumpled dollar bills and gave her one. "See you later, Sugar."

"See you later, Roy," she said, and turned back to the television.

One got to the Blue Creole Cafe by entering a dark, damp passageway off Decatur Street and following it to an alley, then crossing the alley and going through a rusty wrought-iron gate and down a few cement stairs to a forbidding-looking metal fire door with a spring-hinged knocker on it. One could only enter by membership or invitation; it was a place where the bankers and other businessmen of respectable New Orleans took their secretaries and mistresses to lunch or dinner before going to bed somewhere for an hour or two.

When the door was opened for Roy Britt, he said to a massive black doorman who looked like Sonny Liston reincarnated, "I'm here to see Jack Kono."

"He ax you to come?"

"Yeah."

At a nod of the black man's head, Roy entered and was left waiting in an alcove furnished with several expensively upholstered love seats arranged under ornately framed prints of partly nude Tahitian women originally painted by Gauguin. A nervous young blond woman sat on one of the love seats, her knees pressed closely together, worrying the strap of her cheap purse.

She wouldn't be carrying a cheap purse much longer, Roy thought. He leaned on the wall as far away from her as he could, so as not to make her any more nervous about her rendezvous than she already was.

The black doorman returned after a moment and nodded for

Roy to follow him. He led Roy through a dining room of private, draped booths and secluded tables concealed by large potted plants and folding screens. Roy noticed that the understated music backgrounding the room was the same kind Rainey played in the poolroom: the softer, slower Dixieland. At a back booth, with the drapes open, Jack Kono sat eating crab cakes and drinking Pouilly-Fuissé.

"Sit down, Roy," he said, bobbing his chin at the opposite bench. "You want to eat?"

"I ate early, thanks," Roy lied. For some reason his stomach had suddenly knotted up. Jack Kono frequently had that effect on people. He had reptilian eyes in an otherwise softly Cajun face, very white, hairless hands, and a reputation for easy murder. There were some who referred to him as the AntiChrist of the French Quarter. No one, it was said, had ever successfully lied to him.

"I need you to do something for me, Roy," said Kono. "You know my baby sister Angela?"

"Seen her around," said Roy. "Don't really know her."

"Well, I'm having a problem with her. She turned eighteen a few months ago and she's getting unruly on me. Quit the private school I had her going to, moved out of our mother's house, got a job as a shoe clerk." Kono stared at a bite of crab cake, sighed quietly, and shook his head. "I've tried talking some sense into her head but she won't listen. Says she's a grown woman—" he grunted softly, "a grown woman at *eighteen*, can you imagine?"

Roy shrugged. What the hell did this have to do with a fight for him, he wondered.

"I recently," Kono continued as he chewed, "found out she's running around with a guy named Denny Boyle: He's a shanty Irish auto mechanic at a place called Sports Car Heaven across the river in Gretna. You happen to know the guy?"

Roy shook his head. "No."

"I didn't think it was likely you did. I had him checked out and as far as I can tell, nobody really knows the guy. He came down from Birmingham a year or so ago and went to work tuning sports car engines. Customizes cars on the side. Apparently wants to save some money and open his own custom shop some day. A real yokel, right?"

Roy shrugged and looked away. He wished now that he'd gone to answer the ad Verbenia had cut out for him instead of going to the poolroom and getting Kono's message.

"This Denny Boyle is not the kind of guy I want my sister running around with, know what I mean?" Kono said. "He's strictly a dirt-under-the-fingernails type, no class, no future. I want him to stop seeing Angela."

Roy nodded resignedly. No fight at the Legion Hall, he guessed. "You want me to have a talk with him, is that it?"

Kono smiled a barren smile. "If I thought talking would solve the problem, I'd do it myself, Roy."

"So what do you want?"

"I want the guy worked over. But not by hooligans. I don't want it to look to Angela like it was arranged. I want the guy to get in a street fight with somebody who looks like just another guy. But somebody who'll bust him up good and proper for me. Somebody like you, Roy."

Roy shook his head. "That's not my line. I'm not a street fighter; I'm a pro. I mean, I'm *licensed*. I could get sent up for using my fists outside the ring."

"You won't get sent up, I guarantee it. You probably won't even get caught. But if you do, I'll put the fix in. I can buy any judge in Gretna."

"I don't know," Roy said, still shaking his head.

"I'd consider this a personal favor," Jack Kono told him quietly, pointedly. "And there's five hundred in it for you."

Roy stared off at a section of embossed red wall covering. "I was hoping you'd called me over to offer me a fight on one of your cards," he said with soft honesty, keeping his eyes averted.

Kono frowned. "A fight? I didn't even know you were still active. I thought you retired after you lost two or three split decisions in a row. Somebody told me they saw you sweeping out old Rainey's poolroom. That's why I called you there."

"Yeah, well, I do that and I work the truck docks, too, but on'y because I haven't been able to get no fights."

"So what do you want? You want to box again? Fine. Do this favor for me and I'll see that you get back in the ring."

Roy drummed his thick fingertips soundlessly on the brocaded place mat in front of him. Two or three good wins could put him into a main event, he thought. And a good main event might get him a TV fight on ESPN. And if he could beat a ranked contender on TV, with that kind of exposure, who knows, it might catapult him into a title shot. The middleweight division was currently wide open; anything could happen.

"Do you think you could get me a rematch with Sonny Boy Newton?" Roy asked. "I lost a split decision to him in eight last April, but I thought I beat him."

"Newton's boxing the hotel circuit now," Kono said. "You willing to go up to Atlantic City?"

"Sure," Roy replied eagerly.

"Can you make one-sixty?"

"Easy. A week's training."

"Okay, you take care of this little matter for me and I'll match you with Sonny Boy within ninety days. And I'll still give you the five bills. Deal?"

Roy bit his lip briefly, then nodded determinedly. "Deal."

That evening, Roy, Benny, and Sugar walked down to one of the Vieux Carre waterfront cafes for catfish. As soon as they were seated at one of the picnic-bench tables with their basket of breaded fillets and pitcher of iced tea, Benny started in on both of them.

"How was school today, Sugar?"

"Just thrilling, Mama. A real adventure."

"Don't you smart-mouth me, young lady. What did you learn?"

"That the possibility of life exists on the planet Venus."

Benny raised her eyebrows. "Well, that's interesting. I didn't know that." Her eyes shifted to Roy. "Tell me again what Kono said today."

"He said he'd get me a rematch with Sonny Boy Newton," Roy told her. "But first he wants me to have one warm-up bout across the river, a card he's putting on in Gretna."

"I didn't know they had fight cards in Gretna," Benny said.

"This is the first one. They're trying it out. Anyways, I get five hundred for a tune-up six-rounder, and if I win Kono'll make the rematch with Sonny Boy."

"You'll kick his ass this time, Roy," said Sugar.

Benny's eyebrows immediately pinched together and she fixed her daughter in a laser stare. "I cannot believe what I just heard," she said dramatically. "May I inquire where you are learning such talk?"

"School, I guess, Mama," Sugar replied innocently. "You ought to hear how some of those kids talk! They even use the 'F' word."

"That is disgusting. Roy, we have *got* to get out of this Quarter and into that tract of homes out by the airport. I refuse to allow Sugar to go to school down here next year."

"I like the Quarter, Mama," Sugar protested, realizing too late what she might have done.

"I don't care what you like. Be quiet. How much did you say you were getting for the tune-up in Gretna?" she asked Roy.

"Five hundred."

"We can get into a nice little two-bedroom, two-bath, twelve-hundred-square-foot patio home for three thousand down. Only thing is, you'd have to have a steady job. No bank is going to lend money to an unranked fighter who don't even have a manager. Do you think you could get Rainey to say you run the poolroom for him? If you could get him to say you'd worked there five years, and I could get Sam to say I'd worked at the cafe five years, why, I bet we could finance a patio home. What do you think?"

"I bet we could," Roy agreed. He tried never to disagree with Verbenia at mealtime. It made for serious indigestion. Breaking open a fillet with his fingers, he squeezed lemon juice all over it to absorb the catfish taste without neutralizing the catfish flavor, and laced it with salt and pepper.

"I could get a job delivering papers," Sugar suggested.

"You most certainly cannot," Benny squelched her. "You are to come directly home from school every day and stay inside, young lady. I do not want you on the streets of the Quarter. Roy, when is the Gretna fight?"

"Uh, I'm not sure yet. Next week sometime."

"All right. You'll probably be training this weekend, so Sugar and I will take the airport bus out to that new tract and pick us out a place." She patted her daughter's hand. "Won't that be fun, Sugar?"

"Yeah, Mama. A real thrill."

On Saturday afternoon, Roy took the Jackson Street ferry across the Mississippi River to Gretna and hoofed it along used-car row on Route 18 until he spotted Sports Car Heaven squeezed between a recreational vehicle lot and a motorcycle repair shop. A couple of sailors were browsing among the sports cars, bird-dogged by a salesman with a belly that hung over double-knit slacks. There was a lone mechanic in the garage, working on a teal-blue Jaguar. Roy strolled in.

"Help you?" the mechanic asked. He was wearing a grease-stained jumpsuit with "Denny" over the chest pocket.

"You got a phone book I can look at?" Roy asked.

"Sure. Right in the office there." He pointed. "Hanging by the pay phone."

"Thanks."

Roy stepped through an open door into a small, windowed office where the pay phone was on the wall between a water cooler and a Dr Pepper machine. Pretending to look up a number, Roy peered over the top of the telephone directory and studied Denny Boyle. He was a nice-looking young man, twenty-five maybe, the clean-cut lines of his face interrupted only by a nose that was slightly crooked. The sleeves of his jumpsuit had been cut off and Roy could see that the mechanic had good biceps but no real muscle tone; he would be strong but slow. The arms were slightly long, so he'd probably have a couple of inches advantage over Roy in reach. Roy guessed his weight at one-seventy.

Overall, no problem, Roy decided. He could move in quick on the guy, get inside the reach, hook a few quick lefts to the body to bring the guy's hands down, then start busting his face open with straight rights and lefts. Ten, twelve shots ought to do it. The guy would feel like his head had been dragged behind a train.

Putting the directory down, Roy stepped back into the garage. "Thanks a lot," he said.

"No problem," Denny Boyle replied. "Need directions or anything?"

"No, I just needed the number." Roy walked over to him. "What's a car like that cost?" he asked, bobbing his chin at the Jag.

"This model new runs about fifty-five and change," Boyle replied. He stopped working and wiped his hands on a chamois. "I wouldn't buy one, I was you."

"No? Why not?"

"Repair record stinks. Costs a fortune to maintain. You want your money's worth, get a Corvette. Can't go wrong with a 'Vette."

Roy nodded. "You know a lot about cars, huh?"

Denny Boyle smiled. "Cars and nothing else. I been tinkering with engines since I was ten. What do you drive?"

"Nothing right now. But I been thinking about buying one—"

As Roy spoke, a BMW sports car pulled up outside and a young woman got out and came into the garage. "Hi, honey," Denny Boyle said.

"Hey," she greeted him, then went over to his workbench to wait for him to finish talking.

Roy got a good look at her as she passed. She had the same soft Cajun features that Jack Kono had, without the reptilian eyes; hers, instead, were wide, lugubrious, almost frightened-looking. Her lips, too, were different: prominent, healthy, even suggestive. There was no question that it was Angela Kono, Jack Kono's "baby" sister—though from the way her body moved when she walked, there was nothing babyish or childlike about her; physically, Roy thought, she looked every bit the woman that Verbenia was. Roy had seen her around the quarter, at Tradition Hall and a couple of the smaller Dixieland clubs, but this was the first time he had been this close to her. Now he knew why her brother was concerned. With that body and those lips, she was a magnet for sex.

Roy decided to move on. "Listen, I got a friend needs some work on an old Gran' Prix he's got. You fix those?"

"I fix anything with an engine," Denny said. "And I'll work days, nights, Sundays, anytime." He grinned again. "I'm saving so me and my girl there can get married and have our own custom shop."

"That's great," Roy replied. "What time you close during the week?"

"I try to get out by six, but I can stay if there's work. Send your friend around anytime."

"I'll do that," Roy said.

"Nice talking with you," Denny Boyle said as Roy walked away.

That night they had supper at a chili-dog joint because on Saturdays it was Sugar's turn to pick where they ate. Benny complained about it every week.

"I swear, this chili is nothing but grease with a few beans and a little ground beef to give it color. Can't you pick some place different for a change?"

"I like this place," Sugar replied steadfastly. Sugar never relinquished a perk once she got it.

"The chili's not bad if you dip your dog in it," Roy said. Which, of course, caused Benny to turn on him.

"Should you be eating that kind of stuff with a fight coming up? Shouldn't you be eating a salad or something healthy?"

"They don't serve healthy food here," Sugar pointed out. "Just good food."

"This won't hurt me," Roy said, shrugging.

"Just when is the fight anyway?"

"Monday night."

"Are you getting tickets for me and Sugar?"

Roy had been expecting her to ask and was prepared. He shook his head. "It's just club fights, Verbenia. They're holding 'em in a warehouse. It's no place for a woman and a little girl."

"I'm not a little girl, for God's sake," Sugar said crossly.

"Watch that mouth, young lady," Benny warned. "Roy, we have *got* to get her out of the Quarter and into a decent neighborhood. I wish to God I could find her daddy and get the eight years' worth of child support he's behind with." Benny leaned forward to impress urgency. "Listen, Sugar and me went out to that new tract by the airport today; it's called Lazy Acres, isn't that cute? The salesman out there was a really sweet guy named Lance, wore one of those spiffy gold pinkie rings. Anyway, he said if we wanted one of the units—that's what salesmen call the houses: units—anyway, Lance said we should get a down payment in as soon as possible 'cause the units are selling like hotcakes on a frosty morning. So, what I thought was, Sam at the cafe said he'd advance me five hundred on my wages and take twenty-five a week out until it was paid. Then I thought I'd ask my sister Dewanda to ask her husband, Melvin, if they could see their way clear to letting me have a loan of two thousand. Melvin's doing real good now; he's on the road selling manure to plant nurseries and he's pulling in twelve hundred a week commission, so I know they can afford it—"

"I'm not borrowing no money from your relatives," Roy said firmly.

"Well, I know *that*," Benny retorted. "First off, they wouldn't loan *you* no money; it'll be me that's borrowing. Reason I think they'll do it is to help Sugar. They've always felt sorry for her—"

Sugar stuck a finger in her mouth. "You're going to make me barf, Mama—"

"Sugar, I'm going to slap you silly if you don't behave," Benny threatened.

"*They* feel sorry for *me*? Roy, you ought to see *their* kids. Two grossly fat girls and a boy who's a retarded nerd—"

"Melvin, Junior, is *not* retarded, Sugar!" her mother stormed. "He's just a little slow—"

"Not. He's *stopped*."

"That is *e-nough*, Sugar!"

The girl fell silent. Benny turned her attack back to Roy.

"All I want to know is if I can count on that five hundred from you on Monday."

"Yeah," Roy assured her. "Yeah, you can, Verbenia."

* * *

On Sunday morning, Roy went around to Jack Kono's private social club, a storefront on Royal Street with the windows painted black and a MEMBERS ONLY sign on the door. As he was walking up to knock, the door flew back and Angela Kono came striding out with an angry look on her face, muttering what sounded to Roy like obscenities. She glanced at him in passing, then paused, frowning, to stare at him. Roy, feeling himself turn red, knowing she probably recognized him from the previous day, turned away from her, caught the door before it closed, and hurried inside.

Kono was at the bar, watching a replay of the previous night's NBA game, looking very irritated. Roy took a stool beside him.

"Well?" Kono inquired at once.

"Well, I seen the guy," Roy told him. "At Sports Car Heaven, over to Gretna, just like you said."

"And?"

"And I don't see no problem," Roy shrugged. "He's bigger'n me and looks to be pretty strong, but I'll be able to handle him."

"I don't want him just 'handled,'" Kono said grimly. "I want the son of a bitch wrecked. My baby sister Angela was just in here to tell me her and that guy Boyle are talking marriage. She wants to bring him around to meet our mother!"

"You know, he don't seem like all that bad a guy," Roy said tentatively. Kono gave him a withering look.

"Don't try to second-guess me on this, you hear? This is a family matter. My sister is *not* going to marry some Gretna grease monkey who don't even have Cajun blood. Am I clear on that?"

"You're clear," Roy replied.

"Fine. When are you going to do it?"

"Tomorrow night, I guess," Roy decided. "Might as well get it over with. He quits work at six. I'll catch him on the car lot as he's leaving and pick a fight with him. All's I need is about sixty seconds max to do it."

"I want his jaw broken. And his nose," Kono specified. "Work on his kidneys, too, so's he'll pass blood for a while. That'll give him something to think about."

"Okay," Roy said, looking away. He suddenly felt like a man eating tainted food. An urge stirred in him to get up and walk away from the deal. But he had promised the five hundred to Verbenia.

"So you'll do it around six tomorrow?" Kono confirmed. Roy Britt nodded.

"Yeah. Six tomorrow."

"You'll be coming back on the seven o'clock ferry, then?"

"Yeah, probably."

Kono patted Roy's arm and smiled a scant smile. "Good deal."

When Roy left Kono's club, he had walked only a few doors down Royal when Angela Kono suddenly stepped from somewhere onto the sidewalk and confronted him.

"Who the hell are you?" she demanded. "Do you work for my brother?"

"I don't know what you're talking about," Roy said. He tried to move around her but she blocked his way. Her wide, dark Cajun eyes, looking like ripe plums, were seething with anger.

"You know what I'm talking about," she accused. "I saw you in Gretna yesterday, talking with Denny Boyle. What the hell's going on?"

"Nothing. Nothing's going on. You got the wrong guy, miss—"

"My brother is Jack Kono. You just came out of his club. And yesterday you were in Gretna talking to my boyfriend, Denny Boyle. Did my brother hire you to do something?"

Roy felt like a stagecoach surrounded by Apaches. Angela Kono was right in his face. Two people walking by gave them curious looks. Down at the corner he could see a police cruiser turning into Royal.

"Look, miss, I'm a fighter, see? I went to talk to Jack Kono about getting a fight, that's all. And yesterday I only stopped in at that garage to look up somebody in the phone book. Then the mechanic and me got to talking after. If one of 'em's your brother and the other's your boyfriend, that's got nothing to do with me. I'm just doing my own thing, see? Now, why don't you let me go about my business?"

"You'd better not try anything with Denny Boyle," Angela Kono warned. "If my brother hired you to hurt him, you'd better think twice about doing it, because you won't get away with it. I'll go to the police. I'll tell them about both of you. You'll go to jail."

Roy shook his head wryly. "Miss, do you have any idea how many things the police have been told about your brother? Has he ever gone to jail for any of them?"

Angela Kono parted her sensuous lips to speak, to hurl a retort back at this thug with the lumpy scar tissue over each eye, but her words never reached sound. Because there was no retort, and they both knew it. In the Quarter, Jack Kono was above the law.

Turning her face away, Angela swallowed tightly. Roy looked awkwardly down at his shoes. He sucked in on his upper lip for a moment. Why, he wondered, didn't this girl understand that her brother was just trying to look out for her, trying to protect her? Jack Kono was her older brother; not only that, but with their father dead, he was the head of the Kono family. She should listen to him.

"Look," he said after a moment, "I'm sorry you got troubles, you know? But I got some of my own. I gotta go now."

He was glad she did not try to stop him when he stepped around her and hurried along the street.

Roy slept until nine-thirty on Monday morning. He might have slept longer but the bedroom window shade had a crack in it that allowed the morning sun to come in. It woke him and then he could not get back to sleep because he started thinking about what he had to do that night.

Getting up, he pulled on a pair of jeans and a sweatshirt, and went barefoot into the living room. Sugar, in her school clothes, was stretched out on the floor in front of the TV. Her schoolbooks were on the floor by the door.

"Better hurry, Sugar, or you'll be late for school," Roy cracked as he went over to the Pullman kitchen.

"Very funny," the girl said crossly. "I already *went* to school. Mama insisted on walking me there. I had to hide in the girls' rest room for fifteen minutes and then walk all the way back."

"You must really be wore out," he said wryly, opening the half-size kitchenette refrigerator and surveying its contents. "You eat yet?"

"Uh-huh."

"What'd you eat?"

"Mama made me eat cornflakes before we left. When I got back, I had a fried-tomato-and-peanut-butter sandwich and a Cherry 7UP."

Roy shook his head. "You must have a cast-iron stomach, Sugar." He got out butter and peach preserves, spread some of each on two slices of sourdough bread, and poured a glass of milk. Going back into the living room, he sat on the couch to eat. "What are you watching?" he asked, frowning at the gory scene on the screen.

"*Dr. Jekyll Meets Jack the Ripper*," Sugar said.

"Which one is he?" Roy asked, bobbing his chin at the character on the screen.

"That's the Ripper."

"What's he doing?"

"Eviscerating a victim."

"Doing what?"

"Disemboweling her."

"What's that mean?"

"Cutting her open and taking out her insides, Roy," the girl said patiently.

"Isn't there anything else you can watch?" he asked, grimacing.

"Sure," Sugar replied cheerfully. "I can watch the news: war in Bosnia, starving kids in Somalia, riots in South Africa, drive-by killings in Los Angeles, gang rapes in New York—"

"Never mind," said Roy. "Watch what you're watching. At least it's not real."

When he finished eating, Roy went back to the little alcove kitchen and got out detergent to do a sink full of dirty dishes that had been left. Benny never did dishes. "I'm around dirty dishes all day; I can't cope with them at night," was her excuse. Now and then Sugar did them, but mostly it was left to him. Mother and daughter both knew he'd do them because he hated the sight of them.

While he was cleaning up, Sugar came over and lunged against the fridge. "You think you'll like living in Lazy Acres?"

Roy shrugged. "Don't know. Haven't never lived outside the city before."

"I won't like it," Sugar declared. "I'll hate it. There's no place to hang out. No bowling alley, no donut shop, no bus station—"

"Maybe you ought to try school again," he suggested.

"No, school's out for me," the girl replied analytically. "The teachers are boring, the classes are dull, the other girls are unbelievably silly, and the boys aren't interested in anything except looking up dresses. You should see how they purposely drop things on the floor so they can bend down to get them, then turn and look up the nearest dress while they're doing it. They're so juvenile."

"That's 'cause they're young," Roy said.

"Really? Golly, Roy, I never thought of that."

He looked steadily at her. "Your mother's right. We need to get you out of the Quarter."

"Well, if we move to Lazy Acres, I've made up my mind to run away. I'm going to Spain and become a flamenco dancer." She found a towel and began drying the dishes. "Who you fighting tonight?"

"Some dude, I don't know his name," Roy lied.

"I hope he's got a weak jab. I hate it when that right eye of yours gets opened up."

"It's no worse than one of those movies you're always watching."

"It is worse, Roy. It's you." She put an arm around his waist and gave him a quick hug. "I love you, Roy. I wish you were my daddy."

"Good thing I'm not. I let you get away with too much." He rinsed the sink and dried his hands on the dishtowel Sugar was using. "Promise me you won't run away without talking it over with me first."

Sugar shook her head. "Running away has to be spontaneous or it won't be any fun."

"What does 'spontaneous' mean?"

"Impulsive. You know, spur of the moment."

"Promise me you won't do that. It would hurt your mother too much."

"I can't promise that."

"Promise," he insisted.

"Roy-eee! No—"

"Promise!" His voice turned harsh and he gripped her arm.

"All right, Roy, let go!" She decided to concede. Somewhere in the depths of her young mind she remembered her mother saying to another waitress, *"Roy's kind and gentle most of the time, but let me tell you, there's a temper underneath it all. Roy Britt is a guy you never want to push too far."*

"Promise?" he asked for verification.

"Yes, Roy, I promise. I do."

"Okay."

He let go of her arm.

By five-thirty that evening, Roy was on the recreational vehicle lot next to Sports Car Heaven, browsing around as if he were a customer. A salesman had approached him when he first got there, but Roy had put him off by saying he was just waiting for his wife to pick him up. From where he stood he could see Denny Boyle finishing up some kind of work on the engine of a black Datsun 280Z. A light was on in the sports car lot sales office but there was no salesman to be seen. Roy walked around among the recreational vehicles, looking in driver-side windows, kicking tires, always keeping the open repair-garage door clearly in sight.

It was already getting dark, the thin winter air cooling rapidly after the sun went down, a chilling wetness coming in from the waters of the muddy Mississippi and ankle-level fog crawling along the ground from the Gulf. The kind of spooky night that made people seek out jambalaya and gumbo and Dixieland music. Roy realized without knowing why that he really liked New Orleans, liked the French Quarter, more than anyplace he'd ever lived. He'd bummed around the Gulf Coast a lot before settling there—places like Mobile, Biloxi, Panama City, Port Arthur—but no place had ever suited him before. Maybe it had something to do with Verbenia and Sugar being there, he didn't know. All he was sure about was that it now felt like home. Maybe, he thought, if he and Sugar did some real fast talking, they could persuade Verbenia to consider buying an older house there in the Quarter that he could fix up a room at a time—

"So you were lying." A cutting female voice split the silence of his thoughts like a crack of lightning, startling the hell out of him. Roy whirled around to see Angela Kono standing six feet away, eyes riveted on him. "You're here to do something to Denny, aren't you? Did my brother hire you to kill him?"

Roy's mouth dropped open. "*Kill* him? I wouldn't kill nobody—"

"What are you going to do then, cripple him? Break his fingers so badly that he won't be able to work on engines anymore?"

"Hey, I don't do stuff like that!" Roy declared. "What do you think I am, anyway?"

"I don't know," the fierce-looking young woman said. "Why don't you tell me. What are you?"

"I'm a fighter. I told you that yesterday—"

"Oh, yes, I remember. A fighter. What kind of a fighter?"

"A fighter," he repeated impatiently. "In the ring."

"Oh, I see. You mean you fight other fighters?"

"Yeah—"

"Except tonight you're going to fight an automobile mechanic, right?"

Roy felt his face become hot and knew it had turned red. It was almost as if he was a kid and this young woman, who was little more than a kid herself, had caught him doing something nasty and was shaming him for it.

"Listen, this whole thing is your fault, you know, not mine!" he accused. "If you'd listen to your older brother like you should, neither one of us would be in this fix!"

Angela Kono nodded knowingly. "Oh. Listen to my big brother, huh? Is that what I should be doing?"

"Yeah, it is!"

She got right in his face. "Do you know what incest is?" she asked in the coldest voice he had ever heard.

Frowning, Roy turned his face away, not answering. He hated admitting to anyone but Sugar when he didn't know what a word meant.

"You don't, do you?" Angela challenged. "You don't know what incest means." She stepped to the side where he had turned his face, and locked onto his eyes again. "Let me tell you what it means. Incest is where a parent has sex with one of their children. Or," she paused a beat for dreadful effect, "when a brother has sex with his sister."

Roy's face went blank, as if his mind had reset at zero and he was being given his very first piece of knowledge. Then, as he stared at the pretty young woman with the sad eyes, his memory kicked back in and began to help him think. Over the years he had heard dirty rumors now and again of a thing like that but he wasn't sure he had ever really believed them. To him, it just didn't seem possible that a girl's father, or her brother—

Well, it just didn't seem possible, that's all. Why, he wasn't even Sugar's real father, wasn't actually related to her at all; yet she *seemed* like his child, and he knew she thought of him as her daddy. But the mere idea of him doing anything like that to Sugar—

It was disgusting. Sickening. Enough to make him puke.

"You find it hard to believe, don't you?" Angela asked, and now her voice lost its sharpness, its cruel edge, and took on a tone that matched her cheerless eyes. "Well, it's true," she assured him forlornly. "Since I was twelve years old. There were only the three of us left in that big old family house: my mother, who was quite old—I was a late-life baby; Jack, who was nineteen when I was born; and me. Everybody else had died or moved away, and that big old house had all those rooms in it—so many rooms. Sometimes I tried to hide from Jack, but he always found me. He said what we were doing was all right, as long as nobody else knew, as long as I didn't tell anybody. So it went on until I was thirteen, and fourteen, and fifteen, and—"

Her words broke off and she looked down at the asphalt of

the recreational vehicle lot that showed between the wisps of fog, and shook her head in dismal helplessness. Roy felt awful, worse even than at the end of his toughest ten-round split-decision loss. If it hadn't been for Verbenia and Sugar, he'd have wished he was a million miles away.

"I'm sorry, miss," was all he could say. Then he found the words to add, "I didn't know nothing about that. I just thought your brother was, you know, looking out for you."

"I understand," she told him, looking up now, forcing a hint of a smile. "That's what everyone thinks: my mother, our neighbors, the nuns at school. You're not to blame for trying to help him."

"Well, I ain't helping him now," Roy said resolutely. He touched her arm, tentatively, briefly, then quickly pulled away. "You and your boyfriend don't have to worry none about me. I won't lay a hand on him."

"Thanks," she said. "We're getting out of here tonight. Denny's got a friend in Oklahoma City that's going to give him a working partnership in a shop there. It's our chance."

"A chance is all most people need," Roy told her quietly. "Good luck."

On impulse, Angela Kono leaned forward and kissed him on the cheek. Then she hurried off the lot toward the garage next door, toward her future.

Jack Kono was waiting on the Jackson Street ferry dock when the seven o'clock boat from Gretna moored and Roy came off with the other passengers. Kono had a slick young hood named Shimmy with him, a younger guy who modeled himself after Kono in dress and attitude, and who was known to carry a switchblade stiletto to protect his boss with. The two of them fell in with Roy as he started up the dock.

"Well?" Kono asked.

Roy didn't answer or look at him.

"How'd it go?" Kono demanded.

Roy still didn't answer or stop walking.

"Wait a goddamn minute, you!" Kono ordered, stepping in front of Roy to stop him. Seizing Roy's right wrist, Kono pulled up his hand and looked at it. It was clear that Roy's knuckles had not hit anything that night. Kono's face darkened. "What happened?"

"I changed my mind." Roy stepped around him and started walking. Kono quickly got in front of him and blocked his way again.

"Something happened," he accused. "What was it?"

"Nothing you don't already know about, Kono. Now leave me alone."

Again Roy stepped around him and continued on his way. The single, solitary thing he wanted in life at that moment was just to get home to Verbenia and Sugar.

But Jack Kono wasn't going to let him have that. He stepped in front of Roy again.

Roy's eyes turned mean. "I ain't going to move around you again, Kono," he said evenly.

"You won't have to, pug," said Kono, his reptilian eyes narrowing to slits. "Take him, Shimmy," he ordered.

Shimmy's right hand started out of the coat pocket where he carried his blade. But he wasn't even close to being quick enough. Roy pivoted to his left and drove an arcing, plowing right fist low and deep to Shimmy's groin. Shimmy felt his insides shrivel and turn hot as he dropped to his knees, lower body momentarily paralyzed. Then Roy turned back to Jack Kono.

"You low-life scum son of a bitch," he said in quiet, angry words.

Roy's experienced fists went to work in machinelike fashion, went to work on Jack Kono as they were supposed to have worked on Denny Boyle. A left jab set up a straight right that broke Kono's nose and sent a fire-hydrant rush of blood down the front of his silk suit. A right to the liver made Kono bend to that side and half turn, leaving the soft spot over one kidney unprotected. Roy drilled four hard lefts to that spot, all illegal blows had they been in the ring. *See how you like passing blood, you bastard*, he thought. As Kono stumbled backward, Roy stayed right on him. The last punch he threw was a perfectly timed, perfectly placed right hook that generated a barely audible, brittle snapping sound that told Roy he had broken Jack Kono's left jawbone just under the ear.

Miraculously, Kono was still on his feet, staggering around the dock like a drunk man, holding his kidney area with one hand, trying to catch the blood from his broken nose with the other. Shimmy, groaning, was still on his knees.

Roy hurried past several people who had stopped to watch.

"Guys tried to rob me," he said in passing.

He walked away fast until he reached the mouth of an alley, then turned in and ran like hell.

Benny's expression was as barren as a winter desert.

"You mean you've been lying to me, Roy? Everything you told me about the fight in Gretna was a lie?"

"He didn't lie about the money, Mama," Sugar interjected as a plea.

"Sugar," her mother said with rare harshness, "you stay out of this!" Then back to Roy, "It was all a lie?"

"Yeah," Roy admitted. "All except the five hundred, like Sugar said—"

"And you didn't even get that!" Benny fumed.

Roy unwrapped a towel that had four ice cubes in it from around his right hand. His index knuckle was swollen to about twice its normal size and was beginning to take on a greenish-purple color. Roy had known he hurt it from the way his fist impacted on Jack Kono's jawbone; but he also knew the knuckle was not broken, because he could still bend and unbend his finger.

"Want a dry towel, Roy?" Sugar asked, her young face looking older with concern.

"No, Sugar, I gotta get going," he said, putting the icy wet towel in the sink.

"Going? Going where?" Benny demanded.

"I don't know where," Roy told her. "Anywhere. Just out of New Orleans."

"Oh, don't be silly, for God's sake," Benny said. "I'm not *that* mad at you."

Roy and Sugar looked at her incredulously. In some ways she was more a child than Sugar was.

"Verbenia, I'm not leaving 'cause you're mad at me," Roy said patiently. "Right about now, Jack Kono's in some hospital getting his jaw wired. He's gonna have some gorillas after me before midnight. People die for what I done, honey. I gotta get out of town."

He went to the chifforobe in the bedroom and got out the few extra clothes he had and put them in his zippered gym bag. Sugar quickly got his shaving gear from the bathroom, put it in a plastic Baggie, and brought it to him. "I want to go with you, Roy," the girl whispered, her eyes tearing up.

"Don't start," he whispered back. "You got to stay with your mother."

Sugar pouted for a moment, but quickly gave it up and asked, "Don't you have any idea where you're going to?"

Roy glanced at an alarm clock on Benny's nightstand. It was almost nine. "There used to be a bus for Houston left about ten-thirty. I'll prob'ly try for that if it's still running." He put the hand that wasn't swelling under her chin. "Listen, wherever I end up, I'll send a postcard to old Rainey at the poolroom. I'll sign it 'Wingy,' like in 'Wingy Manone' — "

She knew at once. "The one-armed cornet player."

"Yeah. Then you'll know I got away all right. Okay?"

"Okay. But won't we never see each other again, Roy?" The tears left her eyes now and streaked her pale cheeks.

"Course we will," he assured her, knowing it was probably a lie. "I'll figure out something. You just take care of your mother, okay? Promise?"

Sugar promised, but her child's face reflected that it was the most miserable thing she had ever had to do. Standing in the bedroom door, watching him go out to speak to her mother, Sugar's chest trembled with sobs she would not permit herself to release.

"Verbenia, I'm sure sorry about all this," Roy said to Benny, who was sitting at their little breakfast table drumming her nails on its oilcloth covering.

"I know, Roy. I am too," Benny replied without looking up.

"Listen, I hate to ask." He lowered his voice, hoping Sugar would not hear. "But I on'y got a few bucks, and, well—"

"Sure, Roy." Benny rose and got her purse. "I borrowed the five hundred from Sam today. I'll give you a hundred of it, and that's all—"

"That's plenty," Roy said. He noticed Sugar hurry back into the bedroom and kneel at her chifforobe drawer.

"Fall for a guy and end up giving him money to skip town," Benny muttered as she took the money from her purse. "Story of my life. At least this one's not leaving me pregnant."

She gave him the hundred. He started to kiss her good-bye, but she waved him away. "Just go, Roy."

"Okay." He turned away, hurt.

Before he got to the door, Sugar came running out to him and pressed some tightly folded currency into his hand. "Twelve dollars," she said. "I been lagging quarters with some kids in Louis Armstrong Park. I win nearly every day."

"Louis Armstrong Park!" her mother exclaimed, overhearing. "Why, that's all the way up to Rampart Street! What in the world were you doing up there, young lady?"

"Please take the money," Sugar begged Roy, ignoring her mother. "So I'll know I helped you get away. Please, Roy, it's important."

Smiling a slight smile, Roy took the money. He rubbed his painful knuckles briefly against her cheek. "Know something?" he said. "It's important to me, too."

Then he was gone.

The ten thirty-five Greyhound to Houston via Baton Rouge and Beaumont was still running. Roy bought a one-way ticket and sat in a far corner of the terminal, back to the wall, drinking hot black coffee from a nearby vending machine as he watched the street entrance for anyone entering who looked like they might work for Jack Kono. When the departure was announced over the loudspeaker an hour later, Roy was the first passenger to board. He took a window seat about halfway back where he could see through the open boarding-platform doors into the passenger terminal. Settling back, his bag on the overhead rack, he shifted his eyes from the terminal to the other passengers, scrutinizing each one as they boarded. None of them looked threatening in any way. When they were all on board, the bus was only about half full. Least I'll be able to get comfortable, Roy thought. Maybe get some shut-eye. He kept his eyes on what he could see of the passenger terminal.

Two minutes before the bus was due to depart, Benny and Sugar came hurrying onto the boarding platform lugging a couple of beat-up suitcases and looking like a pair of magpies with both their mouths going at once. Benny had Sugar get on to make sure Roy was aboard, then they gave their tickets to the driver and maneuvered their suitcases down the aisle to where Roy stood to meet them.

"Don't even ask," Benny said peremptorily with a wave of her hand. "I couldn't explain this in a million years. Let's just say I'm crazy."

"This isn't very smart, Verbenia," he said, taking the suitcase she handed him.

As Benny slid into a seat, Sugar punched Roy on the muscle. "Don't you blow this, Roy," she whispered a warning. "I went through hell getting her here."

"Still not very smart."

"Just put the suitcases up."

Sugar sat across the aisle, leaving the seat next to her mother for Roy. She noticed as Roy sat down that Benny took his arm and leaned her head on his shoulder. Sugar smiled.

"I gave Sam back three hundred of the five and promised we'd send him the rest," Benny said.

"Okay, honey," said Roy, patting her head.

The driver got behind the wheel. The big passenger door closed with a pneumatic hiss. Several seconds later there was the choking of a diesel engine firing up and a sigh of air brakes being released. The bus began to move.

As the Greyhound pulled back from the boarding platform, Roy looked past Benny out the window and saw Shimmy, the punk he had encountered earlier with Jack Kono. Shimmy was with another hood, bigger and meaner looking. Both stood on the platform and stared hard at the Houston-bound bus as it swung away and left.

Roy wet lips that suddenly went dry. They must have followed Verbenia and Sugar, he thought.

Well, that's all she wrote, he told himself. There'd be somebody waiting every place the bus stopped, watching for him to get off. They had him, and that was that.

He thought about it in the dim light of the moving bus for a while, and finally decided he'd wait until Verbenia and Sugar went to sleep, then get off at the next stop. That way, at least the two of them wouldn't be involved. He didn't want them with him when Kono's hoods caught up with him. He didn't want them to see what would happen.

If they got away, he thought, this was one split decision he would win.

MARCIA MULLER

FORBIDDEN THINGS

Here's something quite different from Marcia Muller, making
her third appearance in this series. It's a memorable tale set in
the modern West, about a young woman searching for her
roots who encounters a mystery that seems inexplicable.

All the years that I was growing up in a poor suburb of Los
Angeles, my mother would tell me stories of the days I couldn't
remember when we lived with my father on the wild north coast.
She'd tell of a gray, misty land suddenly made brilliant by quicksilver flashes off the sea; of white-sand beaches that would disappear in a storm, then emerge strewn with driftwood and
treasures from foreign shores; of a deeply forested ridge of hills
where, so the Pomo Indians claimed, spirits walked by night.

Our cabin nestled on the ridge, high above the little town of
Camel Rock and the humpbacked offshore mass that inspired
its name. The cabin, built to last by my handyman father, was
of local redwood, its foundation sunk deep in bedrock. There
was a woodstove and home-woven curtains. There were stained-
glass windows and a sleeping loft; there was . . .

Although I had no recollection of the place we'd left when I
was two, it somehow seemed more real to me than our shabby
pink bungalow with the cracked sidewalk out front and the
packed-dirt yard out back. I'd lie in bed late at night feeling the
heat from the woodstove, watching the light as it filtered
through the stained-glass panels, listening to the wind buffet our
secure aerie. I was sure I could smell my mother's baking bread,
hear the deep rumble of my father's voice. But no matter how
hard I tried, I could not call up the image of my father's face,

even though a stiff and formal studio portrait of him sat on our coffee table.

When I asked my mother why she and I had left a place of quicksilver days and night-walking spirits, she'd grow quiet. When I asked where my father was now, she'd turn away. As I grew older I realized there were shadows over our departure—shadows in which forbidden things stood still and silent.

Is it any wonder that when my mother died—young, at forty-nine, but life hadn't been kind to her and heart trouble ran in the family—is it any wonder that I packed everything I cared about and went back to the place of my birth to confront those forbidden things?

I'd located Camel Rock on the map when I was nine, tracing the coast highway with my finger until it reached a jutting point of land north of Fort Bragg. Once this had been logging country—hardy men working the crosscut saw and jackscrew in the forests, bull teams dragging their heavy loads to the coast, fresh-cut logs thundering down the chutes to schooners that lay at anchor in the coves below. But by the time I was born, lumbering was an endangered industry. Today, I knew, the voice of the chain saw was stilled and few logging trucks rumbled along the highway. Legislation to protect the environment, coupled with a severe construction slump, had all but killed the old economy. Instead, new enterprises had sprung up: wineries; mushroom, garlic, and herb farms; tourist shops and bed-and-breakfasts. These were only marginally profitable, however; the north coast was financially strapped.

I decided to go anyway.

It was a good time for me to leave southern California. Two failed attempts at college, a ruined love affair, a series of slipping-down jobs—all argued for radical change. I'd had no family except my mother; even my cat had died the previous October. As I gave notice at the coffee shop where I'd been waitressing, disposed of the contents of the bungalow, and turned the keys back to the landlord, I said no good-byes. Yet I left with hope of a welcome. Maybe there would be a place for me in Camel Rock. Maybe someone would even remember my family and fill in the gaps in my early life.

I know now that I was really hoping for a reunion with my father.

Mist blanketed the coast the afternoon I drove my old Pinto over the bridge spanning the mouth of the Deer River and into Camel Rock. Beyond sandstone cliffs the sea lay flat and seemingly motionless. The town—a strip of buildings on either side of the highway, with dirt lanes straggling up toward the hills— looked deserted. A few drifting columns of wood smoke, some lighted signs in shop windows, a hunched and bundled figure walking along the shoulder—these were the only signs of life. I drove slowly, taking it all in: a supermarket, some bars, a little mall full of tourist shops. Post office, laundromat, defunct real estate agency, old sagging hotel that looked to be the only lodging place. When I'd gone four blocks and passed the last gas station and the cable TV company, I ran out of town; I U-turned, went back to the hotel, and parked my car between two pickups out front.

For a moment I sat behind the wheel, feeling flat. The town didn't look like the magical place my mother had described; if anything, it was seedier than the suburb I'd left yesterday. I had to force myself to get out, and when I did, I stood beside the Pinto, staring up at the hotel. Pale green with once white trim, all of it blasted and faded by the elements. An inscription above its front door gave the date it was built—1879, the height of last century's logging boom. Neon beer signs flashed in its lower windows; gulls perched along the peak of its roof, their droppings splashed over the steps and front porch. I watched as one soared in for a landing, crying shrilly. Sea breeze ruffled my short blond hair, and I smelled fish and brine.

The smell of the sea had always delighted me. Now it triggered a sense of connection to this place. I thought: *home*.

The thought lent me the impetus to take out my overnight bag and carried me over the threshold of the hotel. Inside was a dim lobby that smelled of dust and cat. I peered through the gloom but saw no one. Loud voices came from a room to the left, underscored by the clink of glasses and the thump and clatter of dice-rolling; I went over, looked in, and saw an old-fashioned tavern, peopled mainly by men in work clothes. The ship's clock that hung crooked behind the bar said four-twenty. Happy hour got under way early in Camel Rock.

There was a public phone on the other side of the lobby. I crossed to it and opened the thin county directory, aware that my fingers were trembling. No listing for my father. No listing for anyone with my last name. More disappointed than I had any right to be, I replaced the book and turned away.

Just then a woman came out of a door under the steep staircase. She was perhaps in her early sixties, tall and gaunt, with tightly permed gray curls and a face lined by weariness. When she saw me, her pale eyes registered surprise. "May I help you?"

I hesitated, the impulse to flee the shabby hotel and drive away from Camel Rock nearly irresistible. Then I thought: Come on, give the place a chance. "Do you have a room available?"

"We've got nothing *but* available rooms." She smiled wryly and got a card for me to fill out. Lacking any other, I put down my old address and formed the letters of my signature—Ashley Heikkinen—carefully. I'd always hated my last name; it seemed graceless and misshapen beside my first. Now I was glad it was unusual; maybe someone here in town would recognize it. The woman glanced disinterestedly at the card, however, then turned away and studied a rack of keys.

"Front room or back room?"

"Which is more quiet?"

"Well, in front you've got the highway noise, but there's not much traffic at night. In the back you've got the boys"—she motioned at the door to the tavern—"scrapping in the parking lot at closing time."

Just what I wanted—a room above a bar frequented by quarrelsome drunks. "I guess I'll take the front."

The woman must have read my expression. "Oh, honey, don't you worry about them. They're not so bad, but there's nobody as contentious as an out-of-work logger who's had one over his limit."

I smiled and offered my Visa card. She shook her head and pointed to a CASH ONLY sign. I dug in my wallet and came up with the amount she named. It wasn't much, but I didn't have much to begin with. There had been a small life insurance policy on my mother, but most of it had gone toward burying her. If I was to stay in Camel Rock, I'd need a job.

"Are a lot of people around here out of work?" I asked as the woman wrote up a receipt.

"Loggers, mostly. The type who won't bite the bullet and learn another trade. But the rest of us aren't in much better shape."

"Have you heard of any openings for a waitress or a bartender?"

"For yourself?"

"Yes. If I can find a job, I may settle here."

Her hand paused over the receipt book. "Honey, why on earth would you want to do that?"

"I was born here. Maybe you knew my parents—Melinda and John Heikkinen?"

She shook her head and tore the receipt from the book. "My husband and me, we just moved down here last year from Del Norte County—things're even worse up there, believe me. We bought this hotel because it was cheap and we thought we could make a go of it."

"Have you?"

"Not really. We don't have the wherewithal to fix it up, so we can't compete with the new motels or bed-and-breakfasts. And we made the mistake of giving bar credit to the locals."

"That's too bad," I said. "There must be some jobs available, though. I'm a good waitress, a fair bartender. And I . . . like people," I added lamely.

She smiled, the lines around her eyes crinkling kindly. I guessed she'd presented meager credentials a time or two herself. "Well, I suppose you could try over at the mall. I hear Barbie Cannon's been doing real good with her Beachcomber Shop, and the tourist season'll be here before we know it. Maybe she can use some help."

I thanked her and took the room key she offered, but as I picked up my bag I thought of something else. "Is there a newspaper in town?"

"As far as I know, there never has been. There's one of those little county shoppers, but it doesn't have ads for jobs, if that's what you're after."

"Actually, I'm trying to locate . . . a family member. I thought if there was a newspaper, I could look through their back issues. What about longtime residents of the town? Is there anybody who's an amateur historian, for instance?"

"Matter of fact, there is. Gus Galick. Lives on his fishing trawler, the *Irma*, down at the harbor. Comes in here regular."

"How long has he lived here?"

"All his life."

Just the person I wanted to talk with.

The woman added, "Gus is away this week, took a charter party down the coast. I think he said he'd be back next Thursday."

Another disappointment. I swallowed it, told myself the delay would give me time to settle in and get to know the place of my birth. And I'd start by visiting the Beachcomber Shop.

The shop offered exactly the kind of merchandise its name implied: seashells; driftwood; inexpert carvings of gulls, grebes, and sea lions. Postcards and calendars and T-shirts and paperback guidebooks. Shell jewelry, paperweights, ceramic whales and dolphins. Nautical toys and candles and wind chimes. All of it was totally predictable, but the woman who popped up from behind the counter was anything but.

She was very tall, well over six feet, and her black hair stood up in long, stiff spikes. A gold ring pierced her left nostril, and several others hung from either earlobe. She wore a black leather tunic with metal studs, over lacy black tights and calf-high boots. In L.A. I wouldn't have given her a second glance, but this was Camel Rock. Such people weren't supposed to happen here.

The woman watched my reaction, then threw back her head and laughed throatily. I felt a blush begin to creep over my face.

"Hey, don't worry about it," she told me. "You should see how I scare the little bastards who drag their parents in here, whining about how they absolutely *have* to have a blow-up Willie the Whale."

"Uh, isn't that bad for business?"

"Hell, no. Embarrasses the parents, and they buy twice as much as they would've."

"Oh."

"So—what can I do for you?"

"I'm looking for Barbie Cannon."

"You found her." She flopped onto a stool next to the counter, stretching out her long legs.

"My name's Ashley Heikkinen." I watched her face for some sign of recognition. There wasn't any, but that didn't surprise me; Barbie Cannon was only a few years older than I—perhaps thirty—and too young to remember a family that had left so long ago. Besides, she didn't look as if she'd been born and raised here.

"I'm looking for a job," I went on, "and the woman at the hotel said you might need some help in the shop."

She glanced around at the merchandise that was heaped haphazardly on the shelves and spilled over onto the floor here and there. "Well, Penny's right—I probably do." Then she looked back at me. "You're not local."

"I just came up from L.A."

"Me too, about a year ago. There're a fair number of us transplants, and the division between us and the locals is pretty clear-cut."

"How so?"

"A lot of the natives are down on their luck, resentful of the newcomers, especially ones like me, who're doing well. Oh, some of them're all right; they understand that the only way for the area to survive is to restructure the economy. But most of them are just sitting around the bars mumbling about how the spotted owl ruined their lives and hoping the timber industry'll make a comeback—and that ain't gonna happen. So why're *you* here?"

"I was born in Camel Rock. And I'm sick of southern California."

"So you decided to get back to your roots."

"In a way."

"You alone?"

I nodded.

"Got a place to stay?"

"The hotel, for now."

"Well, it's not so bad, and Penny'll extend credit if you run short. As for a job . . ." She paused, looking around again. "You know, I came up here thinking I'd work on my photography. The next Ansel Adams and all that." She grinned self-mockingly. "Trouble is, I got to be such a successful businesswoman that I don't even have time to load my camera. Tell you what—why don't we go over to the hotel tavern, tilt a few, talk it over?"

"Why not?" I said.

Mist hugged the tops of the sequoias and curled in tendrils around their trunks. The mossy ground under my feet was damp and slick. I hugged my hooded sweatshirt against the chill and moved cautiously up the incline from where I'd left the car on an overgrown logging road. My soles began to slip, and I crouched, catching at a stump for balance. The wet fronds of a fern brushed my cheek.

I'd been tramping through the hills for over two hours, searching every lane and dirt track for the burned-out cabin that Barbie Cannon had photographed shortly after her arrival in Camel Rock last year. Barbie had invited me to her place for dinner the night before after we'd agreed on the terms of my new part-time job, and in the course of the evening she'd shown me her portfolio of photographs. One, a grainy black-and-white image of a ruin, so strongly affected me that I'd barely been able to sleep. This morning I'd dropped by the shop and gotten Barbie to draw me a map of where she'd found it, but her recollection was so vague that I might as well have had no map at all.

I pushed back to my feet and continued climbing. The top of the rise was covered by a dense stand of sumac and bay laurel; the spicy scent of the laurel leaves mixed with stronger odors of redwood and eucalyptus. The mixed bouquet triggered the same sense of connection that I'd felt as I stood in front of the hotel the previous afternoon. I breathed deeply, then elbowed through the dense branches.

From the other side of the thicket I looked down on a sloping meadow splashed with the brilliant yellow-orange of California poppies. More sequoias crowned the ridge on its far side, and through their branches I caught a glimpse of the flat, leaden sea. A stronger feeling of familiarity stole over me. I remembered my mother saying, "In the spring, the meadow was full of poppies, and you could see the ocean from our front steps. . . ."

The mist was beginning to break up overhead. I watched a hawk circle against a patch of blue high above the meadow, then wheel and flap away toward the inland hills. He passed over my head, and I could feel the beating of his great wings. I turned, my gaze following his flight path—

And then I spotted the cabin, overgrown and wrapped in shadow, only yards away. Built into the downward slope of the hill, its moss-covered foundations were anchored in bedrock, as I'd been told. But the rest was only blackened and broken timbers, a collapsed roof on whose shakes vegetation had taken root, a rusted stove chimney about to topple, empty windows and doors.

I drew in my breath and held it for a long moment. Then I slowly moved forward.

Stone steps, four of them. I counted as I climbed. Yes, you could still see the Pacific from here, the meadow, too. And this opening was where the door had been. Beyond it, nothing but a concrete slab covered with debris. Plenty of evidence that picnickers had been here.

I stepped over the threshold.

One big empty room. Nothing left, not even the mammoth iron woodstove. Vines growing through the timbers, running across the floor. And at the far side, a collapsed heap of burned lumber—the sleeping loft?

Something crunched under my foot. I looked down, squatted, poked at it gingerly with my fingertip. Glass, green glass. It could have come from a picnicker's wine bottle. Or it could have come from a broken stained-glass window.

I stood, coldness upon my scalp and shoulder blades. Coldness that had nothing to do with the sea wind that bore the mist from the coast. I closed my eyes against the shadows and the ruin. Once again I could smell my mother's baking bread, hear my father's voice. Once again I thought: *home*.

But when I opened my eyes, the warmth and light vanished. Now all I saw was the scene of a terrible tragedy.

"Barbie," I said, "what do you know about the Northcoast Lumber Company?"

She looked up from the box of wind chimes she was unpacking. "Used to be the big employer around here."

"Where do they have their offices? I couldn't find a listing in the county phone book."

"I hear they went bust in the eighties."

"Then why would they still own land up in the hills?"

"Don't know. Why?"

I hesitated. Yesterday, the day after I'd found the cabin, I'd driven down to the county offices at Fort Bragg and spent the entire afternoon poring over the land plats for this area. The place where the ruin stood appeared to belong to the lumber company. There was no reason I shouldn't confide in Barbie about my search, but something held me back. After a moment I said, "Oh, I saw some acreage that I might be interested in buying."

She raised her eyebrows; the extravagant white eye shadow and bright-red lipstick that she wore today made her look like an astonished clown. "On what I'm paying you for part-time work, you're buying land?"

"I've got some savings from my mom's life insurance." That much was true, but the small amount wouldn't buy even a square foot of land.

"Huh." She went back to her unpacking. "Well, I don't know for a fact that Northcoast did go bust. Penny told me that the owner's widow is still alive. Used to live on a big estate near here, but a long time ago she moved down the coast to that fancy retirement community at Timber Point. Maybe she could tell you about this acreage."

"What's her name, do you know?"

"No, but you could ask Penny. She and Gene bought the hotel from her."

"Madeline Carmichael," Penny said. "Lady in her late fifties. She and her husband used to own a lot of property around here."

"You know her, then."

"Nope, never met her. Our dealings were through a realtor and her lawyer."

"She lives down at Timber Point?"

"Uh-huh. The realtor told us she's a recluse, never leaves her house and has everything she needs delivered."

"Why, do you suppose?"

"Why not? She can afford it. Oh, the realtor hinted that there's some tragedy in her past, but I don't put much stock in that. I'll tell you"—her tired eyes swept the dingy hotel lobby— "if I had a beautiful home and all that money, I'd never go out, either."

Madeline Carmichael's phone number and address were unlisted. When I drove down to Timber Point the next day, I found high grape-stake fences and a gatehouse; the guard told me that Mrs. Carmichael would see no one who wasn't on her visitors list. When I asked him to call her, he refused. "If she was expecting you," he said, "she'd have sent your name down."

Penny had given me the name of the realtor who handled the sale of the hotel. He put me in touch with Mrs. Carmichael's lawyer in Fort Bragg. The attorney told me he'd check about the ownership of the land and get back to me. When he did, his reply was terse: The land was part of the original Carmichael estate; title was held by the nearly defunct lumber company; it was not for sale.

So why had my parents built their cabin on the Carmichael estate? Were my strong feelings of connection to the burned-out ruin in the hills false?

Maybe, I told myself, it was time to stop chasing memories and start building a life for myself here in Camel Rock. Maybe it was best to leave the past alone.

* * *

The following weekend brought the kind of quicksilver days my mother had told me about, and in turn they lured tourists in record numbers. We couldn't restock the Beachcomber Shop's shelves fast enough. On the next Wednesday—Barbie's photography day—I was unpacking fresh merchandise and filling in where necessary while waiting for the woman Barbie bought her driftwood sculptures from to make a delivery. Business was slack in the late-afternoon hours; I moved slowly, my mind on what to wear to a dinner party being given that evening by some new acquaintances who ran an herb farm. When the bell over the door jangled, I started.

It was Mrs. Fleming, the driftwood lady. I recognized her by the big plastic wash basket of sculptures that she toted. A tiny white-haired woman, she seemed too frail for such a load. I moved to take it from her.

She resisted, surprisingly strong. Her eyes narrowed, and she asked, "Where's Barbie?"

"Wednesday's her day off."

"And who are you?"

"Ashley Heikkinen. I'm Barbie's part-time—"

"*What* did you say?"

"My name is Ashley Heikkinen. I just started here last week."

Mrs. Fleming set the basket on the counter and regarded me sternly, spots of red appearing on her cheeks. "Just what are you up to, young woman?"

"I don't understand."

"Why are you using that name?"

"Using . . . ? It's my name."

"It most certainly is not! This is a very cruel joke."

The woman had to be unbalanced. Patiently I said, "Look, my name really is Ashley Heikkinen. I was born in Camel Rock but moved away when I was two. I grew up outside Los Angeles, and when my mother died I decided to come back here."

Mrs. Fleming shook her head, her lips compressed, eyes glittering with anger.

"I can prove who I am," I added, reaching under the counter for my purse. "Here's my identification."

"Of course you'd have identification. Everyone knows how to obtain that under the circumstances."

"What circumstances?"

She turned and moved toward the door. "I can't imagine what you possibly expect to gain by this charade, young woman, but you can be sure I'll speak to Barbie about you."

"Please, wait!"

She pushed through the door, and the bell above it jangled harshly as it slammed shut. I hurried to the window and watched her cross the parking lot in a vigorous stride that belied her frail appearance. As she turned at the highway, I looked down and saw I had my wallet out, prepared to prove my identity.

Why, I wondered, did I feel compelled to justify my existence to this obviously deranged stranger?

The dinner party that evening was pleasant, and I returned to the hotel at a little after midnight with the fledgling sense of belonging that making friends in a strange place brings. The fog was in thick, drawn by hot inland temperatures. It put a gritty sheen on my face, and when I touched my tongue to my lips, I tasted the sea. I locked the Pinto and started across the rutted parking lot to the rear entrance. Heavy footsteps came up behind me.

Conditioned by my years in L.A., I already held my car key in my right hand, tip out as a weapon. I glanced back and saw a stocky, bearded man bearing down on me. When I sidestepped and turned, he stopped, and his gaze moved to the key. He'd been drinking—beer, and plenty of it.

From the tavern, I thought. Probably came out to the parking lot because the rest room's in use and he couldn't wait. "After you," I said, opening the door for him.

He stepped inside the narrow, dim hallway. I let him get a ways ahead, then followed. The door stuck, and I turned to give it a tug. The man reversed, came up swiftly, and grasped my shoulder.

"Hey!" I said.

He spun me around and slammed me against the wall. "Lady, what the hell're you after?"

"Let go of me!" I pushed at him.

He pushed back, grabbed my other shoulder, and pinned me there. I stopped struggling, took a deep breath, told myself to remain calm.

"Not going to hurt you, lady," he said. "I just want to know what your game is."

Two lunatics in one day. "What do you mean—game?"

" 'My name is Ashley Heikkinen,' " he said in a falsetto, then dropped to his normal pitch. "Who're you trying to fool? And what's in it for you?"

"I don't—"

"Don't give me that! You might be able to stonewall an old lady like my mother—"

"Your mother?"

"Yeah, Janet Fleming. You expect her to believe you, for Christ's sake? What you did, you upset her plenty. She had to take one of the Valiums the doctor gave me for my bad back."

"I don't understand what your mother's problem is."

"Jesus, you're a cold bitch! Her own goddaughter, for Christ's sake, and you expect her to *believe* you?"

"Goddaughter?"

His face was close to mine now; hot beer breath touched my cheeks. "My ma's goddaughter was Ashley Heikkinen."

"That's impossible! I never had a godmother. I never met your mother until this afternoon."

The man shook his head. "I'll tell you what's impossible: Ashley Heikkinen appearing in Camel Rock after all these years. Ashley's dead. She died in a fire when she wasn't even two years old. My ma ought to know—she identified the body."

A chill washed over me from my scalp to my toes. The man stared, apparently recognizing my shock as genuine. After a moment I asked, "Where was the fire?"

He ignored the question, frowning. "Either you're a damned good actress or something weird's going on. Can't have been two people born with that name. Not in Camel Rock."

"Where was the fire?"

He shook his head again, this time as if to clear it. His mouth twisted, and I feared he was going to be sick. Then he let go of me and stumbled through the door to the parking lot. I released my breath in a long sigh and slumped against the wall. A car started outside. When its tires had spun on the gravel and its engine revved on the highway, I pushed myself upright and went along the hall to the empty lobby. A single bulb burned in the fixture above the reception desk, as it did every night. The usual sounds of laughter and conversation came from the tavern.

Everything seemed normal. Nothing was. I ran upstairs to the shelter of my room.

After I'd double-locked the door, I turned on the overhead and crossed to the bureau and leaned across it toward the streaky mirror. My face was drawn and unusually pale.

Ashley Heikkinen dead?

Dead in a fire when she wasn't quite two years old?

I closed my eyes, picturing the blackened ruin in the hills above town. Then I opened them and stared at my frightened face. It was the face of a stranger.

"If Ashley Heikkinen is dead," I said, "then who am *I*?"

Mrs. Fleming wouldn't talk to me. When I got to her cottage on one of the packed-dirt side streets at a little after nine the next morning, she refused to open the door and threatened to run me off with her dead husband's shotgun. "And don't think I'm not a good markswoman," she added.

She must have gone straight to the phone, because Barbie was hanging up when I walked into the Beachcomber Shop a few minutes later. She frowned at me and said, "I just had the most insane call from Janet Fleming."

"About me?"

"How'd you guess? She was giving me all this stuff about you not being who you say you are and the 'real Ashley Heikkinen' dying in a fire when she was a baby. Must be going around the bend."

I sat down on the stool next to the counter. "Actually, there might be something to what she says." And then I told her all of it: my mother's stories, the forbidden things that went unsaid,

the burned-out cabin in the hills, my encounters with Janet
Fleming and her son. "I tried to talk with Mrs. Fleming this
morning," I finished, "but she threatened me with a shotgun."

"And she's been known to use that gun, too. You must've
really upset her."

"Yes. From something she said yesterday afternoon, I gather
she thinks I got hold of the other Ashley's birth certificate and
created a set of fake ID around it."

"You sound like you believe there *was* another Ashley."

"I saw that burned-out cabin. Besides, why would Mrs. Fleming make something like that up?"

"But you recognized the cabin, both from my photograph and
when you went there. You said it felt like home."

"I recognized it from my mother's stories, that's true. Barbie,
I've lived those stories for most of my life. You know how kids
sometimes get the notion that they're so special they can't really
belong to their parents, that they're a prince or princess who
was given to a servant couple to raise?"

"Oh sure, we all went through that stage. Only in my case,
I was Mick Jagger's love child, and someday he was going to
acknowledge me and give me all his money."

"Well, my mother's stories convinced me that I didn't really
belong in a downscale tract in a crappy valley town. They made
me special, somebody who came from a magical place. And I
dreamed of it every night."

"So you're saying that you only recognized the cabin from the
images your mother planted in your mind?"

"It's possible."

Barbie considered. "Okay, I'll buy that. And here's a scenario
that might fit: After the fire, your parents moved away. That
would explain why your mom didn't want to talk about why
they left Camel Rock. And they had another child—you. They
gave you Ashley's name and her history. It wasn't right, but grief
does crazy things to otherwise sane people."

It worked—but only in part. "That still doesn't explain what
happened to my father and why my mother would never talk
about him."

"Maybe she was the one who went crazy with grief, and after a while he couldn't take it anymore, so he left."

She made it sound so logical and uncomplicated. But I'd known the quality of my mother's silences; there was more to them than Barbie's scenario encompassed.

I bit my lip in frustration. "You know, Mrs. Fleming could shed a lot of light on this, but she refuses to deal with me."

"Then find somebody who will."

"Who?" I asked. And then I thought of Gus Galick, the man Penny had told me about who had lived in Camel Rock all his life. "Barbie, do you know Gus Galick?"

"Sure. He's one of the few old-timers around here that I've really connected with. Gus builds ships in bottles; I sold some on consignment for him last year. He used to be a rumrunner during Prohibition, has some great stories about bringing in cases of Canadian booze to the coves along the coast."

"He must be older than God."

"Older than God and sharp as a tack. I bet he could tell you what you need to know."

"Penny said he was away on some charter trip."

"Was, but he's back now. I saw the *Irma* in her slip at the harbor when I drove by this morning."

Camel Rock's harbor was a sheltered cove with a bait shack and a few slips for fishing boats. Of them, Gus Galick's *Irma* was by far the most shipshape, and her captain was equally trim, with a shock of silvery-white hair and leathery tan skin. I didn't give him my name, just identified myself as a friend of Penny and Barbie. Galick seemed to take people at face value, though; he welcomed me on board, took me belowdecks, and poured me a cup of coffee in the cozy wood-paneled cabin. When we were seated on either side of the teak table, I asked my first question.

"Sure, I remember the fire on the old Carmichael estate," he said. "Summer of seventy-one. Both the father and the little girl died."

I gripped the coffee mug tighter. "The father died, too?"

"Yeah. Heikkinen, his name was. Norwegian, maybe. I don't recall his first name, or the little girl's."

"John and Ashley."

"These people kin to you?"

"In a way. Mr. Galick, what happened to Melinda, the mother?"

He thought. "Left town, I guess. I never did see her after the double funeral."

"Where are John and Ashley buried?"

"Graveyard of the Catholic church." He motioned toward the hills, where I'd seen its spire protruding through the trees. "Carmichaels paid for everything, of course. Guilt, I guess."

"Why guilt?"

"The fire started on their land. Was the father's fault—John Heikkinen's, I mean—but still, they'd sacked him, and that was why he was drinking so heavy. Fell asleep with the doors to the woodstove open, and before he could wake up, the place was a furnace."

The free-flowing information was beginning to overwhelm me. "Let me get this straight: John Heikkinen worked for the Carmichaels?"

"Was their caretaker. His wife looked after their house."

"Where was she when the fire started?"

"At the main house, washing up the supper dishes. I heard she saw the flames, run down there, and tried to save her family. The Carmichaels held her back till the volunteer fire department could get there; they knew there wasn't any hope from the beginning."

I set the mug down, gripped the table's edge with icy fingers.

Galick leaned forward, eyes concerned. "Something wrong, miss? Have I upset you?"

I shook my head. "It's just . . . a shock, hearing about it after all these years." After a pause, I asked, "Did the Heikkinens have any other children?"

"Only the little girl who died."

I took out a photograph of my mother and passed it over to him. It wasn't a good picture, just a snap of her on the steps of our stucco bungalow down south. "Is this Melinda Heikkinen?"

He took a pair of glasses from a case on the table, put them on, and looked closely at it. Then he shrugged and handed it back to me. "There's some resemblance, but . . . She looks like she's had a hard life."

"She did." I replaced the photo in my wallet. "Can you think of anyone who could tell me more about the Heikkinens?"

"Well, there's Janet Fleming. She was Mrs. Heikkinen's aunt and the little girl's godmother. The mother was so broken up that Janet had to identify the bodies, so I guess she'd know everything there is to know about the fire."

"Anyone else?"

"Well, of course there's Madeline Carmichael. But she's living down at Timber Point now, and she never sees anybody."

"Why not?"

"I've got my ideas on that. It started after her husband died. Young man, only in his fifties. Heart attack." Galick grimaced. "Carmichael was one of these pillars of the community; never drank, smoked, or womanized. Keeled over at a church service in seventy-five. Me, I've lived a gaudy life, as they say. Even now I eat and drink all the wrong things, and I like a cigar after dinner. And I just go on and on. Tells you a lot about the randomness of it all."

I didn't want to think about that randomness; it was much too soon after losing my own mother to an untimely death for that. I asked, "About Mrs. Carmichael—it was her husband's death that turned her into a recluse?"

"No, miss." He shook his head firmly. "My idea is that his dying was just the last straw. The seeds were planted when their little girl disappeared three years before that."

"Disappeared?"

"It was in seventy-two, the year after the fire. The little girl was two years old, a change-of-life baby. Abigail, she was called. Abby, for short. Madeline Carmichael left her in her playpen on the veranda of their house, and she just plain vanished. At first they thought it was a kidnapping; the lumber company was failing, but the family still had plenty of money. But nobody ever made a ransom demand, and they never did find a trace of Abby or the person who took her."

The base of my spine began to tingle. As a child, I'd always been smaller than others of my age. Slower in school, too. The way a child might be if she was a year younger than the age shown on her birth certificate.

Abigail Carmichael, I thought. Abby, for short.

The Catholic churchyard sat tucked back against a eucalyptus grove; the trees' leaves caught the sunlight in a subtle shimmer, and their aromatic buds were thick under my feet. An iron fence surrounded the graves, and unpaved paths meandered among the mostly crumbling headstones. I meandered too, shock gradually leaching away to depression. The foundations of my life were as tilted as the oldest grave marker, and I wasn't sure I had the strength to construct new ones.

But I'd come here with a purpose, so finally I got a grip on myself and began covering the cemetery in a grid pattern.

I found them in the last row, where the fence backed up against the eucalyptus. Two small headstones set side by side. John and Ashley. There was room to John's right for another grave, one that now would never be occupied.

I knelt and brushed a curl of bark from Ashley's stone. The carving was simple, only her name and the dates. She'd been born April 6, 1969, and had died February 1, 1971.

I knelt there for a long time. Then I said good-bye and went home.

The old Carmichael house sat at the end of a chained-off drive that I'd earlier taken for a logging road. It was a wonder I hadn't stumbled across it in my search for the cabin. Built of dark timber and stone, with a wide veranda running the length of the lower story, it once might have been imposing. But now its windows were boarded, birds roosted in its eaves, and all around it the forest encroached. I followed a cracked flagstone path through a lawn long gone to weeds and wildflowers, to the broad front steps. Stood at their foot, my hand on the cold wrought-iron railing.

Could a child of two retain memories? I'd believed so before, but mine had turned out to be false, spoon-fed to me by the woman who had taken me from this veranda twenty-four years earlier. All the same, something in this lonely place spoke to me;

I felt a sense of peace and safety that I'd never before experienced.

I hadn't known real security; my mother's and my life together had been too uncertain, too difficult, too shadowed by the past. Those circumstances probably accounted for my long string of failures, my inability to make my way in the world. A life built on lies and forbidden things was bound to go nowhere.

And yet it hadn't had to be that way. All this could have been mine, had it not been for a woman unhinged by grief. I could have grown up in this once lovely home, surrounded by my real parents' love. Perhaps if I had, my father would not have died of an untimely heart attack, and my birth mother would not have become a recluse. A sickening wave of anger swept over me, followed by a deep sadness. Tears came to my eyes, and I wiped them away.

I couldn't afford to waste time crying. Too much time had been wasted already.

To prove my real identity, I needed the help of Madeline Carmichael's attorney, and he took a good deal of convincing. I had to provide documentation and witnesses to my years as Ashley Heikkinen before he would consent to check Abigail Carmichael's birth records. Most of the summer went by before he broached the subject to Mrs. Carmichael. But blood composition and the delicate whorls on feet and fingers don't lie; finally, on a bright September afternoon, I arrived at Timber Point—alone, at the invitation of my birth mother.

I was nervous and gripped the Pinto's wheel with damp hands as I followed the guard's directions across a rolling seaside meadow to the Carmichael house. Like the others in this exclusive development, it was of modern design, with a silvery wood exterior that blended with the saw grass and Scotch broom. A glass wall faced the Pacific, reflecting sun glints on the water. Along the shoreline a flock of pelicans flew south in loose formation.

I'd worn my best dress—pink cotton, too light for the season, but it was all I had—and had spent a ridiculous amount of time on my hair and makeup. As I parked the shabby Pinto in the drive, I wished I could make it disappear. My approach to the door was awkward; I stumbled on the unlandscaped ground and almost turned my ankle. The uniformed maid who admitted me gave me the kind of glance that once, as a hostess at a coffee shop, I'd reserved for customers without shirt or shoes. She showed me to a living room facing the sea and went away.

I stood in the room's center on an Oriental carpet, unsure whether to sit or stand. Three framed photographs on a grand piano caught my attention; I went over there and looked at them. A man and a woman, middle-aged and handsome. A child, perhaps a year old, in a striped romper. The child had my eyes.

"Yes, that's Abigail." The throaty voice—smoker's voice—came from behind me. I turned to face the woman in the photograph. Older now, but still handsome, with upswept creamy white hair and pale porcelain skin, she wore a long caftan in some sort of soft champagne-colored fabric. No reason for Madeline Carmichael to get dressed; she never left the house.

She came over to me and peered at my face. For a moment her eyes were soft and questioning, then they hardened and looked away. "Please," she said, "sit down over here."

I followed her to two matching brocade settees positioned at right angles to the seaward window. We sat, one on each, with a coffee table between us. Mrs. Carmichael took a cigarette from a silver box on the table and lit it with a matching lighter.

Exhaling and fanning the smoke away, she said, "I have a number of things to say to you that will explain my position in this matter. First, I believe the evidence you've presented. You are my daughter, Abigail. Melinda Heikkinen was very bitter toward my husband and me: If we hadn't dismissed her husband, he wouldn't have been passed out from drinking when the fire started. If we hadn't kept her late at her duties that night, she would have been home and able to prevent it. If we hadn't stopped her from plunging into the conflagration, she might have saved her child. That, I suppose, served to justify her taking our child as a replacement."

She paused to smoke. I waited.

"The logic of what happened seems apparent at this remove,"

Mrs. Carmichael added, "but at the time we didn't think to mention Melinda as a potential suspect. She'd left Camel Rock the year before; even her aunt, Janet Fleming, had heard nothing from her. My husband and I had more or less put her out of our minds. And of course, neither of us was thinking logically at the time."

I was beginning to feel uneasy. She was speaking so analytically and dispassionately—not at all like a mother who had been reunited with her long-lost child.

She went on: "I must tell you about our family. California pioneers on both sides. The Carmichaels were lumber barons. My family were merchant princes engaging in the China trade. Abigail was the last of both lines, born to carry on our tradition. Surely you can understand why this matter is so . . . difficult."

She was speaking of Abigail as someone separate from me. "What matter?" I asked.

"That role in life, the one Abigail was born to, takes a certain type of individual. My Abby, the child I would have raised had it not been for Melinda Heikkinen, would not have turned out so—" She bit her lower lip, looked away at the sea.

"So what, Mrs. Carmichael?"

She shook her head, crushing out her cigarette.

A wave of humiliation swept over me. I glanced down at my cheap pink dress, at a chip in the polish on my thumbnail. When I raised my eyes, my birth mother was examining me with faint distaste.

I'd always had a temper; now it rose, and I gave in to it. "So *what*, Mrs. Carmichael?" I repeated. "So *common?*"

She winced but didn't reply.

I said, "I suppose you think it's your right to judge a person on her appearance or her financial situation. But you should remember that my life hasn't been easy—not like yours. Melinda Heikkinen could never make ends meet. We lived in a valley town east of L.A. She was sick a lot. I had to work from the time I was fourteen. There was trouble with gangs in our neighborhood."

Then I paused, hearing myself. No, I would not do this. I would not whine or beg.

"I wasn't brought up to complain," I continued, "and I'm not complaining now. In spite of working, I graduated high school with honors. I got a small scholarship, and Melinda persuaded me to go to college. She helped out financially when she could. I didn't finish, but that was my own fault. Whatever mistakes I've made are my own doing, not Melinda's. Maybe she told me lies about our life here on the coast, but they gave me something to hang on to. A lot of the time they were all I had, and now they've been taken from me. But I'm still not complaining."

Madeline Carmichael's dispassionate facade cracked. She closed her eyes, compressed her lips. After a moment she said, "How can you defend that woman?"

"For twenty-four years she was the only mother I knew."

Her eyes remained closed. She said, "Please, I will pay you any amount of money if you will go away and pretend this meeting never took place."

For a moment I couldn't speak. Then I exclaimed, "I don't want your money! This is not about money!"

"What, then?"

"What do I want? I thought I wanted my real mother."

"And now that you've met me, you're not sure you do." She opened her eyes, looked directly into mine. "Our feelings aren't really all that different, are they, Abigail?"

I shook my head in confusion.

Madeline Carmichael took a deep breath. "Abigail, you say you lived on Melinda's lies, that they were something to sustain you?"

I nodded.

"I've lived on lies too, and they sustained *me*. For twenty-three years I've put myself to sleep with dreams of our meeting. I woke to them. No matter what I was doing, they were only a fingertip's reach away. And now they've been taken from me, as yours have. My Abby, the daughter I pictured in those dreams, will never walk into this room and make everything all right. Just as the things you've dreamed of are never going to happen."

I looked around the room—at the grand piano, the Oriental carpets, the antiques and exquisite art objects. Noticed for the first time how stylized and sterile it was, how the cold expanse of glass beside me made the sea blinding and bleak.

"You're right," I said, standing up. "Even if you were to take me in and offer me all this, it wouldn't be the life I wanted."

Mrs. Carmichael extended a staying hand toward me.

I stepped back. "No. And don't worry—I won't bother you again."

As I went out into the quicksilver afternoon and shut the door behind me, I thought that even though Melinda Heikkinen had given me a difficult life, she'd also offered me dreams to soften the hard times and love to ease my passage. My birth mother hadn't even offered me coffee or tea.

On a cold, rainy December evening, Barbie Cannon and I sat at a table near the fireplace in the hotel's tavern, drinking red wine in celebration of my good fortune.

"I can't believe," she said for what must have been the dozenth time, "that old lady Carmichael up and gave you her house in the hills."

"Any more than you can believe I accepted it."

"Well, I thought you were too proud to take her money."

"Too proud to be bought off, but she offered the house with no strings attached. Besides, it's in such bad shape that I'll probably be fixing it up for the rest of my life."

"And she probably took a big tax write-off on it. No wonder rich people stay rich." Barbie snorted. "By the way, how come you're still calling yourself Ashley Heikkinen?"

I shrugged. "Why not? It's been my name for as long as I can remember. It's a good name."

"You're acting awfully laid back about his whole thing."

"You didn't see me when I got back from Timber Point. But I've worked it all through. In a way, I understand how Mrs. Carmichael feels. The house is nice, but anything else she could have given me isn't what I was looking for."

"So what *were* you looking for?"

I stared into the fire. Madeline Carmichael's porcelain face flashed against the background of the flames. Instead of anger I felt a tug of pity for her: a lonely woman waiting her life out, but really as dead and gone as the merchant princes, the lumber barons, the old days on this wild north coast. Then I banished the image and pictured instead the faces of the friends I'd made since coming to Camel Rock: Barbie, Penny and Gene, the couple who ran the herb farm, Gus Galick, and—now—Janet Fleming and her son, Stu. Remembered all the good times: dinners and walks on the beach, Penny and Gene's fortieth wedding anniversary party, Barbie's first photographic exhibit, a fishing trip on Gus's trawler. And thought of all the good times to come.

"What was I looking for?" I said. "Something I found the day I got here."

BILL PRONZINI

OUT OF THE DEPTHS

A frequent contributor to this series over two decades, Bill Pronzini is one of those rare writers who can be equally effective with his Nameless private eye tales, the Quincannon western mysteries, or non-series surprises like this story of the Caribbean.

He came tumbling out of the sea, dark and misshapen, like a being that was not human. A creature from the depths; or a jumbee, the evil spirit of West Indian superstition. Fanciful thoughts, and Shea was not a fanciful woman. But on this strange, wild night nothing seemed real or explicable.

At first, with the moon hidden behind the running scud of clouds, she'd seen him as a blob of flotsam on a breaking wave. The squall earlier had left the sea rough and the swells out toward the reef were high, their crests stripped of spume by the wind. The angry surf threw him onto the strip of beach, dragged him back again; another wave flung him up a little farther. The moon reappeared then, bathing sea and beach and rocks in the kind of frost-white shine you found only in the Caribbean. Not flotsam—something alive. She saw his arms extend, splayed fingers dig into the sand to hold himself against the backward pull of the sea. Saw him raise a smallish head above a massive, deformed torso, then squirm weakly toward the nearest jut of rock. Another wave shoved him the last few feet. He clung to the rock, lying motionless with the surf foaming around him.

Out of the depths, she thought.

The irony made her shiver, draw the collar of her coat more tightly around her neck. She lifted her gaze again to the rocky

198

peninsula farther south. Windflaw Point, where the undertow off its tiny beach was the most treacherous on the island. It had taken her almost an hour to marshal her courage to the point where she was ready—almost ready—to walk out there and into the ocean. *Into* the depths. Now . . .

Massive clouds sealed off the moon again. In the heavy darkness Shea could just make him out, still lying motionless on the fine coral sand. Unconscious? Dead? I ought to go down there, she thought. But she could not seem to lift herself out of the chair.

After several minutes he moved again: dark shape rising to hands and knees, then trying to stand. Three tries before he was able to keep his legs from collapsing under him. He stood swaying, as if gathering strength; finally staggered onto the path that led up through rocks and sea grape. Toward the house. Toward her.

On another night she would have felt any number of emotions by this time: surprise, bewilderment, curiosity, concern. But not on this night. There was a numbness in her mind, like the numbness in her body from the cold wind. It was as if she were dreaming, sitting there on the open terrace—as if she'd fallen asleep hours ago, before the clouds began to pile up at sunset and the sky turned the color of a blood bruise.

A new storm was making up. Hammering northern this time, from the look of the sky. The wind had shifted, coming out of the northeast now; the clouds were bloated and simmering in that direction and the air had a charged quality. Unless the wind shifted again soon, the rest of the night would be even wilder.

Briefly the clouds released the moon. In its white glare she saw him plodding closer, limping, almost dragging his left leg. A man, of course—just a man. And not deformed: what had made him seem that way was the life jacket fastened around his upper body. She remembered the lights of a freighter or tanker she had seen passing on the horizon just after nightfall, ahead of the squall. Had he gone overboard from that somehow?

He had reached the garden, was making his way past the flamboyant trees and the thick clusters of frangipani. Heading toward the garden door and the kitchen: She'd left the lights on in there and the jalousies open. It was the lights that had drawn him here, like a beacon that could be seen a long distance out to sea.

A good thing she'd left them on or not? She didn't want him here, a cast-up stranger, hurt and needing attention—not on this night, not when she'd been so close to making the walk to Wind-flaw Point. But neither could she refuse him access or help. John would have, if he'd been drunk and in the wrong mood. Not her. It was not in her nature to be cruel to anyone, except perhaps herself.

Abruptly Shea pushed herself out of the chair. He hadn't seen her sitting in the restless shadows, and he didn't see her now as she moved back across the terrace to the sliding glass doors to her bedroom. Or at least if he did see her, he didn't stop or call out to her. She hurried through the darkened bedroom, down the hall, and into the kitchen. She was halfway to the garden door when he began pounding on it.

She unlocked and opened the door without hesitation. He was propped against the stucco wall, arms hanging and body slumped with exhaustion. Big and youngish, that was her first impression. She couldn't see his face clearly.

"Need some help," he said in a thick, strained voice. "Been in the water . . . washed up on your beach. . . ."

"I know, I saw you from the terrace. Come inside."

"Better get a towel first. Coral ripped a gash in my foot . . . blood all over your floor."

"All right. I'll have to close the door. The wind. . . ."

"Go ahead."

She shut the door and went to fetch a towel, a blanket, and the first-aid kit. On the way back to the kitchen she turned the heat up several degrees. When she opened up to him again she saw that he'd shed the life jacket. His clothing was minimal: plaid wool shirt, denim trousers, canvas shoes, all nicked and torn by coral. Around his waist was a pouch-type waterproof belt, like a workman's utility belt. One of the pouches bulged slightly.

She gave him the towel, and when he had it wrapped around his left foot he hobbled inside. She took his arm, let him lean on her as she guided him to the kitchen table. His flesh was cold, sea-puckered; the touch of it made her feel a tremor of revulsion. It was like touching the skin of a dead man.

When he sank heavily onto one of the chairs, she dragged another chair over and lifted his injured leg onto it. He stripped off what was left of his shirt, swaddled himself in the blanket. His teeth were chattering.

The coffeemaker drew her; she poured two of the big mugs full. There was always hot coffee ready and waiting, no matter what the hour—she made sure of that. She drank too much coffee, much too much, but it was better than drinking what John usually drank. If she—

"You mind sweetening that?"

She half-turned. "Sugar?"

"Liquor. Rum, if you have it."

"Jamaican rum." That was what John drank.

"Best there is. Fine."

She took down an open bottle, carried it and the mugs to the table, and watched while he spiked the coffee, drank, then poured more rum and drank again. Color came back into his stubbled cheeks. He used part of the blanket to rough-dry his hair.

He was a little older than she, early thirties, and in good physical condition: broad chest and shoulders, muscle-knotted arms. Sandy hair cropped short, thick sandy brows, a long-chinned face burned dark from exposure to the sun. The face was all right, might have been attractive except for the eyes. They were a bright off-blue color, shielded by lids that seemed perpetually lowered like flags at half-mast, and they didn't blink much. When the eyes lifted to meet and hold hers something in them made her look away.

"I'll see what I can do for your foot."

"Thanks. Hurts like hell."

The towel was already soaking through. Shea unwrapped it carefully, revealing a deep gash across the instep just above the tongue of his shoe. She got the shoe and sock off. More blood welled out of the cut.

"It doesn't look good. You may need a doctor—"

"No," he said, "no doctor."

"It'll take stitches to close properly."

"Just clean and bandage it, okay?"

She spilled iodine onto a gauze pad, swabbed at the gash as gently as she could. The sharp sting made him suck in his breath, but he didn't flinch or utter another sound. She laid a second piece of iodined gauze over the wound and began to wind tape tightly around his foot to hold the skin flaps together.

He said, "My name's Tanner. Harry Tanner."

"Shea Clifford."

"Shea. That short for something?"

"It's a family name."

"Pretty."

"Thank you."

"So are you," he said. "Real pretty with your hair all wind-blown like that."

She glanced up at him. He was smiling at her. Not a leer, just a weary smile, but it wasn't a good kind of smile. It had a predatory look, like the teeth-baring stretch of a wolf's jowls.

"No offense," he said.

"None taken." She lowered her gaze, watched her hands wind and tear tape. Her mind still felt numb. "What happened to you? Why were you in the water?"

"That damn squall a few hours ago. Came up so fast I didn't have time to get my genoa down. Wave as big as a house knocked poor little *Wanderer* into a full broach. I got thrown clear when she went over or I'd have sunk with her."

"Were you sailing alone?"

"All alone."

"Single-hander? Or just on a weekend lark?"

"Single-hander. You know boats, I see."

"Yes. Fairly well."

"Well, I'm a sea tramp," Tanner said. "Ten years of island-hopping and this is the first time I ever got caught unprepared."

"It happens. What kind of craft was *Wanderer*?"

"Bugeye ketch. Thirty-nine feet."

"Shame to lose a boat like that."

He shrugged. "She was insured."

"How far out were you?"

"Five or six miles. Hell of a long swim in a choppy sea."

"You're lucky the squall passed as quickly as it did."

"Lucky I was wearing my life jacket, too," Tanner said. "And lucky you stay up late with your lights on. If it weren't for the lights I probably wouldn't have made shore at all."

Shea nodded. She tore off the last piece of tape and then began putting the first-aid supplies away in the kit.

Tanner said, "I didn't see any other lights. This house the only one out here?"

"The only one on this side of the bay, yes."

"No close neighbors?"

"Three houses on the east shore, not far away."

"You live here alone?"

"With my husband."

"But he's not here now."

"Not now. He'll be home soon."

"That so? Where is he?"

"In Merrywing, the town on the far side of the island. He went out to dinner with friends."

"While you stayed home."

"I wasn't feeling well earlier."

"Merrywing. Salt Cay?"

"That's right."

"British-owned, isn't it?"

"Yes. You've never been here before?"

"Not my kind of place. Too small, too quiet, too rich. I prefer the livelier islands—St. Thomas, Nassau, Jamaica."

"St. Thomas isn't far from here," Shea said. "Is that where you were heading?"

"More or less. This husband of yours—how big is he?"

". . . Big?"

"Big enough so his clothes would fit me?"

"Oh," she said, "yes. About your size."

"Think he'd mind if you let me have a pair of his pants and a shirt and some underwear? Wet things of mine are giving me a chill."

"No, of course not. I'll get them from his room."

She went to John's bedroom. The smells of his cologne and pipe tobacco were strong in there; they made her faintly nauseous. In haste she dragged a pair of white linen trousers and a pullover off hangers in his closet, turned toward the dresser as she came out. And stopped in mid-stride.

Tanner stood in the open doorway, leaning against the jamb, his half-lidded eyes fixed on her.

"*His* room," he said. "Right."

"Why did you follow me?"

"Felt like it. So you don't sleep with him."

"Why should that concern you?"

"I'm naturally curious. How come? I mean, how come you and your husband don't share a bed?"

"Our sleeping arrangements are none of your business."

"Probably not. Your idea or his?"

"What?"

"Separate bedrooms. Your idea or his?"

"Mine, if you must know."

"Maybe he snores, huh?"

She didn't say anything.

"How long since you kicked him out of your bed?"

"I didn't kick him out. It wasn't like that."

"Sure it was. I can see it in your face."

"My private affairs—"

"—are none of my business. I know. But I also know the signs of a bad marriage when I see them. A bad marriage and an unhappy woman. Can't tell me you're not unhappy."

"All right," she said.

"So why don't you divorce him? Money?"

"Money has nothing to do with it."

"Money has something to do with everything."

"It isn't money."

"He have something on you?"

"No."

"Then why not just dump him?"

You're not going to divorce me, Shea. Not you, not like the others. I'll see you dead first. I mean it, Shea. You're mine and you'll stay mine until I decide I don't want you anymore. . . .

She said flatly, "I'm not going to talk about my marriage to you. I don't know you."

"We can fix that. I'm an easy guy to know."

She moved ahead to the dresser, found underwear and socks, put them on the bed with the trousers and pullover. "You can change in here," she said, and started for the doorway.

Tanner didn't move.

"I said—"

"I heard you, Shea."

"Mrs. Clifford."

"Clifford," he said. Then he smiled, the same wolfish lip stretch he'd shown her in the kitchen. "Sure—Clifford. Your husband's name wouldn't be John, would it? John Clifford?"

She was silent.

"I'll bet it is. John Clifford, Clifford Yacht Designs. One of the best marine architects in Miami. Fancy motor sailers and racing yawls."

She still said nothing.

"House in Miami Beach, another on Salt Cay—this house. And you're his latest wife. Which is it, number three or number four?"

Between her teeth she said, "Three."

"He must be what, fifty now? And worth millions. Don't tell me money's not why you married him."

"I won't tell you anything."

But his wealth wasn't why she'd married him. He had been kind and attentive to her at first. And she'd been lonely after the bitter breakup with Neal. John had opened up a whole new, exciting world to her: travel to exotic places, sailing, the company of interesting and famous people. She hadn't loved him, but she had been fond of him; and she'd convinced herself she would learn to love him in time. Instead, when he revealed his dark side to her, she had learned to hate him.

Tanner said, "Didn't one of his other wives divorce him for knocking her around when he was drunk? Seems I remember reading something like that in the Miami papers a few years back. That why you're unhappy, Shea? He knock *you* around when he's drinking?"

Without answering, Shea pushed past him into the hallway. He didn't try to stop her. In the kitchen again she poured yet another cup of coffee and sat down with it. Even with her coat on and the furnace turned up, she was still cold. The heat from the mug failed to warm her hands.

She knew she ought to be afraid of Harry Tanner. But all she felt was a deep weariness. An image of Windflaw Point, the tiny beach with its treacherous undertow, flashed across the screen of her mind—and was gone again just as swiftly. Her courage, or maybe her cowardice, was gone, too. She was no longer capable of walking out to the point, letting the sea have her. Not tonight and probably not ever again.

She sat listening to the wind clamor outside. It moaned in the twisted branches of the banyan tree; scraped palm fronds against the roof tiles. Through the open window jalousies she could smell ozone mixed with the sweet fragrances of white ginger blooms. The new storm would be here soon in all its fury.

The wind kept her from hearing Tanner reenter the kitchen. She sensed his presence, looked up, and saw him standing there with his eyes on her like probes. He'd put on all of John's clothing and found a pair of Reeboks for his feet. In his left hand he held the waterproof belt that had been strapped around his waist.

"Shirt's a little snug," he said, "but a pretty good fit otherwise. Your husband's got nice taste."

Shea didn't answer.

"In clothing, in houses, and in women."

She sipped her coffee, not looking at him.

Tanner limped around the table and sat down across from her. When he laid the belt next to the bottle of rum, the pouch that bulged made a thunking sound. "Boats, too," he said. "I'll bet he keeps his best designs for himself; he's the kind that would. Am I right, Shea?"

"Yes."

"How many boats does he own?"

"Two."

"One's bound to be big. Oceangoing yacht?"

"Seventy-foot custom schooner."

"What's her name?"

"*Moneybags.*"

Tanner laughed. "Some sense of humor."

"If you say so."

"Where does he keep her? Here or Miami?"

"Miami."

"She there now?"

"Yes."

"And the other boat? That one berthed here?"

"The harbor at Merrywing."

"What kind is she?"

"A sloop," Shea said. "*Carib Princess.*"

"How big?"

"Thirty-two feet."

"She been back and forth across the Stream?"

"Several times, in good weather."

"With you at the helm?"

"No."

"You ever take her out by yourself?"

"No. He wouldn't allow it."

"But you can handle her, right? You said you know boats. You can pilot that little sloop without any trouble?"

"Why do you want to know that? Why are you asking so many questions about John's boats?"

"John's boats, John's houses, John's third wife." Tanner laughed again, just a bark this time. The wolfish smile pulled his mouth out of shape. "Are you afraid of me, Shea?"

"No."

"Not even a little?"

"Why? Should I be?"

"What do you think?"

"I'm not afraid of you," she said.

"Then how come you lied to me?"

"Lied? About what?"

"Your husband. Old John Clifford."

"I don't know what you mean."

"You said he'd be home soon. But he won't be. He's not in town with friends, he's not even on the island."

She stared silently at the steam rising from her cup. Her fingers felt cramped, as if she might be losing circulation in them.

"Well, Shea? That's the truth, isn't it."

"Yes. That's the truth."

"Where is he? Miami?"

She nodded.

"Went there on business and left you all by your lonesome."

"It isn't the first time."

"Might be the last, though." Tanner reached for the rum bottle, poured some of the dark liquid into his mug, drank, and then smacked his lips. "You want a shot of this?"

"No."

"Loosen you up a little."

"I don't need loosening up."

"You might after I tell you the truth about Harry Tanner."

"Does that mean you lied to me, too?"

"I'm afraid so. But you fessed up and now it's my turn."

In the blackness outside the wind gusted sharply, banging a loose shutter somewhere at the front of the house. Rain began to pelt down with open-faucet suddenness.

"Listen to that," Tanner said. "Sounds like we're in for a big blow, this time."

"What did you lie about?"

"Well, let's see. For starters, about how I came to be in the water tonight. My bugeye ketch didn't sink in the squall. No, *Wanderer*'s tied up at a dock in Charlotte Amalie."

She sat stiffly, waiting.

"Boat I was on didn't sink either," Tanner said. "At least as far as I know it didn't. I jumped overboard. Not long after the squall hit us."

There was still nothing for her to say.

"If I hadn't gone overboard, the two guys I was with would've shot me dead. They tried to shoot me in the water but the ketch was pitching like crazy and they couldn't see me in the dark and the rain. I guess they figured I'd drown even with a life jacket on. Or the sharks or barracuda would get me."

Still nothing.

"We had a disagreement over money. That's what most things

come down to these days—money. They thought I cheated them out of twenty thousand dollars down in Jamaica, and they were right, I did. They both put guns on me before I could do anything and I thought I was a dead man. The squall saved my bacon. Big swell almost broached us, knocked us all off our feet. I managed to scramble up the companionway and go over the side before they recovered."

The hard beat of the rain stopped as suddenly as it had begun. Momentary lull: The full brunt of the storm was minutes away yet.

"I'm not a single-hander," he said, "not a sea tramp. That's another thing I lied about. Ask me what it is I really am, Shea. Ask me how I make my living."

"I don't have to ask."

"No? Think you know?"

"Smuggling. You're a smuggler."

"That's right. Smart lady."

"Drugs, I suppose."

"Drugs, weapons, liquor, the wretched poor yearning to breathe free without benefit of a green card. You name it, I've handled it. Hell, smuggling's a tradition in these waters. Men have been doing if for three hundred years, since the days of the Spanish Main." He laughed. "A modern freebooter, that's what I am. Tanner the Pirate. Yo ho ho and a bottle of rum."

"Why are you telling me all this?"

"Why not? Don't you find it interesting?"

"No."

"Okay, I'll give it to you straight. I've got a problem—a big problem. I jumped off that ketch tonight with one thing besides the clothes on my back, and it wasn't money." He pulled the waterproof belt to him, unsnapped the pouch that bulged, and showed her what was inside. "Just this."

Her gaze registered the weapon—automatic, large caliber, lightweight frame—and slid away. She was not surprised; she had known there was a gun in the pouch when it made the thunking sound.

Tanner set it on the table within easy reach. "My two partners got my share of a hundred thousand from the Jamaica run. I might be able to get it back from them and I might not; they're a couple of hard cases and I'm not sure it's worth the risk. But I can't do anything until I quit this island. And I can't leave the usual ways because my money and my passport are both on that damn ketch. You see my dilemma, Shea?"

"I see it."

"Sure you do. You're a smart lady, like I said. What else do you see? The solution?"

She shook her head.

"Well, I've got a dandy." The predatory grin again. "You know, this really is turning into my lucky night. I couldn't have washed up in a better spot if I'd planned it. John Clifford's house, John Clifford's smart and pretty wife. And not far away, John Clifford's little sloop, the *Carib Princess*."

The rain came again, wind-driven with enough force to rattle the windows. Spray blew in through the screens behind the open jalousies. Shea made no move to get up and close the glass. Tanner didn't even seem to notice the moisture.

"Here's what we're going to do," he said. "At dawn we'll drive in to the harbor. You do have a car here? Sure you do; he wouldn't leave you isolated without wheels. Once we get there we go onboard the sloop and you take her out. If anybody you know sees us and says anything, you tell them I'm a friend or relative and John said it was okay for us to go for a sail without him."

She asked dully, "Then what?"

"Once we're out to sea? I'm not going to kill you and dump your body overboard, if that's worrying you. The only thing that's going to happen is we sail the *Carib Princess* across the Stream to Florida. A little place I know on the west coast up near Pavilion Key where you can sneak a boat in at night and keep her hidden for as long as you need to."

"And then?"

"Then I call your husband and we do some business. How much do you think he'll pay to get his wife and his sloop back safe and sound? Five hundred thousand? As much as a million?"

"My God," she said. "You're crazy."

"Like a fox."

"You couldn't get away with it. You *can't*."

"I figure I can. You think he won't pay because the marriage is on the rocks? You're wrong, Shea. He'll pay, all right. He's the kind that can't stand losing anything that belongs to him, wife or boat, and sure as hell not both at once. Plus he's had enough bad publicity; ignoring a ransom demand would hurt his image and his business and I'll make damned sure he knows it."

She shook her head again—a limp, rag-doll wobbling, as if it were coming loose from the stem of her neck.

"Don't look so miserable," Tanner said cheerfully. "I'm not such a bad guy when you get to know me, and there'll be plenty of time for us to get acquainted. And when old John pays off, I'll leave you with the sloop and you can sail her back to Miami. Okay? Give you my word on that."

He was lying: His word was worthless. He'd told her his name, the name of his ketch and where it was berthed; he wouldn't leave her alive to identify him. Not on the Florida coast. Not even here.

Automatically Shea picked up her mug, tilted it to her mouth. Dregs. Empty. She pushed back her chair, crossed to the counter, and poured the mug full again. Tanner sat relaxed, smiling, pleased with himself. The rising steam from the coffee formed a screen between them, so that she saw him as blurred, distorted. Not quite human, the way he had first seemed to her when he came out of the sea earlier.

Jumbee, she thought. Smiling evil.

The gale outside flung sheets of water at the house. The loose shutter chattered like a jackhammer until the wind slackened again.

Tanner said, "Going to be a long, wet night." He made a noisy yawning sound. "Where do you sleep, Shea?"

The question sent a spasm through her body.

"Your bedroom—where is it?"

Oh God. "Why?"

"I told you, it's going to be a long night. And I'm tired and my foot hurts and I want to lie down. But I don't want to lie down alone. We might as well start getting to know each other the best way there is."

211

No, she thought. No, no, no.

"Well, Shea? Lead the way."

No, she thought again. But her legs worked as if with a will of their own, carried her back to the table. Tanner sat forward as she drew abreast of him, started to lift himself out of the chair.

She threw the mug of hot coffee into his face.

She hadn't planned to do it, acted without thinking; it was almost as much of a surprise to her as it was to him. He yelled and pawed at his eyes, his body jerking so violently that both he and the chair toppled over sideways. Shea swept the automatic off the table and backed away with it extended at arm's length.

Tanner kicked free of the chair and scrambled unsteadily to his feet. Bright red splotches stained his cheeks where the coffee had scalded him; his eyes were murderous. He took a step toward her, stopped when he realized she was pointing his own weapon at him. She watched him struggle to regain control of himself and the situation.

"You shouldn't have done that, Shea."

"Stay where you are."

"That gun isn't loaded."

"It's loaded. I know guns, too."

"You won't shoot me." He took another step.

"I will. Don't come any closer."

"No you won't. You're not the type. I can pull the trigger on a person real easy. Have, more than once." Another step. "But not you. You don't have what it takes."

"Please don't make me shoot you. Please, please don't."

"See? You won't do it because you can't."

"Please."

"You won't shoot me, Shea."

On another night, any other night, he would have been right. But on this night—

He lunged at her.

And she shot him.

The impact of the high-caliber bullet brought him up short, as if he had walked into an invisible wall. A look of astonishment spread over his face. He took one last convulsive step before his hands came up to clutch at his chest and his knees buckled.

Shea didn't see him fall; she turned away. And the hue and cry of the storm kept her from hearing him hit the floor. When she looked again, after several seconds, he lay facedown and unmoving on the tiles. She did not have to go any closer to tell that he was dead.

There was a hollow queasiness in her stomach. Otherwise she felt nothing. She turned again, and there was a blank space of time, and then she found herself sitting on one of the chairs in the living room. She would have wept then but she had no tears. She had cried herself dry on the terrace.

After a while she became aware that she still gripped Tanner's automatic. She set it down on an end table; hesitated, then picked it up again. The numbness was finally leaving her mind, a swift release that brought her thoughts into sharpening focus. When the wind and rain lulled again she stood, walked slowly down the hall to her bedroom. She steeled herself as she opened the door and turned on the lights.

From where he lay sprawled across the bed, John's sightless eyes stared up at her. The stain of blood on his bare chest, drying now, gleamed darkly in the lamp glow.

Wild night, mad night.

She hadn't been through hell just once, she'd been through it twice. First in here and then in the kitchen.

But she hadn't shot John. She hadn't. He'd come home at nine, already drunk, and tried to make love to her, and when she denied him he'd slapped her, kept slapping her. After three long hellish years she couldn't take it anymore, not anymore. She'd managed to get the revolver out of her nightstand drawer . . . not to shoot him, just as a threat to make him leave her alone. But he'd lunged at her, in almost the same way Tanner had, and they'd struggled, and the gun had gone off. And John Clifford was dead.

She had started to call the police. Hadn't because she knew they would not believe it was an accident. John was well liked and highly respected on Salt Cay; his public image was untarnished and no one, not even his close friends, believed his second wife's divorce claim or that he could ever mistreat anyone. She had never really been accepted here—some of the cattier rich women thought she was a gold digger—and she had no friends of her own in whom she could confide. John had seen to that. There were no marks on her body to prove his abuse, either; he'd always been very careful not to leave marks.

The island police would surely have claimed she'd killed him in cold blood. She'd have been arrested and tried and convicted and put in a prison much worse than the one in which she had lived the past three years. The prospect of that was unbearable. It was what had driven her out onto the terrace, to sit and think about the undertow at Windflaw Point. The sea, in those moments, had seemed her only way out.

Now there was another way.

Her revolver lay on the floor where it had fallen. John had given it to her when they were first married, because he was away so much; and he had taught her how to use it. It was one of three handguns he'd bought illegally in Miami.

Shea bent to pick it up. With a corner of the bedsheet she wiped the grip carefully, then did the same to Tanner's automatic. That gun too, she was certain, would not be registered anywhere.

Wearily she put the automatic in John's hand, closing his fingers around it. Then she retreated to the kitchen and knelt to place the revolver in Tanner's hand. The first-aid kit was still on the table; she would use it once more, when she finished talking to the chief constable in Merrywing.

We tried to help Tanner, John and I, she would tell him. And he repaid our kindness by attempting to rob us at gunpoint. John told him we kept money in our bedroom; he took the gun out of the nightstand before I could stop him. They shot each other. John died instantly, but Tanner didn't believe his wound was as serious as it was. He made me bandage it and then kept me in the kitchen, threatening to kill me, too. I managed to catch him off guard and throw coffee in his face. When he tried to come after me the strain aggravated his wound and he collapsed and died.

If this were Miami, or one of the larger Caribbean islands, she could not hope to get away with such a story. But here the native constabulary was unsophisticated and inexperienced because there was so little crime on Salt Cay. They were much more likely to overlook the fact that John had been shot two and a half hours before Harry Tanner. Much more likely, too, to credit a double homicide involving a stranger, particularly when they investigated Tanner's background, than the accidental shooting of a respected resident who had been abusing his wife. Yes, she might just get away with it. If there was any justice left for her in this world, she would—and one day she'd leave Salt Cay a free woman again.

Out of the depths, she thought as she picked up the phone. Out of the depths. . . .

IAN RANKIN

A DEEP HOLE

Ian Rankin, another newcomer to this series, is a native of Scotland who resides in France with his family. He is the author of fourteen books and was awarded the 1992 Raymond Chandler Fulbright Fellowship in crime and detective fiction. This story, from the British anthology London Noir, *was the winner of the CWA/Macallan Short Story Award for 1994.*

I used to be a road digger, which is to say I dug up roads for a living. These days I'm a Repair Effecter for the council's Highways Department. I still dig up roads—sorry, *highways*—only now it sounds better, doesn't it? They tell me there's some guy in an office somewhere whose job is thinking up posh names for people like me, for the rubbish collectors and street sweepers and toilet attendants. (Usually they manage to stick in the word "environmental" somewhere.) This way, we're made to feel important. Must be some job that, thinking up posh names. I wonder what job title *he's* given himself. Environmental Title Coordination Executive, eh?

They call me Sam the Spade. There's supposed to be a joke there, but I don't get it. I got the name because after Robbie's got to work with the pneumatic drill, I get in about things with the spade and clear out everything he's broken up. Robbie's called "The Driller Killer." That was the name of an old horror video. I never saw it myself. I tried working with the pneumatic drill a few times. There's more pay if you operate the drill. You become *skilled* rather than unskilled labor. But after fifteen seconds I could feel the fillings popping out of my teeth. Even now my spine aches in bed at night. Too much sex, the boys say. Ha ha.

Now Daintry, his title would be something like Last Hope Cash Dispensation Executive. Or, in the old parlance, a plain moneylender. Nobody remembers Daintry's first name. He shrugged it off some time back when he was a teenager, and he hasn't been a teenager for a few years and some. He's the guy you go to on a Friday or Saturday for a few quid to see you through the weekend. And come the following week's dole check (or, if you're one of the fortunate few, pay packet) Daintry'll be waiting while you cash it, his hand out for the money he loaned plus a whack of interest.

While you're only too happy to see Daintry before the weekend, you're not so happy about him still being around *after* the weekend. You don't want to pay him back, certainly not the interest. But you do, inevitably. You do pay him back. Because he's a persistent sort of fellow with a good line in colorful threats and a ready abundance of Physical Persuasion Techniques.

I think the chief reason people didn't like Daintry was that he never made anything of himself. I mean, he still lived on the same estate as his clients, albeit in one of the two-story houses rather than the blocks of flats. His front garden was a jungle, his windowpanes filthy, and the inside of his house a thing of horror. He dressed in cheap clothes, which hung off him. He wouldn't shave for days, his hair always needed washing . . . You're getting the picture, eh? Me, when I'm not working I'm a neat and tidy sort of guy. My mum's friends, the women she gossips with, they're always shaking their heads and asking how come I never found myself a girl. They speak about me in the past tense like that, like I'm not going to find one now. On the contrary. I'm thirty-eight, and all my friends have split up with their wives by now. So there are more and more single women my age appearing around the estate. It's only a question of time. Soon it'll be Brenda's turn. She'll leave Harry, or he'll kick her out. No kids, so that's not a problem. I hear gossip that their arguments are getting louder and louder and more frequent. There are threats too, late at night after a good drink down at the club. I'm leaving you, no you're not, yes I am, well get the hell out then, I'll be back for my stuff, on you go, I wouldn't give you the satisfaction, well stay if you like.

Just like a ballet, eh? Well, I think so anyway. I've been waiting for Brenda for a long time. I can wait a little longer. I'm certainly a more attractive prospect than Daintry. Who'd move in with him? Nobody, I can tell you. He's a loner. No friends, just people he might drink with. He'll sometimes buy a few drinks for a few of the harder cases, then get them to put the frighteners on some late payer who's either getting cocky or else talking about going to the police. Not that the police would do anything. What? Around here? If they're not in Daintry's pocket, they either don't care about the place anyway or else are scared to come near. Daintry did a guy in once inside the club. A Sunday afternoon too, stabbed him in the toilets. Police came, talked to everyone in the club—nobody'd seen anything. Daintry may be a bastard, but he's *our* bastard. Besides, there's always a reason. If you haven't crossed him, you're none of his business . . . and *he'd* better not be any of *yours*.

I knew him of course. Oh yeah, we went to school together, same class all the way from five to sixteen years old. He was never quite as good as me at the subjects, but he was quiet and pretty well behaved. Until about fifteen. A switch flipped in his brain at fifteen. Actually, I'm lying: He was always better than me at arithmetic. So I suppose he was cut out for a career as a moneylender. Or, as he once described himself, a bank manager with menaces.

God knows how many people he's murdered. Can't be that many, or we'd all have noticed. That's why I thought all the information I used to give him was just part of his act. He knew word would get around about what he was asking me for, and those whispers and rumors would strengthen his reputation. That's what I always thought. I never took it seriously. As a result, I tapped him for a loan once or twice and *he never charged me a penny*. He also bought me a few drinks, and once provided a van when I wanted to sell the piano. See, he wasn't all bad. He had his good side. If it hadn't been for him, we'd never have shifted that piano, and it'd still be sitting there in the living room reminding my mother of the tunes Dad used to play on it, tunes she'd hum late into the night and then again at the crack of dawn.

It seemed strange at first that he'd want to see me. He would come over to me in pubs and sling his arm around my neck, asking if I was all right, patting me and ordering the same again. We'd hardly spoken more than a sentence at a time to one another since leaving school, but now he was smiles and reminiscences and all interested in my job of work.

"I just dig holes."

He nodded. "And that's important work, believe me. Without the likes of you, my car's suspension would be shot to hell."

Of course, his car's suspension *was* shot to hell. It was a 1973 Ford Capri with tinted windows, an air duct, and a spoiler. It was a loser's car, with dark green nylon fur on the dashboard and the door panels. The wheel arches were history, long since eaten by rust. Yet every year without fail it passed its MOT. The coincidence was, the garage mechanic was a regular client of Daintry's.

"I could get a new car," Daintry said, "but it gets me from A back to A again, so what's the point?"

There was something in this. He seldom left the estate. He lived there, shopped there, he'd been born there, and he'd die there. He never took a holiday, not even a weekend away, and he never ever ventured south of the river. He spent all his free time watching videos. The guy who runs the video shop reckoned Daintry had seen every film in the shop a dozen times over.

"He knows their numbers off by heart."

He did know lots about movies: running time, director, writer, supporting actor. He was always a hot contender when the club ran its trivia quiz. He sat in that smelly house of his with the curtains shut and a blue light flickering. He was a film junkie. And somehow, he managed to spend all his money on them. He must have done, or what else did he do with it? His Rolex was a fake, lighter than air when you picked it up, and probably his gold jewelry was fake, too. Maybe somewhere there's a secret bank account with thousands salted away, but I don't think so. Don't ask me why, I just don't think so.

Roadworks. That's the information I passed on to Daintry.

That's what he wanted to talk to me about. Roadworks. *Major* roadworks.

"You know the sort of thing," he'd say, "anywhere where you're digging a *big* hole. Maybe building a flyover or improving drainage. Major roadworks."

Sure enough, I had access to this sort of information. I just had to listen to the various crews talking about what they were working on and where they were doing the work. Over tea and biscuits in the canteen, I could earn myself a few drinks and a pint glass of goodwill.

"How deep does that need to be?" Daintry would ask.

"I don't know, eight, maybe ten feet."

"By what?"

"Maybe three long, the same wide."

And he'd nod. This was early in the game, and I was slow catching on. You're probably much faster, right? So you know why he was asking. But I was puzzled the first couple of times. I mean, I thought maybe he was interested in the . . . what's it, the infrastructure. He wanted to see improvements. Then it dawned on me: No, what he wanted to see were big holes. Holes that would be filled in with concrete and covered over with huge immovable objects, like bridge supports, for example. Holes where bodies could be hidden. I didn't say anything, but I knew that's what we were talking about. We were talking about Human Resource Disposal.

And Daintry knew that I knew. He'd wink from behind his cigarette smoke, using those creased stinging eyes of his. Managing to look a little like his idol Robert de Niro. In *Goodfellas*. That's what Daintry would say. He'd always be making physical comparisons like that. Me, I thought he was much more of a Joe Pesci. But I didn't tell him that. I didn't even tell him that Pesci isn't pronounced pesky.

He knew I'd blab about our little dialogues, and I did, casually like. And word spread. And suddenly Daintry was a man to be feared. But he wasn't really. He was just stupid, with a low flash point. And if you wanted to know what sort of mood he was going to be in, you only had to visit the video shop.

"He's taken out *Goodfellas* and *Godfather 3*." So you knew there was trouble coming. Now you really didn't want to cross him. But if he'd taken out soft core or a Steve Martin or even some early Brando, everything was going to be all right. He must have been on a gangster high the night he went round to speak with Mr. and Mrs. McAndrew. In his time, Mr. McAndrew had been a bit of a lad himself, but he was in his late seventies with a wife ten years younger. They lived in one of the estate's nicer houses. They'd bought it from the council and had installed a fancy front door, double-glazed windows, you name it, and all the glass was that leaded crisscross stuff. It wasn't cheap. These days, Mr. McAndrew spent all his time in the garden. At the front of the house he had some beautiful flower beds, with the back garden given over to vegetables. In the summer, you saw him playing football with his grandchildren.

"Just like," as somebody pointed out, "Marlon Brando in *The Godfather*." This was apt in its way since, like I say, despite the gardening, Mr. McAndrew's hands were probably cleaner these days than they had been in the past.

How he got to owe Daintry money I do not know. But Daintry, believe me, would have been only too happy to lend. There was McAndrew's reputation for a start. Plus the McAndrews seemed prosperous enough, he was sure to see his money and interest returned. But not so. Whether out of sheer cussedness or because he really couldn't pay, McAndrew had been holding out on Daintry. I saw it as a struggle between the old gangster and the new. Maybe Daintry did, too. Whatever, one night he walked into the McAndrews' house and beat up Mrs. McAndrew in front of her husband. He had two heavies with him, one to hold Mr. McAndrew, one to hold Mrs. McAndrew. Either one of them could have dropped dead of a heart attack right then and there.

There were murmurs in the street the next day, and for days afterward. Daintry, it was felt, had overstepped the mark. He was out of order. To him it was merely business, and he'd gotten the money from McAndrew so the case was closed. But he now found himself shorter of friends than ever before. Which is probably why he turned to me when he wanted the favor done. Simply, he couldn't get anyone else to do it.

"You want me to what?"

He'd told me to meet him in the children's play park. We walked around the path. There was no one else in the park. It was a battlefield, all broken glass and rocks. Dog shit was smeared up and down the chute, the swings had been wrapped around themselves until they couldn't be reached. The round-about had disappeared one night, leaving only a metal stump in place. You'd be safer sending your kids to play on the North Circular.

"It's quite simple," Daintry said. "I want you to get rid of a package for me. There's good money in it."

"How much money?"

"A hundred."

I paused at that. A hundred pounds, just to dispose of a package . . .

"But you'll need a deep hole," said Daintry.

Yeah, of course. It was *that* kind of package. I wondered who it was. There was a story going around that Daintry had set up a nice little disposal operation that dealt with Human Resource Waste from miles around. Villains as far away as Watford and Luton were bringing "packages" for him to dispose of. But it was just a story, just one of many.

"A hundred," I said, nodding.

"All right, one twenty-five. But it's got to be tonight."

I knew just the hole.

They were building a new footbridge over the North Circular, over to the west near Wembley. I knew the gang wouldn't be working night shift: The job wasn't that urgent and who could afford the shift bonus these days? There'd be a few deep holes there all right. And while the gang might notice a big black bin bag at the bottom of one of them, they wouldn't do anything about it. People were always dumping rubbish down the holes. It all got covered over with concrete, gone and quite forgotten. I hadn't seen a dead body before, and I didn't intend seeing one now. So I insisted it was all wrapped up before I'd stick it in the car boot.

Daintry and I stood in the lockup he rented and looked down at the black bin liner.

"It's not so big, is it?" I said.

"I broke the rigor mortis," he explained. "That way you can get it into the car."

I nodded and went outside to throw up. I felt better after that. Curried chicken never did agree with me.

"I'm not sure I can do it," I said, wiping my mouth.

Daintry was ready for me. "Ah, that's a pity." He stuck his hands in his pockets, studying the tips of his shoes. "How's your old mum by the way? Keeping well is she?"

"She's fine, yeah . . ." I stared at him. "What do you mean?"

"Nothing, nothing. Let's hope her good health continues." He looked up at me, a glint in his eye. "Still fancy Brenda?"

"Who says I do?"

He laughed. "Common knowledge. Must be the way your trousers bulge whenever you see her shadow."

"That's rubbish."

"She seems well enough, too. The marriage is a bit shaky, but what can you expect? That Harry of hers is a monster." Daintry paused, fingering his thin gold neck chain. "I wouldn't be surprised if he took a tap to the skull one of these dark nights."

"Oh?"

He shrugged. "Just a guess. Pity you can't . . ." He touched the bin bag with his shoe. "You know." And he smiled.

We loaded the bag together. It wasn't heavy, and was easy enough to maneuver. I could feel a foot and a leg, or maybe a hand and an arm. I tried not to think about it. Imagine him threatening my old mum! He was lucky I'm not quick to ignite, not like him, or it'd've been broken-nose city and hospital cuisine. But what he said about Brenda's husband put thought of my mum right out of my head.

We closed the boot and I went to lock it.

"He's not going to make a run for it," Daintry said.

"I suppose not," I admitted. But I locked the boot anyway.

Then the car wouldn't start, and when it did start it kept cutting out, like the engine was flooding or something. Maybe a block in the fuel line. I'd let it get very low before the last fill of petrol. There might be a lot of rubbish swilling around in the tank. After a couple of miles it cut out on me at some traffic lights in Dalston. I rolled down my window and waved for the cars behind me to pass. I was content to sit for a few moments and let everything settle, my stomach included. One car stopped alongside me. And Jesus, wouldn't you know it: It was a cop car.

"Everything all right?" the cop in the passenger seat called.

"Yeah, just stalled."

"You can't sit there forever."

"No."

"If it doesn't start next go, push your car to the side of the road."

"Yeah, sure." He made no move to leave. Now the driver was looking at me too, and traffic was building up behind us. Nobody sounded their horn. Everyone could see that a cop car was talking with the driver of another vehicle. Sweat tickled my ears. I turned the ignition, resisting the temptation to pump the accelerator. The engine rumbled, then came to life. I grinned at the cops and started forward, going through an amber light.

They could probably arrest me for that. It was five minutes before I stopped staring in the rearview mirror. But I couldn't see them. They'd turned off somewhere. I let all my fear and tension out in a rasping scream, then remembered the window was still rolled down. I wound it back up again. I decided not to go straight to the bridge site, but to drive around a bit, let all the traffic clear along with my head.

I pulled into a bus stop just before the North Circular and changed into my work clothes. That way I wouldn't look suspicious. Good thinking, eh? It was my own idea, one Daintry had appreciated. I had a question for him now, and the question was: Why wasn't he doing this himself? But he wasn't around to answer it. And I knew the answer anyway: He'd rather pay someone else to do dangerous jobs. Oh yes, it was dangerous; I knew that now. Worth a lot more than a hundred and twenty-five nicker, sixty of which were already in my pocket in the shape of dirty old pound notes. Repayments, doubtless, from Daintry's punters. Grubby money, but still money. I hoped it hadn't come from the McAndrews.

I sat at the bus stop for a while. A car pulled in behind me. Not a police car this time, just an ordinary car. I heard the driver's door slam shut. Footsteps, a tap at my window. I looked out. The man was bald and middle-aged, dressed in suit and tie. A lower-executive look, a sales rep maybe, that sort of person. He was smiling in a friendly enough sort of fashion. And if he wanted to steal my car and jimmy open the boot, well that was fine, too.

I wound down my window. "Yeah?"

"I think I missed my turning," he said. "Can you tell me where we are, roughly?"

"Roughly," I said, "roughly, we're about a mile north of Wembley."

"And that's west London?" His accent wasn't quite English, not southern English. Welsh or a Geordie or a Scouser maybe.

"About as west as you can get," I told him. Yeah, the wild west.

"I can't be too far away then. I want St. John's Wood. That's west too, isn't it?"

"Yeah, not far at all." These poor sods, you came across them a lot in my line of work. New to the city and pleading directions, getting hot and a bit crazy as the signposts and one-ways led them further into the maze. I felt sorry for them a lot of the time. It wasn't their fault. So I took my time as I directed him toward Harlesden, miles away from where he wanted to be.

"It's a shortcut," I told him. He seemed pleased to have some local knowledge. He went back to his car and sounded his horn in a thank-you as he drove off. I know, that was a bit naughty of me, wasn't it? Well, there you go. That was my spot of devilry for the night. I started my own car and headed back onto the road.

There was a sign-off saying WORKS ACCESS ONLY, so I signaled and drove between two rows of striped traffic cones. Then I stopped the car. There were no other cars around, just the dark shapes of earth-moving equipment and cement mixers. Fine and dandy. Cars and lorries roared past, but they didn't give me a second's notice. They weren't about to slow down enough to take in any of the scene. The existing overpass and built-up

225

verges hid me pretty well from civilization. Before unloading the package, I went for a recce, taking my torch with me.

And of course there were no decent holes to be found. They'd been filled in already. The concrete was hard, long metal rods poking out of it like the prongs on a fork. There were a few shallow cuts in the earth, but nothing like deep enough for the purpose. Hell's teeth and gums. I went back to the car, thinking suddenly how useful a car phone would be. I wanted to speak to Daintry. I wanted to ask him what to do. A police car went past. I saw its brake lights glow. They'd noticed my car, but they didn't stop. No, but they might come back round again. I started the car and headed out onto the carriageway.

Only a few minutes later, there was a police car behind me. He sat on my tail for a while, then signaled to overtake, drawing level with me and staying there. The passenger checked me out. They were almost certainly the ones who'd seen me parked back at the bridge site. The passenger saw that I was wearing overalls and a standard issue work jacket. I sort of waved at him. He spoke to the driver, and the patrol car accelerated away.

Lucky for me he hadn't seen the tears in my eyes. I was terrified and bursting for a piss. I knew that I had to get off this road. My brain was numb. I couldn't think of another place to dump the body. I didn't want to think about it at all. I just wanted rid of it. I think I saw the traveling salesman hurtle past, fleeing Harlesden. He was heading out of town.

I came off the North Circular and just drove around, crawling eastward until I knew the streets so well it was like remote control. I knew exactly where I'd effected repairs, and where repairs were still waiting to be carried out. There was one pothole on a sharp bend that could buckle a wheel. That was down as a priority, and would probably be started on tomorrow. I calmed myself a little with memories of holes dug and holes filled in, the rich aroma of hot tarmac, the jokes yelled out by the Driller Killer. I'd never worked out why he'd try telling jokes to someone wearing industrial ear protectors beside a pneumatic drill.

Seeking safety, I came back into the estate. I felt better immediately, my head clearing. I knew what I had to do. I had to face up to Daintry. I'd give him back the money, of course, less a quid or two for petrol, and I'd explain that nowhere was safe. Mission impossible. I didn't know what he'd do. It depended on whether tonight was a *Goodfellas* night or not. He might slap me about a bit. He might stop buying me drinks.

He might do something to my mum.

Or to Brenda.

I'd have to talk to him. Maybe we could do a deal. Maybe I'd have to kill him. Yeah, then I'd just have the *two* bodies to worry about. In order to stop worrying about the first, I stopped by the lockup. This was one of a cul-de-sac of identical garages next to some wasteland that had been planted with trees and was now termed a Conservation Area. The man in the High Street had certainly conserved his energy thinking up that one.

There were no kids about, so I used a rock to break the lock, then hauled the door open with my crowbar. I stopped for a moment and wondered what I was going to do now. I'd meant to leave the body in the garage, but I'd had to break the locks to get in, so now if I left the body there anybody at all could wander along and find it. But then I thought, this is *Daintry's* garage. Everybody knows it, and nobody in their right mind would dare trespass. So I hauled the package inside, closed the door again, and left a rock in front of it. I was confident I'd done my best.

So now it was time to go talk with Daintry. The easy part of the evening was past. But first I went home. I don't know why, I just wanted to see my mum. We used to be on the eleventh floor, but they'd moved us eventually to the third because the lifts kept breaking and mum couldn't climb eleven flights. I took the stairs tonight, relieved not to find any of the local kids shooting up or shagging between floors. Mum was sitting with Mrs. Gregg from along the hall. They were talking about Mrs. McAndrew.

"Story she gave her doctor was she fell down the stairs."

"Well, I think it's a shame."

Mum looked up and saw me. "I thought you'd be down at the club."

"Not tonight, Mum."

"Well, that makes a change."

"Hallo, Mrs. Gregg."

"Hallo, love. There's a band on tonight, you know."
"Where?"
She rolled her eyes. "At the club. Plenty of lovely girls too, I'll bet."
They wanted rid of me. I nodded. "Just going to my room. Won't be long."
I lay on my bed, the same bed I'd slept in since I was . . . well, since before I could remember. The room had been painted and papered in the last year. I stared at the wallpaper, lying on one side and then on the other. This room, it occurred to me, was probably the size of a prison cell. It might even be a bit smaller. What was it, eight feet square? But I'd always felt comfortable enough here. I heard my mum laughing at something Mrs. Gregg said, and pop music from the flat downstairs. These weren't very solid flats, thin walls and floors. They'd knock our block down one of these days. I liked it well enough, though. I didn't want to lose it. I didn't want to lose my mum.
I decided that I was probably going to have to kill Daintry.
I packed some clothes into a black holdall, just holding back the tears. What would I say to my mum? I've got to go away for a while? I'll phone you when I can? I recalled all the stories I'd heard about Daintry. How some guy from Trading Standards had been tailing him and was sitting in his car at the side of the road by the shops when a sawn-off shotgun appeared in the window and a voice told him to get the hell out of there pronto. Guns and knives, knuckle-dusters and a machete. Just stories . . . just stories.
I knew he wouldn't be expecting *me* to try anything. He'd open his door, he'd let me in, he'd turn his back to lead me through to the living room. That's when I'd do it. When his back was turned. It was the only safe and certain time I could think of. Anything else and I reckoned I'd lose my bottle. I left the holdall on my bed and went through to the kitchen. I took time at the open drawer, choosing my knife. Nothing too grand, just a simple four-inch blade at the end of a wooden handle. I stuck it in my pocket.
"Just nipping out for some fresh air, Mum."
"Bye, then."

"See you."

And that was that. I walked back down the echoing stairwell with my mind set on murder. It wasn't like the films. It was just . . . well, *ordinary*. Like I was going to fetch fish and chips or something. I kept my hand on the knife handle. I wanted to feel comfortable with it. But my legs were a bit shaky. I had to keep locking them at the knees, holding on to a wall or a lamppost and taking deep breaths. It was a five-minute walk to Daintry's, but I managed to stretch it to ten. I passed a couple of people I vaguely knew, but didn't stop to talk. I didn't trust my teeth not to chatter, my jaw not to lock.

And to tell you the truth, I was relieved to see that there was someone standing on the doorstep, another visitor. I felt my whole body relax. The man crouched to peer through the letter box, then knocked again. As I walked down the path toward him, I saw that he was tall and well-built, with a black leather jacket and short black hair.

"Isn't he in?"

The man turned his head slowly toward me. I didn't like the look of his face. It was gray and hard like the side of a house.

"Doesn't look like it," he said. "Any idea where he'd be?"

He was standing up straight now, his head hanging down over mine. Police, I thought for a second. But he wasn't police. I swallowed. I started to shake my head, but then I had an idea. I released my grip on the knife.

"If he's not in he's probably down at the club," I said. "Do you know where it is?"

"No."

"Go back down to the bottom of the road, take a left, and when you come to the shops it's up a side road between the launderette and the chip shop."

He studied me. "Thanks."

"No problem," I said. "You know what he looks like?"

He nodded in perfect slow motion. He never took his eyes off me.

"Right, then," I said. "Oh, and you might have to park outside the shops. The car park's usually full when there's a band on."

"There's a band?"

"In the club." I smiled. "It gets noisy, you can hardly hear a word that's said to you, even in the toilets."

"Is that so?"

"Yes," I said, "that is so."

Then I walked back down the path and gave him a slight wave as I headed for home. I made sure I walked home, too. I didn't want him thinking I was on my way to the club ahead of him.

"Short walk," Mum said. She was pouring tea for Mrs. Gregg.

"Bit cold."

"Cold?" squeaked Mrs. Gregg. "A lad your age shouldn't feel the cold."

"Have you seen my knife?" Mum asked. She was looking down at the cake she'd made. It was on one of the better plates and hadn't been cut yet. I brought the knife out of my pocket.

"Here you are, Mum."

"What's it doing in your pocket?"

"The lock on the car boot's not working. I'd to cut some string to tie it shut."

"Do you want some tea?"

I shook my head. "I'll leave you to it," I said. "I'm off to bed."

It was the talk of the estate the next morning, how Daintry had been knifed to death in a toilet cubicle, just as the band was finishing its encore. They were some sixties four-piece, still performing long past their sell-by. That's what people said who were there. And they'd compensated for a lack of ability by cranking the sound system all the way up. You not only couldn't hear yourself think, you couldn't *think*.

I suppose they have to make a living as best they can. We all do.

It was the assistant manager who found Daintry. He was doing his nightly check of the club to see how many drunks had managed to fall asleep in how many hidden places. Nobody used the end cubicle of the gents' much; it didn't have any toilet seat. But there sat Daintry, not caring anymore about the lack of amenities. Police were called, staff and clientele interviewed, but no one had anything much to say.

Well, not to the police at any rate. But there was plenty of gossip on the streets and in the shops and in the lifts between neighbors. And slowly a story emerged. Mr. McAndrew, remember, had been a lad at one time. He was rumored still to have a few contacts, a few friends who owed him. Or maybe he just stumped up cash. Whatever, everyone knew Mr. McAndrew had put out the contract on Daintry. And, as also agreed, good riddance to him. On a Friday night, too. So anyone who'd tapped him for a loan could see the sun rise on Monday morning with a big, wide smile.

Meantime, the body was found in Daintry's lockup. Well, the police knew who was responsible for that, didn't they? Though they did wonder about the broken locks. Kids most likely, intent on burglary but doing a runner when they saw the corpse. Seemed feasible to me, too.

Mr. McAndrew, eh? I watched him more closely after that. He still looked to me like a nice old man. But then it was only a story after all, only one of many. Me, I had other things to think about. I knew I could do it now. I could take Brenda away from Harry. Don't ask me why I feel so sure, I just do.

JUSTIN SCOTT

AN EYE FOR A TOOTH

Connecticut author Justin Scott, making his first appearance in this series, has published fourteen mystery novels and thrillers. This is one of his few short stories, and brought him an Edgar nomination from the Mystery Writers of America.

Hagopian waited for the shooting to stop before he ventured out of his Amsterdam Avenue Luggage Repair. On the sidewalk lay one body only: Ramos, selling crack, cheating his supplier. Hagopian—who was thirty-eight, looked a wizened sixty with three days' beard on his sunken cheeks, and felt seventy—was astonished at how long it had taken someone to shoot the fool.

A small boy knelt over the body, weeping. He scrambled into the crowd as the first of many police cars came screaming like artillery shells. Enormous blue-coated officers demanded to know who'd seen it happen.

Hagopian hesitated, torn between his instinct to hide and a powerful fear that if the police came into his shop to interrogate him they might discover his illegal apartment. If only he had a green card. The eight thousand he had already paid the immigration lawyer—who also happened to be his landlord—bought no peace of mind when a huge policeman asked, "Wha'd you see, Pop?"

Hagopian froze. His English, not yet reliable, failed him under pressure. He couldn't remember "Pop." His first language was Armenian; his second, the Russian they'd beaten into him in the Soviet army; his third and fourth, the Afghan people's Peshto and Dari. The lawyer/landlord had laughed, "You sound like a Polack."

"You see anything? . . . Hey, Pops? Wake up! This your store?"

"Inside, I am fixing," Hagopian managed at last.

"You saw out the window."

Hagopian shook his head. The window of the basement shop was barred, the glass filthy, with luggage heaped behind it.

"What happened when you heard the shots?"

Hagopian gestured at the body. "Is kill-ed."

"Hey, Detective?" the cop called. "Got a live one here."

Hagopian felt his blood congeal. Uniformed militia were one thing, detectives quite another. But he got a pleasant surprise when a pretty blond flashed her badge and said, "Detective Dee. How are you doing, sir? A little shook up?"

"Shooking," Hagopian agreed.

"What is your name, please?"

"Hagopian," Hagopian admitted, swiftly reassessing his predicament. Detective Dee spoke gently, but she had eyes like a blizzard in the Hindu Kush.

"It would appear this gentleman was shot right outside your shop. I wonder if you can help me in my investigation. This *is* your shop?"

Hagopian nodded.

"You repair luggage," she prompted, reading the signs on the railing and the door.

"Luggage. Handbags. Zippers. I am fixing zippers many times."

"What's a 'trank'?"

"Trank? Ah!" Hagopian smiled and for a moment he looked more like the young man he might have been had he made it to Manhattan a decade earlier. "I am drawing—writing—sign when I come-ed," he explained. "Old sign." He pointed at the yellow sign on the stair railing he had hand-lettered in black print. Then he directed the detective's attention to the nearly identical sign on his battered tin door. "New sign. I am meaning 'trunk.' No 'trank.' You get?"

She smiled. But Hagopian was soon back in the ice fields. "Do you know the name of the victim?"

He was careful to first look at Ramos, who had bled into the gutter.

"No."

"Never seen him before?" she persisted.

Conditioned by a lifetime of dodging officially generated misery, Hagopian hunched deep inside the quilted jacket he wore indoors and out, and commenced a drift into anonymity. His body seemed to shrink. His eyes emptied. His cheeks sunk deeper.

"Mr. Hagopian, did you see who shot that man?"

"No."

"Did you hear the shots?"

"No."

"Mr. Hagopian, five shots were heard blocks away. Are you *sure* you didn't hear them ten feet in front of your shop?"

The detective misinterpreted Hagopian's cringe as a shrug. "Let's see some ID, sir. Driver's license? Visa?"

Hagopian swept an apologetic arm over the front of his shop, the barred window blocked by luggage, the bent tin door, the yellow signs with block lettering. "Trank" was the only misspelling. Although every time he saw the squeezed-in "HANDbags," he was reminded that he was no longer a man who planned ahead.

She wrote his name down in her book and lectured him like a schoolteacher: "This isn't a bad neighborhood, yet. But it's gonna get worse until people like you help cops like me. Now come on, Mr. Hagopian. You're a neighborhood businessman, after all, and . . ."

As she scolded and cajoled, Hagopian stared at his feet. He watched from the corner of his eye the body, the ambulance attendants, the cops questioning his neighbors. For relief, he allowed his attention to settle on Consuela, the round and lovely Spanish woman who belonged to Eduardo, dispatcher of the Bolívar Car Service. Consuela tossed him a kind smile. Sadly, Eduardo carried a knife.

"Urban violence won't be stopped until good people stand up and be counted," Detective Dee was going on.

Hagopian almost smiled. Urban violence? One body? Urban

violence was a Russian tank shelling the ground-floor supports of an apartment building until the people upstairs were spilled into the street. Urban violence was a gunship strafing city buses. Urban violence was . . . many things this pretty little American would never know.

She droned on. He let his mind wander to happier things—to the pleasures of his new home. He could buy cooked food from a dozen nationalities in this one block. Bookstores sold tens of thousands of books. The library lent them for free.

Around the corner, ballerinas served as waitresses in the Cafe Lalo. He could splurge three dollars for a cappuccino, heap it with sugar, steep himself in the warm talk around him, the music, the bakery smells, celebrate the winter light streaming in and pretend he was in Moscow, inside a Party-only cafe he had only seen through the window.

Too skinny, the ballerinas. Better this voluptuous policewoman. Or Consuela. Best, the beautiful daughter of the proprietor of the Amsterdam Afghanistan Restaurant. He couldn't bear to go in, but through the window he admired her long black hair and violet eyes—exactly like the girl he had married in the war.

"Oh, god," said Detective Dee, patting Hagopian on the arm. "Please don't cry."

"Excusing, please," he asked, and struggled in a trembling voice to explain. "A person remembered."

Detective Dee looked like she wished she hadn't reported to work that day. "Here's my card, Mr. Hagopian. If you remember anything about the dead gentleman shot outside your shop, please call me immediately."

Hagopian promised he would, to make her go away, and escaped at last into his shop. It was as dim as a cave, ten feet wide and twelve feet deep, heaped floor to ceiling with bags repaired, bags awaiting repair, and bags forgotten—some by his customers, some by Hagopian.

Through these leather and vinyl mountains twisted a narrow ravine. Hagopian followed it past his workbench and through a curtain into his living quarters, a windowless storeroom that contained a single bed, a hot plate, and a humming refrigerator he had found on the sidewalk.

He set his tea kettle on the hot plate and shuffled out to his sewing machine. The boy who had grieved for Ramos was crouched in the shadows of the shop with tears in his eyes and a gun in his hand.

Robbery? Hagopian looked without looking. His money was safe in the scuffed backpack that seemed to be waiting its turn at the sewing machine.

The gun—a cheap and serviceable rust-pitted 9mm auto pistol, Hagopian noted—looked enormous in the little hand. But it pointed so steadily at his face that gun, hand, and the scrawny child himself might have been stamped from the same metal.

Wire-thin arms poked from a dirty red sweatshirt that read RALPH LAUREN POLO and hung like an empty garment bag. His skin was gray, his nose as aquiline as a Spanish grandee's, his hair as black and shiny as that of the South American Indians who delivered for the Korean liquor store. His eyes were red-rimmed, wet, and determined.

Hagopian recognized him from the neighborhood and attempted a cautious smile. "Are kite boy? Yes?"

His little jaw dropped. His eyes narrowed. "Say what? How you know that?"

"Is not pointing gun . . ."

"Why you call me kite boy?"

Hagopian explained that he had seen him flying kites on Eighty-third Street.

"I got no money for kites."

Hagopian asked the boy's name. It was Hector.

". . . Gun, I am thinking . . ."

The gun stayed right where it was, while Hagopian explained how much he had admired the kites little Hector made from plastic straws and tissue paper. The other children had kites from the stationery shop. Hector's flew higher. "Like eagle. Great airplane engineer when grown. Gun is pointing—"

"I got business when the cops split."

"Cops . . . Perhaps I am locking door. Perhaps pointing gun elsewhere."

"Don't move!"

"Please, Hector. I am not telling. I am locking door so cop aren't walking in."

"If you run, I'll bang holes in your back."

Hagopian promised that would not be necessary and walked slowly down the ravine, carefully keeping his hands in sight, and turned the massive Fox Lock. "All safe. See? Safe."

"Stay where I can see you, man. *What's that?*" Hector jumped down from the bags, and leveled the weapon at the whistling behind the curtain. Frightened, he looked even younger.

"Tea boil-ed," Hagopian assured him. "Wanting tea?"

"Got any food?"

"Perhaps we are looking inside refrigerator."

"You got candy?"

"Cookies."

"Get 'em."

Hagopian edged past the gun, poured boiling water on a tea bag in a mug and grabbed the boy a half-eaten bag of Oreos, rustling the plastic first to rout the roaches.

Hector finished the cookies before Hagopian's tea had cooled enough to drink. "What business you are having?" he asked.

"Justice."

"Justice? What is this justice? Police?"

"Not cops. *Justice.* Do right from wrong."

"What wrong?"

"The sonofabitch Luis shot Ramos."

Hagopian covered his ears. "No, no, no. I am not hearing." Hot-tempered Luis Carbona, the most vicious thug in the neighborhood, was a customer. Hagopian was holding a fancy leather bag he had repaired for him.

"I saw him. Luis shot him in the back. Ramos didn't even get to pull his gun."

"That gun?"

"I took it off Ramos before the cops came. So I can bang Luis."

"Why you?"

"Ramos and me, I think we have the same father."

"Wait, wait, wait," said Hagopian. "You're a boy, you can't—"

"Who's going to stop me? You?"

The contempt in his eyes mirrored a helpless old man, but Hagopian persisted. "That not justice. What do you call it? Reverse—? No. Revenge."

"You got it, man."

"Eye for eye, is saying in my country."

"Same here."

"Now everybody blind."

Hector shrugged. "Here, guy bangs you, you bang him back."

"No, no, no. Here—" Hagopian could hardly believe the thought he was about to express; he expressed it anyway because, as much as he feared government, chaos was worse— "Here, seeing murder, you tell cop."

"No way. Cops'll lock him up, two years he's out. I got a cousin, shot in the Bronx? They catch the guy on video? Security camera? Cops a plea? Judge gives him two years in Rikers. He's out in nine months 'cause they got no room. Killed my cousin and he's back on the street. I got another cousin? Amelia? Customs catches her with a little coke at Kennedy Airport. Federal offense. Ten years. Hard time. My mom said she won't get out of jail 'til she's *thirty*. For a little coke? And the guy who kills my cousin, he gets out in nine months?" He stroked the gun. "Luis ain't gonna get out of *this* in no months."

Hagopian shook his head, struggling to explain that even if revenge was justice, it was not practical. "This Luis is very bad?"

"He kills for the drug dealers."

"He has friends?"

"Yeah?"

"Maybe they are coming to you for 'justice'?"

"I don't care, man. They come after me, I'll bang them, too."

"How old are you?"

Hector claimed to be twelve. Outside on Amsterdam a police siren whooped. The boy looked out that way and Hagopian took the opportunity to snap the gun out of his hand.

"Hey! You bastard. You f—. Hey, what are you doin', man?"

Hagopian's fingers flew and before the boy's astonished eyes the gun disintegrated into a tidy heap of metal parts.

"How you do that?"

"Practice."

Hagopian could have added, but hadn't the English, that skills mastered at night, in the rain, while people were shooting, were never forgotten. Just as he would never forget a child, lost on such a night. Shuffling sear spring, main spring, and recoil spring, he emptied the magazine and poked disdainfully at the dirty slide.

"Rust-ed." Hagopian snapped his fingers. "Behind you. WD-40!"

Hector, round-eyed, passed him the spray can Hagopian used to free corroded zippers and snaps. Quickly, methodically, he cleaned the gun and reassembled the now-glistening parts.

It was the first gun he had touched since 1991 when he abandoned his own in the men's room of De Gaulle Airport—a weapon he had carried four years in Afghanistan, home to Armenia, through the Azerbaijan war, all the way across Europe to Paris, fifty feet from the airport security metal detectors.

He wished he could tell Hector how frightening that last fifty feet had been, walking like a naked man. Then maybe the boy would know what "justice" cost.

Suddenly, a fist pounded the tin door. "Hey, open up! You got my bag, man. It's Luis. Open up or I'll kick the door down."

Hector whipped the gun off the worktable.

"No," said Hagopian.

"I'll bang that fucker right through the door. You try and stop me, I'll bang you, too."

"Already you are stop-ed."

"Say what?"

Hagopian held up a tiny steel stud. "How you call? Fire pin."

"You fucker."

"You hiding."

"I'll get another gun, man. You can't stop me."

"Yes, yes, yes. But first, hiding . . . There!" He shooed Hector through the back-room curtain. Luis resumed pounding, but

Hagopian paused at his workbench before he shuffled to the door. He unlocked it and blinked out at Luis Carbona, a Latin with the dead gaze of a mountain wolf.

"Yes?"

"My bag, man. Give me my bag."

As usual, he had left his BMW with the door open and the motor running—a contemptuous dare that Hagopian likened to the custom in his part of the world of massing tanks at the border to remind neighbors who was dangerous.

"Receipt, please?"

"Screw that, man. You know my bag. Black leather. Strap came loose."

Hagopian cast a dubious look into the darkness behind him, then shuffled through the bag mountain, returning with Luis's many-zippered carryall dangling by the broken strap.

"Is not ready."

"*What?*" He seized Hagopian's collar and lifted him off his feet. "I tole you a week ago. You tole me she be ready."

"Is very hard fixing inside. Putting down, please. I show." Luis flung him down and stood over him, his eyes hot, as Hagopian demonstrated how the strap had to be sewn from within. "Is good bag."

"Shit! I'm on a eight o'clock outta Kennedy. I'm leaving *here* at five-thirty. You got two hours or—" he shoved Hagopian against the stack of luggage "—or mine won't be the only bag 'is not ready.' "

Hagopian believed him. Drugs, of course, paid for Luis's airline tickets between North and South America—not that he carried himself, Consuela had assured Hagopian during one of their chats in the morning sun. She called Luis a "mule driver," an overseer of the peasant women so often arrested at Customs, like Hector's cousin. "*Muy malo,*" the liquid Spanish had poured like honey from her lips. *Malo*, for sure. Ask Ramos on the sidewalk.

Cursing his impulse to save Hector from himself, Hagopian hurried to his workbench. He had no illusions about children—not in a world where eleven-year-olds rolled hand grenades into markets—but he did have hope.

Had his son survived, he'd have been Hector's age. And yet the connection he felt with this little boy ran deeper, into his own childhood, when the world had still seemed boundless. Was it possible, he wondered grimly, that Ramos was not the only fool on Amsterdam Avenue?

"Is gone-ed," he called.

Hector pushed through the curtain. "Fix the gun."

"Later."

"I told you, you don't fix it, I'll get another. I know where."

Hagopian did not look up from his sewing machine. "Later."

"When?"

"Eight o'clock. In airport."

"Say what?"

"So neighborhood not seeing you shooting. Yes?"

"Yes!"

Hagopian told him to find out what airplane Luis Carbona flew on: Hector hesitated in the doorway.

"What are you doing?"

"I do what I do." He hunched over his machine.

"Don't forget the firing pin."

Two hours later, Luis Carbona slung his bag on his shoulder, told Hagopian he'd pay him when he got back to Manhattan, and raced off in his BMW. Hagopian hurried next door to the Bolívar Car Service. He fidgeted nervously behind a customer who asked for a receipt, and finally reached the bulletproof window that protected the dispatcher's desk.

"¿Cómo está, Eduardo? I am hiring car."

"Got any money?"

"How much?"

"Where you goin'?"

"Kennedy Airport."

"Twenty-five bucks plus tolls."

"As I am coming both directions, perhaps we are agreeing forty bucks."

"Fifty bucks—plus waiting—plus tolls."

Hagopian had sixty in his tattered change purse. The zipper stuck. Eduardo sneered.

Hagopian apologized: "How you say? 'Shoemaker's children get no Adidas. . . .' Ah, here! We go now."

"You gotta wait. Rush hour. I got no drivers."

Hagopian snatched back his money. "No waiting. Taking taxi."

"I'll drive him," said a honey voice, and there was Consuela, all round and dark, shiny white smile, red lips and fingernails, lush hair like a twist of night. And there was Eduardo, caught between greed for the fifty dollars and his suspicions. "Gimme the money."

As he followed her tight jeans to the car, Hagopian felt years slide from his body like melting snow. Hector ran from Caesar's Pizza clutching a greasy bag.

"Where you going?" demanded Consuela.

"I'm with him."

"Hector, if Eduardo finds pizza on his seats, you're dead meat."

"Where's the gun?" Hector whispered.

"Gun fine. Where's change?"

Hector returned fifty cents. As soon as he finished his slice, he started whispering to see the gun, despite Hagopian's warning nods in the direction of Consuela, who was cursing a fluent stream through the rush-hour traffic. To shut him up, Hagopian asked, "What is Uncle Sam?" He explained how the customer ahead of him at the car service had needed a receipt for "Uncle Sam."

"Don't you know nothing? IRS. Taxes."

Hagopian, ignorant of much in his new land, and glad of any means to distract Hector from out-loud outbursts of "Bang that fucker," asked, "Eduardo pay tax?"

Hector laughed. "You joking, man?" He repeated this absurdity in Spanish. Consuela giggled. Finally, as they passed under the Long Island Expressway, God smiled: Hector, lulled by food and the warm car, fell asleep.

"So where you going?" asked Consuela.

"American Airlines."

"I *know* that. Then where? Who you meeting?"

"We are seeing sights."

"Okay, don't tell me." She pouted, prettily, and Hagopian racked his brain for things to say. But whenever he hit on a subject, he couldn't come up with the words, and they drove mostly in silence into the airport and up to American departures.

Hector woke up fast, eyes glittering. He tried to dip his tiny hands into Hagopian's pockets. "Gimme the gun."

"Later," Hagopian whispered, slapping his hands away, terrified that Consuela had heard. She looked perplexed. "You wait?" said Hagopian.

"Not here. They'll bust me. I'll park and wait for you inside."

"No, no, no. We find you in parking." He looked around the moving maze of cars and buses and hurrying people and spotted the walkway to the parking lot. "By there!" he said, suddenly firm.

Consuela looked surprised. "Okay, if that's what you want."

The car clock read seven-twenty. "Coming," he said to the boy. "Hurry!"

Through electric doors and up the escalator Hector kept pestering him for the gun. But while repairing Luis's bag, Hagopian had rehearsed what he would tell the boy at this point, and had cobbled together some unusually coherent sentences.

"You are knowing what is hit man?"

"Me. Soon as you give me the gun."

"You know how hit man work?"

"I'll bang the fucker second I see him. We split up. Meet at the car."

"No, no, no. This is not rap video. Real hit man is having . . . uuuhhhhh . . . what you call—*teammate*. I am being teammate. Hit man *not* carrying gun. Teammate carrying gun. See target, teammate giving hit man gun."

"Then you watch my back while I bang the fucker."

"Very good, Hector. Now we are finding gate."

They perused a departures screen and located Luis's flight.

"Gate six. Gimme the gun."

Hagopian strode off, following signs. The boy scampered after him, pleading for the gun. Hagopian watched for Luis. He felt his skin begin to crawl, his heart speed up. People rushing with bags, a thousand shoes—clinking, scuffling, rustling—

voices from the ceiling, all hurled him back to Paris, back to those last fifty feet.

Blocking the corridor was a security checkpoint, beyond which only passengers with boarding passes were allowed. It funneled the passengers through X-ray machines and metal detectors. Agents stood in front, directing the flow. Others frisked those who set off the detector. Those studying the X rays stopped the machines for closer looks, and opened bags that didn't pass. In addition, Hagopian noticed a plainclothes agent, an apparent passenger, whose shoulder bag, he would have bet a night with Consuela, contained an assault weapon.

"Gimme the gun."

Hagopian led Hector into the foyer of the men's room, which gave them a clear view of the checkpoint. Hector gasped. Luis came striding out of the men's room, running a comb through his hair.

Hagopian whirled to the wall, lifting one foot as if to tie a shoelace, and enveloped the boy in the folds of his quilted jacket. Luis brushed past them. His shoulder bag skimmed Hagopian's arm, but he did not turn to apologize and the next instant he was on the line forming at the checkpoint.

"Gimme the gun."

"Here."

"Hey, what are you doing?"

Hector tried to squirm away from the barrel pressing his belly, but Hagopian jammed his other hand behind his back, holding him hard against the weapon.

"You are not moving, or you are gut shot. You know what is gut shot? Maybe crack spine."

Hector looked up into the deadest eyes he had ever seen.

"But, but—You son of—But why? Luis buy you off? He pay you to stop me?"

"You want justice?"

"Yeah, man. You said you'd help."

"Watching."

"Hey, no fair, you banging him. *I* bang the guy who killed my brother, not you."

"Watching."

Luis's turn had come. A seasoned traveler, he laid his shoulder bag on the X-ray conveyor and passed through the metal detector, after first depositing his keys and coins in a tray. Flashing a smile at one of the prettier agents, Luis went to retrieve his shoulder bag. But as Luis's bag emerged, an agent took it and beckoned Luis to a table.

"What's he doing?" asked Hector.

Another agent ducked his head to speak into a shoulder mike. "Watching."

The agent opened Luis's bag, zipper by zipper. Luis Carbona checked his watch. A second smile to the pretty agent got a look of stone, and now, as Hagopian held the boy, a swiftly moving cadre of plainclothes agents approached the checkpoint, while uniformed police officers suddenly appeared to steer passengers away.

"I can't see," Hector protested. To his amazement, Hagopian pocketed the penlight he had been pressing to his belly and hoisted him in a swift, sure motion to his shoulder.

"Watching."

He saw Luis arguing, refusing to face the wall, until two burly agents turned him around and slammed him against it.

"What do you see?"

"He had a gun in the bag. It has a false bottom. The X-ray machine nailed it."

"And more?"

Hector watched the agents remove the gun. "Hey, that's Ramos's gun—Wow, Luis tried to get away. This huge cop banged his face on the wall. There's blood all over. Excellent. They cuffed him."

Hagopian lowered him to the floor, stretched his aching back, and headed quickly for the escalator. "We gone-ed. Now!"

From the Triboro Bridge, it appeared as if every light in Manhattan was burning. Hagopian remembered the Milky Way pierced by ice-capped mountains.

"Man, that was great! The Feds'll lock him up forever."

Not so great, thought Hagopian. It would have been greater for him if the hot-blooded Luis had fought to the death.

"Better justice than nine months, yes?"

For the rest of the drive, Hagopian and Hector discussed the possible penalties for the Federal crime of smuggling a gun onto an airliner. If cousin Amelia got ten Federal years for a little coke, it stood to reason that Luis would receive many more.

Suddenly Hector said, "He's gonna get you, man. He's going to know you put the gun—"

"Jail-ed."

"He's got friends. They know where to find you."

Hagopian had already concluded that he had put too much hope in Luis's fighting back. Worse, he had mistakenly assumed that American security agents would open fire like Russians.

"Better justice than small boy killing man. Yes?"

Hector said, "Watch your ass on the street, man."

"No kites in jail," Hagopian persisted. "No airplane engineer. Yes?"

"You better get a gun."

"I don't want a gun." Drained, Hagopian tipped Consuela his last two dollars and went to bed in the back of his shop.

The next day he jumped whenever the door opened. Luis's arrest was on page two of both the *News* and the *Post*. He was pleased to see that his and Hector's estimates of jail time had been conservative. But of course Luis had friends. Sadly, wishing he didn't have to, he asked Consuela if she knew someone who would sell him a gun.

From the many offered, he chose a man-stopping .45 automatic, discounted for a frozen slide that he easily repaired. It was a big weapon, but he had room in the folds of his quilted jacket. No one saw it when he had his cappuccino. But Cafe Lalo didn't feel the same.

That night, as he was closing, the door swung open.

"Close-ed," Hagopian called.

"It's me."

Hector's little face was round in smiles. "Boy, is Luis pissed. He's so mad he's banging his head on the bars."

"How are you knowing?"

"They got him down at Manhattan Correctional. My cousin's uncle is in there. I sent Luis a message."

"What message?"

"Told him I put the gun in the bag when you weren't looking."

Hagopian was appalled. "Why?"

"For Ramos."

"But we make-ed justice for Ramos. Now Luis's friends are hunting you."

"Hey, man, it weren't justice 'til Luis knew I banged him."

CAROLYN WHEAT

UNDERCOVER

For her third appearance in this series, Carolyn Wheat brings us another of her gritty portraits of crime in New York. Only this time there's a difference, as there often is in Wheat's stories. She's one of our most daring and dependable writers.

You can get away with murder if you don't mind copping to something worse. I learned this life truth from Mr. Carlucci. I learned a lotta things from Mr. C. You might say he made me what I am today.

What I was was a cop. In 1952 I graduated the academy with a hundred other micks hungry for the street. Last year—can it really be 1967 already?—I got the three quarters and a bum knee. And nothing to do for the rest of my life but limp around like an old fart.

Chick Dunahee, outa the old one-nine, always starts in on how three quarters is one thing for a guy who's shot, but anything less is just goldbricking.

I say, you gonna grudge three quarters to a guy gave his whole life to the department? Who sat around shootin' the shit after his tour was over on account of the precinct was more like a home than his home? Who spent more time in a black and white than he ever did in his own Chevy it took him seven years to pay for? It don't make no difference how the guy bought it, a shotgun blast or a lousy little fender bender put his knee out permanent.

That accident was the best damn thing ever happened to me is what I tell everybody. I slap the stupid bitchin' knee and say, I got all the time in the world.

Yeah. Time. Time for a third cup of coffee at Klinger's deli, for a fourth beer down to Hanrahan's. Time to play another hand of gin with Harve Petrovich and Chick Dunahee.

Time. Time to sit on a park bench with all the other old farts who don't know what the hell became of their lives. Time to drink too much and time to think too much.

I miss the gun. I can't hardly believe it; I mean, I never fired the damn thing the whole time I was in uniform, except on the firin' range, but the weight of it being gone is like having one less arm. Without the gun, I'm nothin'. Worse than nothin'.

I decided to look up Mr. Carlucci. Notice the "mister." You talk about a mutt, you don't call him mister. You call him Jones or hey, you, or slimebucket, but you don't call him mister. He's just a mutt; he don't deserve no respect. But Mr. C, I don't care how much dope he deals, or how many hookers he's got on the street, or how many guys took a swim in the East River on account of him. He's a gentleman, Mr. C.

I used to stop by the restaurant when I was a rookie hoofing a beat. God, I loved the beat. I loved the feeling that the streets belonged to me, that I was there to take special care of my blocks, my people.

So one night I dropped into Carlucci's, just to see that everything's A–OK. What I seen was an underage busboy carrying a drink to a table. Now, it goes against my grain to hang up a nice place like that over a petty beef, so I call the maître d' over and mention it, casual-like, just so he knows for next time. But the guy's a wiseass, one of your smooth types with patent leather hair. He starts givin' me grief, daring me to write him up, tellin' me his boss has a hook with the State Liquor Authority. I'm about ready to bust the place when I suddenly see the guy's face go gray. Next thing I know this tiny little man with silver-white hair and sharp blue eyes is looking up at me. He don't look like no Italian, but he says he's Mr. Carlucci and what's the trouble here?

I tell him. I don't even look at Patent Leather Hair; it's like he's gone even though he's still there. Mr. C whispers a few words to the monkey suit, and he goes about his business.

Mr. Carlucci apologizes. Not like he's scared or nothin', more like he's pained that I should be treated bad in his place. Like he invited me to his house and somebody insulted me. Then he takes me over to his own personal table, the one with the red carnations in the middle. I sit down. It feels good to take a load off my feet. He snaps his fingers at a kid in a white coat, and next thing I know I'm sittin' in front of the biggest plate of spaghetti bolognese you ever saw. A big glass of vino joins the pasta, and so does a basket of breadsticks, the kind with the little seeds all over.

Some cops always eat on the arm, never open their wallets the whole time they're on the job. Other cops are regular Mr. Cleans, never take so much as a cookie. Me, I was somewhere in the middle. I never took food from nobody I didn't think could afford it, and I never took from nobody I didn't respect.

To me, Mr. C was just trying to make up for the grief his maître d' give me. He was being a gentleman. So I reached for the cut-glass dish of fresh-grated Parmesan and ladled it on thick.

It got to where I stopped in once, twice a month. Not too often, not like I was takin' advantage, but just enough to let Mr. C know how much I liked the food and appreciated the hospitality. In six months I put on ten pounds and hadda get new uniform pants. Nothin' worse for a cop than a beat with good food.

Course, I heard the rumors. How Mr. C was a lot more than just a guy made great manicott'. But I never seen him bring that side of things into his restaurant.

About a year later I got transferred to the four-four. It was a real Bronx Zoo up there, let me tell you. And nothin' to eat but cuchifritos and Shabazz bean pies. I lost the ten pounds, and then ten more.

I haven't gone there since I got the line of duty.

But I gotta take the chance. So I hitch up my pants and pull on the fancy brass door handle.

As I walk through the carved wooden doors, I think of that first plate of pasta. The old decor's gone now: no more hand-painted scenes of Napoli, no more red napkins on starched white tablecloths, no more red carnations. The place has real class: peach-colored napkins folded into goblets like Chinese fans. More forks than a guy could use in three dinners. I liked it better before, but I'd never tell Mr. C. I wouldn't want to hurt his feelings.

There's a new maître d'. I tell him I want to see the boss, but then I start feeling ashamed. What if Mr. C thinks I'm there just to cadge a free meal? I start to mumble something about coming back another time.

Before I can turn my stupid leg around to walk out the door, he's there. Mr. Carlucci in person, his hair just as white and his eyes just as blue and sharp as they ever were. He puts out his hand; I shake it. It feels good when he says, "Officer Sweeney. It's been too long, my friend."

Just like he done that first time, Mr. C ushers me over to his private table. There are peach-colored flowers, real exotic-looking, in the cut-glass vase that used to hold carnations. Like always, his bouquet is bigger and fuller than the ones on the other tables. And none of his flowers are brown at the edges neither.

I sit. It takes a minute to get the freakin' knee under the table. Mr. C looks the other way, like the gentleman he is, and then sits down next to me. He waves a waiter over and orders for both of us.

I'm no Italian, but I know better than to talk business right away. So I tell Mr. C how I busted up my knee, and he shakes his head and says it's a shame. We talk about the old days, what happened to Klinger, the deli owner, how the blind newsie on the corner got robbed again. How nothing's the same since Kennedy was shot.

When the food comes, we stop talking. Fettucine Alfredo, veal piccata, and escarole sautéed in garlic butter. Dessert is espresso coffee with a jolt of anisette. Mr. C takes the tiny slice of lemon peel and rubs it around the rim of his cup. He takes a sip, then leans back in his chair with a sigh of contentment.

That's my signal. Business can now be mentioned.

I come into the restaurant a defrocked cop. I leave a bagman.

I coulda kidded myself. I coulda bought Mr. Carlucci's kind words as he walked me to the door. I can always use a good man, he says, in my business. His business. He don't mean the restaurant, and we both know it. We both know what I am, but he's too much the gentleman to say the word.

He proves it when I go out the first time. He pours me a glass of red wine and gives me my instructions in person. I know for a fact he never done that with the other guys who collected for him. They take orders from Vinnie the Fish.

When I leave the restaurant and start walkin' up the street, it's like I'm breathing brand-new air. It's like spring came overnight, even though I still see patches of dirty snow in the gutter. I belong again. I own the streets; I have my blocks and my people.

First thing I do, I buy a new suit. Like I was starting a new job, only I never had to buy a suit for a job before. I always had the uniform. Funny thing is, I buy a blue suit. Some things never change.

My first collection is from a skinny little Greek who sells fruit and vegetables. He tries to offer me some avocados, free, but I shake my head. Taking them would break both my rules.

Next stop: a Puerto Rican social club. Only thing he offers me is a hard-eyed stare, but it don't make no never mind to me. I get the bag.

Same result at the Jewish dairy restaurant and the jazz joint with a soul food smell so good I almost break the rule. The black mama in the kitchen gives me a big Aunt Jemima smile and says she loves to see a man enjoy his food. I smile back, but I know better than to trust her. The minute my back is turned, I'll find her kitchen knife between my ribs, the lard not even washed off. So no smothered pork chops. Just the bag.

Sometimes I feel bad. But hey, if it's not me, it'll be somebody else, just like if it's not Mr. C, it'll be somebody else. They probably had bagmen in the Old Testament. It's keeping me off the park bench is all I know. All I want to know.

It starts to go wrong about the time the trees in the park behind the courthouse start blooming. All these little pink buds, real nice, like looking through rose-colored glasses. Then the rain comes and the buds fall off and stick to your shoes and who needs it?

It starts with little things, but hey, I'm a cop, or I was before I got the line of duty, and I know how little things can add up

until finally you're up crap creek and somebody stole your paddle.

So even the first time I don't see Mr. Carlucci before I go out to collect I get a funny feeling. Vinnie the Fish tells me Mr. C's home with the flu, and maybe he is. So okay, I take my orders, but I let him know I don't like it, and the next week there's Mr. C and no sign of the Fish.

It was the Fish gave me the new stop on my route. It's a fag bar at the ass end of Christopher Street, which is in the Village, which figures. I start to object; I don't want to go to no fag bar, but Mr. C says these fruits are givin' him a hard time, refusing to pay up, and the place needs special handling.

I walk down Christopher as fast as I can, cursing the limp for slowing me down. There's fag bars all over the place; I can tell even though they gotta be careful. I pass one called Stonewall that I know is run by the mob so there's no trouble about them paying up.

I'm practically in the Hudson River before I reach the joint I'm supposed to collect. It's called Christopher's End, and it's next to the West Side Highway; there are trucks parked on the cobblestones under the road. Skinny guys in black leather jackets and Greek sailor caps lounge around by the trucks. I get the shivers just looking at them, knowing what they're waiting for.

Inside, I expect wall-to-wall fruits. But it's afternoon, and there's only a couple guys sitting at the bar and a foursome playing pool. None of them look faggy; if I hadn't of known, I might not have guessed. The bartender's got muscles like Gorgeous George and a USMC tattoo on his right arm. Hired muscle. No wonder the fags think they can defy Mr. C.

I walk up to the bar. Real quick, before the bartender starts to think I'm there for the wrong reason, I mention Mr. C and say I'm here for the pickup.

The bartender fixes me with the kind of hard blue eyes only an Irishman can have and says, "We're not paying."

Cold, flat. Just like that. I get my Irish up and say, "Who do you think you are, you don't have to pay? Just because the fruits that run this place hire some muscle means they're different from every other fag bar on this street?"

"Hell, yes, we're different," the bartender says. Leans over the bar and gives me an evil grin. "See, I'm not hired muscle. This is *my* bar for *my* friends, and I'm not paying anybody to stay in business. Got that?"

I sit there stunned, like I been hit with a ball-peen hammer. The man was a marine! A United States marine turned fruit. I can't hardly take it in.

He talks about how hard it is to be a fag, what with cops keeping tabs on who comes into the bars, writing down license plate numbers of cars parked nearby, then running a make. He says why should guys get a jacket just for going into a bar? He also says why should they have to pay Mr. C to stay in business?

I turn my head away, thinking what to say next. I look at the guys playing pool. There's this one kid, well built, with dark hair. Never take him for a nelly, the way he eyes the ball, places his cue. Shoots like a master, makes his shot, then grins into the glare of the green-shaded light over the table. White teeth in a tanned face. An actor's face. He catches my eye and gives me a victory salute. Like he wants me to applaud or something.

I turn back to the bartender. "Bad things happen to guys who cross Mr. C," I remind him.

"We'll take our chances," he says. He turns his back on me. I want to say more; hell, I want to rush the bar and beat the shit out of the bastard. The queer punk bastard. Only he ain't no pansy; he's got ten years and twenty pounds on me, and his is muscle, not flab.

So there's nothing to do but go. For now. I turn and hoist my leg off the barstool. As I slide off the leather seat, the kid with the actor's face is standing next to me. I get a noseful of Brut as he whispers, "Can I buy you a drink?"

I run out of the place as fast as my gimpy leg will let me.

As I walk back down Christopher, I look for the cops the bartender talked about. Sure enough, hidden around the corner on Washington there's a beat-up '59 Chevy the department thinks nobody knows is an unmarked. There's one guy behind the wheel, another with a notebook in his hand. Prominent, like they want people to see they're there.

I can't have them gettin' the wrong idea. What if it came back to Chick Dunahee that Biff Sweeney was seen comin' out of a fag bar? I walk over to the unmarked and start thinking fast.

By the time I get the recorder's attention, I got a story all ready. About how I do a little private investigation now I'm retired, about how this father came to me real upset, said his son was hangin' around with queers and he wanted it stopped. About how I only went into the bar to see if the bartender knew the kid.

Nothing about collecting for Mr. Carlucci.

They stare at me with blank cop eyes. I got no idea whether or not they believe me. I open my mouth to add to the story, then realize that would really make me sound like a mutt tryin' to talk himself out of a jam. So I shrug and walk away.

When I get back to the restaurant, the Fish is not happy. Mr. C is not happy. How can a man with Mr. C's rep let a bunch of fairies push him around?

He can't. I have to go back, make noises about how places without insurance have been known to burn to the ground. With people inside. Owner-type people.

But one thing I make clear: Any damage to the bar has to be done by somebody other than me. I may be a bagman, but I'm no hit man. I'm still too much cop for that.

The Fish starts to say I'll do what I'm told, but Mr. C cuts him off. "I understand," he says. Always the gent.

This time I learn the bartender's name is Mick Hennessey. Not just a marine but an Irishman. Go figure. He feeds me a drink. I take it; hell, I need a drink to sit in a place like this, the way I feel about fags.

We talk about fire. I talk about fire. About how dangerous it is, how it can trap people inside and burn them to bacon before they knew what hit them.

Mick talks about sports, about how someday the football leagues are gonna get together and have a big play-off game. Which'll never happen, you ask me. Why should the NFL bother with a bunch of farm teams like they got in the AFL? You think a team calls itself Dolphins can take on the Green Bay Packers?

I don't say none of that; I keep talking about fire. I keep drinking. Things are getting blurry when I smell Brut and turn to see the kid from the pool table sitting next to me. He says his name's Darius. Darius Kroeger. Only he uses the name Cooper when he goes for auditions.

"I knew you was an actor," I tell him. "You got the face for it."

He smiles. That's all, just a smile. But his eyes reach into mine the way no guy's eyes are supposed to reach into another guy's.

I'm drunk. I mean I'm as plastered as I ever been in my life. That's the only way it could've happened. I had to be drunk outa my face. I hadda be.

I wake up the next morning with a large furry animal in my mouth. I think it's my tongue. My head feels like—ah, hell, you ever had a hangover, you know how my head feels.

But that's not the bad part. The bad part is what I think happened between me and Darius.

I lay in bed with the cold sweats, with shakes so bad I can't lift a glass of water to my mouth to pop an aspirin. But it's not the booze; it's the memory.

I never felt like that before. I never knew I could feel like that. Even Monica O'Shea, who gave the best hand job in Hell's Kitchen, never made me feel like that, and every guy at Sacred Heart knew what she could do with those long white fingers of hers.

Oh, I used to brag, just like the other guys. How horny I was, how much I needed a woman. Then I'd go to Monica, get what I came for, and tell my buddies it was great. But I was just blowing smoke; it was okay, but that was all. Just okay.

Same thing with the Times Square hookers we used to bust. They'd offer freebies to stay on the street. You hadda take it once in a while. The other cops would talk about how Crystal or Bobbie Jo, how they did stuff the cops' wives never even *heard* of and wouldn't do for a million bucks. Me, I figured they was okay, but nothing special.

Darius was more than okay. Much more.

I was drunk. I was drunk, I lost my head, and it'll never happen again.

Once doesn't mean you're a faggot.

Does it?

The phone rings. It's as loud as the last trump, and it scares me as much.

I'm right to be scared. It's Mick Hennessey; he asks me how Darius and I got along last night.

He knows. He fucking knows. I didn't think I had any more sweat left in my body, but there's a cold stream trickling down my back.

He knows.

He also knows there will be no fire at Christopher's End.

I put the phone back in the cradle and try to stop shaking.

It rings a second time. I pick it up. What could be worse than what I just heard?

The Fish, that's what.

"So, you're too high-and-mighty to torch a place for the boss," he says, his voice slimy with self-satisfaction. "The truth is you don't want to hurt your fag buddies, do you, *faggot?*"

He spits the last word; it practically jumps through the phone and wets my face.

"You think Mr. C's dumb or something, *faggot?* You think he doesn't watch his back at all times? Well, there better be a nice big bonfire at that fag bar or everyone in the NYPD's going to know you like it with boys. Got that, *faggot?*"

I lean over the bed and throw up on the floor, with Vinnie the Fish on the other end of the line listening to every retch.

I can't believe Mr. C will let this happen. He's too much the gent. But when I ask to talk to the boss, the Fish says, "He's taking a shave. Besides, he's got no use for faggots. Except to collect from fag bars, which is all you're gonna be doing from now on. *After* you light that fire."

"I won't—" I croak, but the Fish chops me off.

"You *won't?* You forget, we own your ass. At least"—he sniggers—"we own whatever's left over after your pretty boyfriend gets through with it. So you *will* light that fire and it will cause great damage to life and property. Won't it, *faggot?*"

The fire. The fire that will cook Christopher's End and Mick Hennessey and Darius Kroeger-Cooper and burn the memory of last night to the ground. To the ground.

Darius. I think about last night, about how he made me feel, and I realize I been undercover my whole life. Thinking it was like this for all guys: that they bragged about women but didn't really like it all that much. But it wasn't them; it was me. It was me that was missing something, and now I found it and I gotta burn it up. I gotta burn it up or be called a faggot the rest of my life.

I seen plenty of fairies on the job. Guys in skirts beat up when the john getting the blow job realized what they had between their legs. Guys caught in men's rooms copping some boy's joint, begging the cops not to book them or the wife'll find out.

I never in my life thought that I—

Once! Once doesn't make you a faggot. Anybody can make one mistake.

I clean up the mess on the floor and start thinking about the fire. How I have to plan. How it has to go smooth as silk, nothing coming back to me.

I think about Mick Hennessey, how talking to him was no different from talking to Chick Dunahee or any other ex-cop. I think about Darius, his white smile, his smooth, dark face. I remember the way his hands caressed my .38; he said he used to go target shooting with his dad. He liked guns; he liked that I was a cop.

I think about burning him to bacon.

It takes me a week to set things up right. To get my alibi in place. To case the joint, working out where the fire should start. How I can get to the site without being seen hefting a can of gasoline through the streets. How I can get away without being spotted.

Every night I dream of Darius, waking with an ache in my groin.

There's only one way I can do this. I gotta become a cop again in my head. I gotta think about it like I was writing up a 61 on a torch job some mope already done. In my mind I start dictating a police report.

At 1500 hours the perpetrator approached the location. Male White, 6', 185 pounds, no limp or other identifying characteristics. Carrying a duffel bag.

It's a half hour after closing. I've got the gasoline can in the duffel bag. My leg's wrapped tighter than hell in an Ace bandage so's I can keep from limping. One less thing to be identified by.

I peer through the windows, just to make sure. There they are, taking a drink together. The two guys I need to eliminate if I'm going to have peace in my life.

The fire originated at the rear exit. Source of the fire was garbage bags ignited by means of an accelerant later identified as gasoline.

I stop a minute before lighting the matches. This is wrong. Everything in my life tells me how wrong. It's like all the priests and nuns I ever knew, all the sergeants I answered to, even my dead mother are standing over me, telling me they're ashamed they ever knew me.

But I have to do it. I have to.

After four tries I get a match lit and toss it onto the garbage bags. Flames jump at me right away; the gasoline is that ready to burn.

Perpetrator ignited a second fire at the front entrance to the location by dousing the wooden door with accelerant.

I slip around the corner and duck into an alley. It's back streets all the way and a quick subway ride. The duffel bag's ash now, along with the garbage. So's the watch cap. I leave the pea jacket in the subway; it'll be gone by morning.

I can't believe I did it.

I need a drink to steady my hands, settle my stomach.

I walk out of the subway. The Ace bandage is killing me; my leg feels like a blimp. But I force myself to walk straight, no limp, past my own car, toward the light pouring onto the pavement from the window of my destination.

I have a report to make.

I open the door and walk in.

"Is it done?"

I nod.

"To a crisp," another voice says. Darius slides off the bar stool and walks over to me. Embraces me in a cloud of Brut, his lips brushing my cheek. Mick Hennessey pours me a drink.

We toast Darius for his acting job. Thanks to him, the cops watching Christopher's End have my license plate number and a description of a man in a trench coat and fedora limping into a fag bar at the same time Carlucci's Ristorante went up in flames.

Who's going to believe a cop set up a phony alibi in a fag bar? Nobody, that's who.

I lock eyes with Darius; we both know how the night will end.

Like I said, you can get away with murder if you don't mind copping to something worse.

I don't mind. I'm with my own now, and I don't mind at all.

BATYA SWIFT YASGUR

ME AND MR. HARRY

Batya Swift Yasgur is the twelfth winner of MWA's Robert L. Fish Award, presented annually for the most promising first story. Many of the previous winners have gone on to successful writing careers, and two of them—Bill Crenshaw and Doug Allyn—became MWA Edgar winners for subsequent stories. We predict the same sort of bright future for Ms. Yasgur.

And isn't it just like my parents to mess it all up for me, just when it was so nice?

So I'm sitting here, in that stuffy green room just outside the principal's office, waiting for that fat, blousy lady, the social worker, to talk to me again. Mrs. Morris. Her voice is thick and powdery and sweet like the makeup she smears on her face; her hair is all puffed and twisted and piled on top of her head. When she smiles, her mouth is like a big cave you can fall into.

"You can tell me everything, dear." She leans over her desk and I shrink back into my chair. It's a big armchair, cozy, like a nest, and I'm a little bird snuggling into it. I won't talk. She can't make me.

She's getting rattled. I can tell.

"Wouldn't you like to talk about it?"

Like hell I would. I make my eyes into little slits, flare my nostrils—just a tiny bit—and tighten my lips. The Satanic look, my mother calls it. Gets them every time.

Now Mrs. Morris is even more rattled.

"I'm only here to help you." Her voice shakes some.

Right, lady. And I'm a flying ant. I'll keep my mouth shut, thanks.

She fidgets with her pen, breathes onto her glasses, and writes something down in a manila folder. I curl myself up into a ball and sink back farther into the chair.

I want Mr. Harry. That's all.

Mommy comes home early every night now. She never used to. Used to work all the time, and I'd let myself in with the key. Made myself cereal and milk and the TV kept me company till she came home. Then it was why didn't I do my homework, and why didn't I make my bed, and why didn't I sweep. Oh, and why didn't I set the table, didn't I know what a long day she had, and how hard she and Daddy work. Then dinner and bath and bed, maybe two minutes of hello from Daddy before he got on the phone. And I used to lie there wondering whether my math teacher would yell at me again for getting the wrong answer, or my science teacher would laugh at me for my "stupid" mistakes.

Until Mr. Harry. Homework times went by so fast with him. I never even thought of TV when I was over at his house. He always had the yummiest cookies and we'd have a great time eating and watching the birds at his feeder. Or that time we shoveled his walk, and we made that giant snowman with a carrot nose and a funny hat, and then he made me hot chocolate.

I hate it when Mommy tries to help me with my homework. "Let's make this a nice family time!" she chirps brightly. "Then how about some pizza?"

I just want things the way they used to be. I want Mr. Harry back.

I'm smoking again. I lift the cigarettes from Daddy's jacket pocket. Mr. Harry got me to stop. Told me all this stuff about cancer, showed me how a cigarette burned a black hole through his handkerchief, and said the same thing would happen to my lungs. "Who cares," I said, puffing away. That's when he hugged me the first time. I swear, he had tears in his eyes. "I care," he told me. And he did.

Why did they have to go and put him in jail?

They won't even let me call him. Or write. Nothing.

Oops! I'm out of cigarettes. Better go get one before Daddy gets out of the shower.

The court is a great big brick building with so many corridors and hallways it's like one of those mazes we built in science class for the poor rats. It's not going to be a trial like on TV, they told me. I'm going to see the judge in his room.

I'm pretty nervous about meeting a judge. I **expect** someone with a black robe, a big wig, and a hammer, who's going to bang and yell "Order!" all the time. But no, he's a little guy with yellow wispy hair, like an old doll's, when I'd washed it too many times. He keeps making grumpy, harrumphy noises in his throat and wiping his nose with a red handkerchief. There are no armchairs.

"When did you first start going to Harry Wrightson's place?"

Another throat noise, another sniffle. I sit up straighter. I don't have to tell this guy anything, even if he is a judge.

I make my slitted-eye face. I can stare him down.

"Answer the question," my mother says, giving my shoulder a squeeze.

I go on staring.

"Yes, yes." The judge clears his throat. "This is hard for you. I know."

No you don't.

He tries again. "When did he touch you the first time?"

I can't hear those words and keep looking at him. I look at the floor. That day, after I failed my science test, when I cried and Mr. Harry held me, warm and tight and cuddly. Stroked my hair and whispered, "Science isn't what counts. Love is. And you're an expert at that." Oh, and I had to ask him what an "expert" is. And he *didn't* tell me to "go look it up."

The judge is asking another question, but I'm not listening anymore.

The school is running this program called "Bad Touch/Good Touch." Mrs. Morris keeps looking at me while they're play-acting these stupid skits on stage, but I make believe I don't see. Mr. Harry's touching—that wasn't bad. Sure, it felt kind of funny at first. But it was—what was his word—*special*. Because I'm special. He said so.

More dumb doctors. One asks lots of questions, you know, some kind of a test. A little like school, but also different. Boxes to fill in, shapes to complete, splatters of ink on some cards, and he wants to know what they look like to me. My mouth is zipped shut. He keeps shaking his head and writing stuff down in this folder. "No little girl has ever behaved like this in here," he says as I'm leaving.

Good. I really am special after all.

They think that 'cause I don't talk, I also can't hear. They're saying more and more in front of me.

I keep hearing them talking about me. Whispers, of course. Lots about a "residence." I *did* look that one up, and it means "home." I don't get it. I already have a home. Correction: I have a house. Only at Mr. Harry's did I ever really feel home.

I'm back in the cozy armchair in Mrs. Morris's office. Mommy and Daddy are there, too. Mommy keeps crying and wiping her eyes with this gross wet tissue that has big holes and is falling apart. Daddy keeps tapping her on the arm and saying, "Now, Bertha."

"Honey." Mommy sounds quivery, like the wings on the hummingbird outside Mr. Harry's window as he used to hover (now *there's* a nice vocabulary word for you, a free gift from Mr. Harry and me) over his feeder.

I won't even turn to look at her. I let the chair cuddle me.

"Talk to Mrs. Morris!" How many times since it happened have I heard Daddy say that in his "punishment" voice. But nothing can make me talk. Not when they yell. Not when they hit. Not when they cry.

"Don't you want to make sure he doesn't do this to another little girl?"

I almost laugh. What we had, Mr. Harry and me, was just between the two of us. He wouldn't do this with anyone else, 'cause no one is special like me.

* * *

Looks like I'm going to be shipped off to this place they call the "residence." Seems like it's some kind of orphanage. I don't get it. My parents are alive. I thought orphan homes are for kids whose parents are dead. Of course, for all I care, they could be. Mr. Harry is gone and that's what matters.

Mommy's eyes are teary all the time, but Daddy does a lot of barking. "Please, honey, won't you even talk to us?" Mommy begs. "You're ruining your life, young lady, I hope you know that!" is all I hear from Daddy.

Who cares.

I hear them talking on the phone. I don't know who they're talking to, but I've picked up on the upstairs extension. They don't know I'm listening, of course. Just like they don't know about the time Daddy yelled at Mommy about the bank and the morgidge (is that how you spell it?) in their bedroom, and I was hiding in my spot in the linen closet outside their door. Or that night when I heard all those strange bumps and thumps and groany noises. Or the time Mommy cried when she thought she was going to have another baby. "I can hardly handle one. How am I ever going to manage with two!" I've got eavesdropping down to a science (probably the only science I'll ever be good at).

"What do you mean, they're going to release him?" Daddy's angriest voice.

"Just what I said." The man I don't know is talking.

"But that's outrageous!" Mommy is crying, as usual.

"Your daughter won't talk, so there isn't enough evidence."

"What she said that time, that wasn't enough? That's how we found out about it in the first place!"

"No."

"What about the other little girl? Doesn't her testimony count for something?"

My hand, holding the phone receiver, turns to ice. I'm afraid I'm going to throw up.

And when I hear myself screaming, Mommy and Daddy drop the phone and are running up the stairs. My voice sounds rusty, like a broken machine that's been lying around too long.

"What other little girl?"

APPENDIX

THE YEARBOOK OF THE MYSTERY AND SUSPENSE STORY

TWENTY OF THE YEAR'S BEST MYSTERY AND SUSPENSE NOVELS

Lawrence Block, *A Long Line of Dead Men* (Morrow)
Mary Higgins Clark, *Remember Me* (Simon & Schuster)
Len Deighton, *Faith* (HarperCollins)
Colin Dexter, *The Daughters of Cain* (Macmillan London)
Peter Dickinson, *The Yellow Room Conspiracy* (Mysterious Press)
Dick Francis, *Wild Horses* (Putnam)
Elizabeth George, *Playing for the Ashes* (Bantam)
Sue Grafton, *"K" Is for Killer* (Holt)
Evan Hunter, *Criminal Conversation* (Warner)
John Irving, *A Son of the Circus* (Random House)
P. D. James, *Original Sin* (Knopf, Canada)
Steve Martini, *Undue Influence* (Putnam)
Ed McBain, *There Was a Little Girl* (Warner)
Walter Mosley, *Black Betty* (Norton)
Marcia Muller, *Till the Butchers Cut Him Down* (Mysterious Press)

APPENDIX

Joyce Carol Oates, *What I Lived For* (Dutton)
Bill Pronzini, *With an Extreme Burning* (Carroll & Graf)
Ruth Rendell, *Semisola* (Hutchinson, London)
Barbara Vine, *No Night Is Too Long* (Viking, London)
Minette Walters, *The Scold's Bridle* (St. Martin's Press)

BIBLIOGRAPHY

I. COLLECTIONS AND SINGLE STORIES

Aird, Catherine. *Injury Time*. London: Macmillan. Sixteen stories, ten new.

Ames, Mel D. *The Ogopogo Affair*. Oakville, Ontario, Canada: Mosaic Press. A single novelette from *Mike Shayne Mystery Magazine* (1984), with photos and nonfiction about a legendary lake creature.

Archer, Jeffrey. *Twelve Red Herrings*. New York: HarperCollins. Twelve new stories, several criminous.

Baxt, George. *Scheme and Variations*. New York: Mysterious Bookshop. A single new short story, published as a holiday gift by the Manhattan bookshop.

Berkeley, Anthony. *The Roger Sheringham Stories*. London: Thomas Carnacki. Eight stories, a three-act play, and a radio play featuring Berkeley's series sleuth, in a limited edition of ninety-five copies.

Block, Lawrence. *Ehrengraf for the Defense*. Mission Viejo, CA: A.S.A.P. Publications. Eight stories, seven from *EQMM* and one from *Mike Shayne,* about a defense attorney who breaks the law on his clients' behalf. Introduction by Edward D. Hoch, afterword by the author. A limited edition.

Capek, Karel. *Tales from Two Pockets*. Highland Park, NJ: Catbird Press. Forty-eight short mystery stories in a 1929 Czechoslovakian collection newly translated by Norma Comrada.

Carr, John Dickson. *Speak of the Devil*. Norfolk, VA: Crippen & Landru. A single novella-length radio play in eight parts, broadcast by the BBC in 1941 but unpublished till now. Introduction by Tony Medawar.

Clark, Mary Higgins. *The Lottery Winner: Alvirah and Willy Stories*. New York: Simon & Schuster. Six stories, two new.

Derleth, August. *The "Unpublished" Solar Pons*. Toronto: Metropolitan Toronto Reference Library. Three previously unpublished Solar Pons adventures written early in the author's career. Edited by George A. Vanderburgh.

Dexter, Colin. *As Good as Gold*. London: Pan Books/Kodak. A special paperback published as part of a promotion for Kodak film, containing the ten tales from *Morse's Greatest Mystery and Other Stories* plus a new Inspector Morse novelette written especially for this edition.

Ellroy, James. *Hollywood Nocturnes*. New York: Otto Penzler Books. A novelette and five stories from various sources, 1986–94. British title: *Dick Contino's Blues and Other Stories*.

Hill, Reginald. *Asking for the Moon*. London: HarperCollins. Four novelettes about Dalziel and Pascoe, one new.

Hornsby, Wendy. *High Heels Through the Headliner*. Mission Viejo, CA: A.S.A.P. Publications. Introduction by James Ellroy, afterwords by the author and Raymond Obstfeld. A single story in a limited edition.

Lovesey, Peter. *The Crime of Miss Oyster Brown and Other Stories*. London: Little Brown. Eighteen stories from various sources.

Lutz, John. *Shadows Everywhere*. Eugene, OR: Mystery Scene/Pulphouse. Twelve stories, 1967–85, all but two from *AHMM*.

Oates, Joyce Carol. *Haunted: Tales of the Grotesque*. New York: Dutton. Sixteen stories of fantasy and terror, a few criminous.

Prather, Richard S. *Hot Rock Rumble & The Double Take*. Brooklyn: Gryphon Publications. Two Shell Scott novellas first published in 1957 and 1963.

Taylor, John. *The Unopened Casebook of Sherlock Holmes*. New York: Parkwest. Six new Sherlockian stories.

Vachss, Andrew. *Born Bad*. New York: Vintage/Black Lizard. Forty-three brief stories and three short plays, a few new.

Yorke, Margaret. *Pieces of Justice*. London: Warner Futura. Twenty-three stories, four new, mainly crime-suspense. One features series sleuth Patrick Grant. A couple are non-criminous.

II. ANTHOLOGIES

Adams Round Table. *Justice in Manhattan.* Stamford, CT: Long-
meadow Press. Ten new mystery and suspense stories in a contin-
uing anthology series. Introduction by Joyce Harrington.
Chase, Elaine Raco, ed. *Partners in Crime.* New York: Signet.
Eleven new stories about pairs of sleuths, one also published in
EQMM.
Cody, Liza, Michael Z. Lewin, and Peter Lovesey, eds. *3rd Culprit.*
London: Chatto & Windus. Twenty-three stories, seventeen
new, plus a few articles, puzzles, and cartoons, in the annual
anthology from the Crime Writers Association.
Coupe, Stuart, and Julie Ogden, eds. *Case Reopened.* St. Leonards,
Australia: Allen & Unwin. Eleven Australian mystery writers of-
fer fictionalized solutions to real crimes in that country.
Cox, Michael, and Jack Adrian, eds. *The Oxford Book of Historical Stories.* Oxford: Oxford University Press. Thirty-six stories,
a few criminous, from various sources.
Forrest, Katherine V., and Barbara Grier, eds. *The Mysterious Naiad.* Tallahassee, FL: Naiad Press. Nineteen new romantic mysteries by lesbian authors.
Gorman, Ed, ed. *A Modern Treasury of Great Detective and Murder Mysteries.* New York: Carroll & Graf. Twenty-five stories
by American writers, 1954–91, from various sources. Introduction and reading lists by Jon L. Breen.
Greenberg, Martin H., and Ed Gorman, eds. *Feline and Famous:
Cat Crimes Goes Hollywood.* Eighteen new stories.
———, ed. *Malice Domestic 3.* New York: Pocket Books. Introduction by Nancy Pickard. Thirteen new stories in the third of
an annual series.
———, ed. *Murder for Father.* New York: Signet. Twenty stories,
eighteen new.
———, ed. *Murder for Mother.* New York: Signet. Eighteen stories, sixteen new.
Haining, Peter, ed. *Murder by the Glass.* London: Souvenir Press.
Twenty-seven mystery and crime stories about drink, from various sources. A sequel to the editor's earlier *Murder on the Menu.*
———, ed. *Tales from the Rogues' Gallery.* London: Little Brown.
A mixed collection of twenty-eight mystery and fantasy tales
about famous villains and murders of history.

————, ed. *The Television Crimebusters Omnibus: Great Stories of the Police Detectives.* London: Orion. Thirty stories and book excerpts featuring characters from popular television series.

Hale, Hilary, ed. *Midwinter Mysteries 4.* London: Little Brown. Ten new stories, three of them also published during 1994 in *EQMM.* Fourth of an annual series.

Hillerman, Tony, ed. *The Mysterious West.* New York: HarperCollins. Twenty new stories set in the modern West.

Hoch, Edward D., ed. *The Year's Best Mystery and Suspense Stories 1994.* New York: Walker and Company. Twelve of the best stories from 1993, with bibliography, necrology, and awards lists.

Hutchings, Janet, ed. *Once Upon a Crime: Historical Mysteries from* Ellery Queen's Mystery Magazine. New York: St. Martin's Press. Thirteen stories ranging in time from the first century B.C. to the 1930s.

Jakubowski, Maxim, ed. *Crime Yellow: Gollancz New Crime 1.* London: Gollancz. Sixteen stories, all but one new.

————, ed. *London Noir.* London: Serpent's Tail. Fifteen new stories.

————, ed. *More Murders for the Fireside.* London: Pan Books. Twenty-one stories from various sources.

————, and Martin H. Greenberg, eds. *Royal Crimes.* New York: Signet. Sixteen new stories involving British royalty through the centuries.

Kaye, Marvin, ed. *The Game Is Afoot: Parodies, Pastiches and Ponderings of Sherlock Holmes.* New York: St. Martin's Press. Fifty-three stories and Sherlockian essays, seven new.

Manson, Cynthia, ed. *Crime a la Carte.* New York: Signet. Nineteen stories from *EQMM* and *AHMM* dealing with food or drink.

————, ed. *Death on the Verandah: Mystery Stories of the South.* New York: Carroll & Graf. Sixteen stories from *EQMM* and *AHMM.*

————, ed. *Merry Murder.* New York: Seafarer/Penguin. Twenty-two stories, mainly from *EQMM* and *AHMM,* chosen from three previous Christmas anthologies.

————, ed. *Murder on Trial.* New York: Signet. Thirteen courtroom stories from *EQMM* and *AHMM.*

————, ed. *Tales of Obsession.* New York: Signet. Fourteen stories from *EQMM* and *AHMM.*

————, ed. *Women of Mystery II*. New York: Carroll & Graf. Fifteen stories by women authors from *EQMM* and *AHMM*.

Murder Most Merry. New York: Zebra/Kensington Publishing. Six new Christmas novelettes.

Mystery Scene magazine staff, eds. *The Year's 25 Finest Crime and Mystery Stories: Third Annual Edition*. New York: Carroll & Graf. Introduction by Jon L. Breen. Twenty-five of the best stories from 1993.

Rae, Simon, ed. *The Faber Book of Murder*. London: Faber and Faber. Some 230 stories, poems, and excerpts from novels, plays, and nonfiction, classic and modern, all dealing with murder.

Randisi, Robert J., and Susan Dunlap, eds. *Deadly Allies II*. New York: Doubleday. Twenty-two new stories by members of the Private Eye Writers of America and Sisters in Crime.

Sellers, Peter, and John North, eds. *Cold Blood V*. Oakville, Ontario, Canada: Sundial/Mosaic Press. Sixteen new stories by Canadian authors.

Slung, Michele, and Roland Hartman, eds. *Murder for Halloween*. New York: Mysterious Press. Eighteen stories, six new, some fantasy. ("Roland Hartman" is a pseudonym of Otto Penzler.)

Smith, Marie, ed. *The Mammoth Book of Golden Age Detective Stories*. New York: Carroll & Graf. Twenty-one stories and novelettes plus one novel, Edgar Wallace's *The Four Just Men*, all from the period 1881–1917.

Spillane, Mickey, and Max Allan Collins, eds. *Murder Is My Business*. New York: Dutton. Sixteen new stories about hit men, plus a reprint of Spillane's 1953 novella *Everybody's Watching Me*.

Stafford, Caroline, ed. *Death Knell*. Norristown, PA: Delaware Valley Chapter, Sisters in Crime. Introduction by Gillian Roberts. Eight new stories, privately printed.

Weinberg, Robert, Stefan R. Dziemianowicz, and Martin H. Greenberg, eds. *100 Crooked Little Crime Stories*. New York: Barnes & Noble Books. One hundred brief crime tales, many from the pulps.

III. NONFICTION

Asimov, Isaac. *I, Asimov: A Memoir*. New York: Doubleday. An autobiography of the famous science fiction and mystery writer.

Bird, Delys. *Killing Women: Rewriting Detective Fiction.* Sydney, Australia: Angus & Robertson/HarperCollins. Seven new essays by Australian women mystery writers. 1993.

Brennan, Neil, and Alan Redway. *A Bibliography of Graham Greene.* New York: Oxford University Press. A complete listing of all novels, short stories, and nonfiction. 1993.

Brubaker, Bill. *Stewards of the House: The Detective Fiction of Jonathan Latimer.* Bowling Green, OH: Bowling Green State University Popular Press. A study of the author's life and his nine mystery novels. 1993.

Bunson, Matthew E. *Encyclopedia Sherlockiana: The Complete A-to-Z Guide to the World of the Great Detective.* New York: Macmillan. A guide to the Sherlock Holmes stories and dramatic adaptations.

Cave, Hugh B. *Magazines I Remember: Some Pulps, Their Editors, and What it Was Like to Write for Them.* Chicago: Tattered Pages Press. Letters and comments by a mystery-horror pulp writer, mainly directed to a writer friend, Carol Jacobi.

Cooper, John, and B. A. Pike. *Detective Fiction: The Collector's Guide. Second Edition.* Aldershot, England: Scolar Press. Expanded edition of a guide for collectors, covering novels and stories by 157 authors.

DeAndrea, William L. *Encyclopedia Mysteriosa.* New York: Prentice Hall. A comprehensive guide to crime and detection in print, film, radio, and television, with listings of bookstores, organizations, and magazines in the field.

Duncan, Karen, ed. *Remembering Anthony Boucher.* Seattle: Accord Communications. A booklet prepared for Bouchercon 25, containing nine brief tributes by authors and fans.

Fuller, Bryony. *Dick Francis: Steeplechase Jockey.* London: Michael Joseph. An account of the famous writer's racing career.

Greenberg, Martin, ed. *The Tony Hillerman Companion: A Comprehensive Guide to His Life and Work.* New York: HarperCollins. A guide to Hillerman's detective fiction and a new interview with him, both by Jon L. Breen, plus an essay on the Navajo nation and a concordance to all characters in his fiction. Includes eight essays and three short stories by Hillerman, with eight pages of photographs.

Haining, Peter. *The Complete Maigret: From Simenon's Original*

Novels to Granada's Much Acclaimed TV Series. London: Box-tree/Granada Television. A heavily illustrated study, concentrating mainly on the film and TV versions of Maigret.

Herbert, Rosemary, ed. *The Fatal Art of Entertainment: Interviews with Mystery Writers*. New York: G. K. Hall/Macmillan. Foreword by Antonia Fraser. Interviews with thirteen well-known American and British mystery writers.

Hubin, Allen J. *Crime Fiction II: A Comprehensive Bibliography, 1749–1990*. New York: Garland. A revised and updated two-volume edition of Hubin's earlier work, listing some 81,000 book titles in the mystery-crime-suspense field, arranged by author. Title, setting, and series indexes are included, as well as an index of films based on the works, together with screenwriters and directors. More than 4,500 listings for short story collections now include individual story titles.

Irwin, John T. *The Mystery to a Solution: Poe, Borges, and the Analytic Detective Story*. Baltimore: Johns Hopkins University Press. A scholarly study of Borges and the influences on his work.

Klein, Kathleen Gregory, ed. *Great Women Mystery Writers*. Westport, CT: Greenwood Press. One hundred seventeen brief essays on women writers, with bibliographies of their mystery fiction.

Leng, Flavia. *Daphne DuMaurier: A Daughter's Memoir*. Edinburgh: Main Stream Publications. A memoir about the author of *Rebecca*.

Lewis, Margaret. *Edith Pargeter: Ellis Peters*. Mid Glamorgan, Wales: Seren/Poetry Wales Press. A critical biography of the author of the Brother Cadfael mysteries.

Lovisi, Gary. *Dashiell Hammett and Raymond Chandler: A Checklist and Bibliography of Their Paperback Appearances*. Brooklyn: Gryphon Publications. An extensive but incomplete bibliography, with notes on collecting Hammett and Chandler, foreign editions, cover art, etc.

MacLeod, Charlotte. *Had She But Known: A Biography of Mary Roberts Rinehart*. New York: Mysterious Press. A biography of the mystery writer and literary celebrity.

McCormick, Donald. *17F: The Life of Ian Fleming*. Chester Springs, PA: Peter Owen/Dufour. A biography of James Bond's creator.

Moore, Lewis D. *Meditations on America: John D. MacDonald's Travis McGee Series and Other Fiction.* Bowling Green, OH: Bowling Green State University Popular Press. Modern culture as seen through the Travis McGee novels.

Parker, Robert B., and Kasho Kumagai. *Parker's Boston.* New York: Otto Penzler Books. A photographic tour of places mentioned in the Spenser novels.

Plunkett-Powell, Karen. *The Nancy Drew Scrapbook.* New York: St. Martin's Press. A publishing history of the teenage sleuth, together with information on film and stage versions and collectibles. 1993.

Reynolds, William, and Elizabeth Trembley, eds. *It's a Print! Detective Fiction from Page to Screen.* Bowling Green, OH: Bowling Green State University Popular Press. Essays on various adaptations of mystery novels to the screen.

Roberts, Garyn G. *Dick Tracy and American Culture.* Jefferson, NC: McFarland. A study of the comic strip sleuth. 1993.

Sampson, Robert. *Yesterday's Faces: Volume 6, Violent Lives.* Bowling Green, OH: Bowling Green State University Popular Press. Final volume of a study of series characters in the early pulp magazines, covering adventurers, rogues, and spies. 1993.

Satterthwait, Walter, and Ernie Bulow. *Sleight of Hand: Conversations with Walter Satterthwait.* Albuquerque: University of New Mexico. An essay by Bulow and two interviews with mystery writer Satterthwait, plus three short stories by him—two from *AHMM* and one new. 1993.

Server, Lee. *Over My Dead Body: The Sensational Age of American Paperbacks, 1945–1955.* San Francisco: Chronicle Books. A brief history with over 100 pages of cover art.

Shelden, Michael. *Graham Greene: The Man Within.* London: Heinemann. A one-volume biography that seeks clues to Greene's life in his writing.

Sherry, Norman. *The Life of Graham Greene, Volume Two: 1939–1955.* London: Jonathan Cape. The second of three volumes in Sherry's Edgar-winning biography.

Swanson, Jean, and Dean James. *By a Woman's Hand: A Guide to Mystery Fiction by Women.* New York: Berkley. Introduction by Nancy Pickard. Over 200 profiles of women mystery writers active since 1977, with index by series character and geographic setting.

Tamaya, Meera. *H.R.F. Keating: Post-Colonial Detection*. Bowling Green, OH: Bowling Green State University Popular Press. A critical study of the British mystery writer's work, with interviews. 1993.

Treglown, Jeremy. *Roald Dahl: A Biography*. New York: Farrar, Straus & Giroux. Biography of the popular author of children's books and mystery short stories.

Van Dover, Kenneth. *You Know My Method*. Bowling Green, OH: Bowling Green State University Popular Press. A study of ten major mystery writers, 1841–1940.

Van Hise, James, ed. *Pulp Heroes of the Thirties*. Yucca Valley, CA: Midnight Graffiti. Sixteen essays on pulp heroes, most reprinted from fan publications, plus two new stories by the editor continuing the adventures of popular pulp heroes.

AWARDS

MYSTERY WRITERS OF AMERICA EDGAR AWARDS

Best Novel: Mary Willis Walker, *The Red Scream* (Doubleday)
Best First Novel by an American Author: George Dawes Green,
  The Caveman's Valentine (Warner)
Best Original Paperback: Lisa Scottoline, *Final Appeal* (Harper)
Best Fact Crime: Joe Domanick, *To Protect and Serve* (Pocket)
Best Critical Biographical: William J. DeAndrea, *Encyclopedia
  Mysteriosa* (Prentice Hall)
Best Short Story: Doug Allyn, "The Dancing Bear" (*Alfred Hitch-
  cock's Mystery Magazine*, March 1994)
Best Young Adult: Nancy Springer, *Toughing It* (Harcourt Brace)
Best Juvenile: Willo Davis Roberts, *The Absolutely True Story . . .
  How I Visited Yellowstone Park with the Terrible Rubes* (Ath-
  eneum)
Best Episode in a Television Series: Stephen Bochco, Walon Green,
  and Davis Milch, "Simone Says" (*NYPD Blue*, 20th Century
  Fox, ABC-TV)
Best Television Feature or Miniseries: Jimmy McGovern, *Cracker:
  To Say I Love You* (*A & E Mystery*)
Best Motion Picture: Quentin Tarantino, *Pulp Fiction* (Miramax)
Grand Master: Mickey Spillane
Ellery Queen Award: Martin Greenberg
Robert L. Fish Memorial Award: Batya Swift Yasgur, "Me and Mr.

Harry" (*Ellery Queen's Mystery Magazine*, mid-December 1994)

CRIME WRITERS' ASSOCIATION (BRITAIN)

Gold Dagger: Minette Walters, *The Scold's Bridle* (Macmillan, London)
Silver Dagger: Peter Hoeg, *Miss Smilla's Feeling for Snow* (Harvill)
John Creasey Award: Doug J. Swanson, *Big Town* (Little Brown)
Last Laugh Award: Simon Shaw, *The Villain of the Earth* (Gollancz)
Nonfiction Award: David Canter, *Criminal Shadows* (HarperCollins)
Short Story Award: Ian Rankin, "A Deep Hole" (*London Noir*)
Golden Handcuffs Award: Robert Barnard
Diamond Dagger: Michael Gilbert

CRIME WRITERS OF CANADA ARTHUR ELLIS AWARDS (FOR 1993)

Best Novel: John Lawrence Reynolds, *Gypsy Sins* (HarperCollins)
Best First Novel: Gavin Scott, *Memory Trace* (Cormorant)
Best Short Story: Robert J. Sawyer, "Just Like Old Times" (*On Spec: The Canadian Magazine of Speculative Writing*, Summer 1993)
Best True Crime: David R. Williams, *With Malice Aforethought: Six Spectacular Canadian Trials* (Sono Nis)
Best Juvenile: John Dowd, *Abalone Summer* (Raincoast)
Best Play: Timothy Findley, *The Stillborn Lover* (Blizzard)

PRIVATE EYE WRITERS OF AMERICA SHAMUS AWARDS (FOR 1993)

Best P. I. Novel: Lawrence Block, *The Devil Knows You're Dead* (Morrow)
Best Original P. I. Paperback: Rodman Philbrick, *Brothers and Sinners* (NAL)
Best First P. I. Novel: Lynn Hightower, *Satan's Lambs* (Walker)

Best P. I. Short Story: Lawrence Block, "The Merciful Angel of Death" (*The New Mystery*)

The Eye—Life Achievement Award: Stephen J. Cannell, creator of *The Rockford Files*

BOUCHERCON ANTHONY AWARDS (FOR 1993)

Best Novel: Marcia Muller, *Wolf in the Shadows* (Mysterious Press)

Best First Novel: Nevada Barr, *Track of the Cat* (Putnam)

Best True Crime: Ann Rule, *A Rose for Her Grave* (Pocket Books)

Best Individual Short Story: Susan Dunlap, "Checkout" (*Malice Domestic 2*)

Best Short Story Collection/Anthology: *Malice Domestic 2* (Pocket Books)

Best Critical Work: Ed Gorman, Martin H. Greenberg, and Larry Segriff, with Jon L. Breen, *The Fine Art of Murder* (Carroll & Graf)

MALICE DOMESTIC AGATHA AWARDS (FOR 1993)

Best Novel: Carolyn Hart, *Dead Man's Island* (Bantam)

Best First Novel: Nevada Barr, *Track of the Cat* (Putnam)

Best Short Story: M. D. Lake, "Kim's Game" (*Malice Domestic 2*)

Best Nonfiction: Barbara D'Amato, *The Doctor, the Murder, the Mystery: The True Story Behind the Bronion Murder* (Noble Press)

MYSTERY READERS INTERNATIONAL MACAVITY AWARDS (FOR 1993)

Best Novel: Minette Walters, *The Sculptress* (St. Martin's Press)

Best First Novel: Sharan Newman, *Death Comes as Epiphany* (Tor)

Best Critical/Biographical: Ed Gorman, etc., *The Fine Art of Murder* (Carroll & Graf)

Best Short Story: Susan Dunlap, "Checkout" (*Malice Domestic 2*)

INTERNATIONAL ASSOCIATION OF CRIME WRITERS HAMMETT PRIZE (FOR 1993)

James Crumley, *The Mexican Tree Duck* (Mysterious Press)

NECROLOGY

Robert Bloch (1917–1994). Well-known mystery and fantasy author of some twenty crime novels, notably *Psycho* (1959), the basis for the popular Hitchcock film. Past president of Mystery Writers of America.

Pierre Boulle (1912–1994). Famed French author of at least eight thrillers in addition to his best-known works, *The Bridge Over the River Kwai* and *Planet of the Apes.*

Charles Bukowski (1920?–1994). Author of a 1983 story collection, *Tales of Ordinary Madness,* containing some crime stories.

Thomas Chastain (1921?–1994). Author of at least seventeen novels, notably *Pandora's Box* (1974) and *Who Killed the Robins Family?* (1983), a best-selling contest novel produced with book packager Bill Adler. Also wrote as "Nick Carter," collaborated on a mystery with Helen Hayes, and authored two novels continuing Erle Stanley Gardner's Perry Mason series. Past president of Mystery Writers of America.

James Clavell (1924–1994). Best-selling mainstream novelist whose work included at least two books with strong elements of intrigue—*Noble House* (1981) and *Whirlwind* (1986).

Maurice Cranston (1920–1993). British author of two novels (both 1946) about Inspector Blunt, unpublished in America.

"Frances Dale" (1909–1994). Pseudonym of Phyllis Craddock, British author of a single suspense novel, *Scorpion's Suicide* (1942), and a popular television cook who authored *The Sherlock Holmes Cookbook* (1976) as by "Mrs. Hudson."

"Jocelyn Davey" (1908–1994). Pseudonym of British author Chaim Raphael, author of seven mystery novels starting with *A Capitol Offense* (1956).

Guy des Cars (1911–1993). French author of sixty novels, at least five of them criminous.

Roger Dooley (1920–1993). Author of a single mystery novel, *Flashback* (1969).

Hal Ellson (1910?–1994). Author of fifteen crime novels, notably *Duke* (1949) and *Tomboy* (1950), plus more than 100 short stories, some collected in *Tell Them Nothing* (1956).

Oscar Fraley (1914–1994). Journalist and coauthor (with Eliot Ness) of *The Untouchables*. Also published two crime novels.

Sidney Gilliat (1908–1994). Coauthor, with Frank Launder, of a three-act mystery play, *Meet a Body* (1955), filmed as *The Green Man*.

Eaton K. Goldthwaite (1907–1994). Contributor to *Black Mask* and author of ten detective novels, notably *Scarecrow* (1945) and *Cat and Mouse* (1946).

Mary Bowen Hall (1932–1994). Author of the Emma Chizzit novels, beginning with *Emma Chizzit and the Queen Anne Killer* (1990).

Hans Herlin (1925–1994). German author of at least four mystery novels, starting with *Friends* (1975).

"Michael Innes" (1906–1994). Pseudonym of British writer J.I.M. Stewart, author of forty-five mystery novels, mainly about Inspector Appleby, as well as mainstream novels and nonfiction under his own name. Notable mysteries include *Hamlet, Revenge!* (1937), *Lament for a Maker* (1938), and *The Man from the Sea* (1955).

Eugene Ionesco (1912–1994). Well-known playwright, one of whose plays, *The Killer* (1960), is criminous.

Marion Jopson (?–1994). British author of a single crime novel, *A Fist in the Sky* (1970), unpublished in America.

Joan Kahn (1914–1994). Well-known mystery editor at Harper & Row and elsewhere, who edited eleven mystery anthologies for adults and younger readers.

"David Keith" (1906–1994). Pseudonym of Francis Steegmuller, author of three mystery novels, notably *Blue Harpsichord* (1949).

Russell Kirk (1918–1994). Author of more than thirty books, including two mystery novels and a mystery-fantasy collection, *The Surly Sullen Bell* (1962).

Margaret Lane (1907?–1994). British author of an Edgar Wallace biography and coauthor with Enid Johnson of three 1930s mystery novels under the pseudonym "Jennifer Jones."

Nancy Livingston (1935–1994). British author of eight novels about retired tax inspector G. D. H. Pringle. Former chairman of the Crime Writers Association.

Frank Belknap Long (1903–1994). Well-known fantasy writer who published pulp stories and nearly a dozen mystery and Gothic novels under his own name and as "Lydia Belknap Long." His science fiction included a story collection, *John Carstairs, Space Detective* (1949).

Ivan Lyons (1934–1994). Coauthor with his wife, Nan, of *Someone Is Killing the Great Chefs of Europe* (1976) and other mysteries.

Margaret Millar (1915–1994). Famed author of twenty-one detective novels, notably *The Iron Gates* (1945), the Edgar-winning *Beast in View* (1955), and *How Like an Angel* (1962). Past president of Mystery Writers of America and winner of its Grand Master award. Widow of best-selling mystery writer Ross Macdonald.

James Moffatt (1922–1993). Canadian-born author of seventeen crime novels under his own name and eleven as "Richard Allen" and "Hilary Brand," many unpublished in America.

"Evelyn Piper" (1908–1994). Pseudonym of Merriam Modell, author of nine suspense novels, notably *The Innocent* (1949), *The Motive* (1950), *Bunny Lake Is Missing* (1957), and *The Nanny* (1964).

Dennis Potter (1935–1994). British television writer who authored the miniseries "The Singing Detective" along with two crime novels, *Ticket to Ride* (1986) and *Blackeyes* (1987).

"Derek Raymond" (1931–1994). Pseudonym of British crime writer Robert Cook, who published his early books as Robin Cook—not to be confused with the American author of medical thrillers.

D. L. (Debbie) Richardson (1951?–1994). Short-story writer, contributor to *AHMM* beginning in June 1984.

Berton Roueche (1911–1994). Author of four suspense novels, 1945–77. Best known for his essays on medical detection for *The New Yorker*, collected in *Eleven Blue Men* and later volumes.

"Miriam Sharman" (1915–1994). Pseudonym of British author Maisie Sharman Bolton, author of nine mystery novels, 1952–71, the first five as "Stratford Davis," all unpublished in America.

Lisa Shepherd (1916?–1994). British writer who published her first crime novel, *The Ladies of Lambton Green*, in 1984 at the age of sixty-eight.

George Starbird (1908–1994). Pulp mystery author of eleven stories in *Black Book, Clues,* and other magazines of the 1930s. Later became mayor of San Jose, California.

John Stevenson (?–1994). Author of one mystery under his own name plus seven as "Mark Denning," sixteen as "Bruno Rossi," and others as "Nick Carter."

Charles L. Sweeney (1918?–1994). As C. L. Sweeney, Jr., author of more than a dozen stories in *Manhunt, AHMM,* and elsewhere in the 1950s and '60s. Reprinted in *Best Detective Stories of the Year* and three early MWA anthologies.

Julian Symons (1912–1994). Well-known British author of more than thirty crime novels and story collections, as well as a large body of critical work in the mystery field, notably *Bloody Murder: From the Detective Story to the Crime Novel* (1972; updated 1985, 1992). His notable novels include *The Narrowing Circle* (1954), *The Color of Murder* (1957), *A Three-Pipe Problem* (1975), and *The Blackheath Poisonings* (1978). A founding member and chairman of the Crime Writers Association, and president of the Detection Club, Symons was honored for lifetime achievement by Mystery Writers of America, the Crime Writers Association, and the Swedish Academy of Detection.

Cay Van Ash (1918–1994). Coauthor of a 1972 Sax Rohmer biography who later published two novels, *Ten Years Beyond Baker Street* (1984) and *The Fires of Fu Manchu* (1987).

Karl Edward Wagner (1945–1994). Writer and editor in the fantasy-horror field, who published one crime novel and a story collection, *Death Angel's Shadow* (1973). Best known as editor of *The Year's Best Horror Stories* for the past fifteen years.

Wayne Warga (1937?–1994). Television writer who published three private eye novels starting with the PWA Shamus Award–winning *Hardcover* (1985).

Terence DeVere White (1912–1994). Author of a single crime novel, *My Name Is Norval* (1979).

HONOR ROLL

ABBREVIATIONS

AHMM—Alfred Hitchcock's Mystery Magazine
EQMM—Ellery Queen's Mystery Magazine
(Starred stories are included in this volume. All dates are 1994.)

*Allyn, Doug, "The Dancing Bear," *AHMM*, March
———, "Black Water," *EQMM*, October
———, "The Cross-Wolf," *EQMM*, mid-December
———, "Fire Lake," *EQMM*, April
———, "Wrecker," *EQMM*, November
Baker, Sybil, "Eensie-Weensie Spider," *AHMM*, August
Bankier, William, "Long Time No Murder," *EQMM*, June
*Barnard, Robert, "The Gentleman in the Lake," *EQMM*, June
Block, Lawrence, "Dogs Walked, Plants Watered," *Playboy*, May
———, "Keller on Horseback," *Murder Is My Business*
Bradbury, Ray, "The Very Gentle Murders," *EQMM*, May
Burke, Jan, "Unharmed," *EQMM*, mid-December
*Burnham, Brenda Melton, "The Tennis Court," *AHMM*, July
Butler, Gwendoline, "The Searcher," *Royal Crimes*
Callahan, Barbara, "The Mists of Ballyclough," *EQMM*, September
———, "Voices," *EQMM*, February
*Carlson, P. M., "The Eighth Wonder of the World; or, Golden Options," *Deadly Allies II*

Caterer, C. M., "Suitable for Framing," *AHMM*, September
Cleeves, Ann, "A Winter's Tale," *EQMM*, mid-December
Collins, Barbara, "Father, Son and Holy Ghost," *Murder for Father*
————, "The Ten Lives of Talbert," *Feline and Famous*
Collins, Max Allan, "Guest Services," *Murder Is My Business*
Collins, Michael, "A Matter of Character," *Partners in Crime*
Curtis, Ashley, "The Ice Cave," *AHMM*, April
————, "Dead Flowers," *AHMM*, August
Davis, Dorothy Salisbury, "Now Is Forever," *Justice in Manhattan*
Davis, J. Madison, "The Measure of His Guilt," *Red Herring Mystery Magazine*, Summer
Dean, David, "Don't Fear the Reaper," *EQMM*, January
Dobbyn, John, "Fruit of the Poisonous Tree," *EQMM*, June
*DuBois, Brendon, "The Necessary Brother," *EQMM*, May
Edwards, Martin, "The Boxer," *EQMM*, January
Emery, Clayton, "Dowsing the Demon," *EQMM*, November
Gallison, Kate, "Plastic," *EQMM*, November
Gordon, Alan, "Do Not Go Quiescent into that Frozen Night," *AHMM*, April
Gorman, Ed, "The Beast in the Woods," *The Mysterious West*
————, "Hunk," *EQMM*, March
*————, "Seasons of the Heart," *EQMM*, August
Grover, Kathleen A., "Traps," *EQMM*, February
Healy, Jeremiah, "Double Con," *EQMM*, March
Hershman, Morris, "The Satisfied Victim," *AHMM*, March
Highsmith, Patricia, "Summer Doldrums," *EQMM*, April
Hoch, Edward D., "An Early Morning Madness," *EQMM*, April
————, "Four Meetings," *EQMM*, August
————, "The Gypsy's Paw," *EQMM*, September
————, "The Theft of Twenty-nine Minutes," *EQMM*, October
————, "Waiting for Mrs. Ryder," *EQMM*, November
*Hornsby, Wendy, "High Heels in the Headliner," *Malice Domestic 3*
————, "New Moon and Rattlesnakes," *The Mysterious West*
*Howard, Clark, "Split Decisions," *EQMM*, December
James, Bill, "War Crime," *EQMM*, April
Jones, Suzanne, "Girl Under Glass," *EQMM*, August
————, "The Good Knife," *EQMM*, January
Lake, M. D., "With Flowers in Her Hair," *The Mysterious West*

APPENDIX

Lamburn, Nell, "Home Is Where the Heart Is," *EQMM*, January
Landis, Geoffrey, "The Singular Habits of Wasps," *Analog*, April
Lepovetsky, Lisa, "Joe Frog's Place," *EQMM*, April
Lewin, Michael Z., "Family Business," *AHMM*, March
———, "The Hit," *EQMM*, October
Limón, Martin, "The Inn of the Marauding Swine," *AHMM*, September
———, "The Mists of the Southern Seas," *AHMM*, June
———, "Night of the Moon Goddess," *AHMM*, October
Linscott, Gillian, "Death of a Dead Man," *EQMM*, mid-December
Lovesay, Peter, "Bertie and the Fire Brigade," *Royal Crimes*
———, "Passion Killers," *EQMM*, January
Luce, Carol Davis, "Shattered Crystal," *AHMM*, March
Lutz, John, "The Chess Players," *EQMM*, May
———, "A Crazy Business," *Feline and Famous*
Matthews, Clayton, "The Jacksboro Highway," *Red Herring Mystery Magazine*, Summer
McCafferty, Taylor, "The Dying Light," *Malice Domestic 3*
McCrumb, Sharyn, "The Monster of Glamis," *Royal Crimes*
———, "Old Rattler," *Partners in Crime*
McGuire, D. A., "Virtual Fog," *AHMM*, June
*Muller, Marcia, "Forbidden Things," *The Mysterious West*
Nevins, Francis M., "Toad Cop," *EQMM*, September
———, "Night of Silken Snow," *EQMM*, November
Olson, Donald, "The French Umbrella," *EQMM*, March
Owens, Barbara, "Bad Habits," *EQMM*, December
———, "Footprints," *EQMM*, January
Powell, James, "A Bequest for Mr. Nugent," *EQMM*, February
Pronzini, Bill, "The Cloud Cracker," *Louis L'Amour Western Magazine*, July
———, "Engines," *The Mysterious West*
*———, "Out of the Depths," *EQMM*, September
*Rankin, Ian, "A Deep Hole," *London Noir*
Reynolds, William J., "The Lost Boys," *The Mysterious West*
Robinson, Peter, "The Good Partner," *EQMM*, March
———, "Summer Rain," *EQMM*, December
Rogers, Bruce Holland, "Hollywood Considered as a Seal Point in the Sun," *Feline and Famous*
Saylor, Steven, "The Alexandrian Cat," *EQMM*, February

288

Schwarz, C. E., "My Obit Habit," *New Mystery*, Winter
Scott, Jeffry, "Hard," *AHMM*, April
——, "The 1944 Bullet," *EQMM*, July
——, "The Passing of Mr. Toad," *EQMM*, October
*Scott, Justin, "An Eye for a Tooth," *Justice in Manhattan*
Sellers, Peter, "Bombed," *EQMM*, June
Slesar, Henry, "The Deal," *EQMM*, February
Spark, Muriel, "The Hanging Judge," *The New Yorker*, May 2
Stevens, B. K., "True Crime," *AHMM*, March
Stodgill, Dick, "A Policy for Murder," *AHMM*, June
Symons, Julian, "In the Bluebell Wood," *EQMM*, February
——, "The Man Who Hated Television," *EQMM*, June
Tigges, John, "The Pasture Mystery," *Murder for Father*
Tremayne, Peter, "A Canticle for Wulfstan," *Midwinter Mysteries 4*
Wasylyk, Stephen, "Crosscurrents and Eddies," *AHMM*, May
——, "The Notes of Morrow's Horn," *AHMM*, mid-December
Westlake, Donald E., "Jumble Sale," *The Armchair Detective*,
    Summer
*Wheat, Carolyn, "Undercover," *Murder Is My Business*
Wilhelm, Kate, "Fox in the Briars," *EQMM*, October
Williams, David, "Second Best Man," *EQMM*, May
Wilmot, Tony, "Skeleton in the Cupboard," *EQMM*, July
Woodward, Ann F., "The Ninth Prince Sits and Talks," *AHMM*,
    February
Wyrick, E. L., "Cruel Choices," *EQMM*, March
*Yasgur, Batya Swift, "Me and Mr. Harry," *EQMM*, mid-December